VISCOUNT OVERBOARD

MISTY URBAN

OLIVERHEBERBOOKS

Published by Oliver-Heber Books

0 9 8 7 6 5 4 3 2 1

CHAPTER ONE

NEWPORT, WALES SPRING 1799

"Gwen, dearie. There's a man at the door. The *front* door."

Gwen, her arms elbow-deep in straw, peered down from the roof of the small sty. Dovey stood on the packed dirt of the rear courtyard, frowning at a small white rectangle in her hand.

"What kind of—*oof*." Gwen sputtered as a bundle of wheat straw sailed upward and smacked her in the face, flattening her against the pitch of the roof. At least she didn't fall off. Little good she'd be to anyone at St. Sefin's if she ended up in the hospital ward.

"Pardon, Miss Gwen." Evans, propped against his crutch, flexed his good arm and turned red to the tips of his ears. "You said toss up the last bundle."

"That I did," Gwen said, rubbing at the burn on her cheek. A sight she'd be, performing tonight for the Vaughns. "Has someone received our guest, if he's a seeker?"

Silence drifted below as Gwen unrolled the whisps of straw and levered the thatch into place with the spar. She knew why neither volunteered, though Evans had lived at St. Sefin's for nearly all the seven years she and Dovey had been running the place. Dovey disliked dealing with strangers, and strangers disliked dealing with Evans.

"He's a *Sais*," Dovey said.

Gwen sighed. "A complaint, then, if he's an Englishman." She tossed the twisted stick to the ground and climbed down the ladder while Evans steadied it with his hand, then she dusted her scratched hands with bravado. "I'll turn him off right quick, shall I?"

Evans scanned the sky, his sidewise glance landing on Dovey. "You may tell Mrs. Van der Welle I'll help her take the linens off the line, as it bodes rain."

Dovey marched toward the shadow of the great stone building, the jagged roof etched against the pearl-grey clouds rolling up from the river. "You may tell Mr. Evans," she tossed over her shoulder, "I don't need his good hand nor any part of him."

Gwen shook her head at their arguing, grown worse of late. "St. Aled's head! What are the two of you chopsing about now?" She stowed the wooden ladder in the small outbuilding that held their other tools, then caught up with her friend. "Mayhap the *Sais* wants to hire a harper and heard none plays the *telyn* so well as Gwen ap Ewyas." They could use the money; they always did.

"He gave me this." Dovey thrust out a small white card.

Gwen didn't catch the gasp before it escaped her. *Mr. Barlow, Bristol. Solicitor.*

"What's it, then?" Dovey didn't read, claiming she was too busy to sit while Gwen taught Dovey's daughter her letters in English and Welsh.

"A legal man." Gwen smoothed the kerchief pinned to the bodice of her grey flannel gown. "Oh, Saint Gwladys, preserve us."

A legal man boded no good. Sleepy Newport thought to grow of a sudden, workers flooding South Wales as the coal fields spread. The new Monmouthshire canal lured more ships to the harbor, reeling goods up and down the Severn in an endless chain. And the *Saeson* poured in too, thinking they owned what was and always had been Welsh land.

Evans pointed behind them with his crutch. "I, uh, think Tomos said the winch on the well needs oil. He struggled with it this morning."

"And I'm to ask Widow to help me take in the linens." Dovey made a beeline away.

St. Sefin's had been Gwen's idea; she had to accept that she was the face of it. She wiped her hands on the woolen shawl at her waist, apron and catchall, and strode through the gardens bristling with spring color. The camelias bloomed red at their hearts and the cherry tree blushed pink as a bride, tugging her heart with a fierce, bright sense of belonging that burrowed deeper each season. This was her home.

A small man stood on the porch, somber and strict in a black wool coat, glaring at the stern walls of the ancient priory. He seemed unmoved by the mellow golden glow of the thick lime-stone walls as they caught the last afternoon sun before it slid between a veil of clouds. Gwen wished she'd paused to pull the straw from her hair and straighten her gown. Fine folk wouldn't hire her to harp in their parlors if they thought she'd turn up in her dirt.

"*Prynhawn da,*" Gwen greeted him, and saw from the slant of his grey-peppered brows that he didn't speak a word of Welsh. "Good afternoon. Do you wish a tour, Mr. Barlow?"

English liked to holiday in Wales, where the woods had not yet been burned up for fuel nor the hills tilled down for farm-ing. Medieval ruins like St. Sefin's were picturesque, and Gwen never turned away tourists willing to place a few coins in her palm for the privilege of seeing where a Welsh nun once slept and said her prayers.

Barlow scowled. "I am not a tourist, Mrs.—"

"Miss," she answered coolly. "Gwenllian ap Ewyas." She made no move to curtsey. This man was not her better, despite his condescending manner. The false name slipped out easily after all these years.

"Can you explain to me, Miss Why-yes—" He stumbled over the pronunciation—"why you appear to be inhabiting a property owned by the Viscount Penrydd?"

Alarm churned in her belly, and instinct shrieked at her to run. Gwen straightened her shoulders.

"You are mistaken, Mr. Barlow. St. Sefin's was abandoned years ago."

The priory, once home to an order of Cistercian nuns, had fallen into quiet ruin when Gwen arrived at its door. She and Dovey made the place as habitable as they could, tacking oiled paper in the openings where the medieval church had held arched clerestory windows, filling in the occasional crumbling block with rough plaster. Mr. Barlow regarded the barred opening in the tower as if Gwen had been personally responsible for melting down the bell that had hung there.

"The property may have been, or *should* be, empty, but I assure you Lord Penrydd holds the deed," the solicitor said.

"I...ah." Gwen flailed, her mind swallowed by one thought. *Someone owned St. Sefin's.* Someone not her. That meant she was a trespasser. They all were.

Barlow's gaze turned hawkish. "Have you gained his lordship's permission to be here? For I have not handled any arrangements for tenancy."

Lie, instinct shrieked. Gwen hated lying. She had lied once, as a child, and the consequences were devastating.

"You'll be well, mam," she'd whispered at the bedside of her mother as she lay, pinched and thrashing, in the grip of childbed fever. "You'll pull through."

But she hadn't. A week later Gwen had stood at the grave-side with her silent, stricken father and understood her mother had been taken, and the infant boy with her, because Gwen had lied, and God heard her.

But if a falsehood would keep a roof over the heads of the people she cared about, Gwen would lie till she choked on it. She pulled her lips into a brittle smile.

"Only a lark, Mr. Barlow. I fancy the place, so I give tours now and again for a bit of silver." She forced out a laugh, a cackle. "No one actually *lives* in this old pile."

"Mistress Gwenllian!" The vicar strolled toward them over the small green hill that led to the gulch dividing St. Sefin's from the parish church. Ifor shuffled behind the vicar, his favorite goat, Gafr, on a rope beside him, both their heads hanging low in shame.

The vicar patted the boy's shoulder. "I'm afraid there's been an upset again today."

Gwen swallowed a groan. "What did Gafr eat this time?"

"I've given Ifor leave to graze his friends in the churchyard, mind," the vicar said. "But it seems that visitors to St. Woolos do not look kindly on our local goats munching grass grown on the bones of their dearly departed. Little as the departed may care."

Barlow stared at the boy's blind, unfocused eyes with an expression of revulsion. Then he turned a disapproving stare on Gwen.

"Perhaps you might show Gafr to his pen, Ifor," Gwen suggested. "I fixed the roof."

Ifor lifted his head. "Did you, Miss Gwen? And without my help even. Well, let's have a look, Gafr." He let his crooked staff and the goat guide him along the pebbled path.

"Your son, *Miss* Ewyas?" Mr. Barlow inquired.

"Heavens, no," the vicar said with a friendly smile. "Ifor was left on the porch of St. Woolos years ago. Miss Gwen saved his life when she took him in. She's saved many a life, if you must know. As much a saint as the good sisters who dwelled here before her, she is."

Gwen held her breath, waiting for a heavenly pillar of fire to reduce the vicar to smoking ash for that heresy. Or scorch her. But the only heat came from Mr. Barlow's tight-lipped glare.

"And all of this taking place, I presume, without the Viscount Penrydd's knowledge or permission, though the property belongs to him."

"Penrydd? Him with the empty estate near here? That's grand for the neighborhood if the new lord's taking up the reins. He's never set foot in Wales." The vicar winked at Gwen. "He's a young one, I hear, and handsome, or least he was before...well, before."

A salty breeze chilled her skin, and Gwen stripped her shawl from her waist to draw it about her shoulders. More proof to her lie wound its way up Church Street, passing the copse of trees that divided St. Sefin's from the growing town of Newport. Tomos's face lit with a placid grin when he spotted Gwen, and he trotted over to slip his hand in hers.

"It won't do, Miss Gwenllian." The tanner still wore his leather apron, reeking of chemicals. He wiped a sheen of sweat from his forehead. "I've tried, and the missus has tried, but our boy's as good as a fart in a jam jar when it comes to the trade."

Gwen tugged Tomos's hand away as he reached, fascinated, for the solicitor's beaver hat. "Perhaps we might apprentice him to the hatter?"

The tanner shook his head. "Fact is, he's too simple for the work, and he wanders off when it takes his fancy. There's the new lady running the pie shop—"

"Where Tomos would eat all the pie." Gwen released a long sigh. "We thank you for your efforts, Mr. Coffin. It's not been easy, I know."

She sent the vicar, Mr. Stanley, a hopeful look as Tomos sensed the tension among the group and began to hum and rock on his heels. Mr. Stanley could busy Tomos for hours, polishing brass at the church. But the vicar watched Barlow and his amazed outrage as the front door to St. Sefin's opened and one body after another spilled outside.

"*Saes!*" Mother Morris shouted, spying the intruder. "*Twll din pob Saes!*"

Mr. Stanley, fortunately, did not understand enough Welsh to translate that particular condemnation. Barlow recoiled at her tone if not the insult.

"Now, Mother." Widow Jones patted the older woman's hand. "All right, here, our Tomos is back! Shall we go in and look out some biscuits for tea?"

Widow Jones was wise in the household arts but too old to go into service. She, like Mother Morris, like the boys, had nowhere else to go.

Mr. Barlow's expression turned as stony as the walls of St. Sefin's. "Five, so far, squatting on milord Penrydd's property. How many more of you are there, Miss Ewyas?"

"*Twll din pob Saes!*" Mother Morris shouted. Widow Jones shook her elbow gently.

"You forget the Penrydds are Cymry, Mother," Widow said. "They only left for London when the mad English king made the old knight a baron. Have you never seen Penrydd Hall, so splendid there up in the hills toward Wentwood? As grand as Tredegar House it is, or could be, with some tending."

"The late Lord Penrydd thought it right to take his seat in the House of Lords," Mr. Barlow said, his lips a grim line. "And the new viscount believes it time to take his lands in hand. Past time, I will hasten to inform him."

"All right, Miss Gwenllian?" Evans limped around the corner of the priory, and Gwen stifled a groan. Normally she relied on his ready hand and good cheer, but he couldn't have turned up at a worse time.

The solicitor curled his lip into a sneer. "Six."

"Yes, six, Mr. Barlow." Gwen grasped at a slim hope. "Six souls in need of shelter. Tell his lordship we wish to arrange tenancy, a proper tenancy, and—and we'll pay."

A strangled cry drew every gaze to Dovey, coming up from the gardens, her basket laden with leeks and spring cabbage. "Pay? Gwen, we've no money for a lease on—" She clapped a hand over her mouth.

"Seven." Barlow recoiled. "And you keep African slaves, I see."

"Mrs. Van der Welle is as free as you or I, Mr. Barlow," Gwen hissed. She fisted her hands in her shawl. She must show restraint. She was at this man's mercy.

Mr. Barlow thrust out his chest, hugging his black leather case as if he suspected Gwen meant to steal it. "I'm afraid tenancy is out of the question for your sort of people. I refuse to propose any offer to his lordship on your behalf."

Evans laughed. "It can't be Penrydd property. We've been here for years."

"The Penrydd boy? *Coc oen!*" Mother Morris swore. "He's a *twpsyn*, he! A ne'er-do-well from the cradle, I've heard, and now that he's been cocked up by the war—"

"Come away, Mother, and let's to tea!" Widow Jones chirped, drawing the older woman away along with Tomos, who rocked and hummed with increasing vigor.

"I had heard young Penrydd was injured in battle," said Mr. Stanley, who took the London papers and thus knew of doings in England and the larger world. "And then to lose his brother, too! Quite a shock. But I'm sure he'll honor the agreement to let Miss Gwen and Mrs. Van der Welle continue their work at St. Sefin's, won't he?"

"I'll eat my hat if an agreement of any sort exists between the estate of Penrydd and Miss Ewyas!" Barlow lifted his nose in the air. "In fact, I will counsel his lordship to bring a suit for the degradation his property has suffered while such...*persons* have made use of it."

Gwen shuddered as a cold wind pinned her to the porch. She wished she could say the situation felt unreal, being cast from the place she'd thought her home, exorcised like a demon, swatted out like an unwanted cat.

But she'd stood in this place before. Twice. And each time found herself cast into the outer darkness, fingers frozen, chilblains blistering her feet.

"You cannot turn us out, Mr. Barlow. We've nowhere to go." Her voice was as thin and sharp as the breeze sweeping off the river, the one promising rain. The kind of torrential rain that lashed with the full fury of Mother Nature, flattening all before her mighty fist.

There was no lease, no agreement. The new Lord Penrydd had no way of knowing his dilapidated medieval priory housed anybody, because she'd never asked his permission. In fact, she'd never taken the steps to discover whether the old abbey belonged to anyone. She'd needed a roof over her head, and so had Dovey, and so had Evans, and she simply grew their community and went about their sustenance without a thought for whose land she occupied. Or whether their tenancy was in fact legal.

Fool. No, greater than a fool. Now they would all suffer for her ignorance.

She couldn't look at their faces. Dovey was her dearest friend. Evans had been part of St. Sefin's from the first. Ifor and Tomos had been disowned by their parents. The widows, like a pair of cuckoos, had no nest of their own. To take their home would be an act of unspeakable cruelty.

But Gwen had learned long ago there was no shield against cruelty. Not humility. Not innocence. Not youth. And certainly not beauty.

"I'm afraid your future actions are not my concern," the solicitor snapped. "My duty is to discharge the wishes of the Viscount Penrydd, and he wishes to divest himself of this property as soon as might be arranged." He firmed his hat on his head. "You must vacate at once, Miss Ewyas, or you will all find a new home in the workhouse, and I promise you it will be far less accommodating than this."

CHAPTER TWO

―――――――

"I would not stake money that the Vaughns will help us," Dovey said when she heard Gwen's plan.

Gwen sucked in her breath to close the last button of her jacket. Her chest hurt, her ribs fragile and bruised as if Barlow's words that afternoon had dealt a physical blow. She winced as she pinned a neckerchief to the lapels of her collar and pricked her skin.

Once she'd been offered rooms of gowns. Hats, shoes, chemises, the finest silks from France, linens white as the snow on the head of Yr Wyddfa. Now she slept in a drafty stone room that had housed a medieval prioress, and her best gown was a redingote with a too-small bodice and a striped silk skirt long out of fashion.

"I would not take their money if I could help it," Gwen said. The Vaughn fortune came from a plantation in Jamaica and part ownership of a slaving ship that sold kidnapped Africans into lives of misery in the Americas, then brought back the fruits of their forced labor in the form of cotton and sugar to British shores. "But I don't know who else to ask."

"Mr. Stanley could take up a collection for us." Dovey

twisted Gwen's hair into one of their precious silk ribbons. The sandy brown curls went free of powder, since they couldn't afford the tax. "Remind his faithful that we keep the poor rates low, since those we take in would otherwise look to the parish for outdoor relief."

"I do not think Mr. Stanley could raise enough even with his flowery words. He did offer to write a letter on our behalf. Perhaps an English lord might heed an English vicar."

Might. An unsteady word to hold such a weight of hope. Barlow had already delivered the order to vacate. Every hour they stayed was a trespass.

Dovey rearranged the lace at her throat, and Gwen knew they shared the same memory. The handmade lace, not as fine as that of Flanders or France, had come tucked inside the wool blanket of an infant deposited on the porch of St. Sefin's six years ago. Desperate mothers often left a badge with their foundling, hoping they might identify the child later when their circumstances improved.

But the babe had died of the bloody flux when they sent it to a wet nurse, and Gwen wore the lace on her evenings out as a reminder. Whatever humiliations or scorn might be dealt her, she would bear it for the sake of the fragile lives that depended on her.

"What shall we tell them?" Worry lurked in the deep brown of Dovey's eyes.

Gwen squeezed her friend's hand. "That I will find a way. We'll not be sent to the workhouse."

Side by side they descended the broad day stair to the refectory. Lancet windows high in the walls let the glimmer of early evening into the wide, smoothened chamber where the nuns had once taken their meals. So solid St. Sefin's was. So safe Gwen had felt in these walls of golden stone, built with prayer and firmness.

An illusion. But wasn't safety always such? Once fancied themselves protected by walls, by love, by a name or full coffers or a mother who bent like a guardian angel over a child's bed. And the next moment the love or the name or the angel could be gone, robbed and not returned no matter the tears one shed.

Normally the residents of St. Sefin's laughed and chattered at their meal, wooden spoons clattering in wooden bowls. Tonight every eye turned to the women on the stairs, faces drawn with fear, mouths worried.

Gwen's stomach pinched, and not from hunger or the too-tight gown.

"Miss Gwenllian!" A young girl peered through the servery window that divided the dining area from the kitchen. In the next instant, she barreled through the connecting door, a bowl of soup curled in each arm, and skidded to a stop before them.

"The bad Englishman did *not* tell us we can't stay at St. Sefin's any longer. Ifor is telling tales," Cerys said.

"Am not." Ifor sat at a wooden table, scooping mouthfuls of *cawl* into his mouth as if his bowl might disappear if left on its own for a moment. The thick native stew was a staple of their menu and Widow Jones put anything she could find in it, thickening the broth with oats and the dumplings she called trollies. Gwen smelled cabbage, leeks, wild garlic, and a trace of beef. The butcher often sent meat he couldn't sell before it went bad.

So many people in Newport supported the mission of St. Sefin's as best they could. If only their voices held some weight with the Viscount Penrydd, but Gwen knew how the gentry thought. They cared only for the opinion of their class, which left her to plead her case with the Vaughns, a family she could never respect and did not much like.

"Are too," Cerys said, pressing her point.

Dovey took the bowls from her daughter. "Only you, little

chick, will be turned out in the street, because you cannot remember you are a young lady and not a goat."

"Right. Spoons." Cerys charged back to the kitchen and returned with her bowl and a trio of utensils. "Budge over, Ifor, I want to sit next to Miss Gwen."

"You smell like wild violet and bluebells, Miss Gwen. Hey, now, Tomos, mind my soup!" Ifor, complaining, slid down the bench as the larger young man pushed in to stroke the silk of Gwen's gown.

"*Pert*," Tomos cooed, pawing Gwen's hair. "Pretty."

"Thank you, Tomos, that is very kind." Gwen gently removed his hand. "Now eat. Tomorrow we find another trade we might apprentice you to."

"Unless the bad man turns us all out into the street, as Mam said," Cerys added around slurps of stew.

"I won't allow it," Gwen said. "I am going to Greenfield to harp for Lady Vaughn, who was bored by the London season and now is bored here. I am sure she will help us."

Lies upon lies, all of them weights upon her soul at the final reckoning. The soup burned her mouth, and Gwen put down her spoon. Her belly refused food.

Cerys sighed. "And there will be lovely ladies with their gowns of silks and satins, and their kerchiefs of lace, and their tiny silk slippers. Will there be dancing?"

Gwen forced a smile. Little Cerys would never see any of the fine things she dreamed about, living as they did. But she saw a way to lift the gloom from their dinner.

"*Saeson* don't know how to dance to a Welsh harp, *pwt*," Gwen said. "Nor whistle, nor fiddle, nor pipe. They only dance to their own English instruments, and quite stiff they are at it. They never bend nor clap, but only promenade and bob up and down, like this."

She climbed over the bench and, one palm in the air,

solemnly processed between the line of tables. She curtseyed to Mother Morris and, when this earned a giggle from Cerys, made a deeper curtsey to Evans, who hobbled toward them with his crutch tucked under his good arm and a bowl in his hand.

"Good eve, Mister Evans," she intoned. "We be *dancing*."

Cerys howled. "That's *terrible!*"

"Most *Saeson* are." Gwen reclaimed her seat. "Good thing your father, God save him, was Dutch, and the way he and your mother danced!" She winked at Cerys. "a scandal, I call it. Nothing but ankle, and your mother as light as a cloud when he twirled her."

"*Fffwt*," Dovey scoffed, for Gwen had never met Lieutenant Jan Van der Welle. But Dovey smiled at the memory of her husband, and Gwen counted it a triumph.

Cerys rested her chin on her hands. "In London there are streets with whole *rows* of shops."

"Perhaps your mother and I might take you to Bristol one day. Or Bath," Gwen said.

"That's asking for trouble, that is." Dovey rose. "Come, Gwen, dearie. If Mr. Evans has done his job and borrowed a horse from the stables, I'll help you hitch up the dog cart."

"Mrs. Van der Welle will find that the horse is already hitched and waiting in the back court." Evans settled himself at the smooth, scarred oaken table.

"Though he might have put it in the front drive and made it easier on a body." As soon as they'd said their goodbyes and left the room, Dovey's face fell into somber lines. "She'll never see London. She'll never be accepted among fine folk, Gwen. You mustn't let her think she can."

The borrowed gelding stood in harness, rolling the bit in his mouth. Gwen would take some of her home-brewed ale to the barkeep at the King's Head in return for the use of his stables. They made most of their way on trade, and Gwen harped, her one skill, to earn coin for the things they couldn't barter. But barter wouldn't work with a viscount.

How much would it cost to buy their freedom? And how would she pay?

Dovey helped Gwen climb into the small cart, holding the creamy linen of her underskirt. Gwen took up the light riding whip.

"Every girl of eight should have her dreams, don't you think? Perhaps she'll grow up to a world where she might be exactly who she is, and loved for it," Gwen said. Her stomach shifted, and she wished she'd eaten.

"Did you ever know such a world? Did I?" Dovey's eyebrows lowered. "By St. David, does that man trust us to do nothing ourselves?"

"Have a care tonight, Miss Gwenllian." Evans came forward and hung a carriage lamp on the hook beside Gwen's seat. "You should have a moon, but you might ask them to send a boy to see you home."

"She knows the way," Dovey said, annoyed.

"There are greater evils than the workhouse." Evans held the side of the cart and met Gwen's gaze. "Don't trade your soul on our account, Miss Gwenllian."

Gwen read the weary resignation in his eyes. She'd never asked Evans about his history, where he maimed his leg, lost his arm. They didn't probe one another's private wounds. It was the one dignity they preserved in a communal space.

"You'd die in that place, and so would we all," she said softly.

He shook his head and stepped back. "There's worse."

Gwen clucked the gelding into a walk, a cold claw of fear in her chest.

She would survive without a home; she had before. She and Dovey could find work. But who would hire Evans, or Tomos, or

Ifor? What would happen to Widow Jones and Mother Morris? Then there were the others who flowed in and out of St. Sefin's, the broken and the hurt, the young mothers in need of shelter, patients they tended in their hospital wing, the travelers to Newport who found themselves lacking the coin or credentials to lodge in an inn but found a bed in the dormitory built for the lay sisters.

An arrogant young man had done this before, shredded Gwen's hopes and the fanciful future she'd built. Now she had something solid, real, and warm beating hearts sheltered in it. She would not allow the Viscount Penrydd to destroy St. Sefin's. She would do whatever it took.

"PENRYDD? Course I know him! Fine chap, absolutely ripping fellow. Never turns down a bit of sport, on the field or... elsewhere."

Calvin Vaughn trailed Gwen through the drawing room of Greenfield and leaned against the delicately painted wall as she seated herself before the *telyn*, the tall Welsh harp in one corner. Lady Vaughn's guests watched them, sharp-eyed, and Calvin peacocked in his waistcoat of bright orange silk. Calvin Vaughn, second son of Sir Lambert and Lady Vaughn, could afford the tax on hair powder.

"Going to the devil as fast as he might." Calvin went on as Gwen pulled the *telyn* onto her left shoulder and adjusted her seat. "But you know how it is with those young bloods who never imagine they'll inherit. Go a bit mad when the title and all that money lands in their lap."

Gwen ran her fingers over the triple row of strings. "You're friends, then? Perhaps you might put in a word for me. I want to buy St. Sefin's from him."

Calvin scowled. "That dank old convent? Heard things

about that place." He looked about the room, then dropped his voice. "Don't see why you'd bury yourself in that pile when you could let a gentleman set you up in a proper establishment."

Gwen bent her head, fumbling in her pocket for her tuning key. "St. Sefin's is a proper establishment, Mr. Vaughn. As chaste as the old Cistercians. I can't imagine what you've heard."

Calvin snorted. "Queer goings-on, that's what." He crossed his arms over his chest, fixing her with his watery blue gaze. "Funny you mention him now. He's coming here, you know. Penrydd."

Gwen looked up to find his gaze settled on her bodice. Her heart ticked to a faster pace, fluttering beneath the lace. "To Newport? What brings him here?" Was he coming himself to turn them out?

Calvin licked his pale lips. "Ran with him in London when I was there, him and Turbeville, chap from Bristol. Invited them down for some hunting. Fought with m' brother a few years back, Penrydd did. Hewitt's at Acre, don't you know, laying siege to Napoleon."

Gwen did know, because Lady Vaughn's elder son, Hewitt, was her ladyship's favorite theme of conversation. "When is he coming?"

"Hewitt?" Calvin's brow wrinkled. "Whenever they squash Old Boney, I suppose."

"Lord Penrydd. The viscount." Gwen applied the tuning key to the bray pins, listening for the tone she wanted, trying to calm her thundering pulse.

Calvin shrugged. "No nailing Penrydd down! He's been a cat on a hot bakestone ever since Tenerife."

Gwen knew only the vaguest outlines of the debacle that had been the Battle of Santa Cruz de Tenerife. She steadied herself with the strings beneath her fingers. Barlow had ordered them to vacate, and the viscount was following to turn St. Sefin's to his own purposes. The room was too small, the ornate cornices of the recessed ceiling descending upon her, the gilded trim on the enormous mirrors closing in. Her head swam. The pattern on the silk draperies clashed with the equally garish tracery of the rugs. The crystal chandelier hung so low that the older dowagers with their towering wigs of a bygone decade had to avoid it for fear of fire. Everything in this room was a trap.

Penrydd was coming. She drew in a long breath. "Perhaps you could arrange for me to meet him."

"Suppose you could *entertain* us while he's here," Calvin said with a leer.

Gwen's hopes swayed like a flat-bottomed dory caught in a tidal surge in the Severn. She had to stay on Calvin Vaughn's good side if she wanted his support. Which meant she, the harper, must suffer innuendos he'd never make to the other unmarried ladies dropping curtsies to his mother. She stroked the lace at her throat, hiding the flush over her chest, reminding herself of that long-lost babe, its lost mother. The promise she'd made to herself.

"I'd welcome the commission to harp for you, Mr. Vaughn." Gwen tossed her head. "If Lord Penrydd enjoys the sound of the *telyn*."

Calvin's smile bared his teeth, crooked and stained. "Want to make sure he enjoys it? Wear something more fetching. A frock that shows a bit more, you know, *here*." He circled a hand over the top of his chest.

Gwen gritted her teeth and pulled the harp firmly against her shoulder, hiding her bosom. She needn't be reminded there were only two reasons a man like Calvin Vaughn, or the Viscount Penrydd, would look twice at a nameless Welsh lass.

But he was coming to Newport. She'd have Mr. Stanley write him and arrange a meeting so she might lay her case before him. Beard the lion in his den, so to speak. She couldn't wait to tell Dovey. Penrydd might have a disconcerting reputation, and she couldn't admire anyone whom Calvin Vaughn considered a crony. But surely a war hero and a lord of the realm would not be so hard-hearted as to turn her away.

"NO."

A man's harsh voice drifted from the housekeeper's parlor as Gwen approached. Her fingers ached from harping for hours and her throat was parched. She hoped Mrs. Harries might make her a posset while she counted out Gwen's fee.

"It wasn't me that had at her," the man said viciously. "She wants coin for her trouble, I s'pose?"

A young woman's voice rose in a cry, the words muffled. Gwen paused in the servant's hallway, candles flickering in their sconces in the wall. She knew that sound. It landed like an arrow in her chest.

"She wants you to take up your part in the matter." Mrs. Harries sounded calm despite the ragged weeping. "She swears the *baban* is yours, sir."

"Not if I say it isn't! And she won't get a Druid penny from me."

The door to the small parlor slammed open and Calvin Vaughn appeared, smoothing the front of his detestable orange waistcoat. Gwen froze as his eyes lit upon her.

"Lurking about in hallways, Miss Ewyas? Not well done of you. Trust you won't spread any lies you hear told about me, eh?"

The pale, weak blue eyes pinned her. Gwen swallowed the words of accusation that surged to her lips.

"I don't spread lies, sir. But as to the truth..." In the heat forcing open her chest, of rage and old, old shame, she saw her own hope cracking and falling away.

Many a young maid had been turned off from Greenfield, sacked, it was said, for trying to ensnare the second son of the house. And now that she'd caught Calvin Vaughn out in his villainy, there would be no help from him with the Viscount Penrydd.

"Mrs. Harries, the harper is here for her fee." Vaughn threw the words over his shoulder, into the room where the weeping ensued, then turned to eyeball Gwen once more. "A fortnight," he snapped. "Penrydd is due in Bristol then, and you can throw yourself at him all you like." His eyelids thinned. "Now see that you don't misunderstand things."

The cad. Buying her silence with the information she desperately wanted. Gwen went to the door of the parlor.

A young woman knelt on the carpet. Her pale, work-roughened hands concealed the face under a white linen mob cap, her slight frame quaking in a plain grey muslin dress.

"You poor dear." Gwen laid a hand on one trembling shoulder. "Poor, sweet *geneth*, sweet girl."

Mrs. Harries sighed. "Mathry, I have done what I could. But you know what Lady Vaughn will require."

The girl drew a quivering sob. "I've nowhere to go. Me mam won't take me, and there's no work in me village for one with a bellyful. *Ach!* I'm not such a *twmffat* I thought that he'd wed me, but to *deny*—" She fractured into sobs.

Gwen couldn't take in one more soul, not when they balanced on the edge of eviction. But she could not simply leave this girl.

"Nothing for it, then," Gwen said, her voice steady. "Mathry must come with me."

Mathry pulled her hands away and looked up. She had a

round face, pleasant and sweetly dusted with freckles, her expression beneath it one of horror. "Oh, not *that* place!" she cried. "It's for...for..."

Gwen waited, one brow raised. "For those that ain't *right*," the girl whispered.

"St. Sefin's is for anyone who needs refuge," Gwen answered. "You may come seek us at any time, but it happens tonight I have a dogcart, so you need not walk. You might collect your things, for I gather you are to be turned off given your circumstances, and I will converse with Mrs. Harries while you do."

"Aiee, aiee!" Mathry keened, rocking on the carpet. "Why'd this happen to me?"

"It's happened to you and a thousand thousands before you, chick," Gwen said, trying to keep the sharpness from her voice. She hadn't collapsed and wailed in pity when it was her in this position. "As Mother Morris says, no use lifting your petticoat after you've peed."

Mrs. Harries shook her head as Mathry rose and rushed off, mumbling through her tears. "I warn them all, when they come," she said to Gwen, though her tone was not without pity. "And I'll be hard put to hire another maid when word gets out yet again."

"This isn't the time to trouble you for my fee, I know—"

"Yes, you'll want extra. The girl will need feeding until you find her a place." Mrs. Harries took a key from the ring at her belt and unlocked a small drawer of her desk, pulling forth a leather bag. "I'll drop Lady Vaughn a hint that you earned more this evening. She'll understand all too well why."

"Perhaps she will have a word with her son about his behavior," Gwen said as Mrs. Harries withdrew several sovereigns from the purse.

"When has that ever availed us?" The housekeeper

squeezed Gwen's hand as she transferred the coins. "Mathry doesn't know what you've saved her from, Miss Ewyas. As you've saved so many."

Gwen hunched her shoulders as memory loomed. A dark sty. The stench of animals, the warmth keeping her alive. Blood on the straw, enough to fill buckets. The frosted ground resisting her small shovel. The silent thing she laid to rest there, wet with tears.

She pushed the shadows away before they overtook her. Mathry, God willing, would carry no such memory to haunt her through her days. Gwen tucked the sovereigns into her pocket, tracing the king's profile with sore fingertips. She hoped by all the saints that these coins would go straight to the pocket of the Viscount Penrydd and win her St. Sefin's. She'd spend the rest of her life paying for it, if need be. She was paying for so much already.

Mathry sputtered with tears as the weary gelding pulled them gently over the hills and vales toward the River Usk. A bright moon silvered the land and the life upon it, a strange, silent glow unseen in the light of the workaday world. Wales lay draped in a veil of magic, but Gwen had not fully seen that until she came here.

Seven years ago, she had arrived in Newport ready to throw herself into the water, or board a boat and sail away from everything. But atop a green hill she'd glimpsed the sun hanging low over a glassy sheet of water which, she'd learn, was the winding Usk pouring into the mouth of the Severn. It seemed she'd reached the edge of the world. The town reminded her of her long-forsaken home, with the medieval castle looming over an ancient port, the ruins of a Roman fort nearby. She stayed, decided to look for a way to live. And then she found Dovey.

Who was waiting up, a candle in the window to light Gwen home, and in short order the two women had a bed in the old nun's dormitory dressed with fresh linens, a pitcher of warm water poured for the exhausted Mathry, and a candle in its holder placed on the small wooden shelf. Rare for a medieval nunnery, the sisters of St. Sefin's had occupied individual cells, the tiny rooms warmed by the kitchens below. It was a far sight better than the workhouse, but poor Mathry sat slumped on the edge of her cot, hair brushed and braided for the night, teeth cleaned, a worn bedgown hanging from her shoulders.

"I can't stay here," she said numbly. "But I've nowhere else to go, have I?" She rubbed her reddened eyes. "Not unless I rid meself of it. No one takes a maid with a *baban*."

Gwen gripped the holder of her candle. "You are welcome to stay here as long as you need, Mathry. We will look after you and any child as well. And if need be, you may leave the child here when you go."

The girl put a hand to a cheek stained with tears. "It's not true what they say, is it? That you...that children disappear here. That you have feasts for the devil, and—"

"Saint Dwynwen's toes!" Gwen cried. "Is *that* what they say? We foster infants until they are taken in by families! Who else around here does that?"

"But you're women alone." Mathry's gaze shifted between them. "And the men come and go, and...you've no one to answer to, and..."

Dovey's face gentled. "And we look after one another and ourselves, just as we please."

Mathry fell back upon the bed, letting out a whoosh of breath. "I've never come and gone as I wished."

"We pay a price for it, don't we?" Dovey reflected as they closed the door on the disconsolate girl. "Well, will the Vaughns turn up our good angels for this, or have they given us naught but another mouth to feed?"

"Mrs. Harries gave me extra, but I don't know if it's

enough." Gwen told Dovey the whole of it as they walked through the dormitory and down the night stair that led to the small chapel beside the old church. Out of superstition, or unarticulated faith, Gwen lit the stub of a candle each night in the small niche dedicated to St. Gwladys. This was where she'd found herself on that first night, leveled to her knees by loss, and she took comfort in the story of the ancient saint, a powerful mother and queen, who had given up everything for seclusion with her God.

"But how can we approach a viscount?" Dovey asked as they made their way back to the old prioress's suite of rooms. "Mr. Barlow isn't likely to make an introduction."

"I'll think of something," Gwen said. "I'll find where he's staying and demand an audience, or...I'll strap my harp to my back and go wherever he's carousing that evening and pose as his musical entertainment, if need be."

"And hope he hasn't heard the same outrageous stories reaching Mathry's ears." Dovey helped Gwen out of her gown and stays, then braided her hair for the night. In Dovey's small bed Cerys slept peacefully, her lips shaped in a smile, undisturbed by their soft rustling or their low, worried talk.

Gwen blew out the candle and crawled onto the straw tick that served as her mattress. Her mind whirled like the eddies one saw in the summer river. She had two weeks to plan how to win Penrydd's mercy, to keep the world she had built here from washing away. But how? What did one penniless Welsh woman offer an English lord?

The leering face of Calvin Vaughn and echoes of Mathry's sobs followed her into sleep while the silver moon sailed the sky in its ancient path, far above human sorrows and fears.

CHAPTER THREE

"Tell her no," Rhydian Price, the 4th Viscount Penrydd, roared to his secretary. "Absolutely not. Under no condition will I do anything so exceedingly boneheaded."

"Milord, if I might take the liberty of reminding you," said his secretary with a sigh, "you perform acts that could be termed exceedingly boneheaded all of the time."

"I won't step into the parson's mousetrap with some girl I've spoken with twice. No matter how much my stepmother wishes me to." Penrydd's leather boots thudded on the wooden floor of the tavern parlor as he swung them off the horsehair chair he'd been lounging in. "What time is it? And where's my rum?"

"It is half six in the afternoon and far too early to begin imbibing. But it is past time we dealt with your correspondence. Sir." Ross tapped his finger on the stack of vellum and foolscap spread over the small table where he sat.

"Bah. I pay you to deal with my correspondence. And deliver my rations of grog." Penrydd glared. "Don't leave off the lime this time."

The secretary rolled his eyes but held his tongue, and Penrydd was glad he wouldn't have to endure yet another lecture. His old navy compatriots poked fun at Pen's affection for the watered rum they'd been rationed aboard ship, flavored with sugar and, when Spain's blasted alliance with France made lemons as well as many other goods hard to come by, the splash of lime juice that prevented scurvy.

The noblemen he knew drank brandy or, if they wanted to be cultured, bourbon. They bought Champagne and Madeira from free traders who had evaded the import tax. They drank cider and sherry and beer.

Penrydd enjoyed those, too, but he liked his rum. Fortunately, he didn't have to begin bellowing or throwing things around, as he'd been obliged to do yesterday to make his point with Ross, who liked all too well to bully him. A scratch at the door announced a young man bearing a tray with Penrydd's glass. He swiped it up and swallowed a long draught and, instantly, the chafing settled. The tremor in his hands ceased, the ache in his head receded, the nervous, fretful feeling changed to one of brief well-being.

And the constant bite of pain faded for one blessed moment. He thought of it as teeth sinking into him. Sometimes it was the teeth of a rat, needle-sharp and annoying. Sometimes it was the teeth of a donkey, a blunt and ever-present pressure. And sometimes it was the teeth of a huge cat like the sailors who had been to India described, the tigers bigger than a man who could take off a limb with one snap.

He wished he could be eaten by a tiger. It would put a swift, tidy end to all the ills that plagued him.

"Where's my dinner?" He eyed the servant. "You might bring more grog with it."

"I won't feed you until you've finished with these letters," Ross said.

Penrydd rubbed his chest. The rum dulled the aches, but his

demons never released their grip. "Aren't I supposed to be giving orders to *you*?"

"You pay me to get the work done," Ross answered, "and unfortunately I cannot do that until—"

"Dinner," Penrydd snarled, slamming his empty glass on the tray of the young boy, who reared back in alarm. "I want a thick flank steak, *not* burned through as it was yesterday, and in a sauce that's a few more degrees above freezing. And leave off anything fancy, or leafy, or green. I won't have French fare at my table."

He glared at the lad, who turned pale. Where was the sweet-faced maid who'd brought his meals yesterday? She'd caught him appreciating her bosom and had given him a saucy wink. He liked a woman who knew what she was about. If a girl was going to put her best wares in the front window, she deserved to have a man enjoy the display.

"They's a gel 'ere to see ye, milor'," the boy stammered, backing toward the door.

Pen brightened. "Did you find me a companion for this eve, Ross? Turbeville had his ladybird with him last night, and it was deuced annoying to be the odd man out."

"I regret to say, sir, I did not have time for the effort. I had other matters demanding my attention. Like your correspondence," Ross said through gritted teeth.

"You couldn't find *one* bit of fluff? In a town the size of Bristol?" Pen scowled at his worthless secretary. His fingers itched for a second glass of grog.

"I am not your procurer, sir," Ross said. "If you desire female company, then you might have taken up the invitation to stay with Mr. Turbeville."

"Aye, and have all three of his sisters lined up at the table like mares at market, and his mother ready to toss on the leg-shackle the moment my gaze alights." Penrydd kneaded his ever-aching shoulder. "I'd rather pay them to go away when we're done."

"Send 'er up, shall I?" The boy scooted out the door, tail end first. "Right, then!"

Ross tapped the table. "We should also discuss the matter of finding you a valet for your stay with Mr. Vaughn, since the one you brought from London peeled off without notice."

"I'll use Vaughn's and count myself lucky to be shot of the blighter." Pen threw himself back in the stiff chair. It couldn't be that he was particularly hard to work with. All his cronies, the titled lords and the gentlemen's sons and the worthless hangers-on looking for a leg up, all of them complained about how difficult it was to find and keep reliable servants. If they weren't sneaking the liquor or feeling up maids in the pantry, they were filching a man's valuables and spending too much time at the pub. Pen had to admit that, if he'd had the damnable luck to have to work for his living, he'd likely be guilty of the same.

But he was a viscount now, the biggest joke yet that an evil-humored Creator had played upon him. A peer of the bloody British realm, with bloody lesser titles and all sorts of properties he now had to look after, including a bloody estate in Britain's back-end, Wales, where there were bloody tenants he had to see to and a handful of crumbling bloody ruins that he had to rid himself of to pay the debts his brother had left behind.

Didn't he hire men to deal with his confounded business so he could concern himself with more important things? Like blunting the pain before it made him a beast. And dedicating himself to the pursuits of a gentleman in the manner of their good Prince George: drinking, wenching, gambling, riding to hounds, and indulging to excess any pleasures that tumbled across his path. Small enough pleasure in the world otherwise.

He did *not* intend to cave to his stepmother's demand that he marry some milky white-livered maiden and breed mewling brats, nor sire a small Penrydd who would grow up to humiliate and defy him in the exact ways he had defied and humiliated his father. Not even if she brought a dowry that might make his brother's bad investments disappear. Being blown to bits on the beach at Tenerife had put paid to any debt Pen might have owed to his nation, his family, his bloodline, or his class.

War had taught him that there was no honor, no higher purpose. He was nothing but a motile, highly destructible piece of flesh. And he meant to enjoy every sensory pleasure this flesh could afford before the next cruel prank of the universe sent him to oblivion.

"Lord Penrydd?"

Pen's boots hit the floor again as he sat up. Speaking of pleasure. His capricious God had consented to smile on him for once. The most exquisite female-shaped creature he had ever beheld stood at the parlor door.

She wasn't dressed like a lady of the night. Her petticoat was clean and white, over it a gown of buttermilk muslin trailing vines of red flowers. It was a quaint style, quite outdated, but one that followed a woman's curves. A delicate lace crossed her bodice, tied at her back. He wanted to unwrap her, like a present.

An absurd cap of lace and silk roses covered curls of a dusty brown, the color of the paths at his favorite hunting property when they had baked in the sunlight on a summer afternoon. Her face was extraordinary. She didn't have the pasty complexion of a woman who never went about in the sun, rather a healthy glow and the tiniest dusting of freckles along a nose that suggested a personality both strong and pert. Independently the wide thick-lashed eyes, high cheekbones, lush lips, and arrowed jaw were pleasing yet unremarkable, but put together, the effect was mesmerizing.

"Fifty pounds," Pen blurted.

Her eyes rounded in surprise. They were some shifting, undefined color, the grey-green of the sea on a cloudy morning. Was she worth more? "A night," he added. He'd pay anything. He wasn't even going to pretend to negotiate.

Ross raised his thick brows. Pen ignored him, as usual.

"A *night*?" Her voice rang clear and fine, trained, the voice of a singer. But her tone held dismay. The lace over her bosom fluttered as she put a hand there. Long, delicate fingers, a fine-boned wrist with an elegant turn. He stared at her hands and imagined them trailing over his skin.

His rough, scarred, contemptible skin. "Not enough? Name your price."

"I hadn't arrived at a number, actually. I suppose I ought to have asked Mr. Barlow."

Who was Barlow? Her flesh broker? Her go between? He envied the man who had any hold over her. But she had a proud tilt to her head, that of an independent woman who answered to no one. He'd make her forget Barlow. He'd make her forget everything but her name. What was her name?

"In truth, I'm not certain what the going rate for such things is," she said.

Pen's head reeled with a grand, desperate notion. She wasn't a hedge whore or a public ledger, open to all comers. But a lady of easy virtue nonetheless, perhaps a high flyer or a quality courtesan. Pen wiped his sweating palms on his breeches. He couldn't afford her. Look at her skin; she wasn't starving or diseased, nor beaten into submission. Her eyes were clear and steady, if her expression was somewhat baffled, and she smelled like spring. A field of bluebells filled his mind, kissed by a warm sun.

Ah, God. For the first time he understood why a man would go to the trouble of keeping a mistress. So he could have sole access whenever he wished and keep her hidden from the outside world. He swallowed. How could he manage to keep her? Most of the letters on Ross's blasted table were bills and accounts of some sort, reminders of funds his rotter of a brother had died owing.

"I'm certain we can come to an agreement." Pen's voice scratched his throat. Where was the boy with the rum? The tremor was starting again, but the need this time was not for alcohol. He couldn't remember the last time he had wanted anything that had to do with another person. Wanted closeness. Affection. Approval.

Ah, yes. He'd wanted affection from his mother, approval from his father, company and camaraderie from his brother. And the evil-minded universe had laughed in his face and stretched him out upon the rack. Pen sweated underneath his neckcloth and worked with a finger to loosen it. This woman wouldn't be withholding, mocking, or cruel. She was warm and soft all over, inside and out.

She blew out a stream of air and Pen stared, arrested by the shape of her anemone-red lips. They would purse in exactly that fashion when he kissed her.

"I don't suppose you would consider simply *giving* it to me," she said. "Out of charity, you know."

Giving her—oh, he'd any number of notions of what he could give her. Starting with certain attentive parts of his body. Then the rest, all of him, for eternity.

Now, where had that bacon-brained thought come from? He was going barking mad with her standing there across the plain wooden room, and Ross watching with his infuriatingly bland expression, and all of this keeping her from where she ought to be, which was in his bed, minus her clothes. He mustn't be *too* stupid; women blessed with this kind of beauty were unfailingly cunning as well.

"What surety do I have that you wouldn't come back and demand something after?" he growled.

He stood and stalked nearer, grimacing as his sore muscles protested. He'd been sitting too long. But he couldn't come off a complete cully, not even to a fine-looking woman. She'd lead him to the cloth market and then later present her bill in the form of a by-blow he was expected to rear. He'd seen it happen to his friends; the Prince of Wales had a dozen such claimants for his paternity, besides the kitlings a certain Mrs. Fitzherbert might be raising in her nest.

"Well." She blinked, and Pen comprehended for the first time why love-struck young men composed sonnets to their lady's various features. He could get tangled in her lashes, caught and left to die there, happily. "I expect we would settle on some sort of contract," she said.

"Contract." His breath came shallow. This was too close to marriage, commitment. Contracts always cost something. He couldn't recall his friends ever mentioning they had a formal arrangement with their birds of paradise. They gave her a slip on the shoulder, carte blanche if they were a generous fool, jewels and silks if she performed in a satisfactory manner, and a dismissal when the performance had lost the power to interest them. Not *contracts*.

She frowned. Pen sweated. Perhaps expensive courtesans did demand written agreements. She could have anything that was his, but he couldn't have claims on his incomes or estates. For one thing, he couldn't support them.

"Ross?" He turned to his worthless secretary. Fortunate he had not removed his annoying self. Perhaps Ross, though born to the yeoman's class, understood these arrangements better than Pen did. "Draw us up a contract."

"Delighted, sir." Without expression, Ross sorted through

the stack of papers on the table before him. "I do not believe we have the pleasure of knowing your name, miss?"

"Why, yes," she said, blurring the words together. Pen strained to identify her accent. West Country, but something more than that? "Gwenllian ap Ewyas."

Welsh. Pen's heart lifted, thrilling to the musical sound of her voice. He could afford a Welsh mistress. Everyone knew the country was full of nothing but sheep herders and potato farmers. How a benighted land had produced such a pearl of a woman was a mystery, but he meant to take advantage of this rare stroke of good fortune. She wouldn't know her own worth, being raised among swine, and she wouldn't object to the coarser elements of the company he kept. He could show her off at the theater, stroll her through the pleasure gardens, and she'd likely be satisfied with paste jewels and a keeper who didn't beat her. He *could* afford her. For a very long time. Perhaps indefinitely.

"And I presume you are here about your interest in the property of St. Sefin's," Ross continued in his bland voice.

"Yes." The word was a whisper. She cleared her throat and squared her shoulders. "That's correct."

"Saint sodding *who?*" Pen barked. She wanted property? The minx! The designing little greedy guts. Then he observed the interesting lift to her bosom granted by her straight-backed posture, and he decided she was worth it. There was no padding, no falseness there. Did she but unveil the lace and let him see the mere tops of them, he was like to sign over anything for her breasts alone.

He needed that rum, devil take it. His mouth was dry as straw. "How much is the property worth?"

"At value, around a thousand pounds," Ross said. "But if one were to arrange a proper lease, the rents over time could amount to much more."

"I am interested in buying outright," she said with a nervous edge to her voice.

"You asked me to give it to you," Pen reminded her. "A regular nunnery, is it?"

Her brows were black and thick, like her lashes, and their pronounced arch made her eyes look larger, more expressive. "Not for some time, sir, though I'm told some nuns still lived there at the time of dissolution. It was the only Cistercian establishment for women in Wales, though I understand—"

"His lordship is inquiring whether you run a brothel," Ross said in the same flat, bored tone. He was clearly unimpressed by her beauty, unbewitched by her ethereal aura. How did he manage to escape her spell, blast the man? Ross ran in the petticoat line, though he wasn't nearly as energetic in his patronage as Pen was.

"A brothel?" she gasped. "No!" The most glorious blush, the pink rose of a sunrise, spread over her cheeks. It accented the height of her cheekbones, the elegant jut of her nose, the finely carved slope where her jaw curved toward her ear. He imagined such a blush spreading all over her body when he—

Her mouth was still moving. "A house of charity, milord!"

"A what?" Blood pounded in his ears, rhythmic as high tide, a combination of outrage, horror, and lust. "I never supported a charity home. Ross! Do I run any charities?"

"That is quite outside your realm of interests, sir," said his secretary.

"We've been there for years, milord. Nearly seven."

Before his brother became viscount, then. "I can't conceive that my father ever approved such a venture," Pen said. "What rents have you been paying until now?"

Up went that chin. He was right about her being pert. "None. Milord." The blush deepened.

"None whatsoever," Ross emphasized.

"We have maintained the property," she hurried to say. "Kept it from falling into disrepair. We haven't the funds to replace the windows, of course, and some of the stonework requires a skilled mason, but we—"

"And you live there?" Pen demanded.

"Yes, with..." She bit her lip as he glowered. With this Barlow, no doubt. Well, no longer. Her old keeper was about to be deposed.

Ross sorted through his pile and produced a set of papers containing a series of sketches. A crumbling ruin of an abbey, in better condition than Tintern but not nearly as picturesque. A rather extensive set of buildings, that! She wanted hectares, with a ruined old church, a solid compound of blocky medieval stone, and assorted outbuildings in the back. For the sheep and potatoes, no doubt.

She twined long fingers together as he stared at her. Those long, clever fingers he could imagine sliding through his hair, down his chest, over his scars, and, yes, a woman who demanded *property* for her favors could damn well tolerate his scars.

"...welcome to come see for yourself, milord, and meet them. There is Evans, and Dovey, that is Mrs. Van der Welle, and Cerys, and..."

A string of meaningless names. Why was she still talking? She'd do better appealing to him if she removed that blonde lace wrapping her bosom.

"It goes on as long I wish," Pen stated. "I get to end it. Not you."

"You mean, you will put a term on our lease?" Her eyes widened. "Er...yes, if you wish that in the contract."

"Write it down, Ross." Pen glared at his secretary, who made an elaborate show of producing an inkstand and quill. He did not, however, commence writing.

"Exclusive access," Pen went on. "You'll have no other men.

Not business associates, not hangers-on, certainly not friends." He knew all too well how immoral men were when it came to beautiful women. No code of honor whatsoever.

"But milord, St. Sefin's has always been open to men as well as—"

"Do you want the property or not?" he barked. "These are my terms."

She scowled. "I am listening." But she clutched the lace at her bodice as if she were steeling herself against a turmoil of inward thoughts.

He had the upper hand, and he knew it. "I have liberty to visit whenever I wish," he rapped out, drawing closer. His leg protested, and he hid a grimace. Blast and damn, he couldn't appear weak now. "No headaches," he insisted. "No excuses. No womanly complaints beyond the, er, usual." Women often had complaints about something, and there were certain days of the month when it was best not to interfere, that he'd learned.

"If you are signing the property over to me, I don't see why we need to submit to your inspection—"

"Not them. Just you. And you'll not complain about the lodgings I give you," he added, recalling friends whose mistresses constantly nagged about their rooms being too small, or poky, or infested.

She blinked, and he was ensnared further. "I intend to continue at St. Sefin's, since I—"

"I'm to live in Wales, the back end of Britain! No, thank you. It's London for me, and for you now as well."

"But you have an estate in Wales, I thought. A few miles from Newport?"

He'd forgotten about that. And he supposed he must visit the bloody place, or Ross would never cease nattering ad nauseum about his responsibilities. He'd been told the fastest way to get there would be to take a pilot cutter across the Bristol

Channel, which was out of the question. He was damned if he'd set foot in any kind of boat.

Though setting foot in a boat was not the problem. The problem was the stepping off the boat into a strafing attack from battlements hidden above the beach, the bodies of men suddenly exploding about him, sand and gore filling the air.

Well, there were roads even in the hind haunch of Britain, weren't there? Pen spoke loudly to drown out the sound of cannon fire in his head. "Very well, we can visit the house in Newport now and again, when you're weary of London. Maybe there's good shooting."

He would have Ross look into it. Wouldn't Turbeville be impressed when Pen turned up tonight with this exquisite creature? He'd try to steal her away immediately. Finally, his mates would have something to envy him for, rather than treating him like the poor broken sod they took on sufferance.

"You keep saying *we*," she noted.

"Well, that's the point of keeping a ladybird, ain't it? A mistress goes with her man. Like a well-trained hound."

Blink. Blink. Blink. He was lost, wrapped in the silky snare of those unending lashes.

"Ladybird?"

For the first time in ages, Ross appeared vastly amused.

"In return for St. What Who's," Pen said impatiently.

Her mouth fell open. She had all her teeth, white, pretty ones. Another point in her favor. "Are you asking me to be your *mistress?*"

"That's what you're here for, ain't it?"

"I came to ask you if I might *purchase* St. Sefin's!" Outrage filled her tone, but well-modulated, controlled. "Since you didn't respond to my letters." She tossed a look of accusation at Ross, who was no more moved by it than he was by any of Pen's scolds.

Pen crossed his arms over his chest. It hurt his shoulder like hell, but he liked the intimidating effect. "And I've said you might have it. On certain terms."

"Becoming your mistress!" she sputtered.

"What, you've another keeper? Barlow treats you better, does he?" Pen snarled, his fury rising. He stepped closer, which was a mistake. The scent of bluebells whacked him over the head, sending his brain awhirl.

She held her ground. He made note of that. Most people quivered and ran when he raised his voice. Except, of course, for Ross.

Up went that altogether too pert chin. "Did you not say before you were willing to grant me St. Sefin's for free, milord? It might do you good to cultivate a charitable interest."

She was cunning in the extreme. He leaned toward her, breaching the bluebells like a wall. He'd walked into cannon fire before this. He could bear the assault on his senses of her unbelievably soft-looking skin, her dusky hair beneath the silly cap, the red of her parted lips, that haunting timbre of her voice.

Her eyes. They were the color of the pond where he'd swum as a lad when his family went to their home in Essex for the summer. His brother couldn't swim, so it was Pen's way to escape him. He'd hold his breath and sink to the bottom and stay there as long as he could bear, watching the rays of sun slant through the grey-green water to light on the weeds and the fish and the utter quiet.

That sensation gripped him again for a fleeting moment. Of being weightless. Caught in a warm, silent world brimming with life. If only he'd met her before. Before he'd lost his family, before he was shot to bits, before he became a cursed viscount, the title thrusting him into a world he never wanted. He might have had a chance with a woman like her, the man he was before.

Ah, he was eight ways a fool. He was born an ass and he'd always be an ass. He narrowed his eyes, steeling himself against her bewitchment. "If you want your St. Sodding, you know what to do."

"You won't accept any other terms?"

The lace over her bodice rose and fell. She was real, every part of her. She was warm and she smelled like paradise, and she was every bright, beautiful thing that life had denied him up till now. He reached out a hand, the right hand that still worked as it should, to run his fingers over the lace and the supple swell of flesh beneath.

She pushed his hand away. "I won't do it."

He scowled. "You bloody well came to *my* rooms. You made me an offer. I accept."

"I didn't offer *that*. My..." She didn't say the word *virtue*, but a courtesan, no matter her price, could make no claims to virtue. She firmed her lips. "I'll pay you. A thou—a thousand pounds."

"Done. And you'll pay in the currency I specified." He smiled broadly. "The cloth market. The blanket hornpipe. Making the beast with two backs—that is Iago's line, you know. Always did think he's the best thing Shakespeare wrote."

See, he wasn't an entire ogre. He was cultured. He'd take her to the theatre. He'd even take her to musical evenings if she persuaded him in the right ways. "I'll tell you when the debt is relieved."

She narrowed her eyes right back at him. "There will be no blanket hornpipe. *Sir*."

"Oh, there will be horn piping." She stepped away, and he grasped the fringe at the edge of the shawl she wore draped over her elbows. It wasn't a Kashmir shawl like that worn by the girls his stepmother tried to make him talk to. It was wool with a red and black print, a serviceable item of clothing, freshly laundered but clearly much worn.

Neither was her cap of a fashionable style, and her gown, for that matter, was a decade out of date, not of silk or satin but hand-painted muslin. The lace that enchanted him was an archaic touch, as fashionable young ladies had put off their laces during the French Revolution. She wasn't expensive.

Which meant he could afford her. Which meant he couldn't let her leave.

"Ross!" he barked. "That contract."

Ross lifted one maddening brow. "Have the terms been decided, then?"

"I just want St. Sefin's." She clutched her lace as if he would tear it from her. Her eyes were wide but not full of fear. Rather anger, sorrow, disappointment—God, how he hated when women looked at him with disappointment. But there was also a hint of despair.

And I just want you. Of course, he wouldn't be such a complete clod as to say it. A woman that beautiful, that graceful, that entirely enchanting should never know despair, not the faintest hint of it.

Instead, he stretched his mouth into a grimace that was his attempt at a smile. He wanted her in his bed immediately. She could start earning her title to whatever properties of his she wanted and he'd strive for that oblivion that would release him, however temporarily, from remembrance, from hauntings, from pain.

"And you know what my requirements are. I'll give you a week to gather your things. And if you don't agree, then I'll come to St. Who's What myself and turn all of you out, every last rat and bedbug."

She whirled away from him, and beneath the flare of her petticoats he glimpsed her feet, clad in sensible leather half-boots, much worn. Her flight to the door left him with the most extraordinary tearing sensation, like a limb being ripped away.

She was leaving, but he understood now that she didn't have any money. Nothing near a thousand pounds. Likely she'd never seen two sovereigns side by side. She had nothing to bargain with but her own sweet, delicious self.

She'd be back.

"Don't make me wait too long!" he called as she exited. "I'm likely to lose interest, and I have a terrible memory."

He smiled as the door slammed behind her. For the first time in ages, Pen had something to look forward to. Something more than a burned flank steak, weak grog, Turbeville's idiocy, and a blinding hangover.

He faced Ross, who looked back with a level stare. "I'll wait on that contract then, shall I?" his secretary said.

Pen rubbed his hands together, the good right against the left that sometimes had full sensation, sometimes not. He felt more alive than he had in ages. As if life had been granted him again. He hadn't felt that even when he woke on the surgeon's cot after Tenerife, unable to move half of his body, beset by a staggering pain that he understood even then would become his constant companion. Finally, undeservedly, but after much suffering, he'd been granted a reprieve.

"I give her two days. Three at most," he said confidently. "Where's my rum?"

CHAPTER FOUR

F our days had passed. Three to go, and then Penrydd would be upon them. Gwen imagined the scenario as she filled her sack with her latest batch of soaps, scented waters, and remedies. He would come with a pitchfork, like men used to pursue witches.

No, he was a titled lord, arrogant and indolent. He'd hire someone else to brandish the pitchfork. Like the sly secretary who had sat and witnessed their interview with great amusement, knowing the whole time what Penrydd was asking her was far, far different from what she was offering him.

Would it be any less embarrassing if they hadn't had a witness? It would have been no less infuriating. No less crushing a disappointment. She would be left in the same quandary.

Become his mistress. Save St. Sefin's. And be taken away to the most enormous and filthy of English cities, far from the hills and rivers of Wales, to become a kept woman, subject to a man's whims and compelled to submit to whatever he demanded of her. A strange, uncomfortable heat snaked through her innards at the very thought.

Or deny him, preserve her virtue, and let them all be cast into the street without shelter or sustenance. Was her virtue really worth that much?

"I won't let you do it." Dovey waited outside the kitchen door, morning sunlight lending her hair and face the high gloss of finished silk.

"Do what? Go to harbor and trade our goat's milk for seaweed? I've been meaning to make laverbread," Gwen answered. "And if the butcher has lamb to give away this week— roast lamb with laver sauce! Wouldn't that be a treat?"

"You won't go back and bargain with that devil," Dovey said.

Gwen picked up the long yoke and settled the curve over her shoulders, and Dovey set a crock of goat's milk, stoppered with cloth, in one basket. Gwen swung the yoke towards her, and Dovey set a wrapped cheese in the second basket. "That's not too heavy, that is?" she asked.

Gwen shifted to balance the weight. With the sack on her back to carry goods home and a few coins tucked into the shawl wrapped at her waist, she was ready for market. "I don't mean to bargain with him. I won't meet his terms."

Dovey blew a stream of air, ruffling the curls at her brow. "All right, then."

"You thought I would?" Gwen exclaimed.

"I expect you considered it," Dovey said, a sharp edge to her tone.

She scanned the sky, and Gwen turned to join her, sniffing the air. Mist rose from the low-lying river, bumping at the knees of Stow Hill, where St. Sefin's shared its high prospect with the ancient church of St. Woolos. Dim through the veil rose the square towers of Newport Castle and the angled supports of the wooden bridge crossing the Usk. Small boats and slender ships with towering masts floated around the wooden wharves and lined the sandy curves of the river, anchored until the next tide. Further south, mist crawled over the marshlands that mean-dered with the river toward the Severn's mouth and the Bristol Channel. Close by, the wallflowers blooming along the old stone walls of the priory teased her nose with their heady aroma, and beyond that she smelled fresh-turned earth where Dovey and Widow Jones were preparing the vegetable beds.

He couldn't take this all away from them. He *couldn't*.

"I considered it," Gwen acknowledged. "But he wouldn't let me stay here, and to pay him with—in—" The cloth market, he'd called it. The *blanket hornpipe*.

The heavy, suffocating weight of a man atop her. That strange disassociation of being joined so intimately, and yet knowing the man above one, taking his pleasure, was not connected to one in the least. It was all so—something she'd never subject herself to again.

Not even to save St. Sefin's.

"I wonder if I could propose something else as a trade," Gwen said. "He's still at the Green Man in Bristol, I under-stand. But he's due at Greenfield in a day or two, and—"

"No," Dovey said.

"But you haven't heard what I—"

"No," Dovey said again. "Make him come to us. Make him turn us out. Let him try." She folded her arms across her chest and shook her head. "He'll have to look us all in the eye as he does it, and if he's the fiend you say, he'll have it in him. But if he's not..."

Gwen felt a wee tendril of guilt that her portrayal of Penrydd had led Dovey to view him as a devil incarnate. He was a self-absorbed brute, coarse and lustful, but those traits were shared by a vast proportion of the male species. He was too handsome for his own good, that was also true, with a fine-featured face, a large rangy frame, a full head of hair and a full mouth of teeth. Looks like that no doubt let him cut a swath among susceptible women, so little wonder he assumed she'd tumble into his arms. But there was something about the way he carried himself, a stiffness to his posture, a hitch to his stride, that made her think the man guarded some deep inner pain. As if his war injuries had not healed aright, and the ache in his limbs was clouding his head.

She shook her head to clear it of fancies. He was the devil made flesh, all right. Promising her what she wanted for a price she couldn't pay. She'd have the pitchfork ready for *him* did his shadow fall across the door of St. Sefin's.

"Mayhap he's drunk himself into a stupor four nights running, and forgot all about us," Gwen said. Perhaps the viscount would turn back to merry old England without giving them another thought. "Most like he's unconscious in a bed somewhere, sleeping off a thick head and snoring enough to bring the roof down." Leaving them to crouch in St. Sefin's in worry and fear until the sly secretary or Mr. Barlow made his move, and their safe home tumbled down about their ears.

MILORD PENRYDD WAS INDEED UNCONSCIOUS. But not in a bed. Gwen stood at the wharf a bare hour later, staring at the small, flat-bottomed dory and its passenger.

"Floated up to me like Moses in his basket," exclaimed the fisherman who'd been casting his nets at the shore and had gathered a small crowd with his excited shouts. "Came out o' the mist like a ghost."

Gwen knelt on the wet, sandy shore and reached inside the light boat that had been drawn up out of the water. The man within lay still as a post, but when she probed the side of his neck she felt the pulse, faint but steady. Unconscious, but alive. St. Aled's head, what had happened to him? Dried blood matted his brow and pooled beneath his head, leaving his brown hair wet and sticky, but she recognized him.

"He's alive," she said, and the cool fog, not quite lifted, touched her neck with a chill. He'd been coming for them.

He was dressed as he'd been during their interview, in buckskin breeches and a clawhammer coat of dark superfine, but his simple blue waistcoat was marred with dirt and the white cloth around his neck stained with blood. His head was tilted one way, his limbs another. He likely had cracked ribs if he'd fallen or been thrown into the boat. It was scarcely a surprise that his wretched conduct might have involved him in an accident or attack. The only mystery was how he'd survived, and what to do with him next.

"This one has Davy Jones looking after him, he has," the fisherman said.

Gwen, glancing his way, saw his baskets brimming with roach, pike, and barbel. On a normal day, she'd have bargained with him. She'd already traded her goat's milk for a basket of laver, the local seaweed, before Penrydd's boat was spotted. A fish stew with laverbread would make a lovely last meal before they were all turned out to starve.

Unless, of course, she agreed to become this man's mistress. Though still and injured, the sheer bulk of him made her shiver. He was a powerful man, title aside.

"Couldn't be out for a row," reported the crab man, emptying his nets and sorting the cockles, razor clams, and mussels into different baskets. "No oars."

Cockles with a dash of vinegar and a hearty laverbread would make a fine lunch later, too, Gwen thought. Might as well make their last meal as fine as could be.

"Forked by a buzzman at the docks down river and rolled over the side to keep him quiet," the laver merchant guessed, coming up with one of his baskets filled with algae. "Then the dory floated up here with the tide, and deuced lucky it caught 'im, if you'll pardon the language, Miss Gwen."

"Forked?" she questioned.

"Cleaned by a diver," he answered. "A sharper. A cut purse. Sure and there ain't a farthing on him. Even 'is stickpin's been snaffled." He pointed at the disheveled neckcloth around the unconscious man's neck.

"I wager the bore got him," someone announced.

"Aye," said the fisherman, brightening. "Did you see it this morn, then? New moon, and the winds just right—big enough to unfoot a land *llob*, I'd say."

That sounded unlikely to Gwen. The famous Severn bore was a tidal wave that roared up the river several times a year, born from the ocean and, when throttled into the narrow estuary, could grow taller than a man and move faster than a horse. But where the mouth of the Severn was wider, as in Avonmouth across the way, the bore made no more than a deep swell, hardly enough to topple an experienced sailor and a former officer of the Royal Navy.

"He needs a doctor." Gwen sat back on her heels. Damp seeped through her linen petticoat and flannel gown. She needed to send him away while he was still unconscious. The man was on his way to turn her out of her home. "Is anyone headed to Bristol this morning? Cardiff? Anywhere?"

The fisherman drew off his wool cap and scratched his head. "No doctor 'round here, Miss Gwenllian. Ain't been a hospital in Spitty Lane since the days of Owain Glyndŵr."

Her breath stuck in the top of her chest. "I can't take him to St. Sefin's." Deliver him to the last place she wanted him to be? She'd be giving the executioner the rope to hang them.

"But where else?" asked the laver merchant, inspecting the still man's face. Penrydd was growing paler by the moment, his breath inaudible, the rise of his chest a shallow heave. They couldn't take him to the workhouse or to a church. There was a barber-surgeon, who was also the local tailor, but Penrydd didn't need leeching. Gwen knew a cunning woman she and Dovey called on for cases they couldn't nurse, but the woman lived past Langstone. It would take time to fetch her here.

And she didn't know the extent of Penrydd's injuries. If he were bleeding inside, he could be dead within the day.

And wouldn't that solve all your problems, said the devil in her ear.

No saint ever suffered the inner struggle that visited Gwen at that moment. All she had to do was walk away. Say she didn't know him, there was naught she could do, and leave him at this pass where fate had brought him. This man was a threat to her livelihood and all she held dear. If he disappeared, the threat would disappear with him.

Until the next Viscount Penrydd took inventory of his properties and wondered why he was encumbered with a crumbling priory in Wales.

She wasn't a saint, but she wasn't capable of leaving him here. She wouldn't leave anyone like this, not a sworn enemy, not the devil himself. She would find someone who would see to his care.

"I'll need help moving him," she said.

"St. Sefin's it is, then," said the crab man with great relief. "Good of you, Miss Gwen."

"No, I—" Her protest went unheard as the men sprang into action, gratified that the problem was to be taken from their hands. The fisherman and crab man found a handcart and the laver merchant threw down a dried mass of weed and bracken to form the semblance of a bed. She held Penrydd's head, her hands under his neck, while the fishermen and crab men hoisted his legs and transferred him to the cart. He was exceedingly heavy. He was thoroughly wet and soiled with blood, muck, briny water, and the sharp ammonia smell of urine. How long had he been in this boat?

And how had he arrived here? Mere days ago, he was a cocky, mocking lord demanding she provide him sexual favors. He'd given her an insolent leer, pawed the lace at her bodice—she felt even now the hot imprint of his fingers on her breast. So much vigor, but also anger and cruelty in him. And now he was this, broken, bloodied, beaten, and silent.

St. Winifred, preserve us, Gwen prayed as the helpful tradesmen arranged everything. The fisherman promised to put about word and find the owner of the dory. The laver merchant arranged her crocks of seaweed in the cart, bracing Penrydd's body, and laid the yoke alongside. Two curious boys who'd joined the crowd of onlookers were enjoined to push the cart up the hill to St. Sefin's and immediately fell to quarreling over which of them should take which handle.

She needed to avoid this man, and now she was bringing him to the very place he had promised to turn her out of. How could she be so foolish? What would Dovey say?

Perhaps he'd be grateful enough for her help that he could be reasoned with. Gwen drew her shawl around her and thanked the fisherman and the crab man by purchasing some of their wares. Then she followed the cart and the quarreling boys and the unconscious body of Viscount Penrydd, lord of the British realm, up Stow Hill to the property he had spoken of with scorn and from which he meant to evict her.

Loss pierced her heart as the straight stone walls of the priory came into view. She *loved* this place. The steepled roof with its clay tiles, so many missing or broken. The bell tower empty of a bell. The roof over the north transept had fallen in decades before and they had no means for repair; they simply mopped up after it rained and tried to keep the mold out, since no one used the church anyway. The men stayed in what had once been the lay sisters' dorter, built to house the women who lived at the priory without taking religious vows. On the ground floor, easily accessed from the storerooms and kitchen, was the infirmary, where she would put Penrydd for now. Until he came to his senses and ordered them to vacate, and she would never see these dignified stone walls again.

She gazed at it all as if for the last time. There was Ifor, grazing his goats in the churchyard. The tune of his pipes drifted on a breeze that warmed as the morning advanced. Tomos clung to the roof of one of the outbuildings, Evans on the ladder behind him, teaching the boy to repair the thatch. Mother Morris and Widow Jones poked wooden tubs full of washing with their long poles. Dovey walked with Mathry along the far hedge, Cerys's curly head bobbing between them as they foraged for mallow, sorrel, and the buds and young leaves of hawthorn. When Dovey spotted Gwen coming up the hill she headed their way and met her in the small open square between the goat shed and the infirmary.

"By St. David! Are we robbing the charnel house now?" Dovey examined Gwen's passenger with alarm.

"I don't know what happened. He washed up ashore at the wharves this morning. Might have been on a boat coming from Bristol." The light dories were made for regular crossings of the channel, bringing goods and people back and forth. But Penrydd had been alone, with no one to steer. Left alone to die, it would seem. Her heart contracted. He might be an obnoxious lord, but no one deserved that fate.

"A drunk landlubber knocked over by the bore," Dovey predicted.

"Or rolled by thieves and left for dead." Evans joined them, peering curiously into the cart. "A nob, looks like. Do we know 'im?"

They both looked at Gwen. She swallowed hard. She

couldn't lie to the faces of her dear ones, but if she said who he was, she'd have a fight on her hands. Dovey would want to know why they should give aid to a man who meant them harm—a man who meant to leave her and her young daughter without shelter or a way to earn their keep. And Evans would argue with Dovey, and Gwen couldn't stomach another quarrel between them, not in her state of fear.

"Let's take him to the infirmary first," she said.

The boys carried the unconscious man to a cot in the long, open room that housed St. Sefin's sick and injured. Gwen let Evans and Dovey tend to the lower portions of their patient, cleaning and clothing him in a pair of loose cotton breeches. It was laughable that Dovey, a widow, should be allowed to button the fall of a strange man's breeches where Gwen, with her maiden status, was not, though her experience with men was no less.

Still, Gwen was happy not to have to deal with the nether regions of the man who had proposed she become intimately acquainted with them. But that left her the more dangerous business of tending to the wound on his head. Her heart stuck in her throat the whole time she cleaned away the encrusted blood. She breathed again to find that, while he had a large goose egg on the back of his skull, the scalp wounds that bled freely were not deep.

"No new injuries down here," Dovey said, unfolding a blanket to pull over their patient's legs. "But Gwen, look at his scars."

A thick raised line, still an angry pink, ran from his left thigh to mid-calf. Gwen's tongue swelled in her mouth, blocking words. In reply she pointed to his bare chest, rising and falling with shallow breaths. His left chest and shoulder were one enormous bruise, and beneath the purpling skin ran a network of raised lines, red and pink and white. His arms and chest were muscular, virile; he was surprisingly fit for a posh lord. But the left side of his body from the neck down was pocked with small craters, a cluster of tiny pink divots that looked like the surface of the moon.

"That's canister shot," Evans said, pointing to the scar on Penrydd's leg. "But that's grapeshot." He indicated the web of scars over his chest. "Someone came at him long and close range, from the looks of it, and he didn't have a scrap of defense." He shook his head. "Poor sod. I wonder where he saw action?"

"Tenerife," Gwen blurted. The sight of his abused body, new injuries upon old, made her stomach feel tangled and sore. He'd been so strong and commanding with her at the tavern, playing the arrogant lord to the hilt, and underneath he was hiding these wounds. Beneath the offensive manner was a young man who had endured incredible suffering.

"This is Lord Penrydd. I met him at the Green Man."

At their shocked faces, she rushed on. "He said he would come turn us out if I didn't agree to his terms. He must have been traveling to Newport, and was attacked or in some sort of accident, and—I couldn't leave him like this."

"The Viscount Penrydd? The one we've been writing to? The one you went to see!" Dovey stepped back, watching the man on the bed as if he were a coiled viper ready to strike.

"What terms did he offer?" Evans asked.

"We couldn't agree," Gwen answered. "And now I brought him here. I'm so sorry."

All three of them stared at the still form on the bed. He was less pale now, his skin not so clammy. His breath seemed calm and even. Gwen picked several long strips of cloth from the bandage basket. In the face of a larger problem she didn't know how to resolve, she liked to focus on the small tasks.

"Help me bind his ribs. I expect the bruising means he

cracked or perhaps broke a few. I think we ought to make a sling for his shoulder as well."

"He's here," Dovey said. "At our mercy. We simply don't let him leave until he agrees to sell. On terms we *can* accept."

"And then we're taken up on charges and transported to the colonies for kidnapping a lord," Gwen said.

Dovey shrugged and lifted Penrydd's right side so Gwen could wrap the bandage around him. It was altogether unnerving to touch him. Leaning over him like this, she felt his heat, and it carried his scent—not foul, not any longer. He smelled like something spicy she couldn't identify, and a trace of the honey she used in their soap.

"I heard a bit about Tenerife," Evans said. He leaned on his cane and watched them. "He must have been one of the first Nelson ordered onto the beach. The Spanish guns mowed them down like wheat."

"St. Brychan's tartan," Gwen whispered. She'd heard Tenerife spoken of as a curse, one of Admiral Nelson's few failures. Hundreds of British men lost to a handful of Spanish soldiers, ships with their captains destroyed. Nelson himself lost his arm in that battle.

Penrydd had all his limbs yet, but he had not been left unscathed.

"Was that why he left the navy?" Gwen asked. She didn't know why she kept her voice low, since they were alone in the room and Penrydd was still unconscious.

"I heard he was out of action for a while, but I gather he sold out when his brother died and he gained the title," Evans said. "Mind, this is all what the vicar told me, since he keeps tabs on the great families hereabout."

"Should we call Mr. Stanley? In case—last rites are needed?"

"No," Dovey said. "We don't tell anyone he's here. Not until we've struck a bargain."

"You're a hard woman, Mrs. Van der Welle," Evans said.

"And you're a fool, Mr. Evans, if you don't think we ought to take advantage of him while we can. He'll be recovering under our roof, wearing our clothes, eating our food. We have every right to press our case with him."

"It's his roof, under British law," Gwen said. At Dovey's dark glare, she raised her hands in the air. "Don't eat me! I agree with you."

Dovey's gaze lingered on her, wary and guarded, and Gwen stiffened. Dovey knew what Penrydd had offered her. Gwen could give up their fraught life in a moment and go on her merry way, the kept mistress of a rich English lord, leaving the rest of them to starve if Penrydd chose to turn them out. After all they had been through, it hurt that Dovey would doubt her for a moment, but Gwen understood why. She had a child to protect.

"He doesn't leave until we've made a bargain," Gwen promised.

Dovey gave her a quick, decisive nod and left to see about dinner, their main meal of the day. Gwen's stomach bit at her insides. She must be hungry. And nervous about the man in the bed, an intimidating presence even if he appeared to be sleeping. He would be the devil to deal with when he woke, sore from his injuries, outraged at the wrong done him.

Taking care not to disturb his dressings, she tucked Penrydd into an old linen shirt, then rearranged the blanket over his chest. His body felt properly warm again, his color improving, his pulse steady. Her hand lingered, fingers lying against the column of his throat as she studied his face. He was a well-made man, in his proportions as close to the ideal as was possible for a man to be, a splendid specimen even with his scars. Many a woman, she imag-

ined, would leap at the chance to earn her keep through intima-
cies with a man not repulsive in his person, though she couldn't
say as much for his character. It would be pleasant to have one's
own rooms, jewels and fine gowns and a carriage, all the things
she had once thought would be hers, but for a lighter price.
Wives had to rear the children and run the household. Mistresses
need merely amuse and provide appropriate bed sport.

No. She wouldn't do it, not even to save St. Sefin's for
Dovey. She had vowed long ago that no man would have that
power over her again. Struggling to keep body and soul together
at least had some honor to it. She would be allowed to keep her
soul.

Dovey brought her dinner, steamed cockles and sauteed
mallow leaves with laver sauce poured over all, and a large slice
of *bara brith*, their native bread. She handed Gwen her knitting
and they kept watch, talking as if it were any given evening and
they sat before the fire in the chapter house with the rest of their
community gathered. They discussed whether they could buy a
side of beef from the butcher. If the Morgans would summer at
Tredegar House this year, and host parties where they might
invite Gwen to harp. Where next to apprentice Tomos, if
anyone would take him, and what to do about Mathry, who
wandered about blank-faced and prone to bursts of weeping.

All the while, the sun inched from the east windows to the
west and the man on the bed breathed, a looming shadow, an
ever-growing threat. Gwen was about to lose her mind and
pounce on him, throttling him awake to demand he pronounce
their sentence and end the suspense.

When it came, the hoarse whisper from the bed nearly
made her shriek and drop her mending.

"Where the devil am I?"

Gwen melted into a puddle of relief. Not dead. She'd been
fearing what she must say to Mr. Stanley, Mr. Barlow, that

awful sly secretary, if Penrydd died. They'd have every reason to think she'd wanted it.

"This is St. Sefin's," Gwen croaked, and then held her breath. Perhaps if he looked about, saw the place through her eyes, his heart would soften toward them.

Dovey sat up and put her knitting aside. She held still as a mouse.

"Who are you?"

His voice was a low rasp. She passed him a wooden cup filled with water from their own well, clear and safe to drink. He tried to raise his right hand, groaned, and let it fall.

"Jesus. Every part of me hurts. What happened?"

Her fingertips tingled as she touched him. Odd. She slid her hand behind his neck and urged his head forward, bringing the cup to his lips. He drank, coughed, and without thinking she dabbed the corner of his mouth with her sleeve. The man was weak as a newborn lamb, yet she still felt a thrill of terror course through her.

She presumed it was terror, at least. Any moment now, he'd recognize her.

His eyes were a reddish brown, like hazelnuts. The outer corners slanted upward, giving him a faintly devilish look. His nose was straight, very aristocratic, and his lower lip was full and almost womanly. What obliterated any impression of soft-ness or femininity was the jut of his chin and the straight, bold jaw, creasing as a muscle clenched.

"Who *are* you?" he breathed.

"Gwenllian ap Ewyas." Her voice scratched from her dry throat, barely audible. It stung that he couldn't recall her from mere days ago, but she mustn't appear weak or simpering. She had to keep the upper hand.

"And who am I?" he asked.

Her breath stopped. "Beg pardon?"

His brows met. "I don't know where I am. I can't say why I feel I've been trampled by a bull. I don't know who you are." He looked up at the ceiling, at the empty room around them, then focused on Dovey. "I don't know who *you* are." He closed his eyes briefly. "And I can't remember my own name."

This was unexpected. Gwen rushed to help him. "You're Pen—*ow!*" She sucked in a breath as Dovey's knitting needle sank into her side. Poking her stays, not her skin, but still.

"Pen?" The furrows deepened on his forehead. "Pen." He repeated it softly to himself. "It feels right, and yet—like that name doesn't belong to me." He met Gwen's eyes, his expression bewildered. "Why should that be?"

"What *do* you remember?" Dovey asked.

He squeezed his eyes shut and thought a long time before answering. "I remember a tree in a meadow. Sunlight. I felt safe there." He paused. "I see a woman's face. I want her to smile at me—is she my mother? I see a tall ship riding at anchor. A naval vessel." He opened his eyes and stared at Gwen, the blank look giving way to panic. "That's it. Everything else is wiped clean. My life—gone."

"You did take a rather fierce blow to the head," Gwen said weakly. "I've heard that can disorient for a while."

"Gwen, dearie." Dovey's fingers clamped around her wrist. "Let's give our patient a moment, shall we? Mayhap he'll remember something more." She dragged Gwen out of the wooden hall of the infirmary into the room next door, the old buttery which they still used for storage.

"He doesn't remember who he is!" Dovey hissed.

"I know!" Gwen clapped a hand to her mouth, pushing back a mad giggle. She had heard tales of people who couldn't recall events after an accident had injured them. There was a farmer in Langstone who had fought in the American colonies and then returned home unable to recall a single incident from the war.

"We can use this," Gwen said. "We can make him see how people need us, and perhaps he won't toss us out after all. We need only explain—"

"Or we tell him nothing," Dovey said.

Gwen frowned. "You mean, let him see for himself what we do here?"

"I mean," Dovey said, with deliberate slowness, "we tell him nothing about *him*. Let him remember on his own time who he is, and what he meant to do with us."

Gwen gasped. "You want us to *lie*?" Her stomach turned over, sending an acidic bite up her gullet. Obliterating the pleasure of that delicious meal.

Dovey's face wore the innocence of an angel. "Lie about what? I've never seen this man before. I don't know him from Adam."

"I can't deceive him. Dovey—I won't be able to keep up a pretense." This wasn't a little white lie to Cerys that there was not in fact a rat in the cellar or that the man leading a calf to the butcher's was taking his pet for a stroll. She wasn't capable of even those beneficial lies that might make someone feel better.

"My darling, darling dear." Dovey gripped Gwen's wrists. "Listen to me. He needs us right now. He needs our help. It may take him a day or two to recover his memory. And when he does —he'll have seen our ways, as you said. He'll understand what we do here. He'll realize what he owes us, and if he's a gentleman, he'll pay that debt." She squeezed Gwen's hands until the blood left them. "All you have to do is not tell him who he is."

Gwen stared into her friend's eyes. She understood. Gwen could walk away from St. Sefin's. She could strap her traveling harp to her back and wrap her few bits of clothing in the shawl at her waist and she could go anywhere. But Dovey had a child to think about, and Dovey couldn't go just anywhere. Not every town welcomed a face that wasn't the same color as all the rest.

Gwen swallowed and waited until her dinner was back where it was supposed to be. "Just tell him nothing," she said.

Dovey nodded in encouragement and loosened her grip. "Let him remember on his own. It won't hurt him."

"It won't hurt him," Gwen repeated.

Dovey squeezed her hands again, but gently this time. "That's my dear girl." She walked back into the infirmary, and Gwen followed.

Late afternoon light slanted across the floor. It lit strands of Pen's hair to gold and burnished his skin. There was a remarkable calm in his voice for a man who had just consulted his memory box and found it empty.

"How did you know my name was Pen?"

"Muttered it in your sleep," Dovey lied blithely.

Gwen's first test came immediately. The hazelnut eyes swung on her. "Do I know you?" he demanded. "You seem— familiar."

Gwen's stomach plopped straight into her worn out shoes. She ran her hands along the fringe of her shawl and prayed to St. Gwladys for strength.

"We are not acquaintances," she answered. "Remember anything else, mi—mmm?" She narrowly remembered not to call him milord.

"Nothing." His throat tensed as he swallowed his panic. Of course he would feel helpless and alarmed. Everything he had, he'd been given because of his name, and now he didn't know what that name was. He was strong, healthy, in the prime of his life, and yet he was reduced to nothing, not knowing who he was, where he belonged, where he might go for help.

She knew exactly how that felt.

"You can stay here, Pen," she said gently. How bold, to

address a lord so familiarly. Only his peers were allowed to do that. "As long as you need to."

His eyes narrowed. "Why?"

"Because," Gwen said, "that is what we do."

The wolf was loose in the sheepfold now, she thought. And she had put him there. How long did they have before his head cleared and the jaws of the wolf snapped shut?

CHAPTER FIVE

Penrydd might have injured his memory, but whatever happened to land him in the dory at the Newport wharf didn't change his personality one whit. He was surly and demanding and insulted everyone and everything.

He didn't like the fish stew that Gwen brought him for a light supper. "As if I'd eat barnacles someone scraped off a ship's hull and boiled!"

"How do you know you haven't?" Gwen challenged him, picking up the wooden spoon he'd tossed onto the floor. She had half a mind to hit him over the head with it. He was sitting up in bed by this point, with pillows she'd helped tuck behind his back, which had required leaning far too close to him and smelling his warm, spicy, male scent again. He ought to have a foul odor and a hideous face to match his temper.

His brows snapped together. "I know ships and sailing. And I don't eat fish."

"How do you know you don't eat fish if you don't remember anything?"

"I just know. And what the devil is in this bread? Seaweed?" He shoved the tray back at her. "God's teeth, I can't eat this! Is this how you treat your patients? By starving them?" With his right hand he rubbed his left shoulder, caught up in a sling. "I need a drink. Something potent. Whisky? Brandy?" He seemed to be searching his mind. "Rum?"

"We've nothing here but what we make ourselves. Cider, small beer, and a bottle or two of rhubarb wine."

"Cow's piss!" Pen spat. "Where's the tavern?"

"There are several down by the wharves, and you're welcome to go there," Gwen snapped. "You've coin to pay for a meal, of a sudden?"

He glared at her. "God, you're a harpy."

"And you're worse than Mother Morris with her tamping." She was tempted to retort that he hadn't thought her a harpy when he'd tried to press her to become his mistress. Her tongue was grooved from biting it so often.

"Tamping?" He glared.

"Angry. Quarrelsome. Prone to wrathful rages."

"Speak English!" Pen barked, then scowled when she answered in a long string of Welsh. It was a verse from an old ballad, the first thing that came to mind, but he didn't know any better, and it gave her some satisfaction to slam the door of the infirmary behind her.

"I'm going to kill him," she hissed to Dovey, who was cleaning up the kitchen. "And then the sin will be on my soul."

"But we'd get to keep St. Sefin's," Dovey whispered back.

Pen sneered at Evans later when he came with Gwen for a last visit before retiring. "You're to help me! Good God, look at you!" He stared at Evans's empty coat sleeve, caught up and pinned to his side. "Between us we make one whole man."

"With two heads and one brain," Gwen snapped. "He's here to help you out of bed, as your carcass is too heavy for me to lift."

"Four heads," Pen said insolently, "unless his manhood went

the way of his arm. Christ, I need a piss! Where's the water closet?"

Gwen pressed her lips together. Even with his memories blurred, Penrydd would figure out from his preferences alone that he was a pampered, high-class dandy. Only fancy homes had water closets. "We have a necessary in the courtyard, where Evans will take you, and there's a chamber pot beneath your bed, if you'd but look."

Penrydd was in pain, Gwen noted as he leaned on Evans and limped out the door, but he clenched his teeth and didn't let a single hiss or moan escape him. Gwen shook out his blankets and lifted the sheets to place a sprig of wormwood on his cot to keep away fleas and bedbugs. She and Dovey had smoked the infirmary after the last occupant had departed, saturating the room with brimstone and sulfur to kill any vermin, but she didn't know what Penrydd might bring with him. Even fancy lords could have lice, though she hadn't found nits in his hair when she'd cleaned his head wound.

The necessary wasn't far, but Pen's face was white and lined with tension when they returned. "This place is falling to pieces," he announced as Evans lowered him to sit on the cot. "It's drafty, it's old, and it smells like a musty tomb. How can you bear to live here?"

Gwen clamped her jaw shut on the first protest that came to mind. This was her home, and she and Dovey worked hard to make it habitable. "Do you have a suggestion then, where they might go, those who have been turned out by their families, or have no families, no living nor any way to make one, mmm?" By St. Gwladys, the arrogance of the man! But she mustn't call him milord, not even as an insult.

"I won't stay here," Pen announced. "Whether I know my own name or not, I won't abide a sty."

Panic gripped her heart. "You haven't given us a chance yet."

"A chance for what? To starve me with your peasant's fare? You can't ask ransom if you don't know who I am. I doubt you could hold me here anyway."

She heard belligerence in his tone, but in his eyes she saw a desperation that matched her own. He knew he had nowhere to go. He was attacking her because he was frightened, lashing out like a cornered animal. She'd seen dogs beaten all their lives that snapped at a hand extended in kindness. Pen's rage was the same, born of fright and helplessness and his hatred of being vulnerable.

He wouldn't tolerate her pity, she knew that. And if he wouldn't accept their help, she couldn't detain him. Disappointment lined her mouth with a vinegar sting. "You're free to leave any time."

"I will." His gaze roamed over the broad, empty room with its carved beam ceiling and bare walls. "Tomorrow morning. Where's the bell if I need something in the night?"

"The what?"

"The bell! To ring for servants."

She wavered between the impulse to douse him with the mug of tea she'd set by his bed or throw her candle onto his bedclothes and light him on fire. "There are no servants here, Pen—" She swallowed the rest of his title before it slipped out. She had to guard herself more carefully lest he goad her into giving something away. "I wish you good night," she said with a hard-won courtesy.

"You're not taking the light with you?" His eyes lost their insolent slant.

"You don't need it, and I won't have you burning the place down simply because you don't like the look of it." She swept out of the room, but not before she had the satisfaction of seeing his mouth tighten into a grimace. She'd steeped his tea with willow bark to help dull the pain and ward off fever, but she didn't feel like telling him that.

"We tried," Dovey said when Gwen found her in their rooms and, as they undressed by candlelight, relayed her conversation with Pen. "If he asks about in Newport tomorrow, perhaps he'll hear good reports of St. Sefin's, and that will sway him."

Gwen doubted it. Mathry's impression of St. Sefin's before she arrived was no more than what many townsfolk were prone to say. That it was a place for damaged, the not-right. Small wonder Penrydd wanted nothing to do with them.

It would be a relief to turn him out. Someone else could deal with his wrath as he went about reclaiming his memory. But she hadn't won him over, and the moment he recalled his mission, he'd be back to complete it. She had to do something to change his mind.

THE VOICE CALLED to her from the vast cavern of sleep. It was huge and dark and she was lost in it, pressed under something heavy. She heard the call again. A man, desperate, in pain.

Gwen threw a wrapper over her shift, found her slippers, and groped for the tin tinderbox. Her fingers fumbled with the flint and steel as the echoing call came again. Finally the splint caught and she lit her chamber stick, then hurried down the stone staircase, shielding the candle flame from drafts. Shadows danced along the high ceiling of the infirmary as she entered, following the call.

Pen tossed on the bed, muscles straining. His face was twisted into a terrifying grimace and the hair over his brow was damp with sweat.

"No! No! No!"

She pressed a hand on his arm. "Pen." Then, as he continued to flail, she worried that he would reinjure his ribs. She set the candle down and pressed both hands to his chest, beneath his collarbone. He was firm and warm. "Pen!"

He clamped his right hand over both of hers. His eyes flew open and the room swirled as he stared at her.

"There was shooting," he said, his voice hoarse and raw. "I was—" He glanced down and saw the bandages beneath his loose shirt, his arm working loose from its sling. "I was injured?"

"Not from shot. You fell into a boat. Do you remember?"

His eyes were wild, glazed. "Blood. Everywhere. Pieces of— ah, God. The screaming."

"You're not there now. You're here."

His throat worked, and she helped him sit, holding the mug to his lips. He drank deep, then curled his lips at the bitter taste of the willow bark. She wiped the side of his mouth with her finger, and he startled and stared at her arm, pale and bare where the sleeve of the wrapper fell away. His gaze traveled up her arm and stopped at her breasts.

She pulled the wrapper around her, crossing her arms over her bosom. Her breasts tingled from his gaze, a strange reaction to have. He roused her nerves to alertness.

"It was a bad dream. A *hunllef*, we call it."

That wasn't exactly true. She suspected he'd been reliving a memory.

He drank again, and she held the mug for him, but this time his eyes wandered around the room, what he could see of it in the small nimbus of light. "I'm in a hospital? Where's Arwen?"

"Who?" Her heart pinched. So there was a woman in his life, someone he cared about. Not enough to be faithful to, obviously, but the concern on his face was real.

So was the puzzlement. "Arwen," he said slowly. "She was sent to the sanitorium. But not this one?"

"You're at St. Sefin's Priory," she said, and at his look of complete bafflement, continued. "In Newport. Wales. Do you remember that much?"

"How am I in bloody Wales, the back end of Britain?"

He'd called it that before. Yet he had a Welsh name for a title and a Welsh estate he'd apparently never seen. Gwen's heart hardened to his distress.

"I'm hoping you might explain that, eventually. We found you in a boat this morning, floated up to shore like you were Arthur of Avalon." No, he was far from an Arthur, that great king of Welsh legend. King Arthur was a leader of men who had fought to keep invaders from overtaking his country. Penrydd was a spoiled bully who summoned his servants with a bell.

"My head hurts." He put a hand there, probing the lump on his skull. "God, there was so much blood. I thought I was being ripped apart."

"Try not to think about it," Gwen said. "Think of something pleasing."

His eyes rested on her face, traced down her cheek to her throat, her collarbone, the swell of her bosom beneath her gown. "Who are you?"

"I told you." It was one thing for him to forget her after several days and a blow to the head. It was quite another thing that he couldn't recall her from hours before.

"My name is Gwenllian. I—run this place, I suppose you could say."

"You own it?" He sipped his tea, his hand steady. Which was fortunate, for she jerked as she sat back.

"I am hoping to purchase it," she said, choosing her words carefully. Should they have this conversation now? Without Dovey, or Evans, or anyone else who had a vested interest in the place?

"Hmm." He swept his eyes down her body, tracing the

curve of her hip, her legs. She'd sat on the cot to lean over him, and now she felt heat reaching from his body through the bedclothes to her skin.

His lips curved in a slow, sensual smile. The heat swirled through her middle, upsetting her sense of balance.

"I wager you'd be a pleasant distraction, Gwenllian. What would convince you to stay with me this evening?"

Sign the deed to St. Sefin's over to me, clear and free, she almost said.

Could she do that—barter her body to secure her future? Could she be that vulnerable again to a man?

He was vulnerable too; lost, alone, hurt, and reaching out to the closest source of aid. His was the act of a drowning man. Not anything to do with her, or even attraction to her, but casting about for relief. Negotiating for help with the only coin he had.

He wouldn't keep a bargain wrung from him in such a state, not when he came to his senses and realized what she'd done. And she didn't like that he thought he had to pay for simple human care. She slid off the cot.

"The next time you spoil my sleep, I'll put a pillow over your face to stop your nightmares."

"Stay and I won't have nightmares." He put a hand to his shoulder. His writhing had worked his sling and the bandages about his ribs loose.

"Here, now, you've undone all my good work. I'll have to take off your shirt to redo these."

"Go ahead, have your way with me," he answered, but without the sultry teasing. Instead, he set his teeth as if in pain as she pulled off the shirt and rewrapped the bindings around his ribs and arm.

"I am sorry to hurt you," she said as he sucked in air. Her face felt hot from his nearness and the heat of his skin singed her fingertips. She was touching a nearly naked man, a man who had offered to—*don't think about it, twymffat.* She tried to focus on his injuries, not the broad expanses of heated male skin, the soft brown hair dusting the planes and swells of muscle. She tucked in the last strip of cloth comprising his sling and opened the small cupboard beside his bed to look for another shirt. His old one was drenched in sweat, warm and spicy.

She'd never been so unsettled by any man she nursed. *He's an ass,* she reminded herself. And it had been a long time since she touched a man, put her arms around a bare chest, ran her fingers over skin. Hers was purely the physical response of woman to man. No more. She would not be drawn again to a man who hid a dreadful character behind a handsome face.

"You're his, then?" Pen's eyes drifted closed as she draped the fresh shirt over his head, then helped him settle against the pillows. "The fellow with the lank sleeve."

"Evans?" She frowned. "I am no one's."

"A woman needs a keeper." His hand covered hers, anchoring her palm over his heart as she tucked the blanket over his chest. "Especially a beautiful one."

She pulled in a breath, but she couldn't rail at him. He was already drifting back to sleep. His hand lay warm and heavy on hers and she left her hand in place for a moment, for far too long, and not simply to assure herself his heartbeat fell into a regular rhythm. With a secret greed she soaked up the compliment and the gentle touch. It had been so long since a man had granted her either.

Dangerous to accept these things from him, and low of her to steal warmth from his sleeping body. She snatched back her hand and stood so quickly that the flame of the candle fluttered in her wake. A woman who turned herself inside out for the flattery of a man was a fool. And a woman who gave herself away for a promise would end up like Mathry, weeping over her belly.

She'd not believe the word of a man until the contract was signed and her future was there on paper.

Like the deed to a property? said the devil on her shoulder.

But not won this way, when he was completely at their mercy. Safety won in this manner would prove no safety at all.

A COCK CROWED in the distance as she left the infirmary, announcing the dawn. There was no point returning to bed. Penrydd had set every nerve alight, made her skin hum with awareness. She snuck to her chamber and pulled a robe of printed cotton over her shift, slipped on her work shoes, and tied her hair up under a cap. She would let the morning air cool her head.

The early dawn was crisp and clear, orange and red ribbons piled across the hills to the east, veiled by mist from the river. Ifor had separated the mother goat and her kid for the night, so Gwen quickly milked the nanny and left them both hay, then stirred up the fire in the kitchen. She found the lump of old dough from the last batch of bread and mixed the yeasty mass with the warm milk, adding flour, eggs, and a pinch of salt. A few tweaks made the dough soft and ropy, and then she turned it into wooden bowls to rise.

It was a task she'd performed a hundred times, and yet she was intensely self-aware of every moment, and aware, too, of the lack of sound from the infirmary. Pen was sleeping, the cad, after robbing her of rest with his troubled dreams and male warmth and jocular invitation to join him. She wouldn't. Of course not.

But if he still meant to leave this morning, where would he go? How would he fare, with no coin and no name to buy his way out of trouble? And when his memory returned, as it soon must, what kind of reckoning would fall on her head?

She pulled out the griddle and mixed oat cakes for breakfast, pressing the rounds of batter flat with more force than was necessary.

"Survived the night, did he?"

She jumped into the air at Dovey's voice. Dovey's apron was starched and white, a lace cap pinned jauntily to her curls, her gown neatly pressed and her shoes black with polish. In comparison Gwen felt frizzled and mussed, rough at the edges.

"I checked on him a few hours ago and he was sleeping." A version of the truth. "Perhaps you can take his breakfast tray, and Evans can help him dress. I see Widow Jones managed to scrub the blood out of his shirt."

Dovey shrugged and left. The rest of the household rose to the daily round of chores, and the refectory filled for breakfast. Cerys strolled in yawning, her hair tangled, her apron tied awry. Tomos reached for a cake while it was still on the griddle and burned his hand, then sobbed as Gwen applied salve to the burn. Mother Morris had a griping stomach, Ifor woke with a putrid throat, and Mathry drifted uselessly about the kitchen, moving things to the wrong places, wafting into the stillrooms or cellars and coming out with empty hands. Gwen heated water from the well and was pouring it over tea leaves that had already been used twice when Mathry's soft indrawn breath made her look up. A scalding droplet splashed onto her wrist.

Pen stood staring at her from the buttery door. Evans had rebound the sling over his shirt and coat, but despite the injury and his restless night he looked awake, alert, and accusing. Mended, and altogether dangerous.

"Oatcakes, Mr. Pen?" Mathry fluttered her lashes. "Or some fresh bread we made?" She indicated the golden-brown loaves, warm from the oven.

"I know what bakers add to their bread," he said. "Alum. Plaster. Chalk."

Where did he think he was, a poor man's tavern? "I would never," Gwen snapped. She put a wrist to her mouth and sucked off the drop of boiling water.

Pen's eyes moved to her mouth, and she dropped her hands. Her nerves jumped like fleas on the goats. And not purely from guilt.

"You came to my room last night." His voice turned silky.

Oh, St. Beuno's bald spot, he was not sporting with her again. Gwen straightened her back as Mathry shot her a narrow look. "Stepping out, are you?"

"I told you I refuse to stay."

Her hopes plummeted. He hadn't given them the ghost of a chance. They'd never had one. She pointed her spatula toward the kitchen door and the short hall leading outside. "*Hwyl fawr!* Godspeed."

He scowled. "I have no reason to stay here."

"That you don't." Gwen turned to the griddle.

"You can't keep me a hostage."

"Nor should we wish to."

"But to go out on your own like that, sir? We'll take care of you," Mathry cooed.

Gwen looked up in time to see Pen's flat expression change to interest. "Just what are you offering?"

"Mathry," Gwen said, "serve the tea. Here's turmeric for Mother Morris's gripe."

"*Saes!*" Mother Morris shouted from the refectory, leaning forward to peer through the servery door. "*Twll din pob Saes!*"

"What is she saying?" Pen demanded to know.

Mathry giggled. "All English are ass—"

"Cerys!" Gwen barked. "Take the bread—the loaves are hot, mind—and help Mathry pour the tea."

Mathry pouted but headed for the next room, skirts swishing. Penrydd's eyes didn't follow her. Instead his gaze settled on Gwen.

"I've met you before," he said.

Her breath hitched and she returned to the griddle. If he was starting to recognize her from their earlier meeting, he was a mere step away from remembering everything. And knowing the hold he had over her, over all of them.

"Where you to?"

"Anywhere. Someone has to know who I am. Surely there are people out there looking for me." He spoke with the solid assurance that he mattered. That he would be acknowledged, welcomed, and obeyed. What a difference it was to be a man in this world.

"Come with me," he said.

She nearly dropped the sizzling cakes as she scooped them from the griddle onto a wooden platter. "Why for?"

He gave her that slow smile again. Sensual. Wicked. "To keep me from bad dreams."

She stood rooted to the old stone floor. A wild part of her *wanted* to go with him. Take up her shawl and her favorite hat and dash off into the unknown.

Leaving everyone who depended on her, those who had nothing and no one. She needed to settle this with him now, before he left. Before he realized they'd known who he was and hadn't told him.

"I—I must see to something." She needed to find Dovey. She couldn't bargain with him without Dovey there.

But Dovey wasn't in the dining hall, and when Gwen returned to the kitchen, Penrydd was gone, too.

She fought to breathe through the crushing sense of panic, of loss. She'd failed. He was gone. Someone about Newport might piece together that he was Penrydd, and what would her gamble cost them? She could only pray it would take him a while to find out. Pray they had a few hours to plan what to do. How to barricade their door if he came back bearing a pitchfork, or worse, Barlow the solicitor.

Stupid of her to feel it a slight that he'd not found her intriguing enough to stay. This wasn't about her, until he realized she'd tricked him, withheld his identity. Then he would rain down the wrath of the outraged aristocrat, and she had no excuse, no defense. And no one to turn to. These people she cared for would lose everything, and it was all her fault.

CHAPTER SIX

S he hadn't spent the hours planning. She spent the day nursing Ifor and preventing Tomos from gnawing the bandage off his hurt hand. She was already exhausted and unraveled when the boy came running up from town to fetch her.

"Mr. Stanley sent me, Miss Gwen. Said you're wanted at the King's Head."

Gwen rose heavily from the side of Ifor's cot, where he'd at last succumbed to a troubled sleep. The King's Head was both coaching inn and public house, a fit place for a reckoning. Pen had found someone who knew him and summoned her to pass sentence. She considered dressing in her finest, but it wouldn't change the outcome. She wrapped her checked red shawl about her and set out.

It was Pen, but he hadn't summoned her to a reckoning. He lay stretched out prone along one side of the stable yard, with Mr. Stanley watching over him.

"A fair handsome lad, or he was, I'm guessing." The vicar scratched his chin. "I mean, underneath the blood and such. The same one you took in, Miss Gwen?"

"Just yesterday morn." Gwen knelt and felt for a pulse. The French had an expression for that eerie sense that one had lived this moment already. Pen was not dead from internal bleeding or some result of his head wound, as she'd first feared. But here he was again, still the viscount who held her fate in his hands, once again unconscious, and in the name of all the saints she didn't know what she was supposed to do with him.

"What happened to him, Mr. Trett?" Gwen asked the innkeeper.

PEN WAS CONSIDERABLY MORE BATTERED than when he'd left, his face encrusted with blood from a cut on his arrogant cheekbone, the dark circles beneath his eyes suggesting he'd been punched in the nose. His hair was mussed, his neckcloth crumpled and untied, his coat had been smudged with dirt, and his breeches had a tear at the knee. They'd barely gotten him cleaned up from yesterday, and now she had to do it all over again. And who knew what internal injuries he'd sustained.

"He's been here since mid-day, giving hisself the barrel fever," Mr. Trett reported. "But I didn't baste 'im. Gossett was in, the great bully, and they was on a spree together until along come Gossett's wife, trying to chivvy him home. The tiff you heard then! The beau didn't like Gossett raising his fists to a woman, and Gossett didn't like the beau in 'is business, so he brings him out 'ere for a brushing." Mr. Trett shook his gingerhaired head. "No more chance than a cat in hell without claws, with a man Gossett's size. And neither paid their shot, too."

Gwen knew of Mrs. Gossett's circumstances. She had hinted more than once that Mrs. Gossett might come to St. Sefin's and bring her children with her. "Oh, he just gets in his cups and his back up, is all. Says I'm not an easy yoke, I am,"

Mrs. Gossett would answer in an apologetic tone, and then turn up to church the next Sunday with a deep-brimmed bonnet hiding her face and eyes.

Gwen sighed. For such a belligerent man, Pen really ought to learn how to better defend himself. "Did Gossett beat your memory back into you, then?" She resisted the urge to nudge Penrydd with her boot and instead poked him in the arm. One did not kick viscounts in the ribs no matter how much they might deserve it.

"You." His eyes fluttered open, and he fisted a hand in the straw beneath him. The knuckles were scraped and bloody. "Gwenllian ap Ewyas." He slurred the words through a swollen lower lip. "Kicked me off her doorstep this morn," he said to Mr. Stanley, who peered at him with interest. "Prettiest harridan I've ever seen."

Gwen propped her hands on her hips. "Well? Did you find your answers?"

"Moses in his basket," he mumbled. "An infant cast upon the sea. What's that old tale? The Fair Unknown? Take me in, princess, and raise me aright, and someday I will rise up and free my people."

Gwen's conscience prodded her. She had to take him in. She had to convince him to look kindly on St. Sefin's and not cast them all into the marsh, which he would be well within his rights to do.

But to continue the deception, to lie to him about who he was—no, they were not deceiving him, exactly. Her stomach boiled at the thought. She was simply—withholding some rather vital information. For Dovey's sake. She gathered her nerve.

"Back to St. Sefin's with you, then. It's right you were to fetch me, Mr. Stanley, but now I must ask if you can help me with this one."

"A shame we can't find where he belongs," the vicar said,

hauling Penrydd to his feet. "His family must be terribly worried."

Guilt bit hard as she stepped close to help. Penrydd mumbled and sagged against her, stinking of rum.

"As drunk as David's sow," she said in disgust.

"Cup-shot? Not I." Penrydd slung his good arm around her shoulders. "A little cut above the head, perhaps. Merely mellow."

"Owes me a bull, he does!" Mr. Trett said as they steadied Pen between them.

She didn't have sixpence on her, much less half a crown. "I will have him come repay the debt as soon as he's able, Mr. Trett," Gwen called. She stiffened as Pen's big, firm body brushed against hers.

"You're completely mauled," Gwen told him. The man would never heal if he kept undoing all her good work. "What have you been *doing*?"

Pen staggered with them as she and the vicar stepped through the arch and onto High Street. "Went to the castle," Pen slurred. "Not in good form! Ferns and such growing from the top of it. Shame. Could give tours and make coin from it, like that abbey—what's it called? Twitterstone—Turntun—place that poet wrote about."

"Tintern Abbey." Mr. Stanley grunted as Pen careened his way, and tried to hold him upright without grasping his injured shoulder or ribs. "William Wordsworth. Excellent collection, the *Lyrical Ballads*. Quite unlike anything I've read."

"Looked in on a pub they said was the old murenger house, whatever that is," Pen went on. "Thought I'd hole up there for the night. Not too shabby for rooms."

"The murenger was responsible for maintaining the town walls, back when we had them. That's what is left of Westgate." Gwen pointed to the pile of stone bricks as they passed into

Church Street, which ended with St. Woolos on one side and St. Sefin's on the other.

Its new commerce was pushing Newport beyond its medieval footprint, the old structures crumbling to make way for works broader and bigger and new. Another religious house in the area, what was called the Austin Friars, had become home to a cider mill. Pen might do the same to St. Sefin's, turn out its residents and use the old buildings for new ventures that actually earned money.

"Went to St. Woolly's," Pen went on. "Climbed the old Norman tower. Great builders, those Normans. But the pater doesn't know me, alas."

Mr. Stanley shook his head, and Gwen let out half the breath she'd been holding. Mr. Stanley, who hailed from an English parish, had interested himself in the great families of the area. He might not have met Penrydd, but he could place who he was given enough clues. There was also the possibility that someone who did know him, like Calvin Vaughn, could come strolling down High Street and end the charade in a moment.

Tell him nothing, Dovey warned in her head. Gwen focused on the task of keeping him upright and not on his hand gripping her side, terribly close to her breast.

"Not from around here, am I?" Pen said. "None at the wharf knew me. Said I floated to shore like a selkie." He frowned. "Some kind of Welsh monster?"

Gwen laughed at his expression. "Selkies are water-folk. They're born on land but choose to live in the sea. They're mythical," she added, in case Penrydd's sodden brain had not grasped this.

"But the women are excessively beautiful and have exquisite voices." Mr. Stanley nodded a greeting to the carter driving his mule and wagon up the street. "If you steal the pelt of a selkie, she has to stay on land as your bride. But she'll always long for the sea, and if she ever takes her skin back, she will don it and leave you forever."

Pen scoffed. "Merfolk."

"No, the *môr-forwyn* is different," Gwen said, wondering how she had been drawn into this ridiculous conversation. Pen drunk had a whimsy about him that she much preferred to the glowering, sober Pen. Or the feckless cad who teased women for sexual favors. He grunted and squeezed her as his foot turned on a stone, and she braced him, ignoring the awakening sensation in her breasts. A primitive instinct, nothing more.

"The mermaid is half-fish, and born in the sea," she said, her voice strangely breathless. She was quite strong; she shouldn't feel his weight so keenly. "And they like to lure men to their doom. There've been many tales of fisherman and sailors sighting them along the coastline, or there used to be, before the canal brought more sailing traffic to ferry the iron and coal. The ships scare the merfolk away."

Pen nodded. "A man on my ship swore he sighted one once on watch among the islands." His brow creased. "Am I a sailor? What islands?"

Gwen's breath swirled in her chest, and she barely eked out a smile for the mistress of the pie shop, who stared at Pen as they passed. "Is your memory returning?"

"Shreds and pieces, like glimpses in a mirror. And never connected to something I can use." He swiveled his head and dipped his chin so his nose was practically in her hair. Gwen startled, alarm and awareness shooting through her.

"You, for instance. I know you. I know your scent—blue-bells." He inhaled deeply. Gwen closed her eyes, feeling faint. "So why do names mean nothing? I can't even remember my own."

"I'm sure it will all come back in time," Gwen said weakly.

He'd remembered Arwen, the woman he loved. He'd remember more soon. She must work quickly to soften him, persuade him to take a generous view of St. Sefin's and their life here. He was quiet and docile as she returned him to the infirmary. She warmed water and witch hazel and set to cleaning the blood off his face, once again stripping off his soiled clothing and wrapping his ribs.

"I will only take you in twice, you know," she said as she cleaned the scrape on his head, hidden beneath his thick thatch of brown hair, but still noticeably swollen. "The third time you go off and get clawed by ruffians, I'll leave you in the ditch where you lie."

His hazelnut eyes held a strange, steady warmth as he regarded her. That slant at the corners of his eyes made him look puckish, up to mischief.

"He was so friendly," he said, sighing as she laid a cloth soaked in witch hazel over the new bruises on his chest. "That Gossett chap. Thought mayhap he knew me, could tell me something. But he beat me hollow and left me all a-mort. Would have filed my pockets if I had any blunt."

"Speak English," Gwen murmured.

He closed his eyes and leaned into her hand as she placed it on his forehead, checking for fever. "My clothes are a gentleman's," he said. "I speak like I've been to Oxford. But I like grog, and flip—have you had it? Small beer and brandy with sugar and lemon. Served it at the pub. I think I'm a sailor, but I fell off a boat. And apparently I'm not very handy with my fives, though the brute said I throw a punch like Jackson." He turned his head against her palm, rubbing like a cat. "Whoever that is."

"Bare-knuckle champion of boxing," Gwen said. "He's held the title since 1795. Even I know that." She kept her hand in place, though the heat coursing through her arm told him touching him like this was unadvisable.

He opened his eyes and held her gaze. "You'd do better to turn me into the street."

That was the advisable thing. Cast him loose and let him come to his senses on his own time. Let someone else take him on charity.

But who? Newport was a small town, barely a thousand souls. Barring Cardiff, the rest of Welsh towns were smaller. It was a risk to travel unknown through these lands, asking for the kindness of strangers. She knew that.

She had built St. Sefin's as a house of refuge. Penrydd, in his current state, was just the flotsam she'd vowed to shelter, with no one else to care for him, no way to provide for himself, injured as he was.

But she could end it in a moment. Tell him who he was, what he owned, what was due him as a peer of the realm. With a word she could restore him to the security, the income, the precedence that was his by birthright and custom and the British laws of primogeniture.

Shame knotted her throat, hot and choking. She was the one denying what was owed him. She was his cruelest tormentor of all.

"Rest," she said hoarsely, returning her cloth to the washbowl and turning away. "I'll see if there's anything left from supper."

"Shame about that poor lad," said Mr. Stanley over fish stew and the last of the bread Gwen had made that morning. He sat at the large kitchen table, chatting with Dovey as she dried and put away dishes. "What do you suppose we should do about him?"

"Wait and let him come to his senses." Dovey fixed Gwen with a firm stare, as though she could see Gwen cracking. "Everything will come right if we just wait."

"For how long?" Gwen muttered as she slipped past her friend to fetch a wooden bowl down from the shelf.

"Telling him puts us at his mercy," Dovey hissed, keeping her voice low while the vicar drank the last of his soup. "I like him better at ours."

But there was no mercy for liars, Gwen thought. And this was her greatest falsehood yet.

SHE HADN'T BEEN to see him in hours. There was noise in the kitchen. It must be mid-morning, and Pen thought he heard her voice now and again. But the light-skirted maid brought his breakfast, winking and flirting the whole time. Pen flirted back—what was a man to do when a woman flattered so prettily?—but he wanted Gwen.

He wanted to hear her. See her. Find out if she'd come again to his room last night. He had a vague memory of gunfire and screaming, some men shouting at him about money, and then the smell of blood turned to bluebells, and the clobber on his head was instead a warm hand and a cool cloth scented with witch hazel. After that he slept without dreaming.

The man with the missing arm, he'd forgotten his name, brought Pen his clothing. His breeches were mended and his coat had been brushed, but his suit was growing shabbier by the day. Was he a dandy, that he cared about his garments? Pen said curtly he could valet himself and sent him away. The sight of the man's empty sleeve and limping walk unsettled him. Made him feel guilty. Why should that be?

Why couldn't he remember a bloody thing about his life?

It was like a great fog in his brain box. Every time he reached for something he should know, it slipped away to airy mist. All that was left were feelings, but no knowledge. He couldn't recall his family. His home. His profession. He knew his likes and dislikes; he knew, for instance, that he badly wanted a glass of rum. But how could he not even know his *name*?

Pen. That was what she'd said. He knew, in some way he couldn't articulate, that was what people called him. But it wasn't his name.

He was turning maudlin, lying in this cot in the empty room, nothing but time on his hands, life going on just out of reach. He was also bloody bored.

He straightened his neckcloth, buffed the buttons on his coat, and walked into the kitchen. Into an uproar.

There was a mad howling going up from some great buffoon who sat in a chair by the wall, rocking and sobbing. Gwen sat beside him holding his hand, bound with bandages. An old crone with white hair and a puckered expression sat in another corner, angrily stabbing knitting needles into a snarled mass of wool and spewing gibberish in the direction of the howling young man.

From a room beyond, a stillroom or cellar of some sort, came the sound of two women quarreling. And the whole room smelled like wet goat. Because an actual goat stood in the door to the scullery, dripping water onto the floor, a rope around its neck leading to the boy who stood within, working a handpump at the basin.

"Good Lord," Pen said, "I'm in Dante's *Inferno*."

"What do *you* want?" Gwen snapped, her head rearing up.

He was surprised. What was she taking his head off for? "There's an awful lot of noise," he said, gesturing to the boy beside her. "Is it because he's an idi—"

"Don't," Gwen warned him, her voice full of wrath. "Tomos

caught his hand in the winch when he was drawing water this morning. He's upset."

"It happened an hour ago," said the crone.

"*Poen*," the boy sobbed.

"Yes, you're in pain." Gwen patted the boy's arm and he leaned against her shoulder. He had an oddly round head, his eyes small slits spaced wide apart, his nose flat between chubby cheeks. A simpleton of some sort. Pen looked away.

"What are the hens fighting about?" He nodded his head toward the small room where bunches of herbs hung from the ceiling, and where the volume of voices, and the acrimony in them, was escalating.

"Cerys has the putrid throat today that Ifor had yesterday," Gwen answered. "We cannot agree on the best remedy."

"Boiled mutton suet and beeswax plaster," said the crone with confidence. "Wrap her from ear to ear and let her be."

"Fetch down to the barber surgeon for leeches," came the voice of the young, flirty maid. "That's what Mrs. Harries always did, and don't tell me you think you know better than she."

"A bolus of conserve of rose mixed with powdered frankincense," came the voice of another woman, older but still mellifluous. "Mr. Wesley says so in his *Physick*."

"There's a licorice tea steeping on the stove," Gwen said. "Just mix in a bit of honey and lemon juice. I think we've one lemon left."

Their arguing was better than a Punch comedy held at seaside resorts in the summers. He must have been to many as a child—what seaside? What resort?

"Add a spoonful of rum," Pen said helpfully. "And then you might give me the rest of the rum, and the lemon."

Gwen stood and moved to stand before him. She was wearing the same plain, worn gown, with that red woolen shawl draped around her waist and a ruffled kerchief concealing what he knew to be a shapely bosom. Why did she go about hiding her assets from the world? At least she wore nothing to hide her hair, which was bound into a loose braid about her head. He wanted to run those ashy brown curls through his fingers. He would wager they were softer than silk.

He blinked as she leaned forward to peer into his eyes, then lifted his hands to look at them. He clenched his fingers to hide the tremor.

"No more grog for you, Pen," she said softly. "We're drying you out."

"No spirits in this fine accommodation? I shall register a complaint with the management." He scowled, hating how easily she saw his weakness.

"And that worked so well last time." She moved to the stove and poured a cup of tea. "Mathry, take this to our little chick. I don't know when Dovey will be back."

The younger maid swished away, tossing Pen an arch look and making sure he got an eyeful of her bosom, which was not in the least concealed. She was rather endowed in that area, and others. Pen watched the progress of her swaying rump out the door, then caught Gwen watching him.

She turned toward the door of the scullery. "Ifor, *bachgen*, it looks like you've managed the worst of it."

"Thought I was about done," a cheerful voice floated back. Gwen scratched the head of the billy goat, which stared at Pen with its golden eyes. Pen, alarmed, stared back.

"Why is the goat wet?"

"It's raining sticks and old women out there," the goat boy said, emerging from the scullery. Pen couldn't help himself; he recoiled at the sight of the boy's blind, scarred eyes. He knew Gwen noted his reaction.

"And Gafr pushed me down and got me all mucky." The

boy scratched between the goat's horns just as Gwen had, then reached out and put his hand on the shepherd's crook leaning next to the door. "Think I'll go back in it and help Evans. He was fixing a tub in the brewhouse and will need a hand."

"Mind your step if it's slippery," Gwen said as the boy departed for the door.

Pen closed his hanging jaw. "You let him wander about like —?" He made a circular motion with his hand.

She gave him a purposefully bland look. He sensed he saw such a look often, from others, and it irritated him every time. "Like what?" she asked.

"Blind!" Pen said, exasperated.

She raised a brow at him. The contrast between her dark brows and light green-grey eyes startled him all over. He would never tire of simply looking at her.

"Blind," she affirmed. "Not witless. That boy sees more than you do, I'd wager."

"Why is everyone so cross today?" Pen bridled.

"Because we've a great deal of work to do," Gwen said shortly. "Tomos, would you like to help me look for morels this afternoon, when the rain stops? We can start in the old orchard, then search in the woods for the hazel trees. Or we might borrow Mr. Coffin's pig and look for truffles, if you'd rather that."

She expressed more enthusiasm over mushrooms than she had over him, Pen thought with annoyance. The second woman came out of the stillroom and looked him over, and his annoyance increased. She was at least two decades older than Gwen, with a black fringed shawl draped about her, and her scrutiny did not conclude with the coy smile that women customarily gave him. Pen might not know much about himself, but he knew he was appealing to women. At least, normal women. Which these were not.

"A man from Merthyr Tydfil was attacked last night at the wharves," the woman in black said to Pen, as if answering his earlier question. "A Jew."

"So?" Pen looked around the room. "No one here is a Jew. And no one here beat him, I'm assuming. Some itinerant looking for work? I ran into a number of them yesterday at the pub. Rough lot. I recall coming in for some abuse myself."

Undeserved, he could have added, rubbing his sore jaw. He had a feeling at least one of his eyes was ringed with purple. Perhaps that's why Gwen was avoiding him, though he hadn't pegged her as missish.

"He was a businessman, they're saying," Gwen said, her tone sharpening. "A prospective financer for some building projects, including the new bridge. And they may call us rude and rough, but Newport is not known for being hostile to outsiders. There's something afoot."

"I still don't follow," Pen said. "You're all British. What have you to fear?"

A torrent of voices answered this, including a barrage of Welsh from the crone.

"We're not British!" Gwen yelped. "We're Cymry."

He stared. "Wales is part of Britain."

She held his stare, challenging. "Not to you."

That was true. Pen glanced at the others, who glared at him with varying levels of distrust. It occurred to him that they considered *him* the outsider. Preposterous! Even the simple boy watched with interest, cradling his hurt hand.

Gwen stomped to a shelf and banged down a basket. "Welsh, you call us. Wales, you say this is. Do you even know what that word means?"

He didn't. He had the feeling he'd had a somewhat decent education. He spoke like he'd been educated, at least. But Wales was Wales, England was England, and Britain was the finest country in the world.

"You *Saeson*," Gwen said, stomping next to a cluster of tools that hung from pegs. "You, the invaders to our land, called us *wealas*. Foreigners." She spat the words. "And that is your name for us even now. We are Cymry. We are proud. But we are not savages. We do not beat men near senseless simply because they are a different race or a different faith."

She was frightened. He took a step toward her. "I won't let them hurt you."

Her eyes flared. "Someone hurt *you*."

He shifted his jaw back and forth. "That was one brute who liked to manhandle his wife. A fellow needed to stand up to him." He felt an odd sort of pride in saying this. As if he wasn't accustomed to standing up for the weaker. As if he had never truly realized, before meeting her, that a man using his fists on a woman was an injustice, not simply the way of the world. Or, if it *was* the way of the world, he could no longer accept that.

"You were attacked before that, and you lost your memory," Gwen said in a low voice. "Someone, or a gang of someones, beat you, robbed you, and left you for dead."

Pen frowned. "You think the attack on me is related to the attack on the Jew?"

"I've no way of knowing. But it's not done around here. And it's not right."

A step sounded in the hallway leading from the door outside, and the dark-skinned woman entered. She was frightfully lovely, with big dark eyes, gleaming skin, every item of her dress pressed and neat as a pin. Gwen was still the more beautiful, Pen thought loyally. But they were like a pair of angels, side by side.

"Cerys?" the newcomer asked.

"Mathry is seeing to her," Gwen answered. Her face grew taut. "What news? Do we bring him here?"

The other woman shook her head. "He's not going to make it. Mr. Stanley said—well, he knows your feelings on such a matter."

"No death under the roof of St. Sefin's," the crone muttered, and though it was in line with all the other senseless things she'd said, the hair lifted on the back of Pen's neck.

Gwen's shoulders sagged. "How terrible," she whispered. "How will his family even know?"

"Mr. Stanley said he will see to it. There's a Jewish community in Merthyr Tydfil, small it is, but he imagines they will want the body for a burial in their own fashion." An attempt at a smile quirked one side of her full, lush lips. "He so badly wants to perform last rites, but knows the man wouldn't thank him for it. A Jew can't be buried on Christian ground in any case. But I daresay our good vicar ran off to say an Anglican prayer in secret, to feel sure his soul is seen off safely."

"He's dead?" Pen demanded. "The Jew who was beaten?"

"He's dying," Dovey said softly. "We'll hear the bells of St. Woolos tolling before nightfall. Mr. Stanley will mark his passing, even for an unbaptized soul."

She met Gwen's gaze and a long, tense look passed between them. Clasping hands, the two women exited toward a different hallway, not the door leading to the dining hall but one leading inside the building. Shamelessly, Pen stepped closer to the wall and cocked an ear. He was an exceptional eavesdropper; he couldn't claim many talents, but that was one.

"We can't tell him." Gwen's voice, low and full of self-reproach.

"No. If we do, and he turns us out—"

Pen's ears pricked. Who did they fear? What man had a hold over them?

"We'd have nowhere to go," Gwen answered. "And you and Cerys—it's danger out there."

"I fear it, Gwen. The town is changing. So many new—"

Their voices fell and diminished. Steps led away. Pen leaned forward, straining to hear, and then leapt back as Gwen suddenly reappeared in the doorway. Her look speared him, accusatory, but underneath it he saw fear.

He moved toward her. He wanted to protect her. He was half a man at the moment, true, with his bruised shoulder and banged-up ribs. But he would lay himself at her feet if she asked it.

"What do you want now?" she snapped.

He panicked at the sudden and unaccustomed surge of protectiveness. He knew this wasn't like him. This woman had overset him, upended all his usual sensibilities. Even though he couldn't say what his usual sensibilities were, she had muddled him. He felt shaken to his core.

"My jordan needs emptying," he blurted.

"Empty it yourself!" It was as if the request broke her. She whirled for the table and the basket she'd left there, swooping up a spade like it was sword and shield.

"Empty my own chamber pot!" he shouted. He was quite certain he'd never done such a thing in his life. "Who do you think I am?"

"I don't care who you are!" She brandished the spade at him, advancing, and Pen debated whether to fall back. "You are here. Under this roof. We took you in. We helped you. And so you will follow *our* rules, mm—Mr. *Pen*."

"Your rules!" he said indignantly.

"And the rule is, everyone helps. Everyone *works*." She pointed toward the door where the boy had exited. "Ifor keeps the goats." She pointed at the simple lad. "Tomos fetches the water and helps mop and sweep. Mother Morris—" that was the crone—"does the mending and the wash. Widow Jones—" the older woman in the black shawl, still rather pretty even for her age—"has cooked most of the meals you've scoffed at, and is the one who fixed your clothing. Dovey, Mrs. Van der Welle, oversees our housekeeping, among half a dozen other duties, and Evans, with one arm, does the work of three men. So you—" she advanced until the spade nearly poked his nose—"can empty. Your own. Chamber pot."

"You needn't take my nose off." Pen put on his most affected drawl. It was all he could offer in self-defense. "And what do you do, besides bark orders and menace people with gardening implements?"

Her eyes flared and he wondered, for a suspended moment, if she were going to strike him. No one *ever* struck him.

No, that felt distinctly untrue. He'd been walloped in Newport several times already. He had the sense he'd been manhandled quite a bit as a youth—the torments felt dim, far away, but deeply entrenched. But no one now dared strike him because—because—he was someone important, devil take it. He did *not* empty chamber pots. He looked down his nose and waited for her to capitulate.

The widow came forward and placed her arms on Gwen's shoulders. "Gwen looks after us all, and earns the coin that feeds us," she said softly. "Gwen *bach*, you needn't harp tonight if you don't wish it. It's been a trying day already, and a fair drive to Greenfield."

"'Tis not so far." Her shoulders slumped. "And it's a small gathering. Lady Vaughn only wants me to play for a family dinner. Though I admit, with what our Mathry is going through, I have no wish to look upon the smug face of Calvin Vaughn."

She froze as she said this, and turned a wide, dreadful stare on Pen. The hairs on his neck lifted again. Was he supposed to know these names?

"You might take me," Pen said, doing his best to hide the desperation in his voice. "Someone might know me. Though it doesn't seem I'm from here." No one had recognized him, though he'd wandered town about the better part of a day. Was no one looking for him? Didn't he matter to someone?

The change in Gwen was alarming. He hated that frightened, hunted look. He wanted the soft woman who had wrapped his ribs and laid her lovely hand on his forehead. His chest hurt, his cracked ribs making it hard to breathe.

"I'll go tonight. Alone. We need the coin." She turned away. "It's time we had meat for a meal, and Tomos needs new boots."

The simpleton stuck out a foot clad in rags and leather, barely cobbled together. "*Llopan*," he said.

Bloody hell. What *was* this place? The roof needed mending, they had to forage for food, and they couldn't even buy the boy boots.

He didn't care about the others, but why was Gwen here, seemingly in charge of this collection of tatterdemalions? A woman that beautiful could simply lift a finger and point to the man she wanted to provide for her. And the lucky fool would eagerly hand over life, name, and fortune for the gift of her body, her promise to be buxom at bed and board.

Not Pen. He didn't want a wife. He didn't want to be here. He'd take to his heels as soon as he bloody well could.

But in the meantime, he wanted to do something that would make Gwen's shoulders slump less. Take away the lines of worry between those clear, soul-searching eyes.

He squared his shoulders, marched back to his room, pinched his nose, and scooped up his chamber pot.

CHAPTER SEVEN

P en emerged from the necessary house to find it was indeed raining with a passion. Puddles formed in the courtyard and churned up mud in the gardens. He couldn't see beyond the woods that hedged the property, couldn't even make out the tower of St. Woolos, though it wasn't far away.

The one-armed man was in one of the outbuildings, cleaning a large wooden vat. The small building reeked of yeast and hops. Pen's stomach growled. He wanted grog, but beer would do. He was not at all in favor of Gwen's edict that she would dry him out.

"Wise to hide out here," Pen said, watching the man work. He seemed surprisingly able for having a maimed leg and but one arm. Most men who came back marred from the wars were left begging in the streets, not at all guaranteed a pension for their service.

How did he know this?

"The women are all a-flutter over that Jewish man who was beaten," Pen went on, trying to drown out the unpleasant emptiness in his head. "You'd think they never knew men to disagree."

He meant to establish a manly rapport, two sane fellows

looking upon the foibles of women and scratching their heads, following age-old custom. Instead, the man swung about, poured a bucket of water into the vat, and resumed scrubbing.

"We don't see many Jews in Newport," he answered. "They mostly stay in Merthyr Tydfil. They don't mix, but they've never been hated here. Not like the *Saeson* hate them."

Saes meant English, Pen gathered. He was as much an outsider, a stranger, as the Jewish man. Did Evans, too, hate the English? Pen prickled as the man looked him over, with no change in expression, then returned to his work.

Pen was used to regard from other men. Envy, if not admiration. He knew that much.

"Gwen is frightened," he blurted out.

"That she is," the man affirmed. He lifted a rake in his hand and scrubbed the sides of the vat with it, scratching out the dried residue of malt. "Miss Gwenllian," he said, with emphasis on the *miss*, "has made St. Sefin's a refuge for those of us as don't have a place to go. She gives us shelter and food and the dignity of supporting ourselves. But she found out she don't own the place. Some *Sais* owns it. And she fears he'll come any moment to turn us out."

Turn us out. Gwen's exact words. So she *did* fear someone.

"Well, if it's this man's property, he's at liberty to do what he likes with it," Pen reasoned. "That's simply the law."

"That it is." The other turned his back on him. Pen had the sense he didn't like what he was hearing. "Ifor!" the man bellowed. "Call in the kid. He's straying near where Dah—where Mrs. Van der Welle planted the monkshood, and I don't have the fence up yet."

The goat boy, who was sheltering on bales of hay stacked under another thatched lean-to, patted his four-footed companion on the rump and gave him instructions in Welsh. Pen watched in astonishment as the billy trotted to the kid, butted it back toward its mother, then resumed his place at the boy's side, as if he were a trained herd dog. The boy patted the goat and walked him toward a cluster of flowering shrubs that stood against a low wall of old bricks, the outline of some former building. The goat fell to eating greedily.

Pen shook off the irritation that needled him at the sight of the stricken child. He wasn't responsible for his condition. Why should he feel guilty? Once again he reached for shreds of memory, for the cause of his unease, and once again his thoughts parted like mist.

"Tell me about her," he said instead. "About Gwen. What is her history?"

"Can't say. Don't know," the man answered.

Evans. That was his name. At least he remembered someone's name. He was improving.

"How can you not know? I thought you've been here for years."

"I have. Came to St. Sefin's almost from the beginning, nigh seven years ago. I can tell you about anyone who's here, except Miss Gwen." He put his shoulder to the vat, pushing it onto its side so the water poured into a nearby drain. Pen watched, impressed at his strength. "I don't even think that's her name."

"What do you mean?" This was interesting. What could she be hiding?

Evans kicked the vat back into place and moved to the one beside it. "Gwenllian is a name with great meaning for the Cymry. One Gwenllian was a princess, daughter of Llywelyn ap Gruffydd, the last true Prince of Wales."

"George is the Prince of Wales," Pen snapped.

"To you, *Sais*," Evans said coolly, and went on with his work. "And then there's Gwenllian ferch Gruffydd, renowned for her beauty, her intelligence, her grace." He spoke in a lyrical rhythm, as if reciting an old ballad. "She married a prince of

Deheubarth and led an army against the Normans at Kidwelly Castle. She might have beaten them, too, if not for the treachery of her own kind."

Gwenllian. The name of princesses, of warrior queens. "Her name really could be Gwenllian," Pen said.

Evans shrugged a shoulder. "True. But she calls herself ap Ewyas. Of Ewyas, that is. 'Tis the name of an ancient kingdom recorded in our stories, before the Saxons, before even the Romans came. A kingdom of power and prosperity and wealth."

"Where was this kingdom located?" Pen asked, fascinated despite himself.

"Here, legend has it," Evans said.

Gwenllian ap Ewyas. Pen tried to wrap his tongue around the strange syllables. She belonged to that identity, a name endowing pride, power, wealth, and high blood. He wondered who she had been before.

It made them alike, in a way. Pen pondered this as he left Evans to his task and Ifor to his goats and, like a sensible person, got himself out of the rain. He had no history. No past. No identity. He could make for himself whatever name he wanted.

As he set foot inside the old priory, strangely welcoming despite its vast stone façade, Pen heard it, through the mist: the tolling of the bell at St. Woolos, low, dolorous, deep. The battered stranger, poor bastard, had left this mortal coil for his great reward beyond.

Pen had seen enough of death to last him centuries—he didn't know how or when, but he knew he was sick of death. Especially useless death. There was no glory, no majesty, no greatness in it. One moment a man was gasping for air, tormented with a mind, a conscience, a soul, and the next—nothing. Ashes and dust.

And yet Gwenllian ap Ewyas had fetched him from the gutter, twice, and brought him to this shabby pile of rocks to keep his worthless carcass alive. He owed her his life. Everyone here did.

What kind of woman came from nowhere, took a new name, and set out to save the dregs of society from washing out to sea?

He wiped the cold rain from the back of his neck, shaking off his gloomy fancies. He wasn't ready to give up his life, nor did he want to fashion a new one. He meant to find his own name, his own life, and go back to it. He couldn't be cursed with this foggy head forever. He'd leave and never again be obliged to deal with harping crones, simpletons, the poor and the maimed and the broken. They would be someone else's problem. Not his.

But there was a danger beyond these grounds; he felt Gwen's fear. He couldn't just throw himself defenseless on the world and expect it to treat him kindly. He needed to find where he belonged. Then he'd leave and never look back.

But, he admitted to himself as he roamed the ancient pile that was St. Sefin's, he wanted one thing from the mysterious Gwen before he left. He wanted her to see him as more than another burden, one more broken soul. He'd pierce that high curtain wall she'd constructed around herself. She would look at him with an expression that was not scorn, not exasperation, and not pity, but softness. Admiration. Perhaps even desire.

Yes, that would be a neat way to tie up his time here. He would change her opinion of him no matter what it cost him.

And *then* he would leave and never look back.

SURVIVING AT ST. Sefin's, Pen soon found, required more skills than he possessed. He discovered this a few mornings later when Gwen, pronouncing that he was healing well, laid off his sling and made him tie his own neckcloth.

"I don't know how to tie my own neckcloth," Pen snapped,

enraged by this discovery. "Maybe I don't wear neckcloths in my real life. Or suppose I have other people to do it for me."

"Who's to do it for you here?" Gwen snapped back.

Pen glanced around at their audience. Evans, who was in the infirmary as chaperone, held up his one hand apologetically. The man's own neckcloth was a simple twist, something he could manage himself. Pen turned his scowl on the woman Evans stiffly referred to as Mrs. Van der Welle and everyone else called Dovey.

"Oh, very well. I did it for my husband scores of times." She stepped forward and with a few efficient yanks had a tolerable knot to show him in the hand mirror. "But Gwen's right. Henceforth you'll do it yourself."

"And be sleeping in the men's dorter, as you call it," he grumbled. "No more comfy infirmary all to myself."

"You won't want it when we bring someone infectious in," Gwen said, stripping off his sheets before he had barely risen from the bed. "It's time you start shifting for yourself, mm—Mr. Pen."

It was time he started looking for ways out of here. He'd been here for over a week, taking his meals in the infirmary, exploring the priory, walking the grounds to regain his strength. He avoided the other inhabitants as much as possible, except for Gwen.

"Aren't you going to wrap my ribs again?" He enjoyed Gwen's nursing, the moments when her soft arms came around him and her hair pressed against his nose and the scent of bluebells filled his head. A man needed some pleasures in this dismal life.

"They don't need wrapping now that the swelling's gone," she answered. "Best you use your muscles. Mind you don't exert yourself, but take deep breaths. It will keep fever from settling in your lungs."

Pen put a hand to his left side. He'd seen the scars as he undressed by candlelight in this broad, shadowed room. What kind of life had he lived? The endless ache in his rib and shoulder felt familiar, and Gwen, drat her temperate eyes, wouldn't give him rum. Instead she made him drink willow bark tea. He'd never admit to her that it helped, and left him without a thick head later.

"Now to work with you," Gwen said briskly. "You're ready to help with chores."

"I'm emptying my own chamber pot," Pen said. "I'm quite sure I've never done that in my life, either. What more do you want from me, woman?"

He followed her through the storerooms to the kitchen, where the black-clad widow was singing over a stove while the crone sat in a straight back chair, mending what Pen recognized as his own silk stockings. The simple boy sat at the table, lining up asparagus stems by size after a young girl, who looked to be Dovey's daughter, snipped off the ends. And there was the blind boy and the goat on its rope lead, moving its mouth in chewing motions, staring at Pen with its slitted eyes.

He was taken aback by the warm, bustling atmosphere of the place, the friendly conversation going back and forth.

"I want any number of things from you," Gwen said in answer to his question.

He gave her the best lascivious look he could affect. It was wasted as she turned to pick up a wooden bowl and dumped a clump of boiled oats into it. "This morn, I want you to help Ifor take the goats to the south pasture. We're not to stray into the churchyard today. Then you might help Tomos fetch the water and walk him over to St. Woolos, where the vicar has some tasks for him. You might ask Mr. Stanley if you can help as well. It was he who sent the boy to fetch me when he found you in the stable yard of the King's Head the other day. You might still be lying there if not for him, so you owe him thanks."

"You're sending me off with a blind boy and the idiot?" Pen looked at them in turn, not hiding his horror.

"And then you might help Evans set up the fence around the poison garden so the goats don't get in," Gwen said.

"Yes, I imagine he could use an extra hand," Pen said acidly. "What's a poison garden?" He picked up a spoon and poked at the brown lumpy mass in his bowl. When he ate it, he found raisins and a trace of wild honey. Delicious. Food tasted good to him again, which was a surprise.

"The herbs that are poisonous if not used correctly. We fence them off so others don't take them unknowing."

"Wouldn't everyone here know better?" He spooned up his oatmeal quickly. He'd prefer to wash it down with grog but knew better than to ask.

"Our gardens, especially our vegetable beds, are open to anyone in town who wants to come harvest from them." Gwen scooped oats into a bowl for herself. She'd served him first, Pen noted. "There are too many who don't have enough to eat, so we share what we can."

They didn't have much, Pen thought, looking around. And yet, to keep the doors open to anyone in need? Astonishing that they hadn't all been killed in their beds some dark night.

"Ready to head out, your worship?" the goat boy said cheerfully, putting his bowl in the scullery sink and picking up his crooked staff. "Gafr wants a stretch."

"Why are you calling me your worship?" Pen said, rising from the bench. "I'm not a judge." He didn't think. Dispensing justice and settling disputes did not strike him as work he had an affinity for.

"You've a lordly air about you, you have," said the boy. "Like you're better'n all of us."

Gwen suddenly grew busy with the dishes, clanging spoons and bowls together. "Off with you! His worship needs to earn his keep, just like the rest of us."

"What I need is to get my memory back," Pen muttered, and set off to follow the goat boy into his next circle of hell.

HE WAS RUBBISH AT EVERYTHING, Pen learned. Had he not learned a single skill in his life? Or had it all been knocked out of him with that clunk in the crown office?

He was no good as goatherd. The goats wouldn't mind him no matter how much he shouted. He shredded his breeches chasing the kid through a patch of stinging nettles. The nanny butted him in the rear when he bent to right the bucket of mash she'd upended. And when he stood too long once, daydreaming about Gwen and whether he would have any reason to cross paths with her once he returned to his real life, he looked down to find the big goat, Gafr, chewing on his leather boot. Gwen and the others had laughed merrily when he stomped into the refectory that night for the evening meal, complaining about bone-headed goats.

The simple boy was worse. He made Pen nervous. Trying to march him out to the well in the mornings to draw the day's water was irritating enough, when the simpleton wandered at a snail's pace and pointed to everything, muttering words Pen didn't understand. But it was excruciating to accompany him on afternoon excursions to the neighboring St. Woolos when he went in the same meandering, lackadaisical fashion. The child wanted to stop and smell every sodding flower, then stand for a long time admiring the tall square Norman tower and the stained glass window of the nave. He was a man of direction, Pen discovered. He liked to get things done, not dally along enjoying the scenery. He must be a man of discipline and focus in his real life. Perhaps he was a soldier? Or held a profession of some sort?

Soldiering would explain the nightmares that continued to plague him. Terrifying dreams he nightly found chased away by a cool hand on his sweating brow, a musical voice murmuring calmly to him in Welsh or singing him scraps of old ballads. A soothing tea held to his lips, and the sweet smell of bluebells lingering in the air as she sat next to his bed, embroidering or mending or knitting something until he fell asleep. Gwen, mistress of St. Stodgy's, might play the harridan with him in daylight hours, but at night, when the dreams came, she was an angel of mercy.

As he'd done before, the vicar gave the simple boy a polishing cloth and set him to dusting the artifacts in one of the chapels. Pen stood examining the Romanesque carvings above the portal that led to the rest of the church. He was surprised to find anything so stately or refined here in Wales, a land of thatched huts and muddy sheep.

"You're not from Newport, are you, lad? I gather you're English."

The vicar had not approached Pen since the day he'd helped haul him home from the King's Head. Now he spoke as he would address the simple boy, friendly, straightforward, without condescension. Kinder than the hilarity and teasing Pen had encountered at the tavern all those days ago when he'd admitted he didn't know his family, his history, his occupation, or his name.

It was all still a frustrating blank, locked in a part of his brain he couldn't access, memories wafting beyond his grip like gauzy curtains in the breeze.

"I wish I knew where I'm from," Pen said. "I wish I could remember anything."

"I'm sure someone's looking for you," the vicar said. He was a soothing presence, soft-spoken but direct, without guile or hidden motives. Pen liked that about him.

"What if they're not?" Stanley's kind manner struck a nerve. He couldn't recall details, but he could recall feelings. And Pen had an awful fear that no one in his life would much care if he tumbled off the edge of the world.

His shoulder burned, and he rubbed it for relief. "What if I'm stuck here, friendless, alone, never knowing my name? Useless and castaway in St. Sow's Sty for the rest of my life."

With Gwen. At least he would be near Gwen.

Stanley merely stood next to him, linked his fingers, and regarded the set of carved arches. To Pen the thick stone triangles looked like teeth. They might close on a man if he dared step through.

"An interesting history to this church," the vicar remarked. "Gwynllyw, a wealthy and respected Welsh prince, retired here sometime in the fifth or sixth century and took up the life of a hermit, building his cell here on Stow Hill. His wife, Gwladys, set up her own hermitage not far away. After his death they say a timber church was built here, and it became a place of pilgrimage.

"After it burned down—sacked, I would guess, by the Northmen, or Vikings as they are called—it was rebuilt in stone by an Anglo-Saxon king who had converted to Christianity. Then the Normans came and built their new port and castle and gave the church its tower. At some point it became Woolos —I suppose the Saxons couldn't pronounce Gwynllyw."

Pen didn't say anything. He couldn't pronounce these Welsh words either.

"Then in the uprising of Owain Glyndŵr, St. Woolos was destroyed again. And rebuilt again. And now it is what you see today."

Pen couldn't see that it was anything impressive, with its

single tower sticking out of the hill like a sore thumb, brambles growing nearly to the door, the stained glass letting in a muddy light, and half the gravestones tipping over in the churchyard. But he waited until the vicar came to his point.

"It was destroyed many times, and rebuilt each time. Each time was a chance to make it better."

He paused, and Pen refused to meet his inquiring gaze. Was the vicar hinting that *Pen* had an opportunity to rebuild his life? What foolishness. He didn't need to reinvent anything. He needed to *find* who he was, because of a certain, he was someone important. Maybe rich. That would be nice, to return to a life of luxury and never have to empty his own chamber pot, or eat gruel, or play nursemaid to a simpleton again.

It stung, though, that the people of St. Stiffin's thought *he* was the simpleton. That night Tomos was welcomed warmly for dinner and invited to talk about his experiences. Pen got a bowl plunked in front of him full of something they called onion cake, which looked to him like sliced potatoes covered in cheese. Apparently everyone else thought this a treat. He ate it, and wasn't about to admit there was anything tasty about it. In his real life, his rich life, he had five course meals and footmen to place each dish before him. Or would have, someday.

The thought that his real life was elsewhere, and he would return to it soon, kept him going through the next hideous days. The old crone, Mother Morris, made him mop the floors—stone floors! With cracks everywhere! A nightmare!—and then laughed and jabbered at him in Welsh when he upset the bucket of filthy water and suds over the scullery floor he'd just mopped. She repeated the story at dinner, in English this time, and everyone laughed, even the simpleton.

The Widow Jones thought his horror and revulsion hilarious when she asked Pen to take the laundry out of the soaking bucket and, when he held his nose at the strong scent of ammonia, informed him that the "chamber lye" was made up of the contents of chamber pots.

"Just the liquid portion, mind you. It's called lant, and it's wondrous at lifting stains. Makes the fabric workable."

He was so desperate to wash his hands that he grabbed the nearest pot of water and poured it over his palms, scalding his fingers. The widow clucked and scolded as she fussed over him, but she didn't let him leave his post. Instead, she set him to poking the laundry with a stick while she poured the rest of the hot water into a bowl, scraped a few shavings from a bar of soap into it, and whipped it into a sudsy froth. The wet fabrics were heavy to stir and wring, then rinse and wring again, then spread over the lawn and every available surface to bleach. His sheets alone weighed a stone. His muscles hurt by the end of the afternoon, and the scents of ash and lye burned his nose. By God, he'd never do a lick of manual labor when he went back to his life, Pen swore.

But that was all the others did. Dovey was always in the garden or whisking about the house. Her daughter was ever underfoot, running errands and singing snatches of song as she went. Evans never seemed to sit still except in the evening, after their light supper, when the group sat together on the front porch when the weather was fine. If the weather was less fine, they gathered in a room they called the chapter house, which was built like a large parlor full of uncomfortable benches and chairs. Once in a while they lit a fire in the hearth and sat around chatting, telling stories and playing games.

Some nights Gwen sang and played on a small traveling harp of hers, and those were the only moments when Pen could bear the place. These weren't his people. He was quite sure he was accustomed to being around men with their plain speech and rough ways; in his real life, he didn't waste his time making idle, polite speech with women. But when Gwen played the harp, it was like a heavenly spirit came among them. The room warmed; the angry chatter in his head subsided. Even his ribs and shoulder hurt less when he listened to her voice. She was an uncommon gem and she was buried here, in this hinterland. How could she bear it?

Those were his times of peace: the rare evenings when Gwen sang, and the nights he woke in the solid dark to the scent of bluebells and honey and her soft, soothing voice rousing him from a nightmare. They were becoming more frequent and violent, the dreams. As if some urgent message from his past was trying to break through the fog in his mind.

One morning, remarkably, he woke with the sense that he had slept. He felt refreshed in a way he hadn't felt since—well, he couldn't remember. The small casement high in the wall of his room let in light telling him the sun had climbed Stow Hill, and motes swirled in the air like a smattering of pixie dust. He started as his fingers brushed something soft and warm, and looked down to find that his hand rested on the back of a woman.

Gwen's rear end was seated on a small stool beside his cot but she had slumped forward in sleep, her head pillowed upon arms crossed upon the side of his bed. A wrapper and shawl covered her shoulders, and her half-loose braid spilled thick ashy brown hair over his hip. Her face was turned toward him, and an ache spread through his belly at her relaxed features, achingly lovely. Her dark lashes and brows stood out against her lightly tanned skin. The shape of her face was so elegant, brow and nose and chin almost stern in their clarity, but her lips, red and full, betrayed her soft heart.

He stroked her hair, feeling he touched a holy relic, one too pure for his handling. Her lips curved in a smile and her eyes opened, that soft grey-green of a deep forest where a man could wander, enchanted, and become lost forever.

"What is that awful racket outside?" he whispered as a clatter of noise poured in the window, which flickered with the shadow of passing wings.

She said a stream of words in Welsh, then translated. "We have a pair of choughs nesting above the chapter house. That's the cry you heard—there. The others—" She paused, listening. "Chaffinch. Thrush. That little peep—that's the nuthatch. Tomos loves them particularly."

He stared at her as the noise became music. He'd never cared to listen to the natural world before. He'd never had someone to translate it for him.

He'd never woken with a woman in his bed and wanted to stay there with her. She was only halfway on his bed, having fallen asleep at her bedside vigil. He felt guilty for robbing her of rest at the same time he relished having her all to himself. Her hair beneath his palm was a river of silk, the skin beneath her light wrapper firm and warm. He wondered what she would do if he pulled her into bed and fit the delicious length of her against him. He knew his ribs were not quite healed, but his lower body was very interested in the image.

"You stayed with me all night?"

"You didn't want me to leave. Your nightmares are getting worse," she said softly. He nodded, his throat stuck. "And I feared you might throw off your blankets and develop a chill, you were sweating so."

She laid a hand on his brow and he clasped his other hand over hers. He ought to be burning up with embarrassment that a woman should see him so weak and vulnerable, pursued in his sleep by memories he couldn't summon in the light of day. But she was calm, unaccusing.

"I'm not sure I want to remember everything," he said.

The corners of her eyes tightened and her lashes fluttered as she looked away. He didn't want her to withdraw but she did, taking away her hand and straightening on the stool.

"Perhaps the dreams would cease to be a torment if your memory returned."

With a haunted look, she stood and left, departing toward the stair that led to the kitchens. Her lost warmth left a hollow space in his blankets. In his chest. He was a fool, pulling on his clothes in haphazard haste to follow her, but she drew him like a siren lured doomed sailors to the shore.

The kitchen was empty, a surprise. Perhaps everyone else was already at their tasks. He saw a crust of bread wrapped in cloth and a hunk of cheese on the table, he guessed left out for him. If he took it to Gwen, would she eat with him? She'd woken with her guard down, for the first time not wary or distant or short with him. He wanted more of that Gwen.

But then she came into the kitchen in her day gown and customary red woolen shawl, tying a kerchief over her hair, and he feared the golden moment was lost.

"*Bore da*," she said. "Good morning."

No, no, no, she couldn't retreat. That moment when she looked in his eyes and smiled had woken something in him. If she turned away now that raw, aching thing in him would still be there.

"What are you doing?" He tied, or attempted to tie, his neckcloth as she put a copper kettle on the stove, then went to the scullery and emerged with an earthenware bucket. "What's that?"

"Soap lye infused with oil. It's time I made a new batch of soap." She sent him a wry half-smile as his eyes flared. "It's not chamber lye, 'tis pot ash and quick lime, with a bit of goat's milk. Your delicate sensibilities won't be offended."

"I'm not the least bit delicate," Pen said, stepping closer.

She snorted. "All right. Then you can go to the King's Head

today with Evans and help shovel out Mr. Trett's stable. You ran up a tab the other day when you were drinking with Gossett, before you let him knock you senseless in the stable yard. I promised Mr. Trett you would pay your debt." She built up the fire and took up a stick to stir her concoction.

"Aren't you worried I'll be beaten again? They still haven't found who fell upon that Jewish man." Perhaps preying on her nurturing instincts would get him somewhere.

Concern flashed through her eyes. "That's why Evans is going with you."

He stepped closer. Appealing to her nurturing side was the wrong move. It wasn't nurturing he wanted from her.

"Are you certain I'm up to the task? I don't think my ribs have healed yet." Though they hurt far less than they had. He had the vague feeling that they'd hurt much worse before his beatings. He'd spent a long time contemplating his scars, wondering how he'd gained them. All that rose to his waking mind were sensations of white-hot agony and red flashes of blood. He could move easily now, and it felt strange, like he hadn't done so in years. Gwen had healed him.

"Don't strain too much, and stop when you're weary. You need to keep your lungs clear." She tapped his chest. "Deep breaths."

He caught her hand and held it. She'd touched him again. He didn't want her to play nurse with him, either. He wanted her to see him as a man.

"Is that why you've been setting me to all these ridiculous tasks," he growled. "And then laughing at me when I'm rubbish at all of them." His pride still stung from being the joke of St. Stuffy's. Everyone else had a place, had a part, made a contribution. Except Pen. "And now I'm to play stableboy?"

"Half a stableboy, with one good arm," she said archly. "With Evans, you make a whole man. Like you said."

He moved closer, crowding her, her hand still anchored on his chest. He hoped she didn't notice the accelerating beat of his heart. "I would like you to know I'm a whole man. Very whole." A step closer and she'd be acquainted with his manliness, pressing against her hip.

She froze, and the playful teasing in her face evaporated. Fear fled over her features, followed by wariness and stiff reserve. They were back to the guardedness. The smiling girl, kin to the songbirds, was gone.

"Then we've been good for you." Her voice sounded strained, breathless. "Staying here at St. Sefin's has helped you. Will you admit it?"

He frowned. "Helped me? I've been a prisoner. The moment I have a place to bolt to, I'm breaking out." He lifted his free hand and stroked a curl that refused to stay beneath her kerchief. "You might come with me."

"And do what? Go where?" Her eyes were wide, fathomless pools, sucking him in.

"I don't care where we go. And as for what we'll do..." He leaned toward her, leaving but an inch between their faces. She needed to close that last distance; he wanted her surrender. Wanted her to admit what flared between them. That beneath her impatience and dismissiveness with him was a deeper yearning. He felt it, too.

A pointed pressure against his left side brought him out of the swirl of fantasy. He stepped back and she lowered the stirring stick.

"You're shoveling muck today. That's what you're doing," she said.

"All day," he said. "You won't want an interlude, or—" He rubbed the lock of hair wrapped around his finger. "Even a brief few stolen minutes with me?"

"I will be making the soap," she said, deliberately turning

away.

But her hands were unsteady as she stirred the kettle on the stove. At least he had the satisfaction of knowing he'd unsettled her. But she was no pure maiden to blush and titter when a man showed he desired her. He'd eat his hat if she wasn't an experienced woman who knew exactly what he was proposing.

But she didn't desire him. Or she did, but refused to act on it. Worse yet.

"You needn't deny yourself, or me," he said peevishly. "And I don't see why you would want to stay in this ramshackle place. Whatever I can offer you would be better."

She whirled back to face him, stick raised, her eyes narrowed. "We help people here," she hissed at him. If she were a Medusa, he'd be stone already. "We helped you, only you're too thick-headed to admit it. I belong here. This is my home. And even if it weren't, don't think I would leave it for the kind of man who—" She cut off the next words.

"What?" he challenged her, stepping towards her again, a different heat shooting through his veins. What had she meant to say? "What kind of man am I?"

She turned her back and plunged her stick into the liquid on the kettle, stirring madly. "The kind who leaves," she said shortly. "If you're going, begone with you. If you come back, bring a barrow full of manure, if Mr. Trett will spare some. Dovey can use fertilizer on the garden."

Impossible, interfering, *irritating* woman. She was lying to herself and denying him. A dalliance would be the one good thing to come of his cursed time here. Pen looked for his hat, a battered old wool cap he'd borrowed from Evans, and set out.

The girl Mathry met him as he crossed the yard to fetch Evans and the wheelbarrow. She wore a shawl about her waist in what seemed the manner of these Welsh women, who used it for apron, basket, and cleaning cloth. He guessed in a few months' time, Mathry would be using hers as a sling for a babe. She had that ripe look of a woman increasing, a glow to her skin, her uncovered bosom swelling in generous curves. He took a moment to appreciate the view, but it didn't improve his mood.

"Mr. Pen." She paused before him with a coy look, setting one hand on a curving hip. "Where you to?"

"Shoveling muck with Evans, it seems. A Herculean task to be sure."

The reference was lost on her. She wouldn't know who Hercules was, much less his seven labors. He bet Gwen would recognize the allusion. And then scoff at his comparing himself to Hercules. She still saw him as inept. Inadequate. One more thing she had to take care of.

Mathry made a sympathetic click with her tongue. "Poor darling," she cooed. "You haven't had much to make your stay here agreeable, you haven't." Her sweat smelled spicy. Did they not bathe at St. Sodding's? But Gwen always smelled like a summer afternoon, and occasionally whatever she'd been cooking.

Mathry drew closer. Her hand, cradling a shawl full of plant cuttings, nearly brushed his groin. Did the lass know what she was about? He suspected she did.

She pitched her voice low. "If I can help you in any fashion, Mr. Pen, I will." She slid her tongue over her lips.

He watched, fascinated. Had he fallen for such lures in his past life? There was something vulgar about her obvious offer, though he had to credit her good sense. He was a cut above the other men in her orbit. He was merely surprised she'd waited this long to make her play.

"The only thing that would help me right now," he said with complete honesty, "is finding out who I am and going back to my life."

She leaned in, which gave him a near-entire view of her

breasts, lifted as they were by her tight stays. "Take me with you."

"You and your babe?" His lip curled. "A merry little band of three?"

She faltered, withdrawing, the sultry look turning to concern. "How did you—"

"I don't dally with mothers," he said shortly. "Sink your hooks into a man who's a better bet than I am." And he stalked across the shorn yard to take out the rest of his irritation on Evans, who was man enough to handle it.

Maybe he'd just walk on from Newport and never come back. Leave Evans and all the rest of them to the manure and the poisons and the chamber pots and the bloody belligerent goats. He owed Gwenllian ap Ewyas nothing; she had no hold over him.

Or if she did, he wouldn't heed it. He would cut rope the instant opportunity presented itself.

Proving her right after all: that he was a man who ran.

CHAPTER EIGHT

"He's back." Dovey came in from the garden, setting a basket of rosemary leaves on the kitchen table.

"Pen?" Gwen stirred a handful of salt into her copper pot and reached for the basket. With her stove already hot, she'd steam the oils from the rosemary and add it to her soap. It would make an aromatic blend, and she could sell or trade with the town merchants and finally get a new set of boots for Tomos.

"The solicitor from Bristol," Dovey said with a grim set to her mouth.

"*Coc oen*," Gwen swore, and for once Dovey didn't laugh that she'd adopted one of Mother Morris's curses.

She used her kerchief to wipe the sweat on her brow from hours of standing over the stove, then wiped her hands in her shawl and followed Dovey to the front porch of the church. There stood Mr. Barlow in his black wool suit and hat, glaring at her from beneath bushy white brows.

"Mr. Barlow." He was as menacing as she remembered. She'd had dreams that he'd appear just like this to turn them out. They woke her sweating and ready to scream, like Pen and his nightmares. A sick sensation slipped and slid around in her belly. Where was Pen?

"Would you—like to come in?"

"I bear a message from the Viscount Penrydd. The owner of this property," he reminded her, as if she didn't recall that very well, every moment of the day.

St. Tybie's tears. Pen had regained his memory. How had he set the solicitor on them so fast? He'd departed with Evans that morning. He must have run into Mr. Barlow in Newport and all had been made clear. And what was the first thing Pen did upon reclaiming his life? Set his solicitor upon the people who had saved his life. She clenched her hands in her shawl.

"And what has his lordship to say to us?" She struggled to keep her voice steady. Dovey drew in a long breath, bracing herself for a blow.

Barlow consulted a slip of paper in his hand with an expression of haughty disdain. "His lordship will allow you to purchase the property of St. Sefin's in its entirety, free of lien or any other obligation," he said, drawing out the announcement, "for the price of—fifteen hundred pounds."

"Allow us...purchase...?" She felt as if she'd tumbled off the roof and had the breath knocked out of her. Heavy and yet weightless at the same time. The miracle, the solution she needed—tossed in her lap. At a price she could never, given a lifetime, be able to afford.

Dovey reached out and clasped her fingers. Her palm was as cold as Gwen's.

"How soon does he want the money?" Dovey asked.

"His lordship requests payment in full at the earliest possible convenience. Or he will tender the offer to other parties."

What other parties? Gwen wanted to cry. No one else

would love this place as she and Dovey did. No one else would keep its mission of gathering and tending lost souls.

"Pay...in full?"

Barlow attempted to look down his nose at her, a difficulty as they were the same height. He settled for a look of exasperation. "What is your answer?"

Gwen's knees wobbled. Pen was gone. He was Viscount Penrydd again, a lord of the realm. The man whose nightmares she'd soothed, whose wounds she had doctored, who had raised all those alarming and unwanted sensations within her, he'd disappeared. She should be happy the danger was in focus now. She should be glad the lie was done.

"We do not have that amount at hand, Mr. Barlow. We would need to arrange some method of payment."

"So you cannot accept."

"We accept!" Gwen rushed to say. "But will his lordship not —can we not speak with—"

She blinked. She could speak with Pen right now, for here he came up the hill to St. Sefin's, larger than life and sturdy as a plow, pushing a wheelbarrow full of manure. Evans limped beside him, carrying a sack across his shoulder.

The Viscount Penrydd, lord of the realm, pushing a barrow of dung, looking as hale and hardy as the day he was born. Gwen's jaw unhinged.

Barlow glanced at the approaching men with the same expression of dislike that he cast over the empty bell tower, the centuries-old façade of the church with weeds growing along its base, and then Gwen herself.

"I will not vex his lordship with a petty counteroffer," Barlow said. "What answer shall I take him?"

Gwen sent a look of appeal at Pen, despair tugging at her gut. She could not lose St. Sefin's. But she could not buy it at this price.

"His lordship knows we wish to buy St. Sefin's," she said. "But he must also be aware we cannot produce fifteen hundred pounds at his asking. It will take time to collect the funds."

Pen set the barrow down. "Fifteen hundred for what?"

She stared at him.

Bewildered, Gwen glanced at Dovey to find her engaged in some swift and unspoken exchange with Evans. He read the tautness about Dovey's eye, the tic of muscle in her cheek, as well as Gwen could.

"We've been at the King's Head all afternoon," Evans said in a bland tone. "Quiet day among the horse's rumps. Fifteen hundred to buy St. Sefin's then? That's the offer?"

"That much?" Pen looked with disbelief upon the pile of stone. "Is there gold hidden in the foundation?"

Gwen stared some more. Would he be generous and lower the price to a figure far more within her reach? Or was he here to watch them all turned out with whatever poor possessions they could carry?

"I don't think *you*," Barlow said with a look of the greatest contempt at Penrydd, "are in any position to challenge his lordship. I wouldn't expect a rough-hewn rustic to know the worth of this land or the rents it might obtain."

What game was this? Gwen reeled with confusion. Surely the solicitor recognized his employer. Pen hadn't changed *that* much in two weeks.

Pen slapped his hands to his hips and scowled, every image of affronted masculinity. "Rough hewn? Rustic?"

He acted as if he didn't recognize Barlow, either.

"His lordship can't be persuaded to a lower price?" Evans, the peacemaker, jumped in.

"Lower? He ought to demand more for what has been taking place on his property without his knowledge or consent!"

Barlow glared at Dovey. "Harboring runaways and no doubt other stolen goods."

Dovey sucked in a whistling breath. Barlow turned his sneer on Gwen. "Very like there is drinking and no doubt gambling taking place here. You're fortunate the parish hasn't complained before this about disturbances to the peace. But what can one expect of guttersnipes best left to die in the street."

Pen stepped forward, his face dark with menace. "Guttersnipes! You will apologize to the lady."

"Lady!" Barlow stumbled backward, huffing with outrage and clapping a hand to his hat. "Keep your hands off me, you filth! Or I will have you in the parish lockup so fast your illiterate head will spin."

"Filth!" Pen roared. "I'll dip your jobbernole in my wagon and we'll see who's filth then."

The solicitor turned and bolted down the drive, moving as fast as his polished boots could carry him. Pen wiped his hands as if he'd won a fight. "Showed him, didn't I?"

Gwen groped for words. "Jobbernole?" she finally asked.

"Jolly knob. Crown office." Pen pointed to his head. "Called me filth, he did!"

Tomos wandered up to them. "*Twll din pob Saes*," he observed.

Pen returned to his barrow and hoisted it with a grunt, favoring his left shoulder. "You said it, boy. He's a cod's head." He paused before Gwen. His jaw was set with anger, his eyes alight with righteous wrath. "Don't fret, Gwen. We'll deal with this arse of a lordship, and anyone else who dares complain about you."

She had the insane urge to take him by the face and kiss him. She conquered it.

"Cod's head," Tomos said, falling into step with the men.

"Yes, very good." Their voices retreated toward the garden

with their load of fertilizer. "Can you say numbskull?" Pen asked.

Gwen gripped Dovey's hands. "He didn't recognize Penry-dd," she hissed. "Because of the way he was dressed?" It wasn't the cleverest disguise, though most city men wouldn't see past a wheelbarrow full of manure, whoever held it.

"More like Barlow has never clapped eyes on his lordship," Dovey guessed as they hurried toward the kitchen. "All their correspondence could take place through his secretary."

"So Mr. Ross would have written to Barlow about the offer," Gwen reasoned. "Did Penrydd decide to sell before he set out for Newport? Maybe he wasn't coming to turn us out, but to negotiate." No pitchfork. No snarl. No devil at all, as she'd feared.

Widow Jones hummed about the kitchen, pouring soap into molds. The scent of fresh rosemary warmed the air. Gwen's heart darted like a swallow in her chest.

"And Barlow is simply dispatching his business." Dovey tied her shawl as an apron around her waist. "Does he even know the viscount is missing?"

"Did he understand we did not decline? We simply don't have that money." Gwen's breath clenched painfully as she selected a knife to chop rosemary leaves. "Will he offer St. Sefin's to someone else?"

"But he'd need Penrydd's approval, and Penrydd is here." Dovey kept her voice quiet so Widow Jones didn't hear.

"With no idea who he is." A wild giggle bubbled up. "Did you see the way he went after Barlow?"

Dovey's eyes danced with shared laughter. "He did not take kindly to the insult!"

Of course he wouldn't. In his proper life he was a viscount. Men bowed and scraped and licked his boots, seeking his patronage, influence, favors. Women vied for his attention, hoping to become his viscountess.

Her lungs squeezed again, caught in that odd grip. Did he have someone in sight already? The mysterious Arwen?

Gwen pondered the incredible exchange, and hopeless ways to raise fifteen hundred pounds, while she crumbled chopped rosemary atop the molds filled with simmering soap. They'd dry in an aromatic top layer and, when used, soothe the skin. At least there was one task she could manage, right now, while everything else was tumbling about in her head.

"Brought you something."

She startled as Pen appeared at her elbow. He had changed into a suit of Evan's old clothes. His hair was damp, curling over his forehead, and he smelled like her soap. He held out a canvas sack.

"Evans and I mucked out Trett's stables, then went to the butcher's and moved some offal about for him. His wife sent this. She says a proper Welsh soup must have salted bacon. And swedes."

Gwen unwrapped the paper to find a thick packet of bacon. Her mouth watered. "This is..." Astonishment bound her tongue.

"You're welcome." He looked smug, so pleased with himself for bringing something to the table. She had expected nothing but complaints over the task he'd been assigned.

"Trett says Gossett hasn't been back in since he trounced me. But Mrs. Gossett's been seen at the miller's, with two perfectly sound eyes." He rubbed a hand over the back of his neck and grinned at her.

Gwen hauled out the frying pan with unsteady hands. He had mucked the innyard's stables, performed a service for the butcher, and brought home food. And he had known she would want to hear that Mrs. Gossett was enjoying a reprieve from her husband's fists.

He hadn't recognized Barlow the solicitor. And Barlow hadn't recognized him.

"That's good news, it is." She sliced the bacon while Widow Jones stepped into the cellar.

"Swedes!" Pen called after her, rolling his left shoulder. "I've a hankering to try them."

"I think we have some left from last autumn." Gwen kept her eyes on her knife.

She wondered if the day's work had been a strain on his injuries. She'd make him a rub for his sore muscles before bed, though she doubted the wisdom of offering to apply it herself. He was so large, so clean-smelling. So confident. She'd seen a sweet, calm side of him when she awoke on the side of his cot and listened to birdsong while the morning sun fell through the window. The moment bound her like a golden net, catching her every time she turned, tapping at some deep, soft space in her heart that had long been buried.

"Have they found who murdered the Jewish man from Merthyr Tydfil?" Dovey asked.

"No news, but Trett says there've been reports of ark ruffians and knights of the blade lurking about the wharves and the common houses, robbing and threatening and bullying people. Some gang from Cardiff or Bristol, not sure where. I've not found yet how I got caught up in it, but to be sure there's some cloven foot in the business."

"Cloven foot?" Gwen asked. If he was asking around town about who attacked him, he would eventually find out who he was. Her knife wobbled and veered over the meat on her cutting board.

"The devil's in it," Pen said. "Hey now, don't be stingy! I

earned that bacon, and I'll have nice thick rashers, if you please."

He reached for her knife, sliding his hand over hers, and the contact rattled her to her core. She leaned back, bumped into his shoulder, and leapt away.

"I wonder what they want. These ruffians," Gwen gasped. There were new elements coming in droves into sleepy Newport, immigrants seeking work in the coal fields and mines, but most found honest if brutally demanding employment. "There are always some who will try thievery, but in the past the men have settled it."

"Could be the crimps again." Evans entered, he too having cleaned up from his day. "They're the ones as kidnap men for the East India ships and the African slavers."

"*Twpsyn!*" Dovey cried, shaking a wooden spoon at him. "You're tracking your muddy boots all about my clean kitchen, you are! Cerys has more sense than you do!" She made shooing motions and Evans ducked into the storeroom, where Widow Jones scolded him for stepping on the swedes.

"Better him than me," Pen whispered in her ear, and Gwen smothered a laugh.

This light-heartedness was absurd in her, not at all suitable. Her emotions were such a tangled skein—the panic with Barlow, her confusion when the solicitor didn't recognize his employer, the entwined hope and despair that Pen had offered her St. Sefin's, and his being with them now, at ease with the crowd in the kitchen, though he owned this place and held sway over all of them. She couldn't find her feet. She retreated to the stove, and he followed her.

"Do I stink?" he asked, leaning close.

She shivered. He smelled *good*. She wanted to press her nose into his neck. Heat crept down her back and she focused on arranging the rashers of bacon on the griddle.

"That's an outrage, woman!" She sucked in air when he wrapped his hand about hers, taking possession of her wooden spatula. "You can't cook the bacon that hot, you'll burn it. You want to build the heat, slow and easy, and then bring her to a nice, hot sizzle. Just like handling a—" He cast her a sidewise look. "Never mind."

Gwen bit back an infatuated smile. She didn't want him to see she'd grasped the innuendo, that his flirtatiousness made her bloom like a daffodil. "And when did you become an expert in preparing pork, mm—Mr. Pen?"

"I can't say. Perhaps while I was soldiering? It's a skill women admire, isn't it?" Aware she was watching, he slid the spatula along the pink curves of the bacon as if he were caressing the body of a lover.

She swallowed again, this time fighting embarrassment. Curse the man and his ability to unsettle her. It had been easy to dismiss him when he was rude and presumptuous. This Pen, with his mesmerizing smile, relaxed confidence, and messily tied neckcloth, was impossible to ignore.

That night the residents of St. Sefin's, still buzzing with the gossip over Mr. Barlow's offer, watched in shared surprise as Pen dished and passed round bowls of *cawl* brimming with thick chunks of bacon and braised vegetables, with fresh, hot laverbread served alongside. He accepted the praise and exclamations as if he'd made the meal himself.

Gwen opened a jug of last fall's apple cider and they feasted merrily and long. For the first time in weeks, Gwen felt free from the fear that Barlow would turn them out at any moment. Pen had named his price, and it was in respectable pounds sterling, not sexual services.

She watched him, drawn into his good humor as he boasted of how he'd beat Evans in filling the wheelbarrow, telling lively stories of what they'd seen at the tavern, who had been at the butcher's, what ships had tied up at the wharf. He was amusing and held the center of attention with careless ease. But he didn't flirt with any of the others, and he avoided Mathry's sultry, come-hither looks. It was only Gwen who was the target of his probing stares and seductive smiles.

She couldn't reconcile this man with the sulking, snappish Penrydd she'd met in the Bristol tavern, the arrogant lord who moved as if he were in pain and assumed she was for sale. Nor could she square him with the demanding, quarrelsome knave she'd patched up after a beating, twice. This was a new side of him entirely.

"You don't have the money, do you?" Pen asked quietly when Gwen came to his door at bedtime. He'd moved into the men's wing, a short hall of tiny rooms that had once housed travelers and visitors to the priory. He'd claimed the chamber furthest from where Evans slept, explaining that he didn't want to wake the man in the night with his screaming.

"I don't have one tenth of it," she answered. She stepped into the room, following him as he shed his coat, then began unbuttoning his waistcoat. The sturdy wool, cut for a smaller man than he was, outlined the planes of his shoulders and the lean length of his back.

"Then what will you do?"

"Ask about for loans, I suppose."

Though who had money to back her, she didn't know. The Vaughns wouldn't support a place for the poor. She could try the Morgans of Tredegar; Charles Morgan was respected in the area, a soldier in the Coldstream Guards who had been a prisoner at Yorktown during the trouble with the American colonies. But she suspected he would prefer to invest his money in his lands and the support of his young family, and he was not at home to apply to.

Other great houses nearby, like Caldicot Castle or Llancaiach Fawr, their landlords had rented out as farms. There would be no rich benefactors there. The great castles of Chepstow and Abergavenny were no more than stops on tours of picturesque Wales, the glories of the Norman Marcher lords and Tudor barons now a ruined memory. And the Marquess of Bute, who owned a number of castles in Cardiff and Caerphilly, might want St. Sefin's for himself as he seemed to have an affection for ruined monuments. She didn't dare approach him for help. A marquess, ranking above a viscount, was even further from her orbit.

"There's the money I earn harping," she said. Pen cast his waistcoat aside and began untwisting his neckcloth, and she swallowed through a suddenly dry throat. His ease at revealing his body to her was almost more intimate than his becoming disrobed.

"We'll find the money somehow. I only hope—we have the time." Her stomach skittered about. It was so strange trying to barter with him when he didn't know the hand he held.

She startled as he shed his shirt and sat on the bed, back to her. They'd done this a dozen times, and yet the sight of his strong straight back, webbed with scars, made her throat go dry again. The man was all muscle, strengthened by his recent physical labor. He'd been working hard in support of St. Sefin's. For them all.

"He called me filth." His voice held hurt and outrage.

She unscrewed the jar of camphor liniment and dipped her fingers into the balm. "Of course, you're not. None of us are." She needed him to remember that when the time of reckoning came.

"Just because I had a wheelbarrow of manure."

She smoothed the ointment over his injured shoulder and side. The treatment was working; he was healing from the attack at the wharves, and she wondered if he were finally healing from his war injuries too. At St. Sefin's his days were spent in active labor, his nights in rest. His food was simple, not at all like what rich folk ate, and his alcohol consumption was less. He'd been an absolute bear to live with in the first days of withdrawal, but he'd stopped demanding rum.

With a return to health would come the return of memory. She had to be prepared for that to happen.

"I hope I'm more important than he is in my real life. I'll cut him down to size."

Pen still sounded affronted, though his voice was muffled. He dropped his head and she massaged his neck, the muscles warm and pliable. All this strength and power beneath her hands, but leashed for the moment, and quiet. Even without his name and title, he was a powerful man. A twist of something—apprehension, perhaps—snaked low through her belly. The candle on the shelf flickered in a small draft.

"Why has no one come looking for me?"

Now he simply sounded baffled. And hurt. Guilt bit at her heart. Barlow, a man he employed, had likely never met the current Lord Penrydd in person, given he'd looked him in the eye and didn't know who he was. Who else in his own life might not recognize him, lowered as he was? And he was at this disadvantage—as much at Barlow's mercy as any of them, really—because of her. Because she continued to lie to him.

The snaking feeling twisted and hissed.

"Maybe no one misses me. Maybe they're happy I'm gone. Maybe my wife and children are relieved to be shot of me, and —" He paused. "Though I'm certain I don't have a wife or children. Yet."

Her stomach turned over as she moved to his ribs, gently rubbing ointment over his old scars. "What about Arwen?" The woman he'd called for from the depths of his first nightmare, though he hadn't asked for her since.

A long silence unspooled. Gwen moved back to his shoulder and started working down his arm.

"I lost her." His voice was low and tense. "I don't know how. I can see her face—small and pale, like a pixie. I can *feel* that I cared for her, and when she died, I was in a rage of guilt and grief—but I can't remember her last name, or what she was to me, or how she died. Nothing." His voice switched to outrage, the cornered animal again. "How is that possible?"

Gwen worked a thick scar on his upper arm that extended across his shoulder and chest. "Did you know the ancient Celtic bards memorized hundreds, if not thousands of verses? Histories, genealogies, tales of valor and war and romance, and they could sing any one of them on command."

"Blah blah blah, the Welsh are wonderful, blah blah," Pen grumbled. "The English have long poems, too."

"Yes. But the druids believed their knowledge and teachings were too sacred to write down, and as for our Cymric literature —well, you know how you *Saes* feel about us using our language. So the bards preserved the old books by memorizing them, piece by piece."

"So did the Greeks. That's why we have Homer."

"But how did they do it?" She slid her hands down his forearm and started kneading the tendons in his hand.

"The same way I learned my Latin. Endless recitation and having it beat into me. I can't tell you my own bloody name, but if you ask nicely, I'll bet I can give you one of Cicero's speeches in its entirety."

"No doubt you could. It's a trick of rhythm, and meter, and other poetic devices that help you memorize long passages," Gwen said, concentrating on his fingers. "At least, that's how I was taught. But the great poems are also a matter of finding the connections. The way one piece relates to the next." She lay his hand on his legs. "Your memory will come back, Pen. You'll find the connections."

She could only hope, when the time came, he would not want to kill her in his rage for having deceived him.

"Why aren't you sickened by my scars?"

She met his eyes. His gaze was clear, steady and curious, the pupils wide and dark.

"Because they were earned in combat for an honest cause. They are badges of honor."

He snorted. "I'm not so certain it was honest. Or worth anything, in the end. But you don't pity me, for all that."

"We all have our scars. Some earned in different ways."

"Then you'll do my leg as well?" He patted his left thigh, giving her a look of invitation. He was still clad in his breeches, but she knew the scar on his leg was thick and deep, still an angry red after all this time. His limp emerged at the end of the day, when he was weary, or when the weather was damp.

"Do it yourself." She thrust the jar of camphor liniment at him.

"You're not going to give me anything, are you?"

She stared. "We've given you a roof, and food, and—"

"*You*," he whispered, his eyes kindling with a slow heat. "You're not going to yield an inch of you."

Her breath whirled out of her throat, wisping away like a fog. "I'm giving you a rub for your scars. Here it is."

She held out the jar. He closed his hand over hers, and, like a fool, her eyes fluttered shut at the warm strength of his fingers curling about hers. He felt *safe*. And that was the most dangerous thing about him.

"I'd swear I knew when a woman fancied me," he said, his voice a low rasp. She couldn't meet his gaze, focused so intently on her face, examining every feature as if she were a perplexing piece of art. Her cheeks heated—she couldn't fight the blush—

and he chuckled. The sound stirred her like the scrape of his hand over her skin.

"You *do*. But you won't take what I offer. Unabashed, uncomplicated pleasure." He left her hand and drew a fingertip over the inside of her wrist. The delicate skin flamed to life. He drew his finger upward, trailing his rough fingertips along the sensitive skin, and a fiery current raced up her arm and arrowed into her breasts. She shifted, uncomfortably warm, and tried to draw away. He didn't let go.

"Mindless pleasure," he purred, rubbing a thumb along the crease inside her elbow. Sensation pulsed to her nipples. "The kind that will make you forget who *you* are for a minute. What's the harm with a bit of—cavorting?"

The word was the dash of ice water she needed. She uncurled her fingers, letting the jar of liniment drop onto his bed. She looked away from his bare chest, the layers of heat and muscle.

"It doesn't bother you?" she blurted. "The mindlessness."

His smile tensed. "I've already had my mind blotted out, remember?"

"But you don't know if you can trust me." He couldn't. She was lying to him, keeping him away from his business, his estates, his friends. His family. "I could be tricking you. I could be out for something. I could try to rob you, or—" She bit her lip on the guilt breaking through. She was supposed to make him trust her!

He dropped her arm. "Rob me? I have nothing. These aren't even my clothes." He scooped up the jar of ointment, clenching it in his fist. "You can't blame a man for wanting a bit of human comfort when he has nothing else."

Comfort. She hadn't thought of it that way. She'd assumed his impulses were purely primal, a man who wanted a conquest for the sake of conquest, or a man who liked his pleasures varied and continuous, and would take them from whoever was near at hand.

Had he been seeking comfort with his offer back in the Bristol tavern, when he invited her to be his mistress? Did he want companionship, warmth as well as pleasure—from her?

"A woman pays a dear price for her comforts," she murmured. "We are not allowed to—*cavort*."

She didn't take her leave, and he didn't acknowledge her departure. She left him the candle and the camphor, making her way down the broad night stair and through the hall to the narrow turret where she and Dovey kept their rooms.

She wouldn't be so foolish again, coming to his room alone and at night. He could tend his own damn scars. She couldn't afford to be this upset by him, by what he wanted of her. By what she wanted of him.

For it was more than St. Sefin's that he held over her. And she couldn't meet his price.

CHAPTER NINE

Something had happened to Penrydd.

He'd been puzzling her for days, but Gwen put her finger on it the afternoon he burst into the kitchen with Ifor, both coming in for their dinner. They scraped the mud off their boots and Pen announced, sounding quite pleased with himself, "I learned a Welsh word today."

Gwen, in the middle of steaming herbs for oil, simply stared. His face was turning tanned and healthy, no longer the complexion of the pasty lord who slept all day and caroused all night. His eyes were clear, perceptive, and often glowing with amusement. His hands didn't shake in the mornings. His hair was growing long, curling over the collar of the borrowed coat.

He met Gwen's eyes with a cocky smile. "*Gafr* means goat."

She felt the broad tug of an answering smile cross her face. His delight called up the same warmth within her. "He," Pen said, turning to gaze at Ifor, "named his goat, Goat."

Ifor grinned. "He's a fine goat."

"Exemplary," Pen agreed. He picked a burr off the boy's collar, quite casually, and tossed it aside. "The Platonic ideal of a goat."

"A plodding what?" Ifor asked.

"Plato, *gwashi*," Gwen said without thinking. "An ancient Greek, one of the three fathers of philosophy."

Pen stared at her as if taken aback that she knew this. Of course, they lived in Wales—how did the Welsh know anything of Western intellectual tradition? Gwen turned back to the stove and busied herself with her steaming apparatus but kept one ear cocked toward the scullery as Pen primed the hand-pump and washed their hands, explaining Plato's theory of ideal forms to Ifor. She met Dovey's expression of wonderment and shrugged, as surprised as she at Pen's kindness toward the boy.

The day Barlow insulted him, something had switched in Penrydd. He'd gone from antagonistic and sullen to cooperative, almost cheerful, and terribly easy to like. His sarcasm didn't abate, but his insults did. Instead of holding himself apart, sneering at the ways of St. Sefin's and all Welsh, he pitched in to do his share. She was surprised at how easily he fell into the rhythms of the place. Into life with them.

What would that mean when he found out what she'd done to him?

"What's dinner?" She jumped as he appeared at her elbow, clean and smelling like soap. He set off those butterflies in her belly, every time.

"We call them St. Sefin's sausages. Chopped vegetables bound with egg and old breadcrumbs. We've no meat."

"Time to hire myself out as stable mucker again." He gathered two plates and carried them into the refectory, placing them on the table where Widow Jones and Mother Morris had set their knitting aside. "Mother, my shoulder says we'll have rain soon. What say your knees?"

"Ah, *bydd*, bodes the *glaw mis* tonight." Mother Morris rubbed her right hip and picked up her knife. "First rain of May. Good for the eyes, and kills the lice on the cattle."

"May already!" Pen said. "Widow, I would have brought you morels, but Ifor and I have a funny story about that. What do you say again when everything's gotten cocked up?"

"*Cachu hwch!*" Mother Morris said gleefully, diving into her dinner.

"It's all pig's poo," Ifor translated, bringing Tomos and their plates to the table to join them. Gwen stared as Pen slid along the bench so the boys could sit on either side of him.

"*Cachu hwch!*" Tomos chuckled.

"Aye, that describes my mushroom experience, but don't say that before Mr. Stanley, lad, when we go to clean the bronze tomorrow. He won't appreciate the sentiment."

"I want to go." Cerys, denied a spot next to Pen, claimed the place across from him, burrowing next to Widow Jones. "I want to look for the treasure."

"Treasure at St. Woolos?" Pen said. "A hair of the saint's head, or maybe the tip of his ear? I saw St. Alban's shoulder blade once." He lowered his knife, his voice changing with surprise. "Though I don't know where, or how."

"It's a real treasure that—"

"Cerys, little heart," Dovey said, bringing in a plate piled high with sausages. "Don't bore Mr. Pen with old legends." She slapped the plate on the table next to Cerys and then waltzed off with her nose in the air, swishing past Evans and pretending not to see his nod of thanks.

Gwen tsked to herself as she fixed a plate for Mathry. What had Evans done now to offend? But she was more interested in watching Pen, the center of attention at the dinner table, and enjoying the banter with the children.

"St. Sefin's was wealthy." Cerys ignored her mother's warning and assumed an air of self-importance as she explained. "The priory took in travelers and ran businesses, probably weaving and brewing, so say me mam and Miss Gwen. There was a poem on the riches of St. Sefin's some *Saes* wrote down in his book. There was silver plate and jeweled caskets and a gold chalice they used for the Eucharist, said to be the same one Jesus used at the Last Supper. But when the knights of fat King Henry tromped in to take everything, where was the treasure?" Her green eyes grew wide. "Gone!"

"Gone," Tomos whispered, his eyes equally wide.

"Stolen already." Pen nodded.

"No, Mr. Pen, it was never found! The nuns hid it away. That's what the poem says. And it's not anywhere here, or I'd have discovered it by now, since I've been searching for *years*. So I think it might be hidden at St. Woolos. And when I find the treasure, Mam and Miss Gwen can pay the lord and we can all stay here and have a roof over our heads and not be thrown into the workhouse or the street." She beamed, pleased with her logic and the scope of her dreams.

Penrydd's gaze met Gwen's as she and Dovey took seats next to the older women. Gwen looked away from the question in his eyes.

She'd ceased her visits to his room after his talk about comfort. His nightmares still troubled him, but she made him a tea each evening to help him sleep. There would be no more coming again in the dark to soothe him, no chance of falling asleep again on his cot or, worse yet, falling prey to his charms. Fortunately—so she told herself—he'd ceased with his teasing looks and seductive invitations.

Instead, he watched her. And listened. When she mentioned she needed a pot or a barrel fetched from a storeroom, it was sitting on the table when she next entered the kitchen. She'd caught him once, early morning, helping Tomos with his chore of fetching the water, cautioning the boy against getting his hand caught again in the winch. He helped Ifor turn out the goats and he helped Cerys gather hay for their feed.

He carried baskets of wet laundry for Widow Jones. And he could often be spotted about the grounds of St. Sefin's, working on some task with Evans, the two of them tossing masculine banter back and forth. There were no more sneers at Evans' lank sleeve, but instead a steady extra hand when he needed one. When men came from the wharves needing help to free a ship stranded in a sandbar at the mouth of the Usk, Pen went with them, speaking rather knowledgeably about draught and ballast.

She hadn't once had to empty his chamber pot.

One morning, when his nightmares struck just before dawn, he gave up on sleep and came into the kitchen to find her starting the morning bread. Pen ate a bun at the table and talked with her while she mixed Mother Morris's favorite gripe water and found she'd used the last of the dried fennel. She'd looked around to find him gone and was surprised at her own disappointment. She was coming to enjoy their conversations in the times when he was quiet and serious, or as serious as he could be. Just as she chided herself for foolishness, feeling a sense of loss at his departure—he didn't have to declare his business to her!—he'd come through the back door, tall and calm and shaking morning dew from his hair, bearing a fistful of fennel.

Those marks of attention and companionship were more seductive, and touched her more deeply, than any innuendo or talk of cavorting. She didn't dare tell him that.

But she felt he knew.

"How'd you lose your arm, Evans?" Pen asked one night as they sat around the fire in the chapter house, all disposed to their different tasks. Cerys sat at her mother's knee, her hands spooled with yarn for the scarf Dovey was knitting. Mother Morris made stockings, Widow Jones mended a shawl. Gwen sorted through a box of donations that had been left on the porch, separating the clothes that needed to be mended from what could be used right away. Ifor and Tomos played backgammon, and Mathry sat with a barely begun infant gown on which she was making little progress. Everyone stared at Pen in the wake of this question as if he had suddenly proposed a country dance.

He stared back. "What? Is he your household brownie who turns into a boggart does anyone mention he's missing a limb?"

"Nay, we simply don't—talk of our pasts here," Dovey said, her voice carefully neutral.

Pen shrugged and sprawled in his seat. By silent agreement everyone had given him the bishop's chair, a huge oak piece with ornate carvings along its arms, legs, and high back. It looked as if a canopy of cloth of gold should be erected over it, and Pen lounged as naturally there as if something in him remembered he was a lord.

"I can't bore you all by prating about my past," he said. "So I want to hear yours."

Gwen set aside a men's shirt that might be cut down for Tomos. She couldn't imagine the Penrydd she'd met in Bristol caring a whit for anyone's life beyond his own. But now everyone watched Evans to see what he might say.

"Gibraltar," Evans said. "I joined the British Army as a lad, which was a laugh since I grew up on the water, but I wanted to see the Americas. Instead I was sent to Gibraltar and eventually made a gunner at the fort. Took some heavy fire from the Spanish and French." He rolled his wounded shoulder, remembering.

"The Siege of '82," Pen guessed. "When the French came in with their floating batteries, armored warships they were? I heard it was a rain of hellfire, days upon days of it. But they didn't take the strait."

"Nay," Evans said, rubbing his injured leg. "They didn't."

"Then what?"

"I came back to Pembrokeshire. Rented a farm in Angle. My sweetheart took me back, just as I was. Many grand and happy years we had, with the *babanod*. Five of them, sweet lads and lasses." He stared reflectively into the fire. "Then the typhus came."

Dovey put down her knitting and stared at Evans as if she had never seen him before. "You lost someone," Gwen said softly.

He bowed his head. "I lost them all."

A heavy silence fell across the room. Cerys sniffled. Evans shrugged. "So I wandered east, looking for a good place to drown myself. And I found Miss Gwen and Dah—Mrs. Van der Welle here in Newport, trying to rebuild this gloomy old pile, and thought, I have one good hand to give them."

Dovey stared at her lap. "But to lose your family," she whispered.

"There's not many as have one year that happy, much less ten," Evans answered.

"Well!" Pen adopted a bluff tone, but Gwen saw the story had affected him. "Anyone care to top that tale?"

"Mine's obvious." Mathry sat beneath the mullioned window, the setting sun casting a gold nimbus about her head. She pouted and pointed at her belly. "He said he loved me and would always take care of me, and I, like a *tymffat*, believed him."

"My spineless son turned me out because his wife didn't like me," Widow Jones said. "I thought I had raised him better, with a shred of sense. But his loyalty is to her now."

"Mother Morris? What about you?" Pen watched as the older woman bit off a length of string.

"*Twll din pob Saes,*" Mother Morris cried. She leaned forward and muttered a musical cadence of Welsh, her mouth turned down at the corners.

"An Englishman came after her husband died and took her farm for the coal," Widow Jones told them. "The *Saes* said the land belonged to him. Her sons were put to work like animals and the mines killed all three of them—cave in, poisoned air, lung fever." The widow shook her head while Mother Morris hugged herself and rocked in her chair. "The

Saes never paid a penny to their families when they died. She lost one daughter to childbed, and the rest found new husbands. Mother was sent to the workhouse here, and that's where Miss Gwen found her."

Widow Jones turned to the older woman. "Not all *Saes* are like that, Mother," she said, indicating Pen.

"*Dim*, he's Cymry," Mother nodded. "One of us."

Gwen, startled, glanced at Pen to see what he made of this acknowledgement. But he simply turned to survey the boys at their game, his face thoughtful.

"Ifor was brought to St. Woolos when he was three," Gwen said. "He'd gone blind by then. His mother served the sailors at the wharves and caught the English pox."

Pen scowled at her. "The pox is the French disease."

"And the French call it the Spanish disease." Evans managed a smile. "At any rate, it's rare that the children survive. Ifor's a fighter."

"Mr. Stanley couldn't raise him, of course. A bachelor priest? But we could," Gwen said.

"Me," Tomos said, looking up from the board.

"Ah, *bachgen*. Tomos's mother brought him here because—" She hesitated. "They had so many mouths to feed, and he's a strapping boy, isn't he? She asked if he could work here for his keep."

"*Bwyd*," Tomos said happily, separating his game pieces from Ifor's, which were carved with a mark.

"Yes, you earn your food and more," Gwen told him.

"And Dovey." Pen's eyes settled on her. Cerys stilled, listening.

Dovey focused on her needles, her long lashes hiding her eyes. "My mother was born on a sugar plantation in the West Indies. She was given to the planter's daughter as her companion and went with her at her marriage. Turns out the husband liked my mother as well as he liked his wife. He, my father, brought them both to England when he retired from his government post, and I was raised in Bristol."

She paused, turning the needles in her hand to begin a new row of stitches. "He left papers freeing my mother and I when he died, but he didn't leave any money, and his widow didn't see it her place to look out for us, though my mother had served her so long. Maman took in sewing and I worked for a hatmaker, as a hairdresser, as a lady's maid."

Her needles clicked steadily. Gwen continued sorting clothes, knowing this story already, but the others listened, rapt. Only Evans seemed detached, staring out the window above Mathry's head. Pen was as riveted as Cerys.

"My husband was a Dutchman who came to Bristol to learn English shipbuilding and help the Dutch Navy rebuild its fleet. It didn't take him long to win me. We married in Bristol and took a small set of rooms." Dovey's gaze settled on her daughter, and she smiled. "He was wild about you, my darling. He boasted that you have his eyes."

Cerys's green eyes shone, but Dovey looked back at her work as if she couldn't, for the moment, bear the sight of her daughter's glowing face. "Because he knew the Baltic Sea, Jan was hired to help take a ship filled with riches to Catherine the Great, Empress of Russia, in St. Peterburg. So many riches—artwork, fabrics, fancy metalwork. I'd never seen such fine things. They promised a commission that would have bought us a house."

"But it didn't," Pen said somberly.

Tears gathered on Dovey's lashes. "They sailed too late in autumn and the storms blew them into the Archipelago Sea. It's known as a graveyard for ships. Hundreds have gone down there. Including Jan. His friends in the navy searched, they told me. But they've never found a trace of his ship. Not a bolt, not a plate. Not a man." She fell silent.

"Full fathom five thy love lies," Pen said in a low voice, "and of his bones are coral made."

Evans's head swung round, his expression darkening in rebuke, but Gwen recognized the poetry. "Nothing of him doth fade, but doth suffer a sea change into something rich and strange," she murmured. At Dovey's small frown, she explained. "When we read *The Tempest,* remember? Ariel sings a lament to Ferdinand to tell him his father has been lost at sea."

"And where did you learn Shakespeare, Miss Gwen?" Pen asked, his voice soft but somehow dangerous. "You haven't told us your tale."

"Ah." She lifted a shift from the box, a woman's gown, nearly new. She ran a hand over the fine linen, soft as silk. "Does anyone care?"

"Everyone else shared their histories," Pen said. "Those of us who could."

Gwen nodded and put the gown aside. A shift that fine would have been prized by its owner, worn as often as possible. It could only be sorrow that brought it to St. Sefin's barely worn.

She cleared her throat and kept her eyes on her task, aware of how the late golden light in the room fell in thick shafts, catching the dust motes in their dance. Outside the songbirds began their evening chorus.

"I was born in Merionethshire, to the north. When the family I was living with turned me out, I traveled south, moving lake to lake, following the rivers. I don't know what I thought—

of drowning myself, perhaps? Or sailing away. When I came to Brynglas, the rise above Newport, I stopped and saw the Usk where it emptied into the Severn, and the sea spreading beyond, and I...I thought, 'I will lose myself there.'"

She pulled out the next item, a child's shirt, and quickly set it aside. Too small for Ifor. "But I needed a place to stay for the night, and I saw spires and towers, so I made my way here. St. Woolos was locked, but St. Sefin's was open. Abandoned. Anyone could just walk in. I couldn't believe a place so grand, so holy, had been left to crumble."

She didn't look at Pen. She didn't want him to remember this later as a rebuke against his family. "And I found St. Gwladys. You've seen her chapel downstairs. How intact the stained glass is, and all the carvings. I sat with her, and I—I prayed, if you could call it that. And she...spoke to me."

She looked around at their intent faces. "If anyone sneers at me, just one of you—" She looked pointedly at Pen—"I'll forget to boil the nettles before I put them in your soup. But I had a vision. Gwladys said to me, 'I found peace here. And you shall, too.'" She wiped beneath her eyes and bent to her task, unfolding a woolen petticoat. "The next day I met Dovey."

Dovey nodded. "I'd come to Newport looking for work. Heard one too many comments in Bristol about my missing husband and my half-breed child. I thought Wales might be better."

"So you simply moved in," Pen said, curious but not accusing. "And found out later someone else owns the place."

She met his eyes, her heart sinking. Was this the moment that everything ended? Perhaps their sharing their pasts had drawn back the veil on his. "So it seems."

He twisted his mouth in thought. "And you don't have fifteen hundred pounds between you. You don't have half that."

Dovey shifted slightly. She knew to the ha'penny their

savings, the small bit they'd hoarded from Gwen's fees, like the coins Mrs. Harries had paid her to take Mathry. It wasn't one tenth his asking price.

What else could she do? "I'm earning what I can harping," Gwen said. "In fact, I'm engaged at Greenfield tomorrow evening. Shall I practice for you tonight?"

To distract Pen and his sharp, considering gaze she took up her traveling harp, the small instrument she'd brought with her on her flight south. The only thing she'd brought with her, having lost or left everything else. The music soothed away the hurts and sorrows they'd bared to each other, knitting them more deeply with what they now knew.

And it was Pen, of all people, who had brought forth these confessions. He had united them before as Viscount Penrydd, the threatening landlord whose black-clad solicitor had called for their eviction, but that was a union of fear and mistrust. Now he had opened their eyes to one another.

When would it be safe to confess to him who he was? He was softening, just as she'd hoped. But every moment she delayed gave him more with which to accuse her, for taking up this deceit in the first place. For denying him his name, his place in the world, and all the power and wealth that came with it.

HE FOUND her in the stillroom later that night, sorting through her jars for willow bark for his tea. A thrill shot down her back when he spoke at her shoulder—how did the man manage to tread as soft as a cat when he was so large and solid?

"You didn't explain where you learned Shakespeare."

She fumbled with the cloth stopper in the jar. "The house I was in for a while—they had a tutor."

"For an education like that, you'd have had some birth and

breeding," Pen said. "You didn't learn Plato or Shakespeare from a Methodist minister's traveling school."

She poured the hot water over the bark and other herbs and let it steep. She'd told him enough already. Not that it mattered; no one was looking for her. She'd closed the door on her past when she came south, and she didn't need anything that might lie behind it.

Unlike Pen, who desperately wanted to unlock that closed door in his head, and deserved to. He was a viscount, and she had him herding goats and mucking stables.

She looked for the tea strainer and found him holding it. "You were right, what you said." His hazelnut eyes burned in their intensity. "I should wonder if I can trust you."

Her breath caught.

"Everyone else, they're an open book." He handed her the strainer, and their fingers touched. A tingle surged up her arm. "But not you. Gwenllian ap Ewyas. Keeper of secrets."

"We've only ever tried to help you, mi—Pen."

He must not resent her too much when the time came. It had been good, tonight, for him to learn their histories. She ought to have suggested it before.

"You don't trust me, either," he said. His voice sent a shiver down her nape, as potent as a caress. She poured the tea, spooned in honey, and handed the cup to him. He closed his fingers around her hand, heat pressing from both sides. "You trust no one."

A hard lesson, but she'd learned it well. "Do you think you might trust me?" she breathed, unable to withdraw her hand. He was so close she felt the heat of his body, reaching out to embrace her. A weakness wove through her knees.

"I don't have a choice." He drew the cup from her fingers, but his eyes held hers, and his body loomed. "With no memory, no possessions, no name? I'm completely at your mercy. It's strange, though."

He touched her cheek with a finger, pushing back a strand of hair stuck to her face. His hands had grown callused from work. She hadn't missed his flirtatious remarks and teasing; she *hadn't*. But she leaned into his touch as if he were an anchor holding her ashore.

"I don't believe you're being honest with anyone," he murmured. "Not with me. Not with your closest friends. But I trust," he said slowly, "that you will show mercy."

And he left the room.

That night, when she heard the hoarse shouts in the wee hours, Gwen curled her fists into her pillow and pulled it over her head. She would not go to him. There was nothing she could do for him, she told herself.

If she went it would prove nothing but that she wanted him. Wanted to touch him, soothe him, be near him, and every time she drew close to him, it was harder to pull away. But she couldn't risk exposing herself. She had far too much to lose.

CHAPTER TEN

G wen would have enjoyed the opportunity to chat with
some of Lady Vaughn's guests at Greenfield, but Calvin
Vaughn stuck to her side, regaling her with his various griev-
ances, which primarily consisted of how tedious he found
Newport and its environs.

"No entertainments whatsoever," he complained. "Not the
least bit civilized."

"I take it the Viscount Penrydd has not made good on his
promise to visit." Gwen strove to keep her tone light, disinter-
ested. "Have you heard aught of his whereabouts?"

She knew it troubled Pen that no one from his life had yet
located him. It troubled her, too, for people must be searching—
his secretary, if no one else. She could not hide him much
longer. An English lord would not be allowed to simply
disappear.

"Penrydd? He's buried in drink and women in Bristol or
somewhere else, that's my guess." Vaughn leaned back in the
rout chair he'd placed beside Gwen's harp. "I told Turbeville to
come anyway, but he had a tangle with some local blokes who
left him in rather bad shape. His secretary, Penrydd's that is,

told Turbeville sudden business called the viscount away." He sneered. "Wager he tupped the wrong woman and took to his heels when her husband set out after him."

Gwen hid her face behind the glass of lemonade that a circulating footman had brought her. "So no one has seen him," she probed. "Not his solicitor, or anyone?"

Vaughn narrowed his watery blue eyes at her. Gwen sweated beneath her lace neckerchief. The spring evening was warm already, and with the smoke of many candles and oil lamps added to the perfume drenching the guests, the room was suffocating. She longed to open the window beside her harp, but Lady Vaughn was a firm believer in the dangers of exposure to outside air.

"Speaking of business," Vaughn said. "Don't set that blows-abella on me again."

"I beg your pardon," Gwen said, chilled by his shift in tone.

"Our old chambermaid. Mrs. Harries said she's at that place you run. The home for idiots and thieves and those the work-house won't take. She came here today, wailing that I'd made vows to her. Turned her off with a few firm words, and I won't take kindly to future visits."

"Mathry?" Gwen tried to remember if she'd seen the girl that day. Mathry had been lackaday about chores from the beginning, often complaining of fatigue or overwork, but the last few days she'd been subdued in her manner. She hadn't even flirted with Pen.

"If she's putting about that I'm the father of her child, it won't speed my suit with the Sutton family," Vaughn said. "And we need their money."

Gwen struck a discordant note on the harp and pressed the strings between her palms to stop them vibrating. Her face heated as others glanced their way. Lady Vaughn frowned at her son, chatting in the corner with Gwen instead of charming their guests.

"Su—Sutton?" Gwen stammered.

"Yes. Daughter's a prosy bore, but a large dowry covers a multitude of flaws."

"Where—where does she live?" Gwen, fumbling with her tuning pin, gave up and shoved it back in her pocket with trembling fingers.

He frowned. "Vine Court in Llanfyllin. You wouldn't know it."

"How could I," Gwen echoed in a faint voice. "And Anne is —coming here?"

"We'll marry there, I s'pose, and then roam abroad for the wedding trip. She wants to go someplace heathenish, like Scotland or Ireland. Her brother's a prime buck, always ready to sport his canvas, so at least—how did you know her name is Anne?"

"Oh—didn't you say it? Anne Sutton. Of Vine Court." Gwen licked her lips, sticky and sour with lemon.

"You're not about to flash the hash, are you? You look peaky."

"It's—dreadfully hot in here. Won't your mother open a window?"

"Come." He stood abruptly. "We'll take a turn about the garden."

"I—I shouldn't. They're expecting music." But her head was spinning. Far better to be sick outside than here in the drawing room. Sir Mark Wood had engaged her to play at Pencoed Castle a few nights hence in honor of his daughter and her new husband. She desperately needed a down payment toward the price of St. Sefin's when Barlow—or Penrydd—came demanding it.

The medieval Greenfield Castle had been destroyed in the

rising of Owain Glyndŵr and rebuilt as a late Tudor manor house, sturdy in its walls of local red brick. Vaughn led her down a dark hall to an outside door opening on a high walled garden, hemmed by tall hedges of hornbeam and English holly. Light spilled from a first-story window, but the garden was close and dark. It was air, however, and Gwen drew deep gulps of it.

"Ah," she said after the cool evening air had done its part to calm her. "I am better now. I should return."

"Something to confess." Vaughn blocked the narrow path. Behind him stood the door to the house and the light and safety of the crowd. Fear darted through her. Oh, why had she been such a fool to come here alone with him?

Because she hadn't had the least expectation that Vaughn would be a menace to her. "We ought to go back inside," Gwen said, retreating.

"I've developed the most violent attachment to you." Vaughn advanced down the path.

"Violent?" Gwen said with dismay, backing into a hedge. Prickles of blackthorn caught her gown and stabbed at her lace.

"Go mad if I can't have you." He said this as if they were discussing the weather. Gwen nearly choked on a wild gasp of laughter. Was this his notion of wooing?

"This is—sudden." She looked about for an avenue of escape. He was not much taller than she, but portly, and she flinched when his hands seized her shoulders.

"I am sure the madness will pass," she said. "Let us go back inside and have a glass of cool lemonade, and—"

His frame pressed against her, and she turned her head to the side as his hot, sour breath wafted over her face. She tried shrinking further into the hedge as his fleshy body nudged against hers. No, he wasn't wooing her.

"Give you—what you want." His face descended, lips parting.

"No," Gwen gasped, twisting in his grasp. "I don't want—this."

"Will in a moment. Hold still." His hands slid to her breasts, squeezing, moaning, as his wet mouth probed for hers. Slobber trickled down her cheek and neck. She knocked his hands aside, and he grabbed her waist.

"Trollop," he muttered, panting as he tried to lower his mouth to her breasts. "Coming here taunting me, pretending to be so pure. I know what you are." He pushed his hips against hers and groaned.

Gwen's heart stopped beating for a moment. Had Anne said something? No, Anne didn't know what Gwen had done.

Unless her brother told her. Panic and furious shame roared through her head. "No," Gwen said fiercely, pushing her elbows between them and turning to the side. "*No.*"

"Hedge whore! Don't think I'll pay for it. You've been *begging* me from the first." Vaughn clamped his hands to her bottom, churning his groin against her. "Know how to satisfy a woman. Bet the others at your place can't. Runts and cripples. Half men."

Gwen froze against her will. What did he know? Had he heard a new man was at St. Sefin's? He might make the connection to the missing Penrydd, if so. A fresh fear gave her strength.

"I said *no.*" She drove her elbows apart and broke his grasp. In his moment of surprise she twisted away from him and the hedge, lunging for the path.

"I *do* have to pay you?" He whirled and followed as Gwen backed down the path, one arm held out before her. His pale eyes glittered in the light from the window above. "Come back here, wench, and we'll settle this. How much?" He stalked down the dark path toward her. "Don't price yourself too high, now. You're a Welsh piece."

Gwen moved swiftly toward the doorway, safety and

escape. Now that she'd gotten him off her, she felt bold again. She could outrun him if she had to, even in her skirts.

"St. Sefin's is not what you say! Nor are its men."

He sneered. "Every woman has a price. For most, it's pretty words. 'I love you. I'll take care of you always.' What's your price, Gwen of the gutter?"

Gwen lifted her chin and crossed her arms over her chest. "Fifteen hundred pounds."

He heaved out air. "Fifteen hun—you complete biter! No woman's worth that price."

"Anne Sutton is!" she flared. "Her dowry is twenty thousand pounds. What do you think she'll do if I she finds out you accosted me? Or if she hears about Mathry, or any of the others?"

"You wouldn't dare." His face was mottled with shadow, his teeth bared. "I'll run you aground. Every last of those thatch-gallows under your roof."

"You'll leave us in peace. Say a word against us, one foul whisper, and I will tell Anne how many women you've ruined hereabouts, how many maids have left this house because of you. She will believe me."

The threat stopped him cold, but he still had the upper hand. "Don't dare go back in that house, you sly boots. I'll tell my mother you threw yourself on me. Stripped to your diddies and begged me to take you. Whining like a bitch in heat." He adjusted the fabric at his crotch. "Won't get a shilling more out of her. Nor anyone else around here."

"Your mother knows what you are," Gwen said.

He lunged for her, and she ran.

GWEN RETURNED the horse and dogcart to the King's Head and walked up Stow Hill, alert and trembling. Normally she would be unafraid of the night or the darkness. The evil lurked in the houses like Greenfield, where soulless men thought they could take what they wished without asking. Here in Newport, the honest merchants and the tradesmen's families slept peacefully in the rooms above their shops. And, thanks to her and Dovey and the others, the desperate had somewhere to go.

But someone had attacked and killed the Jewish man from Merthyr Tydfil, and they still didn't know who had attacked Pen. The reports continued of rough men from Cardiff starting quarrels at the wharves and hectoring ships' captains about their cargoes. Gwen kept an eye on the darkest corners as she walked, pulling her shawl tightly around her.

St. Sefin's was a refuge for those who would otherwise be left without relief. She had made it so. She would tear Calvin Vaughn's guts out and dance on his entrails if he took this sanctuary away from them.

Her own rage astonished her. It wasn't like her to be vengeful. But somehow, of all the English gentry in Wales, he knew the Suttons. And with that name he raised all her ghosts. They capered about her, mocking, screeching, tormenting her with what she had lost.

She'd put them in danger already, by deciding to take in Penrydd and then lie to him. When the wolf awoke, he would swallow them all. Penrydd had far greater power to destroy them than Calvin Vaughn.

Something was wrong at St. Sefin's. A candle bobbed along the upper passage, where the women had their rooms. Everyone should be abed at this hour. Gwen stepped into the kitchen, her heart still beating erratically from her confrontation with Calvin Vaughn. A keening cry came from above, and a cold shiver ran down Gwen's spine.

Dovey met her at the bottom of the night stair leading to the women's dormitory.

"Who—?" Gwen started.

"Mathry." The shadows hollowed her cheekbones and thinned her lips, turning Dovey's beautiful face into a frozen death's mask, like those on Egyptian mummies. "She tried to purge the babe."

"She went to the midwife?" Gwen gasped and tossed her cloak on its peg.

"Not ours. She went to the cunning woman in Bassaleg, and now she's convinced the woman laid a curse on her and she's going to die."

She led Gwen to the source of the keening. Another candle burned in Mathry's room. The girl lay in bed, her gown drenched and stuck to her with sweat. She struggled to her elbows and stared at Gwen with wide, terrified eyes.

"Don't let it die."

"Mathry, *dynan*." Gwen hurried to her, pressing a hand to her brow. The girl was clammy, but not feverish. "Dearie. What did you do?"

"He told me to get rid of it." Mathry burrowed her forehead into Gwen's palm, her face crumpling. "He said he'd take me back if I did. So I went to the woman he told me of—another maid at Greenfield went there, and she was free after, and found work again. But the place was so horrid, Gwen, and she said some awful spell with smoke and incantations, and she made me drink a brew, so bitter...I'm sure she poisoned me."

Mathry shook her head and sobbed. "As soon as I drank, I knew—I don't want to lose it. I don't want it gone." She reached out both hands, tears running freely down her face. "Please help me."

Gwen met Dovey's eyes, her stomach slithering with fear. They didn't need to speak. If the woman knew her herbs, she would have given Mathry something highly effective, something that could not be reversed.

"Are you bleeding? Vomiting? Voiding?" Gwen pressed Mathry's cold hands between her own.

Mathry's soft, dumpling face drew taut with pain. "Me belly feels like there are snakes in it. And I've been puking me guts out." She nodded toward the chamber pot near Gwen's feet, which exuded a noxious aroma.

"But bleeding," Gwen said, just as Mathry leaned over the side of the bed to add to the contents of the chamber pot. Gwen held back her hair as she heaved. Dovey rubbed her shuddering back.

"No." Mathry wiped her mouth with the sleeve of her shift. "Not yet."

"Then there's a chance," Gwen said. "She might have only given you a purgative. Or a laxative, if she didn't know better. Did she say what was in the brew?"

Mathry shook her head in misery. "She only asked if I had quickened. I told her no."

"We might be able to stop you throwing, but only if she gave you something for the bowels and not the womb." Gwen scooped her hand under Mathry's trembling arm and Dovey moved to her other side. "We will make a tea. And walk. And pray."

"*Ein Tad*," Mathry began obediently, swinging her legs over the bed and sliding on her slippers. "*Yn y nefoedd, sancteiddier dy new...*"

"Not the Lord's Prayer," Gwen said. "Pray to St. Elen, mother of Constantine. And we will go light a candle to St Gwladys, mother of Cadog the Wise."

Dovey grabbed Mathry's wrapper off its peg and they shuffled down to the kitchen, the girl between them moaning with every few steps. In the kitchen, Mathry ran into the scullery to puke into the sink, then collapsed in a chair while Dovey built up the fire in the stove to heat water. Gwen ducked into her stillroom, blessing again the housekeeper at Vine Court who had imparted her knowledge of herbs. Anne Sutton's family had given Gwen much, before they robbed her of the things she most wanted.

"What will help me?" Mathry whimpered, clutching her middle. "Anything?"

"Cramp bark and black haw," Gwen answered, carrying her precious stores into the kitchen. "Here, *pwt*, chew some fennel. Pen picked it for Mother Morris, but it might help your belly if she gave you a purge."

"Hedge witch," Mathry muttered, taking the stalk.

"That's the Roman church that burned cunning folk for witches," Gwen said, going through her herbs. "And the English church took up the torch. In Merionethshire, we went to the cunning woman for all our remedies. I don't know this one in Bassaleg, and I haven't heard well of her."

Mathry wrapped her hands around her middle and bent forward. "I don't want to lose it. Is it terrible that I didn't know that until now?"

"Mathry, child." Dovey took a cup from the shelf. "No mother has a simple path. And no one, man or woman, should judge you until they're in your slippers." She reached across the table and squeezed Mathry's hand. "What it is, is not easy."

"But you knew. You wanted Cerys."

"I did, but I had a home and a husband who loved me. Neither he nor I knew I'd be raising her alone." She looked at Gwen. "I don't mean—"

"I know, *enaid*," Gwen said softly. "You've had me and Evans, but we're not a husband and father."

Mathry dropped her head into her hands, moaning. "I'll be punished. The babe will be taken, or come out—come out like Ifor, or Tomos. I've brought a curse on it, haven't I?"

Gwen turned to the fire, preparing the tea. "You cannot

think that. If wishing made it so, then every wanted babe would come out whole and perfect and—and nothing bad," she ended lamely, her throat closing.

Mathry looked up, blinking in surprise. "You speak as if you've carried."

Dovey stirred. "Gwen's never—"

"I have," Gwen said quietly.

She met both their stunned faces, then turned to Dovey. "I never meant to lie to you. I simply—could not speak of it. The hurt...I was blind with it, when I came here. And you had Cerys, so small and fragile, and I couldn't bring that shadow on you. Or her."

Dovey's face softened. She placed a warm hand on Gwen's arm. "Ah, dearling."

"Will you tell me what happened?" Mathry said, her eyes wide and dark. "Please."

"'Tis not a happy tale, Mathry."

"But I want to hear it. I don't know *anything*, and it's so much—I want to know what might go wrong, so I can stop it." She clutched her belly. "If I have the chance."

Gwen nodded. The others had shared themselves, after all. And perhaps she could lay these ghosts dancing around her, mocking her with their terrible cries. Perhaps she could keep her past from reaching out and strangling what she had here.

"Drink," she said. "We will visit St. Gwladys. And then we will walk, to hasten the purging and help the work of the herbs."

The old medieval church was cool and quiet, the grey stones holding the chill of the spring night. Doves cooed and shifted in the timber beams of the ceiling. In the small chapel, in the section that still had an intact roof, St. Gwladys smiled from her narrow window. The lead cames that held the stained glass showed through her red-blue gown and the green hill behind her, where stood a lamb and a Celtic cross.

"Were you married?" Mathry asked. They walked the church laid out in its cross pattern, down the length of the empty nave, around the short arms of the side chapels, then back to the stone altar, long stripped of its valuables. "Or were you like me?"

"Exactly like you, lass. After my mother died, my father sent me to live with an English family in Llanfyllin. They were rich from lead mines and wanted a companion for their daughter. I was tutored with her and treated as one of the family. Her brother..."

Her throat grew tight. The skirts of their gowns swished on the cold stone floor, and the candle in Dovey's holder flickered. Every so often Mathry put a hand to her belly, as if willing any movement there to halt.

"He was a few years older, but headstrong, selfish. Swore he loved me. Insisted his family would allow us to wed, once they knew how he felt. I ought to have been wiser, but with no mother, no guidance, and having been raised the equal of his sister..."

"You believed him," Mathry said grimly.

"He might have meant it," Gwen said. "But when his family disapproved and cast me out—he did nothing. I couldn't go back to my father. He'd married again, a woman quite young, and forgot all about me. I went to stay with a friend of the family, outside of town. I wrote him, the brother, to say where I was so he might come claim me and his child. I heard nothing from him except—" She swallowed hard. "Except the news he was betrothed to another. I knew her. She was English as well, the daughter of a baronet, with a dowry almost a large as Anne's. That was the girl, my sis—almost sister."

"She did nothing?" Mathry asked, wincing at another cramp.

"She may have wanted to, but she was even younger than I

am, and about to come out in society, as the English do. When it was clear I was increasing, I had to leave my friend's. I had nowhere to go, so I tried to find work. But when you are a young woman with a belly—"

"Yes," Mathry said, nodding. "Did you cast it, then?"

"No. I wanted her. I wanted her more than my life. I had no one else to love me, you see, but my own mam had loved me so fiercely, and I'd been so devoted to her. Anne's mother was cold. I vowed I would do better. But I had nothing—no help. No home."

Dovey's eyes were a deeper black than the darkness, and the candle picked out the sheen of tears. "What happened?"

"It was winter. I was staying in the sty of a kind farmer who let me bed with his animals. She came early, and I was alone, and I knew something was wrong, but I didn't know what to do. It was—a difficult birth. She came out feet first, with the cord wrapped around her neck."

Gwen drew a deep breath, reliving that pain turning her inside out. It seared to the core. Dovey reached around Mathry to touch her shoulder.

"It doesn't always kill, I know that now," Gwen managed. "A good midwife might have helped me turn her, or untangle her, or—" She caught Mathry's horrified eyes. "We'll have the best we can find when it's your time. I promise you. But I—as I said, I didn't have help." She let out a shuddering sigh, watching the floor. One step at a time, one foot before the other. "I buried her as best I could, in the hard ground, and came south with my heart frozen. All I wanted was to go as far away as possible. To let the sea carry me off."

"Not you, too," Dovey said quietly.

Gwen summoned a wavering smile for her friend. "I found St. Gwladys, as I said, and she told me to stay here. And that's when you found me."

"And then you found me," Mathry said. She sighed, her shoulders drooping. "God above, how does any woman survive this? And how does she let a man touch her again, after?"

"Would you want another child, Gwen?" Dovey asked as they circled the church for the dozenth time. The deep shadows felt warmer, safer, with these women at her side. The ghosts had ceased their screaming.

"I don't know if I can. Something—happened with the birth. Part of my womb collapsed. I shoved it back in, and by some miracle didn't take a fever," Gwen said. Dovey flinched at this image, and Mathry made a horrified squeak. "But I imagine something weakened or was broken," Gwen said. "I won't bear children again."

"Cerys is as good as your own," Dovey said stoutly.

Gwen nodded. "She is, and we could fill St. Sefin's with babies if we wished. I don't need a womb to mother."

"We need that lord to let us stay here," Mathry said. "I want my babe to have a roof. And mothers." She leaned her head on Gwen's shoulder, and a small piece of Gwen's heart that had been hard for years pained her, though not in a harmful way. It was the pain of a frozen piece of flesh beginning, at long last, to thaw.

"You haven't bled yet," Gwen said softly.

Mathry nodded. "And the cramping's stopped. I think your tea worked."

"I'll make another dose, with something to help you sleep. And tomorrow I'll start you on red raspberry leaf and nettle tea. Do you want someone with you tonight?"

"I'll stay with her first," Dovey said. "You're weary from harping."

Gwen nodded. She hadn't told Dovey yet about Calvin Vaughn pressing her into the hedge, or what it meant. There would be no more harping fees from the Vaughn family. Now where were they to find money?

The three women stood for a moment, heads bowed, hands pressed together, before the flickering smile of St. Gwladys. Then Dovey led Mathry to bed, smoothing the girl's hair from her brow in the same gesture she used with Cerys.

Gwen stood a long moment, communing with her saint. She needed guidance. Strength. She'd purged something in finally speaking of her past. She'd been foolish and she'd suffered, but she no longer felt, quite so strongly, that losing her daughter had been a punishment for lying in sin with Daron Sutton. Her child's death had simply been the way of Nature, of life and of death.

Her heart gulped in her chest when she heard a footstep from above. She reared back, looking up, to see a man's shadow on the stair leading to the bell tower. No one used that stair; she didn't imagine it was safe. Was it a ghost? Vengeance come upon her? Was she to pay again for past sins?

Who would take care of St. Sefin's if a murdered ghost came at her from the dark?

It was Penrydd. He reached out and put his hands on her quivering shoulders. He was warm and solid and she had that odd notion, once again, that he was *safe*.

He wasn't safe. No man was, least of all him.

"I'm sorry I frightened you. I was in the bell tower. I like to go up there when I can't sleep."

"You—were all the way up there? And the stair didn't collapse? I thought those boards were rotten." She peered into the dark above them.

"Many of them are. I ought to repair it, in the daylight. But one can see a long way from a tower atop a hill. Puts things in perspective."

He couldn't sleep because she was no longer helping him fight his nightmares. Guilt squeezed her throat. And shame.

"You heard us?"

"I didn't mean to eavesdrop. But I couldn't not hear. Mathry seemed in distress, and I didn't want to interrupt."

"Or stop all our hearts, swooping down like a *pwca*."

"Like a what?"

A lock of his too-long hair fell over his brow, casting an impish shadow on his face. He adjusted her shawl around her shoulders, snugging it about her neck.

"The Welsh Puck. He leads travelers by night to the edge of a cliff, and then he blows out his lamp and leaves them there. Do you want me to make you a tea for sleep and sweet dreams?"

His frown deepened. "Your lace is torn."

Gwen lowered her eyes and sucked in a breath. The scrap of blonde lace she and Dovey shared, the token of that long-ago babe left on their doorstep and their pledge for what they would build together, had been torn by Calvin Vaughn's fumbling, unwanted hands.

Rage made her voice shake. "Mayhap Mother Morris can mend it."

He walked with her as she turned toward the hall leading to the kitchen. "You told them your story."

St. Teilo's toes. He'd heard every part of her confession. Her sordid, sob-filled history. Gwen stopped in her tracks. The candle danced in its holder.

"You heard—all that?"

He nodded and put a hand at her elbow, drawing her down the corridor. His lips formed a hard line. "Am I the reason Mathry tried to cast out her babe?"

"Why would you think that?" she whispered, watching his face.

He winced and stepped back to let her precede him into the

kitchen. The fire still glowed in the stove, casting heat into the room. "She, ah, invited me into a dalliance. I declined. I may have led her to believe it was about the babe, when in truth—I did not wish to dally. With her," he added.

Gwen poked at the fire and then swung the kettle on its hook. "It wasn't you. She went to see Calvin Vaughn today, to ask for his help."

A small line appeared between his brows, but he didn't seem to recognize the name. Perhaps Vaughn had been puffing her up about their association, a knight's lesser son vying for a viscount's attention.

"And Vaughn, ass that he is, sent her to a cunning woman to be rid of it. As fortune would have it, the woman didn't know—or Mathry couldn't pay for—the right herbs."

"Is he why you don't trust me? The father of your babe. Is that why you mistrust all men?"

He stood close, and she felt the intensity vibrating through him, awareness, heat. He packed the tea strainer with willow bark and chamomile, and Gwen stared. The man who had asked for a servant's bell in the infirmary, who had wondered who would empty his chamber pot, stood in the kitchen with her, fixing tea.

"He has no hold over me any longer," Gwen said. "I'm glad to say."

"I can keep your secret, you know."

He turned to face her and the heat from the fire soared up from her toes, traveling through her entire body. Her fingertips tingled. The hair on the nape of her neck rose.

For a moment the sick memory of Calvin Vaughn attempting to kiss her, Calvin Vaughn rubbing his groin against her, flushed through her body. She pushed it from her mind.

"It needn't be a secret. I know it's supposed to be shameful, a girl having a child out of wedlock. But it happens all about Wales, and I would guess England, too."

"Is it shameful? To want to join your body with the person you love? For I am supposing you loved him."

Ah, this was the more shameful confession yet. "Perhaps at the time I believed that. I had looked up to him, and—the feelings were exciting. Desire is so powerful when one is young. I wanted so much to have someone of my own, and—the longing was stronger than my good sense."

His voice was a husky murmur. "Desire is powerful at any age."

Oh, indeed it was. Gwen let her eyes drift closed as a shiver passed through her body. She leaned toward him, riveted by his warmth. His solidity. The delicious scent of him, leather and sweat and the barest hint of rosemary from her soap.

Calvin Vaughn's lust had left a foul imprint on her. She wanted it erased. She wanted to immerse herself in Pen instead. The thrill that went through her at his very nearness tore free the parts of her she held so tightly. The sheer intensity of wanting him cleared her mind and cleansed, somehow. The man had plucked a burr from Ifor's collar before it could prick the blind boy. He had let Cerys lure him into her hunt for St. Sefin's lost treasure.

He had, that very afternoon, come back from mucking stables around Newport with a new set of boots for Tomos. In truth an old set that the cobbler had repaired, in return for Pen's help in making deliveries. But he had brought boots.

She turned to him and drew a deep, steadying breath. "Will you kiss me?"

"What?" His eyes widened, growing dark, and his voice was thick and deep.

"I asked will you—"

The rest of the words disappeared on her lips as he swooped

in. This was no tentative foray. His hot mouth fell upon hers and she opened her lips eagerly to his seeking tongue. The contact summoned a wave of molten desire, swift and shocking. She'd expected him to know how to kiss a woman. She'd expected to enjoy it. But this—she dug her hands into his hair to hold his head so she could kiss him forever, let the whole world fall away and leave just them, just this, his warm mouth, his clever tongue, the scent of the man making her head swirl. Kissing Penrydd felt like the most important, the most profound, the most necessary thing she had ever done in her life.

Behind her, the kettle screamed.

She panted for breath as he lifted his head. His eyes were dazed with passion, and she felt a burst of triumph along with the other hot sensations roiling around her insides. He'd been affected. *She'd* affected him.

"Your tea," she said weakly.

She could tell he wanted to kiss her again. She wanted to kiss him. But she pushed his cup at him, then tended to Mathry's tea and avoided meeting his gaze. She needed some air, a bit of distance to get a rein on her emotions. He was too much, suddenly.

"Let me know when you want that again," Pen said, and she closed her eyes against the delicious heat that flared and danced. And the bolt of satisfaction, too. He wanted her.

She turned to bank the fire for the night so they would have warm coals in the morning. "I need you to keep another secret. Calvin Vaughn fathered Mathry's child."

He merely nodded. "I hope she'll be all right," he said softly.

She stared at him, soaking up every line of his strong-featured face, the gleam in his eyes, the shape of his lips still damp from their kiss. The shadow of stubble along his jaw, the strong column of his throat. That deep, steady ease within him.

When had that happened? The Penrydd she'd met in the

Bristol tavern couldn't sit still for a second. Even his hands had quavered. The Penrydd who'd floated to her shore injured and wiped of his memory had paced and snarled like a caged cat. This man stood quietly, as if he'd reached peace within himself. Knew his own strength, and knew how to use it wisely. The Penrydd of before might have taken Calvin Vaughn's part in the matter of a cast-off mistress. This man cared that Mathry not be hurt.

She lifted her fingers and traced them over the prominent line of his cheek, where the bruise from his beatings had faded. "I knew there was a good man in there," she whispered. Solid, and decent, and *good*.

He caught her fingers and kissed them. "I had a thought up there, in the bracing cold, while I listened to you," he said. "What if I have a Mathry out there?"

"What if you—?" She stumbled on the words, her lips growing thick.

"What if there is someone looking for me? Someone who's in trouble because I am gone." He held her hand cupped against his cheek, his stubble prickling her palm. "Or something I need to make right."

She nodded, her throat closing. She needed to make things right with him.

She would talk to Dovey first. It wasn't fair to do this without her consent, considering all they had at stake. But it was time for the charade to end.

She needed to tell Pen who he was.

And she would have to bear losing him once he knew what she'd done.

CHAPTER ELEVEN

S he was going to kill him.

Not on purpose, Pen knew. But not having Gwenllian ap Ewyas—not being able to hold her, touch her, win her for his own—was going to shred him into a million tiny fish-bite sized pieces. And she would doubtless laugh as she fed his chum to the salmon he'd seen fishermen hauling by the netful out of the River Usk.

He'd claimed the privilege of driving her to her harping appointment at Pencoed Castle. That was the first foolish thing.

What hadn't been foolish was kissing her. But not kissing her again was going to drive him out of his mind.

He borrowed a horse and trap from the King's Head, with Mr. Trett's blessing, and she insisted on checking the harness before they set out. Yet another instance in which she refused to rely on anyone else, yet having heard her story, he could understand. She'd lost her mother, her remaining parent sent her to strangers, and then she'd been dishonestly wooed by the son of the house. Pen had no doubt the lad had pursued her with everything he had in him. A girl of her beauty, with the grace of a queen and that quick mind and sweet nature, under his roof and his for the taking? She hadn't a chance.

And after trusting the boy's blandishments and empty promises, she'd been turned out of that home, too.

Pen tried to imagine giving birth alone and unaided in the bleak of winter, with nothing but a dead babe to show for the effort. How had she not become hardened and cruel?

Yet at her lowest point, she'd found her way back to life by caring for others. Dovey. Evans. Everyone else who came to her, turned out of their rightful home. He could see how it weighed on her that she could lose the place and didn't have the money to buy it from this lord, whoever he was. The lord represented by the black-clad solicitor who had looked at Pen holding a wheelbarrow of dung and called him filth, because of the work he did and the poor appearance of his clothing, when he knew nothing of Pen himself.

Of course, Pen knew nothing of himself, either, but the man's insult had burrowed deep. It was unfair and it was untrue. He hoped, in his real life, he was a better judge of character and didn't dismiss people by sight.

But some deep, lurking fear told him he hadn't been any better. Some evil came roaring out of him at night, in his dreams —it had to be evil, to have such a terrifying grip on him. And he had a sense, a knowing that came with the bloody torments of his dreams, that he too had been in a position like Gwen's, torn apart body and soul, hanging to life by a thread. And instead of rising and pulling himself together, building something that could shelter himself and others, he had chosen a path of self-destruction and selfish absorption, if not outright cruelty.

But he could change. Just as he could prove he wasn't the scrum that the solicitor had called him, he could build himself back as a man of integrity and honor. Gwen had given him that chance, dredging him from the river and knitting him back together. He was doing his best to show her he was worthy of saving. He was even coming to appreciate those other broken souls. He didn't care for them as Gwen did—he wasn't *that* soft-hearted, or soft-headed, either—but he knew better than to scorn them for their poor state. He knew what they'd survived.

Gwen had survived. And so had he.

"Hawthorn blossom for your thoughts," Gwen said.

They drove along a rutted track eastward, with wooded hills rising to the north and tidy farms to the south, dotted with barns and houses. He insisted on driving and she, after walking around the trap to study its wheels and construction, had accepted. Now she reached out and broke a blossom off a hedge crowding the narrow lane. The hawthorn was in bloom, along with the apple trees and everything else. The season of rebirth, it was.

"I was thinking how scenic this countryside is," Pen said. "I hear Wales spoken of often for its beauty. And its wildness."

He felt comfortable with her, jostling side by side in the small trap. She wore what he recognized as her one good gown, the redingote riding dress, with the delicate blonde lace that Mother Morris had carefully mended. Her woolen shawl protected her skirts from the dust of the road, but not all of her ash-brown curls consented to stay pinned beneath her bonnet. With her refined features and elegant figure she had the kind of beauty that would capture attention in court and the ballrooms of the great—somehow he knew that, without recalling how he had any knowledge of the doings of the great, much less royalty. Yet she seemed happiest in the open air, unfettered by so-called courtesy or custom.

"It's the most beautiful land God ever made. That," she pointed to the forested hills to the northeast, "is Coed Gwent, the great and ancient forest of the kingdom of Gwent. The English call it Wentwood. Its lords have been doing their best to whittle the trees down for their ironworks, and it's said that the Royal Navy prefers Welsh oak for its battleships."

Pen's neck prickled at the mention of the Royal Navy. That meant something to him. But she was still chattering, her arm pointing due north. "Had we followed the river we'd come to Caerleon, a center of trade for the Silures long before the Romans came and built their fort. The amphitheater and baths are still standing. St. Cadog built a church there, and Geoffrey of Monmouth said it was Arthur's capital, home of the Round Table."

She paused, turning the hawthorn blossom around in her hands before she handed it to him. "Cromwell's troops camped on Christchurch Hill before they came down and destroyed Newport Castle. It was never rebuilt after, which is why it looks as you saw it."

She was making another sly dig about English destruction in Wales, no doubt. But she was also showing him how much she knew, and cared about, this land. She might not choose to come with him when he left. His throat tightened at the thought.

"What am I to do with this?" he asked.

She smiled. "Eat it. Best while the leaves are young and before the flower buds have opened."

Cautiously he put the sprig in his mouth. No one in his life, he thought, besides Gwenllian ap Ewyas, would ever encourage him to eat roadside shrubbery. Of course, no one else in his life knew the plant was edible.

She laughed at his expression. "Nutty!" he exclaimed. "Surprisingly good. How did you know you could eat it?"

"Much of what's around you is edible, Pen. In fact, on our way home tomorrow, we'll stop to gather. That's chickweed, good for treating a variety of ills, and tasty in salads. The gorse flowers are delicious and make good wine. And I want to harvest the ramson, the wild garlic, before the flowers have died. It can flavor most anything."

"And ward off vampires, I've heard."

She laughed. "Vampires are for European countries. We have the Gwrach y Rhibyn, the hag who waits at the crossroads. She'll drink the blood of your children unless you keep them close."

She fell silent and fingered the lace at her throat. He glanced at her delicate fingers, the slender line of her neck, then away. The urge to be foolish and kiss her again was strong upon him, but he wasn't sure she would welcome his embrace in the light of day. She'd been vulnerable that night in the kitchen, as she never had before, but today she was calm, poised, self-possessed.

She didn't flirt with him as did virtually every other woman he encountered. She didn't cast out lures or try to entrance him merely for the sake of conquest. He had the awful sense that when she regarded him with her clear, steady eyes, as she was doing now, she saw deep inside him.

And he wasn't certain there was much of anything to show there.

"How did you learn it all? How to forage, I mean."

Her eyes clouded and she looked away. "My mother taught me first. I don't think we were poor, for our house was pleasant, built of wood and a tiled roof, not mud and thatch. But she used everything around us. Then, at Vine Court, the housekeeper knew herbs, and there was a cunning woman nearby who made remedies that had been handed down to her. Not written but taught, woman to woman, for centuries, much like the bards and ancient druids learned their verses.

"And then when I was—on my own, and had no way of earning food, I learned by trial and error what around me I could eat." She broke off a hawthorn blossom for herself and popped it in her mouth. "It helps us now, at St. Sefin's. When we are able to find our own food."

Her little community, living half-wild in the abandoned shell of a medieval religious house, on the edges of a society that had broken them. And he had found himself, unaccountably, fitting in. Best not to examine why.

"I thought cunning folk were witches," he said.

She frowned. "The priests like to call them witches. And burn them for it. I fear what is lost when learned men and their instruments of torture come to take from the simple folk. And to what purpose?"

He was one of those, Pen thought. The men who came with guns and fire to force others to their will. His nightmares told him that.

She had saved his life, but he did not see how she could come to care for him. He was too different, foreign in more ways than just being English. He'd never been taught what she knew. And he feared that, when in the past he'd had the chance to help another or advance himself, he'd advanced himself, every time. She couldn't love that.

He cleared his throat. When had his thoughts grown so foolish as to turn to love? He'd been thinking of kissing her, of peeling off the lace and the woolen shawl and the outdated gown and browsing on the treasures beneath. None of which had aught to do with *love*.

"When did you learn to harp?"

"Ah, my mother played. She had a small *telyn* in our house. I brought it with me when I went to the Suttons. Anne's mother let me sit in on her lessons, and I liked to play, and was told I had some skill at it. So when they turned me out, I took the harp with me. I imagined, at the time, Daron would find us a house of our own, and I would set up like a lady." She fell silent for a long moment. "In any event, I learned I could play for the occasional meal or coin. I am no Marged ferch Ifan, though."

"Who?" Pen pulled their trap aside to let a farmer pass with a wagonload of straw. The farmer touched the brim of his cap, and Pen returned the gesture.

"Queen of the Lakes, they called her. She lived in the north. It was said she could shoe a horse, make a boat, play the harp and the violin. And she could out-wrestle any man." She sent him a sly, mischievous smile.

"I will be happy to help you improve your wrestling skills," Pen said, straight-faced. "Any time."

"Have a care what you offer, Pen," she teased. "Wales is full of fierce women. Have you not heard of Jemima Fawr, hero of the Battle of Fishguard?" At his scoffing look, her eyes widened. "It was but two years ago! When the French troops landed at Llanwnda, she and a group of women caught and captured a dozen French soldiers, armed with nothing but a pitchfork. The soldiers had been drinking, but still. She locked them in a church for the night, and the next day the French surrendered, and that will teach any foreigners who try to invade Wales again."

"She sounds fearsome indeed," Pen agreed.

She plucked at the fringes of her shawl. "I heard she was awarded a lifetime pension by the crown. If only I could do something as brave or noble, and be granted St. Sefin's as a result."

Finally, an opportunity to be useful. "Have you sent word to the solicitor yet? Would it do to approach this lord and ask him to lower the price?"

She looked away, evading the question. Did she not have the courage to face an English lord? He could help with this. "I mean—"

"Stop," she said suddenly. "I mean, stop the horse. Here."

He turned the horse off the road, where the verge disappeared into woodland. The ground was violet in every direction, a carpet of fragrant bluebells. Gwen scrambled down from the trap and ran into the midst of them like a nymph of the wood.

"I can distill these into perfume," she called. "The women pay for it. Come help me gather, Pen."

He looped the reins around a tree limb while the horse took the opportunity to munch the red clover growing along the road. But at the edge of the patch he paused, arrested by the delicate fragrance. Something stirred in the fog of his head.

"Bluebells," he said. A memory formed. The shape of her standing in a room—not a room he recognized, but she was wearing that dress, that shawl. "I know that scent."

She turned her head, arms outstretched but frozen, as if she were a woodland fairy caught at frolic by human eyes. "Do you remember something?"

Yes. He had been struck by her, her beauty, her anger—she was angry with him about something. And he remembered bluebells.

He opened his mouth to say all this when some inner voice warned against it. He'd never in his life, he would guess, been a man who listened to his inner voice. But this time he did. It cautioned him to say nothing. If he asked how he knew her from his former life, then this idyll—driving together, playing for a dance at Pencoed Castle, the closeness that was growing between them, and their cozy rhythm at St. Sefin's—all would come to a cold and violent end.

He moved toward her. "You always smell of bluebells. I love that scent on you."

He wasn't certain she would yield to him, not even when he slipped a hand about her waist. But when he laid a finger beneath her chin she tipped up her head to kiss him, and he fell again into that new land where every color was brightened, every sense apprehended more beauty, where the world seemed shot through with wild joy. Or perhaps that pulse was his heart hammering as she curved against him in surrender, slipping her arms around his neck, pressing her body into his.

He groaned with pleasure and kissed her deeply, tasting hawthorn blossom and her own delicious warmth, a well he wanted to drown in. He kissed her endlessly, their bodies fused, a dance of lips and tongue that was like delirium, while his hand slid up her side slowly, fingers skimming her ribs and the shape of her stays beneath, sliding beneath her arm, then closing over one perfect breast. Her heart pounded as wildly as his own.

But she stopped and pulled away, as if she felt her nipple piercing his palm as sharply as he did. "Bluebells," she muttered, her eyes huge grey-green pools.

"Yes." He tried bending his head, but she turned her chin, then peeled herself from his arms. He stifled a groan of disappointment and frustrated desire.

"We'll be late if we stop to gather bluebells," she said. "Tomorrow."

Tomorrow, would she consent to lie with him? Perhaps here in this very field. He could strip her naked, lie her down on a silken carpet of purple-blue blooms, and every part of her would smell, and taste, of bluebells. His arousal bobbed in agreement.

"I was hoping we would wrestle," he said, his voice thick. He took a moment to gather his composure before returning to the trap and helping her climb in.

She looked ahead, a flush climbing her cheek. Her throat knotted as she swallowed. At least he had the satisfaction of knowing she wasn't unaffected by that deluge of a kiss.

"Tell me why I love the scent of bluebells," he said. That image of her in the room, staring at him with wide accusing eyes, seemed burned now into his brain. Had she known him in his former life? And if she did, why had she said nothing about it?

Had she forgotten meeting him, while he remembered her, even though he could remember literally nothing else?

He took the reins and urged the horse to walk on, giving her a moment to compose herself. He sensed she would not be entirely truthful.

"They mean humility, for some," she said, watching the road ahead. "Everlasting love, for others. There's an old superstition that you aren't to pick bluebells or bring them into your home because they are beloved of fairies. You can call a fairy by ringing a bluebell, but a bluebell patch like this is thick with magic."

Oh yes, he felt that. Thick with magic.

"But you can pick bluebells," he said. She was lying. Or withholding. Why? "Because you are a fairy?"

"Because the bulbs help pass water and stop bleeding," she said. "But don't eat these plants, mind! They're poisonous."

A woman who handled poisonous plants fearlessly. Who faced life and all its injuries and losses, fearlessly.

But there was something she wasn't telling him.

He watched her carefully, waiting for his moment as they arrived at Pencoed Castle, a majestic structure sitting incongruously at the end of a farm lane. Gwen pointed to the tall rectangular gatehouse as they approached from the west. "The same red sandstone used to build St. Sefin's," she said. "Isn't it a lovely color?"

But instead of proceeding through the gate to the courtyard at the front of the house, Gwen directed him around a tall stand of trees toward a dower house and the outbuildings to the side, which included the carriage house. Inside she was warmly greeted by the housekeeper and shown the room she was given for the night, high in the third story among the servants' quarters.

Pen was greeted with friendliness, too, but he felt odd entering the house from the back. Perhaps his former self used the front entrance to such homes. Pencoed was a fortified manor house on a grand scale, with the ruins of an old wall encasing the front courtyard and battlements along the roof. Inside, the walls of dressed stone and timber-framed ceilings lent a severe beauty to the large staterooms, while the leaded glass windows let in gracious light and the plentiful hangings and thickly upholstered furniture offered luxury. Gwen looked as at ease in the grand surroundings as she did in the kitchens of St. Sefin's. While the guests gathered for their dinner and Gwen set up with her harp in the formal parlor among the other musicians, he thought with her beauty and quiet grace she belonged more among the gentry at the table than she did among the servants.

That was where Pen was, pressed by the butler to help serve at table and then carry refreshments among the guests as the diners mingled after, chatting and only half-listening to the music. An impressive livery was found and brushed for him, the thick cotton finer than anything he'd worn at St. Sefin's. He wondered what Gwen would think when she saw him in the saffron breeches and stockings, the embroidered gold waistcoat and cuffs over a cutaway tailcoat of navy blue with large bronze buttons. He looked well in it—so he was informed by the glances of the maids and the female diners alike—but all he cared for was Gwen's smile when she saw him moving about holding a platter of Champagne flutes, one gloved fist behind his back.

Something told him he had never done this in his life— served a crowd of people, donned borrowed livery in a rich man's house. He vowed he'd never do it again, when one too many of the self-important gentleman ignored him as if he were furniture, simply a man-shaped sideboard holding his beverage, and one too many of the women managed to run a gloved hand along his arse or thigh. He clenched his teeth and looked unaffected. But he swore, deep down, that when he went back to his former life, he would never again treat someone in his employ like a furnishing. He would never demean a man for honest labor, even if it were shoveling shit. And he would never, under any circumstances, lay hands on a woman unless she had unambiguously specified he might do so.

"Aren't you tired yet?" he asked Gwen when he found her in the servery as he went to refresh his platter of glasses. The evening was well-advanced, the revelry growing louder as the guests imbibed. They were a free-spirited group to begin with, most of them military men and their wives, friends of Sir Mark and his daughter's bridegroom. Major James Blackwell had served in India and recently married Miss Maria, daughter to Sir Mark by a local woman who had been his Indian wife during his time with the Bengal engineers in Calcutta, and the union was new enough to still provide grounds for celebration.

Pen sensed that in certain English circles, high sticklers would look down on a match with a wife who was not British, not legitimate, and only half-white, but this group regarded the new Mrs. Blackwell with admiration for her beauty and her established situation, for it was said her father had settled three thousand pounds on her at her marriage. The musicians carried on, but Gwen had been instructed to fetch refreshments, for the others, a viol and a cello player, were men, and she was expected to serve them. Pen gauged by the shadows under her eyes and the red marks on her fingers that she was weary and her hands growing sore, but her sweet smile at him, her eyes heavy-lidded, brought the memory of their kiss in the bluebells leaping to life.

"It's a pleasant group. Sir Mark intends to pay well, and I like the house."

Pen set aside the platter he held and the one she'd taken up. The music continued, and he held out his arm in the form a country dance. He remembered how to dance, at least.

"You should be mistress of a house of your own, one as grand as this," he said. "With a husband who adores you, as Mrs. Blackwell's husband dotes on her."

She paused a moment, watching him with wide, wary eyes that color of a forest's heart. Some inner struggle took place, and he held his breath, hoping that he would win. That this pull between them, this cautious new trust—and, yes, the heavy current of desire—would draw her to him more than whatever cautions held her back.

Then she laughed and lifted her hand to his, and the tight fear in his chest broke and fell free. She moved with him, beginning the simple figure, turning one way while he turned the other, his bow to her curtsey. They turned again, hands touching, and her hip brushed his leg. The confines of the servery pressed them close, and her heat, her scent, her intoxicating touch wrapped around him as they went through the familiar steps.

"I, too, thought I would have those things once," she said, and her voice held an odd, strained note. Her eyes moved over his face. "But I am certain you will. Have a grand house, that is, and an adoring wife."

He hadn't wanted a wife before. But he did now. He knew that with an utter, profound clarity. It stilled him mid-figure.

She paused, too, following his lead. He stared into her eyes, caught by how perfectly in tune she was with him. Against his will, against all wisdom, his head lowered. He oughtn't kiss her here. It was too easy to be surprised. It was already enough that they should be dancing; a kiss would end whatever reputation she had, were they caught by someone who wouldn't turn a blind eye. He feared the Pen of before had never been the kind to consider a woman's reputation; he did so now. But he could no more resist trying to kiss her than he could keep the sun from rising in the east.

She was wiser. She stepped away, her eyes dark with desire —he was gratified to see it—but something else. Her expression looked as if she were torn in two.

"Gwen," he said, his voice rasping from a dry throat. "Would you ever consider if—"

"I cannot," she said. She caught up a tray of glasses as if she were an embattled knight and he the dragon on the attack. "I must—they'll be looking for me."

And she was gone, leaving the imprint of her on his hand, and his heart.

She knew what he'd meant to say. Something he had never offered any woman, never thought he would want to offer a woman. What he wanted to spread before her like the lavish courses set upon that glittering table, his heart laid out and ready for carving.

And she didn't want him in return.

CHAPTER TWELVE

"What did you say it was called?" Pen asked as they rattled down another rutted farm lane, this one lined with brambles and blackthorn.

Gwen was tense this morning, her eyes heavy and shadowed from staying up late harping for Sir Mark's guests, and then dancing again in the kitchen as the Pencoed servants cleaned up after the great folk and enjoyed the leftovers of their lavish supper. Pen had perhaps nipped too much of the leftover drink. The revelry had lasted far into the night, but all Pen really recalled was dancing with Gwen. Gwen's face glowing with laughter as she looked up at him, Gwen's blush when he put his hands on her waist to lift her or let a hand slide over her hip as they completed a figure. Gwen's indrawn breath when he stole a kiss in the shadowed hallway before she squeezed his hand and went upstairs to bed.

That Gwen was gone. She was prim again in a traveling gown, her wild hair stuffed under her bonnet, her hands in leather gloves because she wanted to stop every few yards to gather weeds from the roadside. It would take them hours to get back to Newport as it was, and the fine day was turning on them. The sun that burned off the mist that morning as they left Pencoed Castle had given way to clouds rolling in from the east, a low grey ceiling threatening rain. He'd wanted to head straight back to town to stay ahead of the weather, but Gwen insisted on a detour to the north, another great house that she wanted him to see.

"It's called Penrydd."

Gwen was driving this stretch, and she had a steady hand on the reins. Pen didn't mind being her passenger; it gave him a chance to study the countryside. "That's the name of the house," she said. "And the title given to the family."

Her eyes flickered to him. She said the name as if it meant something to her.

He knew it meant something to him. He felt a pull deep in his mind. That name had some hold over him—what?

"Why is everything around here Pen-something?"

"It's the Cymric word for 'head.' Pencoed means 'head of the forest.' Pendragon, the title given our greatest heroes, means 'head dragon' or 'chief warrior.'"

"So Penrydd means—" The word felt familiar in his mouth. But why? His head hurt, as if his mind were stretching.

"Headrest, literally, or place to rest your head," she said softly. "Here we are."

The trap emerged from a stand of alder and black poplar into a large field hemmed by a low stone wall and gate. On a green rise stood a small castle of grey stone, a fortified manor in the Jacobean style, built for show and not defense. Four cylindrical towers rose from the corners of a low curtain wall topped with battlements, but despite the medieval design the manor house was every bit as grand as Pencoed, with tall, narrow windows incised along the three floors and attics above. To the right, outside the stone wall, clustered modern outbuildings and offices, also dressed in grey stone. A few sheep browsing the far pasture lifted their heads and began to nose in their direction, until the corgi standing watch warned them back to the herd.

Gwen cleared her throat. "Do you want to go inside?"

"What, just stroll in and ask for a look around?" Their horse startled, flicking its ears at his sharp tone.

"You could," she said.

"No," Pen said. He knew strongly, though he couldn't say why, he did not want to go into the house. Not yet.

But he knew it. He'd seen this house in a picture. A painting. He tried to remember where. It hung on a wall in a large hall—a foyer of a house he knew. A large house, in a large town. London. He had a house in London, and a painting of this house hung in the foyer, and he saw it every time he came in or out—for yes, he used the front door of great houses, particularly his own. And this painting hung in pride of place because this castle belonged to him.

His mind strained in several directions at once, trying to remember everything. He *was* important. He was possibly rich.

"Tell me about the family," he said. The horse, still alarmed, shifted its feet as the dog trotted toward them.

Gwen held the horse steady, though her voice wavered. "They're a Welsh family, an old one. Knights, possibly princes if you go back far enough. They fought for Welsh freedom with Owain Glyndŵr. Then they stood for Henry Tudor during the War of the Roses and were raised to barons by Henry VII. They changed their name to Price, from ap Rhys—son of Rhys, that is —and became, like many, English lords with a Welsh estate. After the baron fought with George II at the Battle of Dettingen, and then defended the king during the Jacobite uprising, he was raised to a viscount. He spent most of his time in London, I'm told, and though the family seat is here, his heirs have never seen it."

He'd meant to come here. The knowledge slithered over

Pen like cold water poured on his head. *He* was the heir. He hadn't wanted to be, hadn't been raised for it, had run away from it in fact and joined the army. No, not army; navy. He'd been an officer in the Royal Navy. Not a half bad one, until he was blown up on the beach he saw in his nightmares. But this estate, and this family, were connected to him.

"Bloody hell," he whispered.

"Does this mean anything to you?" She trembled like a dragonfly on a tender branch, rippling and iridescent, ready to dart away at any moment. But she reached out a hand to him, and he took it. He wanted something to anchor him. He wanted *her* to anchor him.

"Why are you showing me this?"

Her eyes were the grey of the rain-filled sky, as sad and stormy. "I want you to remember who you are." Her voice was a thread. "I thought this might help."

She knew. Pen's entire body recoiled as the realization hammered him. This house belonged to him, and Gwen knew that and had brought him here. She knew his history. Did she know why he'd been attacked, tossed into a tiny Welsh rowboat, and turned out to sea?

Why hadn't she told him?

Thunder burled over them, low and threatening. The corgi eyed the sky and trotted back to his flock, barking instructions. The horse stamped its hooves.

"Let's go," Pen said roughly. He almost said *home*, but St. Sefin's wasn't his home. He didn't know where his bloody home was. London? Here? Somewhere else?

Pen. *Penrydd.* She had known his name. He *had* met her before, in the room with her anger and the scent of bluebells. She had kept this from him and he wanted to know why. Anger boiled like lava within him, but stronger than the anger was a voice of caution that warned him to wait until he understood more. Exactly who he was, and how much she knew, and why she hadn't shown him any of this right away.

He needed action. He took the reins and she handed them over without a word. The silence held as they drove back to Newport. She spoke only to give directions or ask him to stop so she might hop out to gather weeds or flowers by the side of the road, cramming her harvest more quickly into the cloth bags she'd brought as the clouds drew dark and close. At last they clattered over the wooden bridge spanning the Usk, where the scent of the marshes and a fringe of smoke from the riverside kiln lay heavy in the air.

The hair on the back of Pen's neck rose an instant before two men emerged from the shadow of the ruined castle and stepped into the road, blocking their way.

"Stay, travelers!" called the large one, a tall man with thick shoulders and a too-small leather coat. Gaps showed among blackened teeth. "We be the toll masters, and yer to pay a toll."

"There is no toll on Newport bridge," Gwen said sharply, curling her hand into a fist around her riding crop. The horse shied, sensing her fear, and Pen held the reins steady.

"They is now. Hey, Minikin!" the large man called. "These two don't know 'bout the toll."

A fellow about half his height strolled forward, wearing a short leather jerkin and breeches and a feather in his tricorne hat. "Tsk, tsk," he drawled. "That's twice the fee then, innit?"

"Tha's what I thought." Gap-tooth grinned. "Let's have a look at the bags, aye?"

"You will not!" Gwen exclaimed. "That's food and medicine, and I will not have you dirtying it with your paws."

"Dirty paws, is it!" The large man glared. "Les'see how you like the dirty paws on you, moll!"

"Touch her and I'll part that paw from you," Pen said coolly.

"Oh, the mort's yours, then? Well, can the cove handle his

fists? If you don't pay the toll, you pay a forfeit. And if you don't post the cole, you pay with the moll."

"I will not be payment for anything!" Gwen fumed. "Let us go before we call the watchman."

Thunder rolled through the sky, and the horse huffed. The little man took the bridle and held it as if guessing Pen had thought about driving the animal on, running the men over if need be.

"Squeak for the kenchin!" the thief chortled. "We'll beat him all hollow when he comes, but we'll chafe your cove first, little cat!"

"Oh, very well," Pen said with a sigh, handing Gwen the reins and descending the trap. "Let's have this done then, shall we?" He began unbuttoning his rough woolen coat.

"Pen, don't," Gwen said. There was no one about, the shops being shuttered and the citizens in their homes, buttoning up against the storm. Pen only hoped he could make a better account of himself than he had the last time he'd stood up to a larger man.

"This won't take long," he told Gwen with a bravura he didn't feel. "I'll comb the brute's head, and we'll go."

"We owe them nothing!" Gwen exclaimed. "Besides, that's the *glaw taranau* coming, the thundering rain. We'll be wise to take shelter."

Pen rolled up his sleeves and took his stance. The combatants circled, taking the other's measure. The taller man had a larger reach and a huge advantage in weight, but he was clumsy. Pen rolled to the balls of his feet in readiness but the other stood back on his heels, counting on his mass rather than his movements to win the day. He was right to do so; one solid punch from that claw would lay Pen out on the ground. But he couldn't shame himself before Gwen.

"Ye look like a gentry cove I tossed the other day," Gap-tooth said, cracking his knuckles. "Remember, Minikin? Th' one on th' boat."

"He do look 'im," the little man observed, peering at Pen as clouds closed in.

Rage reared through Pen. "You attacked me at the wharves? You were the ones?" He threw a punch that snaked beneath Gap-tooth's guard and landed in a fleshy rib.

His assailant grunted. "Throws a punch better'n he did, though."

"Do you know what you *did* to me?" Pen roared. If this was the man who beat him senseless—robbed him of his memory, of everything he knew—he saw red. He dove in and swung, again and again, and the jolt and burn of pain told him his punches were finding a place.

"Hey, now!" the little man cried. "'Twas just business. We does what we's hired to do."

"Steal from passersby and call it a toll?" Gwen called. "Some business! We'll have you all thrown in the watch house."

Which was nothing but a lean-to in the back of King's Head stables, Pen knew. It wouldn't hold these ruffians. He paused in delivering a flurry of punches to the chest and ribs of the larger man and reared back, shaking the hair from his eyes. He was already pouring sweat—or was it raining?—but he felt deadly cold.

"Who hired you?" he growled.

He never heard the answer because a brick exploded beneath his cheek, and he saw stars. The world tilted and he toppled like a felled tree to the hard-packed ground.

"Stop!" Gwen screamed. Above him, her outline stood etched against the pearled sky, arms outspread like an avenging angel. She plunged a hand into one of her bags and then threw something into the air as if she were scattering pixie dust. Powder glittered and spread, and Gap-tooth started choking.

His companion, Miniken, let go the bridle and turned away with a terrific sneeze.

"Pen?" Gwen's face was just above him now, blurred and concerned. He let her pull him up. "Can you get back in the trap?"

"Not...finished," he wheezed, trying to suck air in his lungs.

"Yes, we are." She pulled his arm around her neck and heaved him to his feet. He staggered against her the few steps back to the cart, where the horse shook its head, snuffling. There was something in the air, tickling his nose. Gwen's nose twitched, too. Gap-tooth bent over, holding his ribs while he sneezed violently, and Minikin had half-disappeared behind an enormous printed handkerchief.

"What...was that?" Pen managed to get his breath back as Gwen drove them down High Street towards Stow Hill and St. Sefin's. At the pie shop a curtain moved as a woman looked out, then quickly retreated.

"I've never seen those men before," Gwen said, her jaw set with anger. "I can't imagine they'll be let stay there to intimidate people. I'll tell Mr. Stanley at once, and he can talk to the constable and the magistrate. Sir Robert still has the position, I think."

"What was the powder?" His ribs felt tight as she drove into the yard of St. Sefin's and helped him down from the trap.

"Sneezewort," she said. "Chewing the root is good for toothache. I carry a powder of it when I travel to deter anyone who wishes to meddle with me."

Pen laughed, though it made his chest hurt. He hadn't thought Gap-tooth had landed any punches to his midsection, but he might have missed something in his red haze of fury. His face was on fire. Gwen told him to lie down in his room while she boiled comfrey leaves to make a compress.

He didn't want to leave her, but bed sounded wonderful.

He was weary from little sleep the night before. He'd been given a blanket to roll out on the kitchen floor at Pencoed beside several other traveling servants whose masters had elected to stay the night. Then there was the day-long battle to keep from trying to kiss Gwen at every opportunity. On top of that, the emotional turmoil of recognizing Penrydd Castle, and his connection to it—how did he own a bloody castle, and come from a line of viscounts? And that was before Gap-tooth had dealt him a facer.

As he left, Dovey came into the kitchen, her eyes wide with alarm. Pen paused in the hallway, pricking his ears.

"Who beat him now?" Dovey whispered, feeding the stove to heat water.

"A pair of ruffians at the bridge, who appear to have been stowing away in the castle. I'll tell Mr. Stanley about it." A pause. "I think they admitted to attacking him before. One of them said they'd been hired."

A small gasp. "What if he thinks it was *us*?"

"He could. We have to find out what those men are doing. And who was behind the attack."

"Did you say anything?" Dovey said after a moment of silence. Pen pressed against the wall, holding his breath.

"I took him to Penrydd," Gwen said in a low voice. "Showed him the house."

"And he remembered?"

"He had some reaction to it. As if it seemed familiar. But he didn't say much."

"Then we don't know what he knows," Dovey said quietly.

"Dovey *bach*," Gwen said after another moment passed. Pen leaned in to hear over the steaming hiss of the kettle. "I know you want to let him remember—"

"Until we can come up with a good reason for—"

"But what if he's in danger here? What if those men are after him?"

There was a clatter, a brief pounding, then Dovey's voice, low and urgent. "What happened while you were away?"

"I kissed him. Again."

Pen reared back, surprised at the confession. He would have lied, himself. Surely Gwen was a great hand at lying. Her voice changed, became muffled. "We—danced. We talked. He's—"

Pen willed his heart to stop pounding in his ears so he might *hear*, damn it.

"Different," Gwen said finally. "Not the man I met at the tavern."

"He'll go right back to that when his memory returns," Dovey said.

"Will he? I wonder. Maybe it's best if we..."

Tell me. The inner voice had turned frantic. *Tell me everything!*

"Gwen." Dovey's voice was threaded with fear. "You said it yourself. There are dangerous men out there. If he turns us out, what happens to Cerys and me?"

"I'll take care of you," Gwen said. "I promise."

"How, dearling? You don't have any money either."

Utter silence fell in the kitchen. Pen peeked around the doorframe. Gwen stood at the table, wrapping a clump of wet leaves in a strip of linen. Dovey moved close and touched her arm.

"Can we wait a bit longer? At least until the men are gone and the danger is over. Cerys can't be out there alone. Not like this."

Gwen placed a hand over her friend's. "I'll wait," she said. "But if he is starting to remember..."

Dovey nodded and wiped the corner of one eye. "I know."

Gwen turned toward the door, and Pen leapt for the stairs to his room so he could pretend he'd been there all this time. He was wrestling with his waistcoat when Gwen rapped at the doorframe and walked in.

"A compress of comfrey for your face," she said. "Helps with swelling. Here, let me."

She handed him the small bundle of linen and he held it to his cheek. The warmth soothed, though his vision in that eye was already clouding.

"At least he clobbered me on the right side. Balancing things out, so to speak."

He willed his heart to calm as Gwen worked the buttons of his waistcoat and peeled it off him, then hung it next to his coat. He sat on the bed and kicked off his boots, but it hurt too much to bend over and take off his stockings. She knelt and dealt with them, making a pile of laundry that someone else would tend to, probably Widow Jones.

They might have been keeping his identity from him, but they'd tended to his basic needs. He'd remember that when the time of reckoning came. But his heart didn't slow with that realization. If anything, with Gwen's scent surrounding him, her soft hands on his face as she checked the compress, it beat all the faster.

"I'll take your shirt and work out the stains."

"Blood?" Pen said, holding out his arms as she lifted the shirt over his head.

"Not yours." She smiled. "You trounced him, Pen, and he was three stone heavier than you."

"Do you think he's the one who beat me before?"

Cool air tingled over his feverish skin, and he sat nearly naked before her. They were alone here in this narrow stone room, with the last light leaving the sky. It felt like they were wrapped in a secret, a world known only to them. Like the field of bluebells, save here was a bed he could draw her down upon.

Like that intoxicating dream of a dance, but with a door they could lock against the outside.

"We'll find out." She sat beside him, her eyes roaming his bare skin, looking for injuries. She lifted a finger and traced the scars webbing his left shoulder, chest, and ribs. "You seem better."

"I don't feel the pain from before." Somehow he knew that. Like she'd said, the connections were forming in his mind, deep, too slow for his patience, but all would be clear in time.

She lifted troubled eyes to his. He drank her in. "I'll make it right, Pen."

"You'll stay with me, then?" Because that would make everything right. He didn't even care if she would choose, even now, to use her body against him, as a forfeit or a trade, a distraction, or defense from all he might accuse her of. He didn't care how she came into his arms, only that she arrived there.

"Comfort?" Her voice was low, a note of sadness in it that didn't bode well for his chances of success. Her lashes feathered across her cheeks as she watched him rub, without conscious thought, his left thigh and the old wound there.

"Or reward," he suggested. "For my defending you so gallantly against those villains."

"I owe you much." She stood, and the air turned cold against his skin. "More than you know."

A confession? But of what? He waited, watching her face. Her throat worked as if she struggled to say something, but then she turned away, touching a hand to her brow as if in pain. "Rest," she said. "Call if you need me. I—"

But she didn't finish that thought, merely took his clothes and left him with the compress, his throbbing face, his other aches. His hollowness that couldn't be filled with anything other than her.

He threw himself back on the bed, deflated. He'd been this

low before, he told himself, and had come out of it. If only he could remember how. He cast his mind back to the castle, the painting, the house. If only he could remember the house.

HE REMEMBERED THE BEACH.

Admiral Jervis and his fleet had been savaged in their attack on Cádiz, so Jervis moved his attention to the harbor of Santa Cruz at Tenerife. If the British could capture the Spanish ships ferrying gold and treasure from the Americas, they could cut off Spanish aid to the French, Britain's enemies. This was the gist of their orders. The Canary Islands were plums ripe for the picking. It would be almost as much fun as sacking Spanish frigates in the West Indies.

The assembled force had been magnificent: Nelson leading with his flagship *Theseus,* Troubridge with *Culloden* and Hood sailing the *Zealous,* flanked by half a dozen frigates, hired cutters, and mortar boats. Pen had been assigned to his old friend Bowen on the *Terpsichore.* They were guaranteed success, and Spanish gold to divide between them.

The first attack was a disaster. They failed to take Valleseco, couldn't raise the guns high enough to fire on the Spanish fort. Nelson called back the gunboats and moved them down the coast. Pride was at stake, now that the Spanish had been warned.

They'd said the guns at San Cristóbal wouldn't reach that far. Or Troubridge and Hood, leading the land assault, would take the fort before they landed. They covered the oars in cloth and approached by night. It didn't help. They had no covering fire; he learned later the British gunpowder had been ruined with damp. Mortar fire from the fort lit up the sky, falling on the boats at the shore in brilliant rockets of flame. As the men poured onto the beach, the guns turned on them.

And hell exploded. With the dazzling bursts of flame and spark it was hard to see what was happening, but Pen heard screams as men were hit, ripped apart. It was like the fireworks at Vauxhall, he'd thought stupidly, watching the mortars cartwheel through the sky and rain down on them. Bodies fell about him as they rushed up the beach. These were his men, his friends, his comrades. Blood, bone, and gore erupted around him like carnival confetti. The air reeked of iron and powder and smoke.

He felt the thud in his leg and kept running. Bowen's men had been ordered to rush the battery and spike the guns. How had the Spanish known they were coming? Someone shouted that they were firing from the town, grapeshot pouring from houses and windows as the citizens took up their guns. Pen dropped his weapon as a huge claw sank into his chest and shoulder. A second claw followed, digging deep into his ribs, spinning him as he fell. The sand was cold and damp against his cheek. Wet. He knew it was his blood.

He couldn't cry out. The battle rage was upon him and he wanted to run, to fight, to move. But something heavy lay across his lower body, and his legs wouldn't work. His arms were useless. His mouth filled with the iron taste of blood. He lay on the beach and watched the fireworks wheel through the night sky as he grew weaker, lighter, and the sounds faded into the distance. He closed his eyes and waited for what came next.

"PEN."

There was light, a tiny candle, but light, pure and steady. "Pen?"

A woman's voice. Something damp on his brow, cool—not blood. A cloth. He clutched the hand. A woman's hand, fine-boned, delicate, the skin as soft as cream.

Bluebells. The beach smelled of bluebells. He was dead.

God, that was a relief. He wouldn't have to face the failure. To learn who had died, who had been torn apart, how many good men had been lost in the bloody hunt for treasure and glory.

"Wake up. It's another *hunllef*. A nightmare."

"I'm alive?"

He felt alive. Blood rushed through his body. His arms worked. So did his legs. A woman's form hovered above him—exposed to the guns and flames. She'd be shot and killed.

"Cover!" he shouted and pulled her down, rolling her under his body. She was warm and soft and yet at the same time delightfully firm, her body lithe and strong. And very shapely. He felt every line of it against his body. His alive, not bleeding, not maimed body.

"Pen!" Her muffled shout was a half-cry, half-laugh. One hand slapped his cheek, but gently. Her other arm snaked around him, her hand sliding over his back from waist to shoulder. He wasn't wearing a shirt and her soft, hot hand blazed a trail over his bare skin.

"You're at St. Sefin's."

Not Tenerife. He dropped his head into the crook of her shoulder, burying his face in her soft, warm, scented skin. He wasn't dead.

Bowen was dead. Nelson lost his arm, removed mid-battle so he didn't bleed out from his injury. Jervis had been made Earl of St. Vincent.

And he, Lieutenant Rhydian Price, had been recovering in a naval hospital when the black-edged letter came. His brother had caught pneumonia on a hunting trip to Scotland, some foolish dare to swim an icy Scottish loch. Not something the sensible Viscount Penrydd would do. So Rhydian was discharged to the house in London, limping, still swathed in bandages, his pain bone-deep and constant.

His sister Arwen was dead, too. The consumption had killed her in that awful sanitorium while he'd been playing buccaneer in the West Indies. His mother was long dead, buried in the lovely estate in Essex that she had brought to her marriage. His cold-eyed stepmother and his brother's helpless wife had been at the London townhouse to receive him. Edwin hadn't sired an heir, so Rhydian was now the Viscount Penrydd, fourth of that title. He owned the London townhouse, the estates in Essex and Cumbria, a hunting box in Scotland, a house and assorted properties in Wales. And all the obligations and duties of his grandfather, and his father, and now his brother had devolved upon him. Along with their debts.

There was a lot of debt. Something else the otherwise sensible 3rd Viscount Penrydd should never have dived into. Edwin was the heir, the sportsman, solid marks on his university exams, a pedigreed wife. Rhydian had always been knocked about by his father, his brother, his cousins, his own heedless exploits. He was the second son, an annoyance to his solid, competent, respectable brother. He was perpetually in a scrape, in a temper, or in trouble of some sort, living from one spree to another. Until he inherited the title, two viscountesses to support, the houses and estates. And Edwin's mistakes.

He'd come to Wales for something to do about that. Recent events were still hazy. He held still, breathing in the woman below him who lay supple but alert, waiting for him to collect himself. He'd needed to sell properties to pay money his brother owed. He'd never seen the Welsh holdings, so they could go. He'd met up with a friend from his Eton days, Turbeville, a worthless sot but a great deal of fun. There'd been another man he'd agreed to see, a knight's son who'd been sniffing around his brother's widow back in London. Prunella wouldn't wed again unless she could improve her station, but the knight had some property in Wales, so Pen thought to approach him as a buyer.

And then—something happened. He'd been hit over the head by bluebells.

"You're back?" Gwen whispered.

"I'm awake." He drew his nose along the line of her neck, then trailed kisses along her collarbone. She shivered. She was in her shift and wrap, hair in a loose braid. She smelled of night air and everything in the world that was pure and clean and lovely.

He couldn't remember why she had come to him. He didn't know why she hadn't told him who he was. He couldn't remember what he wanted in Wales, but he wanted Gwenllian ap Ewyas. More than he'd ever wanted anything in his life.

When she shifted, her legs parted slightly, and he slid his knee between hers. Her breath hitched.

"How do you feel?"

"I need something," he murmured. The skin of her shoulder tasted oh so faintly of rosemary. Soft. Delicious. Her hand moved over his back again, inching downward this time, fingers trailing soft fire along his shoulder blade, ribs, then down to the waistband of his breeches. He'd fallen asleep wearing them.

When was the last time a woman had caressed him? He couldn't remember that, either.

"Tea?" she whispered. "Another compress?"

He lifted his head to look in her face. Her eyes were enormous, shadowy pools. He didn't care that he was falling into them.

"You."

Her lips parted, and he swooped in and kissed her. She slid her other hand into his hair and held his head, kissing him back with a matching hunger. He dragged his hand from her shoulder down the side of her body and felt her hard nipple graze his palm. She was responding. She wanted him.

He groaned and kissed her more deeply, shifting his weight to the side so he didn't crush her, slipping his hand beneath her bottom to cradle her against him. He dipped his tongue into her mouth and she caught him, meeting his passion, his need. He drew from her mouth as if he could draw out the essence of what she was. The truth of what lay between them.

"Stay with me tonight." He nipped her earlobe, kissed down her neck and then back up her chin, pulling her lip between his teeth. His arousal rose between them and he barely restrained himself from pressing into her, urging her, begging. He wanted her to choose him. To come to him gladly, without artifice, without regret.

"What is this, Pen?" Her voice was throaty with desire.

"Whatever you want it to be," he said.

She'd lied to him. He was deceiving her, wanting to retain the upper hand for a moment when she'd had the advantage of him for so long. They were on equal ground, both liars. Both desirous. Both adults with no promises to another. There need be nothing more beyond this room, this night. He'd lived in a blank for weeks; he wanted that blank filled with Gwen. Whatever she offered, he would take it. Even if she was simply bartering her body for his goodwill. Even if loving her made him a fool.

"Let me up," she whispered.

He stifled a groan and closed his eyes, holding himself in as he rolled to his side and eased away from her. He wanted to shout, to rage. He was a viscount, for God's sake! He was rich—somewhat rich—and could have anything—most anything—he wanted. What would make her want him?

He watched in despair and hunger as she moved to the door,

the wrapper clinging to her delicious shape, the candlelight gleaming on her skin. She closed the door and turned to him.

Her gaze met his, steady. She was uncertain, but she wanted him. She wasn't afraid, and she wasn't ashamed.

He held out his hand, letting his hunger, his need, and a promise show in his eyes.

She came back to the bed and finally, finally, into his arms.

CHAPTER THIRTEEN

"Tell Mr. Pen to hold still, or I'll get his hair crooked," said Cerys, waving her shears.

Pen, sitting with a towel around his shoulders, widened his eyes at Gwen. "Tell Miss Cerys I'm here for the barbering, not the surgery."

With a look of intense concentration, Cerys pulled Pen's wet hair straight with her comb and, at her mother's direction, made a few careful snips. Gwen smiled and turned back to the scullery sink, where she was washing the equipment to make a batch of small beer. Watching Pen move about St. Sefin's like he belonged among them made her heart feel as if it were being squeezed into a bottle.

Since their first night together, her days—a week? Nearly two?—had been filled with stolen kisses, whispered promises, caresses snatched in passing when they thought no one else might see. She slipped into Pen's room each night and woke each morning entwined with his naked body, heavy and satisfied, more alive than she'd ever felt. They orbited in a strange limbo, a dreamworld of passion in the dark, and in the daylight hours they fell into a growing rhythm of companionship, a connection deeper than anything she'd ever shared with a man. The cold truth hovered around them, waiting to snap shut its ruthless jaws, but she'd shut her eyes against it like a child safe from monsters as long as she didn't see.

"Cyw hungry," Tomos announced, kicking his boots against the doorframe to shed them of mud.

He entered the kitchen carrying Pen's latest addition to their community, a chicken. Pen had engaged Gossett to improve his fighting skills, and Mrs. Gossett, who hadn't sported a black eye in weeks because her husband had other places to spend his energies, had gifted Pen the poultry, a game fowl that Gwen suspected had been retired from Gossett's cock-fighting brood.

Tomos took immediate charge of the creature and named it the Cymric word for chick. When the thing wasn't clucking, scratching, or diving beneath one's boots for a bug or worm, Cyw was content to be carried about by Tomos like a fat feathered infant or minor god. Tomos's glee over his pet was as enormous as Gwen's joy in her stolen time with Penrydd, and they were both, she feared, in for eventual heartbreak.

"And here's licorice." Mathry entered, shaking dew from her shawl and holding up a basket full of slender brown sticks.

"Licorice! How is it you have licorice?" Pen started from his seat and earned an immediate reproof from Cerys.

Mathry sauntered his way, a hand curving over the tiny bump of her belly. In the past few days she'd quickened and had settled into making infant clothes like a woman on a mission. She pitched in to help with a new zeal, was pestering Gwen to teach her herb lore, and moreover had dropped her flirtatious manner toward Pen.

Gwen wondered how much Mathry or any of the others knew of what was developing between her and Pen. Even the sound sleepers must notice how he took every opportunity to be near her. And how she melted with delight each time he did.

What *was* developing between them? She didn't know what to call it. His kiss made her forget where she was. His touch made her body feel as if music sang through her veins. She craved him and couldn't get enough.

"A priest brought licorice plants to St. Sefin's from Turkey during the Crusades." Gwen busied herself with her task so she didn't stand there gaping at Pen with that broad, foolish smile. "Or so the legend goes. Cerys never found the treasure, but she found the old records of the priory bundled in an altar cloth and stuffed in a trunk in the abbess's rooms. It's been growing wild for a long time, but good enough for all that."

Pen bit into a licorice root, and Gwen stared too long at his straight teeth, the flicker of muscle in his firm square jaw, the pleasure on his face. She was going soft in the head. Licorice was a feeble return for what she'd done to him. Was doing.

"My turn for a trim?" Ifor stepped into the kitchen with Gafr on his lead and a boy near his age behind him. "Here's a lad from Greenfield to see you, Miss Gwen."

"*Bore da,* Gareth," Mathry said with surprise. "Is everyone well?"

"You're all right, that's clear," the boy said with a bold grin. Then his eyes flickered over Pen and he ducked his head in instinctive deference. Gwen's throat closed before she realized Pen hadn't been to Greenfield and the servants there wouldn't know him.

She wasn't ready to lose him. She'd agreed to keep up the ruse, telling herself it was for Dovey's sake, that she still needed to win him to the cause of St. Sefin's and persuade him to let them stay. But the truth was that, like a greedy harlot, she wanted her hands on him every minute, and she didn't want to give him up.

She'd have to. She knew that. But since he appeared to be in no hurry to reclaim his memory, even after seeing his estate, she saw no reason to rush him out the door. Not when she could spend one more night, one more day with him.

"They want you at Greenfield for dinner tonight, Miss Gwen." The messenger boy sat at the table next to Ifor, who pulled a steaming plate of cakes their way and offered him one.

Gwen spoke above the sudden roaring in her ears. "They can't want me to harp."

Gareth licked a finger. "They've guests from Llanfyllin and want you to dine with them. A fancy pair, they are."

The prickle along her neck told Gwen that every eye in the large kitchen was fixed on her. She felt Pen's stare like the heat of full sun in summer.

Dovey swooped in, scolding the boys as she slid the plate away from Ifor's nimble fingers. "My *picau ar y Maen*, is it! I made those cakes for Mr. Evans and Mr. Pen to take to town today, and if you eat them all, then you feed two hungry men when they return."

Gwen kept her voice level, despite the wild skitter of her heart. "Lady Vaughn can't pay me enough to return to Greenfield. I've no interest in meeting her guests."

"None?" Dovey questioned. They still needed money, after all, to buy St. Sefin's from Pen.

Gwen shook her head. Calvin Vaughn would leer at her. She couldn't bear facing Anne after all that had happened. And if Anne's brother had come with her—

"No." She struggled for air.

Gareth sighed. "Mr. Vaughn won't like that answer," he said.

"Calvin Vaughn knows why it's a no." Gwen reddened and dragged a brace of bottles towards her.

Mathry slid her basket onto the table. "Ah, Gwen *bach*. Did he—?"

"Tried to put a slip on your shoulder, didn't he?" Pen ducked out from beneath Cerys's shears and shook off the towel, ignoring her outcry. In two long strides he came to the sink to Gwen's side and with a warm finger under her chin turned her face toward him. His brows lowered as he read her expression.

"I knew he was a dirty dish," he swore softly.

Alarm rose from the rush of soupy heat that filled her at his touch. "How did you know?"

"Er—gathered. From Mathry's tale of woe." He dropped his fingers from her chin and ran a hand through his damp hair. She wanted to take his hand and draw it back to her face. She wanted to put both his arms around her and lean into him like he could be the only thing she needed, the pillar that held up her world.

"What's a slip on the shoulder?" Cerys asked.

"Nothing you'll let a man give you, *pwt*," Dovey said. "All right, Tomos, take a seat."

"Who're the grand folk that want Gwen?" Mathry asked.

Gwen flinched. She'd tried so hard to run from her past, and now the shadows were reaching out to swallow her. How had they found her, after all this time? And what did they want with her now? It couldn't be to make amends. The time for that was long past.

"Vaughn thinks to marry Anne Sutton," Gwen said, eyes on her task. "That's the girl I was companion to before her family turned me off. Can you believe the cursed luck? Of all the families in Wales, he's settled on her."

"The gentry world's a small world, and the great world smaller still." Pen said this as if he knew the great world, and alarm prickled Gwen's scalp.

"Does she know of Mr. Vaughn's reputation around here?"

Dovey draped the cloth around Tomos's neck as he settled in Cerys's chair.

Gwen's shoulders slumped, and Pen lifted a hand to rub the back of her neck, loosening the knot of tension. She sighed and leaned into his warm, strong fingers. Those clever, clever fingers had been on every part of her body, mapped every inch of her, and yet this small, intimate touch was just as thrilling.

"She deserves to know," Gwen said. "But she might have to marry him just the same. I'll wager her parents decided the match, and Anne would never go against them."

Men of means were not expected to limit their affections. The higher the class of man, the more businesslike his marriage. His wife provided pedigreed heirs, and he searched elsewhere for pleasure. Her throat ached and she reached unthinkingly for the water heating over the stove. She forgot to wrap her hand with a cloth and cried out when the searing pain registered. Stifling a curse at her stupidity, she crammed her scalded fingers in her mouth.

Pen would expect a similar arrangement in his marriage. He wouldn't marry a girl from the Welsh hills. Though he might offer to make one his mistress.

Pen tugged her hand from her mouth and examined the reddened tips. "Shall I call Vaughn out and maim him for you? Geld him, perhaps."

Dueling was illegal, and only gentlemen had the right to call each other out in a supposed matter of honor. Rougher men used their fists to settle an insult. Was Pen remembering he was a gentleman?

But why would he remain here with them, if that were the case? A rush of helpless longing weakened her knees as he kissed her burned fingertips.

"You're not still soft on him, I hope?" Pen growled.

She knew he wasn't speaking of Vaughn. "I've no wish to see him again. Ever."

"Good." Pen moved closer and she shivered as the warmth of his nearness teased her skin. He smelled like freshly turned earth and a hint of honey. "I've been trying to blot him entirely from your mind," he whispered beside her ear.

His breath wafted across her neck, stirring the delicate hairs, and the flare of awareness plunged through her body, lighting an instant sliver of heat between her legs. St. Meleri's marrow, how could he enflame her with a mere whisper? Was she that desperate for the touch of a man?

Not just any man. This one.

She turned toward him like a flower unfurling in the sun. The unholy gleam in his hazelnut eyes said he knew he'd aroused her, exactly as intended. The man played her body as confidently as she strummed her harp, and she thrilled to his handling. He knew how to satiate them both, and each night he feasted on her sighs and tremors as if her satisfaction heightened his.

No need to tell him the pleasure they found together far surpassed anything of her experience. Or that he was quickly erasing the possibility that she could ever want anyone else.

"Perhaps a bit more blotting is called for," she murmured.

She smiled as his eyes narrowed and he gripped her waist with a warm, heavy hand, thumb brushing her ribs. "As much as it takes," he said, his voice a low rasp.

Evans thumped into the room, and Gwen broke free of the spell. Her head had been moving toward Pen's, mouth tipped up to invite a kiss, in front of nearly every person she knew in the world. St. Teilo's teeth, what had come over her? Did she want everyone to know she was tupping the man who held all their fates in his hands?

Pen's hand fell from her waist and cool air rushed in when

he stepped away. She barely heard what she said in farewell as the men took their leave, Gareth with them.

Dovey watched her, one hand on her hip, wooden spoon raised in the air. Her eyes bore lines of strain and worry.

"What are you about, dearie?" she whispered as the others shuffled off to their tasks.

Gwen turned to the stove, cheeks burning. "It's not to barter with him, much as it might appear," she said. "And it's nothing to do with his earlier offer, either. What it is, is—"

A torrential passion that had upended her world. Like the merfolk of legend he'd called to her and she'd followed, the foolish maiden risking her future and her life for the sheer bliss of being desired by him.

"I fancy him, is all," she said lamely.

"Fancy," Dovey said. She popped a licorice stick in her mouth and chewed.

"Well, I can't say I blame you a bit." Mathry took the basket of licorice root into the stillroom. "He is a lush one, though I take a fright when he gets all lordly."

But he didn't belong to her, and he wouldn't stay in her world. Gwen knew this as she collected her bottles. *She* was the mermaid, stealing him from his life. And keeping him because she loved who she became in his arms, a woman confident, capable, desirable. With Pen she wasn't spoiled by betrayal or broken by loss. With him, she was whole.

The dream wouldn't last. No dreams did, not even for those more deserving than she.

GWEN HEARD the delicate footsteps first, then saw the woman's shadow fall over the hard-packed dirt. That was all the warning she had. Her heart dropped into her belly, though she couldn't see the figure framed in the doorway of the brewhouse, outlined in shadow by the afternoon sun, the blooming dogwood on one side and the crimson rhododendron on the other.

"Gwenllian! Is it really you? I thought I'd never see you again."

The woman's soft voice held the cultured accent of the upper-class English. The stick Gwen was using to stir the vat of malt slipped through suddenly nerveless fingers.

"Anne." Her voice scraped through a throat gone dry. "You ought to have come to the front door."

"I knocked. No one answered."

Anne Sutton of Vine Court, and she had found Gwen in the outbuildings, cap discarded and shawl tied up, sweating like a scullery maid.

No. Working in good faith to tend the home she had built with her own two hands. Why did she fear Anne Sutton was here to take everything away from her? Again?

Gwen wiped her hands on her shawl. She had abandoned her friend along with everything else when she left Vine Court all those years ago. Anne might have believed what her parents told her, that Gwen was a grasping orphan who had tried to seduce, then trick Daron into marriage, and had been turned out on her conniving ear.

"Come into the kitchen," Gwen finally managed to say. "There's *bara brith* for tea."

Anne Sutton was accustomed to fine tea in formal parlors served from dainty porcelain dishes, and Gwen smelled like beer malt and sweat. Even so, Anne untied the ribbons of her bonnet and seated herself at the huge oaken worktable in the kitchen as if she'd come to tea at St. Sefin's every day of her life.

Dovey barreled in from the hallway. "Gwen, there's a *Sais* at the—" She faltered and drew up short.

"Hello," Anne said coolly.

The timid girl Gwen had known was now a calm, self-possessed young woman. She'd be four-and-twenty, one year younger than Gwen. A surprise she wasn't already married. Had her family hoped for higher and had to settle for Calvin Vaughn?

"Anne, this is Mrs. Van der Welle, widow of Lieutenant Jan Van der Welle of the Dutch Royal Navy. Dovey, this is Miss Anne Sutton, daughter of the Suttons of Llanfyllin."

Dovey curtsied, her face a mask of exquisite politeness. "And this is Cerys, Dovey's daughter," Gwen added as Cerys, peering from behind her mother's skirts, gazed wide-eyed at the grand lady. "Dovey is my friend and partner in running St. Sefin's."

"Yes, I'd heard the Vaughns' housekeeper say you ran a house of refuge for the indigent." A smile floated over Anne's lips. "How like you to take up charity, Gwen."

"It turned out a good fit for my talents, since my plans for marriage didn't unfold as anticipated."

Now where had that bitterness come from? It wasn't Anne's fault Gwen had been turned out and forced to birth a stillborn daughter in a sty in the middle of winter. No, her brother was solely to blame for that debacle. Gwen would not ask about him. It was shock enough that Anne had come here, that she could so easily stir the old hurt Gwen thought she had long set aside.

And why was Anne here? What could she want?

Gwen pulled down the tin with the good tea, the kind they purchased rather than making up with their own cuttings. She nearly dropped the precious leaves all over the floor at Anne's next words.

"We didn't know what else to do when you turned down our invitation to dinner. Daron and Mr. Vaughn will return as soon as they've completed their errands in town. My brother is wild to see you again."

Daron. Here. The man she'd given her body to, who had

planted a child within her, then left both her and the babe to freeze in the Welsh winter.

"I thought your brother didn't want anything to do with me." Gwen forced the words through a throat gone hot and tight.

"Gwen." Anne's voice was gentle, full of sorrow. "My family treated you abominably. I regret what my parents did to you."

Gwen's hands moved like thick clumps of clay she couldn't control. Against her will she knocked one of their precious jasperware teacups to the floor. The bowl shattered, pieces falling apart like petals of a flower past its blooming.

"Your parents behaved as might be expected, considering they would feel the girl they had taken in and nurtured betrayed their trust." Gwen knelt to pick up the china shards and hissed as a sharp edge sliced her finger. "Your brother, on the other hand..."

Dovey nudged her aside and cleared the broken pieces, handing Gwen a cloth. Cerys swung the kettle over the fire, warming water for tea. Gwen wrapped her cut finger, trying to calm her galloping pulse.

Anne's mouth twisted. "I believe he promised to marry you."

"That, and more." Gwen sank into a chair across from her former friend, this girl who had once been as dear as a sister. Anne's buttery blonde hair was piled in a smooth braided chignon atop her head, with perfect curls hanging at her brows and temple. Her skin was as pale as skimmed cream. Gwen guessed that her high-waisted muslin gown, with the ruff of lace at the jacket-shaped bodice and embroidered hem, was the latest London fashion.

"But I thought there was a—?" Anne moved her gloved hand in a delicate motion around her middle, her eyes cutting to Cerys.

"Didn't survive," Gwen said, throwing up the wall in her mind against that old agony. Even now, the memory hurt.

Anne relaxed. "That's a relief."

Dovey whirled, her yelp of surprise matching Gwen's. "What?"

"I only meant—" Anne's cornflower-blue eyes widened. "It will make things easier. There will be no explanations that need be made when you marry. We will simply say you were parted, but have been faithful to my brother all this time." She raised a pale eyebrow. "Might we?"

Gwen stared. "Faithful," she echoed. An image swirled to mind of her entwined with Pen in his bed, moist and gasping.

"For that's why we've come, of course," Anne went on. "So Daron might offer his hand and make good his promise. Finally."

Gwen reeled in her chair. "Did your parents die?" she blurted.

"No." Anne winced. "Though your father passed. You did not know? I am very sorry."

Blood throbbed in Gwen's finger and her head. Her father, dead. But he had been lost to her long ago.

"His widow wouldn't know where to find me, to tell me," she murmured.

"Well, I am happy we found you at last." Anne reached her small gloved hand across the table. "Gwen. Everything can be better now."

"Better how?" Daron had simply changed his mind, and she was expected to come to his hand like a pony eager for the treat long denied her? She stared at Anne, at the woman she'd matured into from the meek, dainty girl. Anne represented the life that had ended for her when Gwen received Daron Sutton's scrawled note that he was marrying another. Ruined, penniless, as good as orphaned and carrying a child, she'd been cast whole-sale from polite society, Anne's world.

Pen's world.

Not her world. Not any longer. There was no going back.

Anne watched her, eyes wide with innocence. As if Gwen could simply step away from her new life back into the old one. As if there wasn't a chasm between them large enough to bury her.

"Daron wants to marry me?" Gwen repeated.

"That is my greatest hope," Daron Sutton said.

He stepped through the door leading outside, entering the kitchen as if he owned the place. Dovey and Cerys grew as still as the air before a storm whirled up from the bay.

Gwen gaped. He wasn't as tall as she remembered. He wore a bright blue coat of superfine tightly fitted about his broad chest and middle. His pale blond hair swept forward over his cheeks and brow. His deep-set eyes looked smaller than she remembered, his nose larger. His lips still had their childish, Cupid's bow shape, but his jawline had grown soft and fleshy.

Nothing remained of the boy she'd wildly adored, who had so excited her with his whispers and touches that she'd snuck off to the castle ruins at the edge of his property and let him plow her in the grass as if she were a dairy maid. His face registered surprise, a hint of shock he quickly hid, and then a gleam of approval, even satisfaction, as if he recalled those stolen moments, too.

But he didn't raise a flicker of excitement in her. Not anymore.

"Daron," Anne said, "Gwen doesn't know that her father—"

"Our condolences, I'm sure." Daron swept her a courtly bow, then reached for Gwen's hand. She leaped to her feet, wild with the urge to escape.

"Gwen, darling." His voice boomed. "Caught you off your

guard, I see. But surely Anne told you why we came?"

"She said you wanted to see me." Her words came high and thin. Dovey stood behind her. She had allies. She was on her own turf. He had no power to cast her out—not here. "I cannot imagine why."

"This is your welcome for old friends? Gwen. My soul." He bent to one knee, quite prettily, though his waistcoat strained across his middle as he reached out to grasp her hands in his. The Suttons' English cook had been feeding him well. "I've come to fulfil my vow at long last. You must forgive me for how long it took."

"I thought you married someone else." She felt as if she'd lost too much blood, dizzy, heart pounding, though the cut on her finger was but a scratch. He'd sent the note. She'd read it. He was to marry a coal mine owner's daughter, one with more money than Gwen would ever see in her life.

He pouted, his lips thin and sulky—had they always been so? Nothing like Pen's firm, well-shaped lips, full and yet somehow masculine. Pen's nose was assertive but not nearly so heavy, and the lines of Pen's jaw were etched as firm and clear as dressed stone. Pen's eyes had a mischievous slant. Daron's eyes were round and childlike, his lashes so pale his lids shone through them. His hands were sweaty without his gloves.

"I was—mistaken in her," Sutton said. "Gwen! You can't imagine the agonies I've endured without you. How could you leave without word?"

"How could I?" Gwen pulled her hands from his and went to the fire, taking a cloth to wrap about the handle of the hissing kettle. She felt like that, boiling and ready to scream.

Sutton lurched to his feet and cleared his throat. "As to the matter of the—little stranger that, er, was of some concern to us—"

She waited, against her will wanting to hear what he would

say about the babe he had denied.

Anne came to his rescue. "Not an issue," she said.

Sutton relaxed. "Then all is well!" he said heartily. "Where should we have the banns read—your parish or mine? I imagine there will be many improvements you wish to make to Vine Court, and I for one—"

"I'm good enough for Vine Court now, am I?" Gwen asked. The hot water seethed as she filled the teapot. "What changed your mother's mind?"

"Oh. Er. You see..." Sutton glanced at Anne. Her delicate brow furrowed. "Ah, well, the mater has come round," he said. "Persuaded of my affections, and all that."

"I see," Gwen said. "Your affections have persisted all this time? And you suppose I've likewise been biding here, waiting to marry you, all this time."

Cerys sucked in a breath and fisted a hand in her mother's skirts. The remaining teacups trembled as Dovey set them in a line.

"Well, no one else'll have you!" Sutton blurted. "Ruined as you are."

Gwen stared at him. He dared come here, after *years* of silence, and presume she would tumble happily into his arms? Without even an apology for the way he'd destroyed her life, without the least effort?

She had the fleeting and unworthy wish that she'd worn a gown more fitting for such a dramatic moment. She'd dreamed of this reunion, in those first early dark and hopeless nights. She'd dreamed Anne Sutton would seek her out, weeping and penitent about her parents' cruelty. A hundred times she'd imagined Daron Sutton crawling back, begging for forgiveness, a return of her love. And here she stood in her worn flannel gown, her much-used woolen shawl, her hair straggling free of its ribbon like Medusa's snakes.

"Can't see why you refuse me. Me!" Daron looked truly surprised.

"You cannot?" Her voice strangled in her throat. "Past circumstances aside, I have nothing to offer you. I have no dowry. No property. No family, not any longer. What possible interest could you have in me?"

Anne stirred. "Gwen, dear, your father—"

"Not now, pet," Sutton said. He advanced toward Gwen with a fulsome smile. She held the teapot before her as a shield.

"Rushed my fences, I see!" he exclaimed. "Too much, too soon. Of course, you're overwhelmed. Take a day or two to consider, Gwen, but I know what your answer must be. You gave your heart and your troth to me long ago, and I have come to claim them." He placed a pale, fleshy hand on his embroidered waistcoat beneath the elaborate cravat.

Gwen glanced at Dovey. Her friend clutched Cerys's hands, her face brave and resolute. At Gwen's look she briefly nodded, as if giving her permission to depart.

The longings Gwen thought dead and buried stirred in the ash of her old sorrows. This was the fantasy that had sustained her through many lonely years. Daron before her. Asking her to be his wife. Offering her a home.

Vine Court was a beautiful place, and she would be its mistress. She liked Llanfyllin, a market town nestled on a river near the foot of the mountains. People would know her yet, though it had been eight years since she left. There were other great houses nearby that could offer her society, and she would be considered a gentlewoman. She would be safe. Supported.

She would not have children to raise, not with the damage the previous birth had done to her womb. And Daron would be her husband, the boy who had pleasured himself with her body in tall grasses and dark halls, moaning desperate vows that came to nothing when his family intervened. He would be a husband who followed his whims wherever they led and he would expect to be obeyed.

She would have his name, but, she suspected, not much else. And for that, for Vine Court, she would give up the home she'd built here with Dovey and the others. She would give up her freedom to carry her basket around town upon her own business. He might ask her to give up harping.

And she would have to give up Pen.

Pen wasn't hers anyway. She stifled a bolt of pain at the thought. She was stealing him and would have to give him back eventually. But in his embrace she had healed at last of the wound dealt her soul when she was cast out of her former life. With Pen she was desired, adored. Cherished. He was her match in passion, in intellect, in determination. And in him she had found a man of wit and humor, a man who had himself struggled to heal, and who had learned self-awareness as well as compassion for others. He had changed.

Daron Sutton was simply an older version of the boy he'd been, petulant, self-interested, glib of tongue and shallow of nature. Daron Sutton and Vine Court were not what she wanted, not any longer.

Penrydd was the man she wished she could have. Pen and St. Sefin's and her life with her people here, even though she knew one or all would be taken away from her. She couldn't have Pen any more than she could have had Daron, all those years ago.

A sudden grief surged through her breast, climbing her throat in a choking wave. She had to escape before any of them saw her tears.

"I'm afraid I must decline the great honor of your hand, Mr. Sutton," she said, clinging to the last shred of her self-control. "I—"

She rushed from the room.

CHAPTER FOURTEEN

She thought Dovey might pursue her, or Daron, to press his incredible suit. But it was Anne who found Gwen in the brewhouse, poking the vat of mash with her stick.

"After all this time." Gwen stabbed at the thick, lumpy liquid and wiped tears from her cheeks. "For him to find me—to tell me—to think that I—" She stared at Anne, groping for words. "Why?"

Anne withdrew a delicate handkerchief and rubbed the lid of an upturned cask before she sat upon it, arranging her muslin skirts about her legs. Then she sighed.

"We haven't any money."

Gwen pushed a dank lock of hair away from her face. "Your parents have wealth enough and more."

Anne stared into the distance. Outside the small enclosure, grey clouds inched up from the Severn, slowly overtaking the watery spring sun.

"It's gone. My father made poor investments, then borrowed to recoup his losses. Then he was voted out as magistrate, so he couldn't collect fees from that anymore. About a year ago he put every last farthing into a shipping venture to the West Indies."

Anne swallowed, her slender throat tensing. "The ship was seized by buccaneers and the cargo was lost. He had a tiny insurance settlement that we've been living on. But if we don't marry well, Daron and I, we'll be paupers."

She stared at Gwen, her eyes a shimmering blue. Gwen rubbed her brow with a knuckle, the reek of yeast puckering her nose.

"Surely the Vaughns will help you once you marry." She could understand, if not appreciate, Anne's dilemma. Gently reared, she had always had money, and now that the money was gone, she must cast about for someone to replenish her funds and take charge of her. It would not occur to people like the Suttons to make do with less, or to earn their own keep.

Anne bit her lip. "Mr. Vaughn won't have me unless my parents can furnish the dowry he was promised. And Sir Lambert has said he won't support my parents. They'll never agree to support you and Daron, too."

Gwen stirred the heavy liquid, poking at the bubbles. "What happened to the girl Daron told me he would marry?" The baronet's daughter he'd left her for. The reason he would acknowledge neither her nor her babe.

Anne shook her head. The silk ribbon on her bonnet fluttered. "She ran off with her Italian dancing master a few months after you left us. My father sued hers for breach of promise, but the money wasn't much and Daron soon spent it."

"So find another rich heiress. Surely there are a few about."

Anne hesitated. "There are, but—"

But why would a family bestow its richly endowed daughter on mere gentry when she could fetch a much higher rank? Gwen would not have been Daron Sutton's first choice, not ever. She could no longer tell if the moisture on her face was from sweat or tears.

"I haven't any money either, despite how it looks. St. Sefin's doesn't belong to me. We bring in barely enough income to support ourselves. And I need money myself so I can buy the priory from—"

"Gwen!" Anne blinked in surprise. "Don't you know your father left you everything?"

Gwen swiped at her stirring stick as it slipped from her grasp again. "Everything of what?" she asked.

"Come over here and sit down," Anne said.

Gwen sat and listened, but she didn't comprehend. She knew the property she grew up on, her father's land, held a small mine. Her mother had warned Gwen away from the mining camp with its many dangers and rough-mannered workers, male and female alike.

But now she learned that, shortly after her mother died and Gwen was sent to live with the Suttons, her father discovered new veins of lead-silver on his property. Then he married the widow of a rich landowner and found deposits of copper on his wife's land. The new mines made him rich, and when he supplied the British Navy with copper to plate the hulls of their warships, King George made him a knight.

And so her father, born a Welsh farmer, had died Sir David Carew, the cross of his order buried with him. And excepting the jointure due to the twice-widowed Lady Carew, he had bequeathed both his estates, with their farms and mines and houses and rich yields of ore, to his only surviving issue, Gwenllian.

His solicitors had followed Gwen to the Suttons, and the Suttons had come in search.

She needed air. She needed to move. Gwen stood and lunged outside, stepping into the courtyard just as Daron Sutton emerged from the kitchen. He gave her a confident smile and swaggered toward her. He cut a gentlemanly figure in his tailored coat and snug-fitting breeches. But he was a dumpling compared to Pen.

Even now, when she thought his betrayal laid to rest, Gwen's chest hurt to know the only reason Daron could want her was mercenary. He wasn't overcome with remorse or yearning for their long-ago, childish infatuation. No, it was a different self-interest. He needed a wife with money, and how could Gwen refuse him, ruined as she was? Rich merchants might lock up their virginal daughters, but Gwen's honor could be repaired if she married, and the Sutton fortunes could be repaired with her mines.

Pen, at least, had wanted her for herself. A warm weight in his bed to keep the nightmares away, but there was something more honest in being wanted for her body than for her supposed inheritance.

Losing Pen was going to hurt her far more deeply than losing Daron ever had. Gwen knew that with a sudden flash as if the sun had broken through the grey press of clouds. Losing her lover and her child had so scarred her heart that she feared she might never care for another again. But she'd dared take that risk, to open her heart again. And now she knew that Pen's leaving would bring her to her knees.

"Fair Gwenllian!" Daron attempted a bow, but his coat was too tight to allow much movement. "Has Anne finally persuaded you to be my bride? You will make us both very happy."

"Gah! Get off, you stupid beast!" Calvin Vaughn's voice startled them all. Gwen looked about for a place to bolt, recalling her last interaction with this man.

"Ass of a goat! I'll have it in stew."

Vaughn stomped into the courtyard. His scowl changed to calculation as he took in the tableau: Anne regal and pretty in her pale gown, Daron hovering, and Gwen with her grey flannel worn and dusty, her woolen shawl in need of a wash, her hair a frightening tangle from being tossed about all day by the wind. Medusa indeed, facing down another cocky warrior come to cut off her head.

Vaughn's smile turned sly. "All wrapped up, then? Celebration in order?"

"Gwen has not yet accepted my hand." Daron gave her a reproachful look, tapping his hat against one plump thigh.

"What could Miss Ewyas be holding out for?" Vaughn sneered. "She won't get a better offer than you, Sutton."

"Ewyas?" Anne fumbled with the Welsh pronunciation.

At the sound of her chosen name, the muddle in Gwen's head shifted and fell apart. After years of isolation and loneliness, she had awakened that morning in the arms of a man who handled her as if she were a bolt of precious silk or a thread of priceless saffron. She didn't owe Daron Sutton anything.

Her past did not define her. She wouldn't allow it.

"Not get a better offer?" Gwen heaped a false sweetness into her voice. Sutton and Vaughn both owed her an apology that she would never hear. "I receive offers all the time. If I recall, you yourself, Mr. Vaughn, ardently expressed your admiration for me the last time I was at Greenfield."

Anne frowned. "What do you mean?"

Daron sputtered. "Vaughn! Care to explain?"

"Ah. Ger." Vaughn's pasty face turned a brilliant red. "Misunderstanding! She's telling bouncers. What can you expect of a female." He swung on his friend. "Have it done with, will you, Sutton? I want to be free of this shithole before that blasted goat eats my boot."

"Gwen," Daron began with a flourish of his hat. "My soul."

But Gwen was done with the charade. "Let me understand," she said, pressing the rage from her voice, clinging to calm. Had she ever cared for this man, this petulant child who assumed all should bow to him? How had she been so foolish as to believe his promises?

"You wooed me when I lived under your roof with declarations of love and marriage," she said. "Then, when I fell pregnant, you let your family turn me out of the house. You left me to give birth alone, and the child died because I had no help. I came here starving, destitute, ready for death because neither you nor my father would have ought to do with me." The rage swept through her, fast and searing.

"And now, because you believe me heir to my father's holdings, and because no other match is available, you think to come here and ask for my hand? Or rather, command it, as if I am yours to bid."

She advanced on Daron and he stepped back, eyes wide with alarm. She thought she'd moved past this wish to shriek at him for his betrayal and abandonment, but here it came roaring up from the deep, like the mythical Welsh dragon of Merlin's prophecy uncovered in the hill.

"What it is, Daron Sutton, is I will never give you my hand. I will never forgive what you did to me. I will never entrust my future to a man like you." Gwen dug her nails into her palms, using the nip of pain to hold back tears. She turned to Anne. "You needn't marry if you don't wish it, Anne. You may come here and we will take you in."

A wild thought kindled behind the rage, burning bright. If her father had in his guilt or desperation found no other heir, if she gained from his death the merest pittance, she might use whatever she had to buy St. Sefin's from Pen, free and clear.

All could be settled between them. She could find what lay between them once her lies were at an end.

Daron curled his lip in distaste, regarding her as he would a poisonous viper. He snapped his fingers at his sister. "Come, Anne! We won't stay and listen to this vicious diatribe. If this person has no sense of the honor I do her in offering her my hand, I won't stay to importune her. Vaughn?"

Daron hastened toward the carriage standing in the drive. Anne wavered with indecision. Vaughn glared at Gwen, his pale eyes glittering with malice.

"You fool," he spat. "You stupid tart, so high and mighty. Your mines could keep both our families plush in the pocket if you weren't so selfish." His thin lip curled, and the glint in his eyes turned to lust. "What are you holding out for, then? Want my hand instead of Sutton's? Leave him and his puling sister in the cold. He's got nothing, but I'm son to a knight. Bit more tempting, is that?"

He moved closer, and with a sick rush Gwen remembered the press of his fleshy body against hers in the shrubbery, his slobbering lips, his member probing at her hip. She shuddered with revulsion.

"I'd rather you kill me before you try to mount me again, *drewgi*."

Red blotches sprouted on his pale face. "Mind your manners, you filthy trollop. You don't know what I could do to you. Bring evidence to the magistrate that you're running a disorderly house. Strip you of everything and see you locked in the bridewell besides."

Gwen lifted her chin and hid her shaking hands in her shawl. "There is no evidence. You have no case."

"Don't I?" He thrust his face near hers, spittle flying from his lips. "Whole town knows you're an odd lot. Wouldn't take much to convince a justice you're running a brothel of some sort. Men coming in and out of here all the time."

"What men?" Evans asked.

He stood in a gap between the outbuildings and the tall back of the priory. He leaned on his cane and held a sack slung over his shoulder from which emanated the distinct smell of fish. Pen, as if remembering Barlow's scorn, stepped behind Evans and pulled down the brim of his woolen cap, hiding his face.

Gwen's stomach dropped into her old worn boots. This was the end. Pen would recognize Vaughn, or any moment Vaughn would look at Pen. She'd wanted the lies to end, hadn't she? But not like this. Not so soon. She steeled herself for the killing blow.

"Miss Gwen?" Evans searched Gwen's face. Then he looked to Dovey, who had come out of the kitchen without Gwen noticing. "Mrs. Van der Welle," he said gently. "Is everything all right?"

"We had guests for tea," Dovey said. Her expression was taut, her cheekbones standing out as she clenched her teeth. "Friends of Gwen's."

Gwen held back a sob of breath. Dovey stood to lose everything, too. When Pen recovered his memory. If Vaughn made good on his threats.

"We're leaving." Vaughn's pale, watery eyes flicked over Evans, then passed with the same contempt over Pen, who studied the ground as if watching for snakes. "Tea at Greenfield tomorrow, Gwenllian, and we'll settle this proper," Vaughn said. "Mayhap my intended can remind you how to behave like a lady." He extended an elbow to Anne.

Anne glanced at Dovey, then Gwen. A wistful expression crossed her face. "I'd like to be sisters again, Gwen," she said softly, and took Vaughn's arm.

They headed for the carriage. The moment they left, Pen lifted his face. Gwen froze at his expression, as flat as stone and as unreadable. He dropped his own sack, and the top burst open to reveal the glassy eyes and speckled silver scales of salmon, an enormous catch. Then he strode into the brewhouse.

Gwen bolted after him.

. . .

SHE FLINCHED as Pen threw down a wooden cask with a crash. She'd seen before how he needed exertion to vent his emotions. She supposed it was the reason he had taken up sparring with Gossett.

His growl was that of a wounded bear. "He wants to marry you."

He reached for a bucket from a high shelf. "No!" She leapt forward, snatching the bucket from his hands.

"No, you don't want my help? Or no, your old lover didn't ask you to marry him, and then Vaughn made you an offer straight after?"

"No, you can't put that in our brew. It's not malt." Her voice was unsteady, and she clutched the bucket to her middle as if it could hold her together. The cut on her finger throbbed as her heart drummed.

He scowled. "Looks like grain."

"This is darnel. Delerium grass. I spent all day picking it out of our barley, and I put it high so the goats can't find it." She moved to replace the bucket on the shelf. "It looks like regular grain, but its effects are worse than drunkenness. A man can go mad, hallucinate, develop tremors. Too much will void the stomach, enough will stop the lungs."

Pen reached for the bucket, his warm, strong fingers clasping hers. She wanted to sag against him, let herself bask in the heat of his touch. But he was angry, and she had to know why.

He stared into the bucket of innocuous-looking seeds. "And you put that in beer? Or bread?"

"Of course not. It's poison."

Slowly Pen tugged the bucket from her grasp. "I want to use it."

On them? Her heart clenched with fear. "Why?"

Lines fanned from his eyes as his face tensed. He'd grown tan from working outdoors, wearing the face of an honest laborer as well as the attire of one. Next to Daron's or Vaughn's milky whiteness and silk waistcoats, he exuded virility, assurance, strength. A tendril other than fear curled through her belly. Simply being near the man made her vibrate like a string on her harp.

Seeing only his rough clothes and ungloved hands, Vaughn had dismissed the Viscount Penrydd as a rough laborer, just as Barlow had. But had Pen recognized Vaughn?

He swiped up an empty bucket and stomped to the well. "Are you going to take him back?"

"No."

He grunted as he hauled on the winch, muscles flexing across his shoulders and back, visible beneath his rough woolen coat. She longed to touch him, to smooth away the tautness in his body, the grim lines around his eyes. She longed to hide within his arms and let the rest of the world float away.

"But he wants you." He unhooked the full bucket and set it on the ground. She passed him an empty bucket and shivered as their fingers brushed.

"Wanting isn't having," she said, heartache in her voice.

He lowered the second bucket into the cold depths of the well. His tense, coiled strength sent a thrill through her, but she couldn't tell if it was danger or desire.

"Isn't he rich? He could give you the money to buy this place from that lord you mentioned. Take you away, give you fine things. Treat you like a queen." A long pause filled with the creak of the rope as he hauled up the bucket. "Isn't that what you want?"

"I want to keep St. Sefin's." Her voice shook. Was this the reckoning at last?

"You wouldn't give it up to be a rich man's wife?" The second bucket sloshed as he dropped it to the ground.

"Daron isn't rich any longer. He came here because he thought I have money. That's the only reason he offered."

His snort startled her. He lifted the heavy buckets with ease and strode back to the brewhouse. "Gwenllian ap Ewyas. Are there no mirrors in this place? Neither of those men wants you for a dowry."

Was he trying to tell her that was how *he* felt about her? It was purely a sexual urge, the instinct of a man to sow his seed?

She watched as he returned to the brewhouse and poked at the oven, spreading the fire to heat the water he poured into a second vat. The first, the ale she'd made that morning, belched the thick, yeasty smell that told her it was ripe and nearly ready to be poured into casks.

"Why do you want the darnel?" she asked again as he took the bucket of poison from the shelf. The grains held the blackish tint of the fungus that caused hallucinations. She'd learned the hard way how to distinguish them.

"Revenge." He emptied the bucket into the vat of fresh water.

Her heart stopped. "On us?"

He scowled and, with a long stick, poked at the sodden mash in the vat. "Are you the only one allowed to keep secrets?"

Her throat closed completely. He knew she was lying to him. He just didn't know how much.

What would he do to her once he knew?

He dropped the stick and stalked toward her. Gwen backed up until the rough wooden wall of the brewhouse bumped against her rear. He braced an arm against the wall and leaned in, and her head swam with the delicious scent of him, earthy heat and virile male. She was lost to coherent thought when he stood this close to her.

"That girl, the sister, didn't recognize your name. Ewyas. What's your real one?"

She stared into his eyes. "Gwenllian Carew."

He stared back, waiting.

"My father was ambitious. He wanted to be accepted by the *Saes*." Her voice was a whisper. It felt good to speak the truth at last, like setting down a stone she'd dragged behind her far too long. "But my mother was Cymry to the core."

"So your name *is* Gwenllian, at least. Where were you born?" His breath brushed the hair above her ear, sending tingles down the backs of her knees.

She bit her lip. "We lived in a small village in Merionethshire called Llan Festiniog. The Moelwynion mountains to the north, a spectacular set of waterfalls, and Roman ruins close by—it was a lovely place to grow up. My father's family farmed for centuries, and my mother's family ran the Pengwern Arms."

"Why ap Ewyas? For your false name."

She sucked in a breath as he dragged a hand from her hip along her side, brushing her belly and ribs, resting in the curve below her breast. The wicked man knew his touch made her thoughts scatter like curlews startled from the riverbank. He knew, too, how she craved him above all else, couldn't deprive herself of his nearness.

"When St. Gwladys told me to stay here—I had to be from somewhere, and I didn't want my past. My father had told me never to contact him until I had redeemed myself. I had no friends who could take me in. The man I'd trusted had betrayed me, and I'd buried my child."

His gaze held on her steadily, without accusation, without scorn. She ran her tongue over her lips, and his eyes followed. "The old histories sing of Eudaf, Earl of Ewyas, who battled for the Silures against the Romans. He was father to Elen the saint, who became the mother of Constantine and the wife of Macsen Wledig, Maximus the Great. I wanted to be from a place that bore such strong, fearless women."

His gaze dropped to his hand, continuing its path up her body. One thumb circled her breast, teasing but not touching the tip. He knew her body so well. She wanted, at last, for him to know all of her. For the pretense to be done.

"Properly it should be *ferch* Ewyas, since I am a daughter, and *ap* means son. But I was no one's daughter. No one's wife. No one's mother. I never wanted to be hurt again in the ways a woman can be hurt." She swallowed the hard lump in her throat. "A man can be free to make his way in the world. So can a saint. And so would I."

He raised a hand to her throat, placing a finger in the delicate hollow between her collarbones. "You hid your past, and I lost mine. But you don't want your past back. I wonder what you can tell me of mine."

Her breath scraped like gravel in her throat. His eyes held a guarded look again, a veil she couldn't see through.

"Dovey," she said, choking on the word.

He frowned. "What?"

"I—I have to talk to Dovey."

His hand tensed at her throat, and she had a quick, wild thought that he wanted to throttle her into telling the truth. She too wanted to tear down this last wall between them. He'd never hurt her, and she wanted to stop hurting him.

"All this time," he said in a low voice, "you've been protecting Dovey. I ought to have guessed it." He drew a long breath, as if steadying himself, and then with deliberate slowness let his hand drop as he stepped away. "If I know anything about you, it's that you would step in front of a cannon for Mrs. Van der Welle or her child." His mouth lifted on one side, not a smile, yet not a sneer. "Would that you felt such loyalty to *me*."

Gwen gasped for air. Her chest couldn't take in enough.

She'd let this go on far too long. She wanted to tell him everything. How ashamed she felt that she had ever let a boy like Daron Sutton use her. How Pen had awakened her heart. How much it hurt that Calvin Vaughn would threaten to say foul things about St. Sefin's when she had worked so hard to make a place of refuge for those like her whom life had broken.

Pen wouldn't just hate her for lying to him for so long. He'd refuse to sell St. Sefin's to her, too, and then she and her people would be in exactly the position she'd tried to avoid: turned out without a roof, without sustenance, without hope.

She'd be left with nothing. Again. And this time, she didn't think she would survive.

CHAPTER FIFTEEN

P en woke to an enormous racket of birds. He sniffed the air and from outside his window smelled the sea and the morning mist rising from the river. The day promised sun. He had lived here long enough to know the time by the slant of light, if the tide was coming or going, and whether the air carried rain.

Gwen lay with her head on his chest, her hair a wild tangle. He was torn between waking her to talk to her and watching the complete innocence of her sleep. When she came to his room last night, her face lit by the flickering candle, her expression unsure of her welcome, he hadn't been concerned with explanations or just desserts. It was as if he lost every instinct for self-preservation when she was around. He craved the peace he found in her arms above every other thing.

He didn't even care about her motives, though that made him a fool. He would be a fool for her. She had rescued him the way she had so many others, knit his broken places, made him whole with that gift she had for life and strength and hope. He'd never felt this contentment, this bone-deep ease with himself. He had a roof over his head and nourishing food in his belly. His body felt stronger than it had ever been from his days of honest labor, and his head was clearer without daily immersion in rum.

With Gwen in his arms, he found a part of himself he'd never known existed. With her silken body beside him, her hair spilling over his arm, her quiet, steady breathing and her face angelic in sleep, he woke to a world made new. The realization tilted the earth on its axis, made him dizzy though he lay in his bed.

There was his world with Gwen in it, and there was the world without her.

With her, his world was complete, even with the gaps in his memory. Without her, he wouldn't survive.

Rather terrifying thought, that.

He still didn't know how much she knew about him, or why she would withhold that knowledge from him. But he sensed it wasn't what he had first feared, that she meant to humiliate him. No, what humiliated him was to have a man like Calvin Vaughn look past him as if he were nothing.

Calvin Vaughn had been his toady back in London, eager to lick Pen's boots in hopes of courting his widowed sister-in-law, who had a sizeable jointure. Vaughn had accompanied Pen on many nights of carousing at the theatre and gambling den. He'd applauded Pen's every win at cards, every insolent compliment to a lady, every barbed setdown of another man. But here, just like that black spider of a solicitor who looked at Pen holding the wheelbarrow and saw filth, Vaughn had seen a laborer in a workman's woolen jacket and cap and ignored him like the dirt under his feet.

Without his lord's clothes and his lordly mien and his noble title, perhaps he *was* nothing. A worthless excuse for a man who preyed on others and expected the world to conform to his desires. Much like Vaughn.

In his real life, he had power. He could end livelihoods in an instant by closing a pension or turning tenants off an estate. He could improve the lot of thousands with a wise investment or cripple the lives of millions with an investment somewhere else. He was a bloody. English. Viscount.

And before he came to St. Sefin's, he hadn't possessed one quality that would make a man like Barlow, or Vaughn, respect him when the title was set aside. The only thing he'd ever managed in his life was to not die on the beach at Tenerife, and that was due to the luck of grapeshot landing two inches shy of his heart, and the field surgeon binding his leg before he bled to death.

Gwen shifted and put a hand on his ribs. She met his eyes, blinking sleepily, and her slow, sweet smile hit him like a mallet in the chest.

"It's noisy out there," Pen murmured. "Is that the thrush?"

She tilted her head and listened. "Garden warbler. They like to nest in the cemetery next door." She paused. "Behind it, the one that sounds like my harp, skylark. And there—that's the swift. A sign that summer is near."

He combed his fingers through her glorious hair, soft as spring grasses. She was a wild creature, his Gwen. She would love his estate in Essex. Acres and acres of woodland and pasture to tromp about in. He would take her fishing and swimming in his favorite lake and he would eat whatever she wanted to pull out of the shrubbery.

The daughter of farmers and innkeepers. Finally, she'd told him the truth of her background. It wasn't the lowest possible birth, but not nearly high enough that he could raise her to a viscountess without damning them both to misery. The judgments and contempt from those of his class would kill that free, independent spirit of hers that he loved. People would cut her, despite her title, and he would be ridiculed for stooping so low. He would be laughed out of Lords, shut out of his clubs, and when they were pariahs in his world, not invited anywhere, what then could he offer her?

If Edwin had been alive and doing his duty, damn his eyes, Pen could marry where he pleased. He could marry a farmer's daughter and everyone would think it another of his freaks, like when he had decided to live in a cave for one summer, or pretended there was a monster in the lake on their estate in Essex. Like when he and his mates at school had painted a farmer's entire herd of cows one night for a prank, or when he had bought a commission into the navy when extra Price sons had always gone into the law. Rhydian's way, his family called it, the mantra accompanied by a disappointed sigh.

But many men of his station kept mistresses. It was practically *de rigueur*. The Penrydd townhouse had a carriage house where she could be close at hand, though those quarters were rather small. Perhaps a house next door, or just off the square, would give them room to entertain when they wished. He'd buy her a coach and pair and a roomful of gowns. In a proper frock he could take her anywhere, the theatre, the pleasure gardens, dinners with his friends, and she would shine down any of the high-born women. He'd be the envy of all who knew him. For once.

And he could take her with him when he traveled; many men of his class brought their mistresses to house parties. Prince William, Duke of Clarence, lived openly with his actress, Mrs. Jordan, and they had a handful of little FitzClarences. Pen would support any children and love them with his entire being. He would settle a generous annuity on her and wouldn't revoke it even if she wearied of him, as she was bound to do, since he seemed to be the sort that wearied people.

His heart tightened painfully as she scattered little, thoughtful kisses over his chest. Her lips were warm and soft as velvet. What if he offered her everything he had, his life, what remained of his fortune, and she didn't want him? How could he bind this woman so deeply to him that she'd never let go? He wanted to be sure of her before he made his move.

He wanted her to trust him enough to tell him the truth.

"Gwenllian ap Ewyas," he said softly. "What are you doing to me?"

Her eyes widened, and she smoothed her hand down his belly, fingers moving in sure strokes. He let her play. He loved how bold and unashamed she was. The pleasure she took in him, with him, added to his satisfaction in ways he'd never experienced.

"Besides that, minx," he said, his voice roughening.

She hesitated, and that shadow he hated came into her eyes. She was preparing to skirt his question.

"Do you want more than this?" she whispered.

What else mattered but the world they built together? He liked the man he was with her. And he was fairly certain Gwen liked him better as plain, nameless, blank-slated Pen than anyone had ever liked him as the Honourable Rhydian Price, or Lieutenant Price, or The Right Honourable The Viscount Penrydd. If she would only look at him like this all the time, be this easy and open and loving with him, then he didn't need anything else.

But there were any number of people who depended on the Viscount Penrydd for their survival. He wasn't at liberty to lark off to whatever corners of Britain he liked and hole up there with a pretty maid, leaving Ross to run the estate. Damn Edwin, damn him, *damn* him for dying.

He caught her roving hand and held it to his chest. "I want you," he said roughly, "to tell me what *you're* after."

Her eyelids tensed, and he recalled that she still needed the money to pay off that lord who'd offered to sell the place. Something tugged at the last blank spot in his mind. His memory was coming back in long skeins, but the days before he'd showed up at St. Sefin's were dark. Probably due to the blows he'd taken to the head, though thanks to the pair who had accosted them at the bridge, Pen had a lead on who was responsible for the beating that had left him insensible in a boat in Newport.

Once he got that sorted and had his revenge, there was no reason to stay here. And no reason not to carry Gwen away with him when he left.

She had to come with him. Leaving Gwen would tear him apart worse than being shot on the beach at Tenerife.

She splayed her hand over his chest as if listening to the agonized rhythm of his heart. She shifted and laid her body atop his, her breasts to his bare chest. The contact staggered his senses, as she always did. Then she put her hands along his jaw in that way that made him want to bow his head and surrender to her completely.

Fool. Wasn't it weakness, to not be able to resist her? To not *care* if she destroyed him in the end, as long as they had this first? It felt exactly like stepping off the boat onto the beach at San Cristóbal. He knew he was going to be shot to hell, and he was going to do it anyway, for the glory of the act itself and the impossible hope of reaching what lay beyond.

"Dress yourself," she said softly, "and come to breakfast. Dovey should be back this morning. She and Mathry went to attend a childbed, the woman who runs the pie shop. We will speak when they return."

"Evans and I promised to stop over to St. Woolos and do some repairs for the vicar." No reason to jump to her tune like a trained spaniel. He had to cling to some shred of pride. "And we have that project we've been working on."

She smiled. "The reason for all the blasts in the back pasture?" She nipped at his jaw, breath tickling his ear, and the pleasant arousal he'd awakened with turned to a hard ache.

"I feel like there's something I'm forgetting. One more thing I need to attend to this morning." He slid a hand down her sleek, long back and cupped the soft curve of her derrière. The muscle flexed as she drew up her knee, settling her hips against his groin. His arousal slid along her core, slick and hot and inviting, but she paused to touch his lips with her fingers.

"Remember this, Pen," she said softly. "Every moment with you has been a gift to me. This was real."

Was. Not *is*. She kissed him, and he kissed her back, deeply, hungrily, despairing. He hauled her against him until there was no air between their bodies. What did she mean by *real*? She'd lied about her name. She'd shown him his family's house and told him their history but she'd told him nothing of himself. She'd saved his life after not just one beating but two, and she'd wrecked him. He was changed. As Pen of St. Sefin's he'd become a different man than the insolent, wounded, occasionally vile Viscount Penrydd, and he didn't want to go back to that empty life.

Yet he had to. He feared that when the time came, she would let him go. And without her, what joy would life hold?

He kissed her anyway, swallowing a groan as she lifted her hips and then slipped her body down upon his. Being inside her like this was a bliss for which he'd pay any price. He was hers, body and soul. With that strong, elegant hand and those fingers callused from harping, Gwenllian ap Ewyas had smashed through his every layer of defense, all the walls and guards he'd spent years carefully erecting. She broke through his every barrier as if it were wet paper and clenched his heart in her fist, raw and beating.

And he, useless clodpole that he was, lacking a single shred of self-preservation, didn't have the will to take it back.

· · ·

PEN NEEDED ANSWERS. It was time.

Gwen stood in St. Sefin's herb gardens under a spring-blue sky, her mind only partially on the task of instruction. "And this is yarrow," she said to Mathry, plucking a long stem. "See the feathery leaves and the way the flowers cluster in the center of the petals. Attracts ladybirds and useful insects, and the starlings like it for their nests. Some call it thousand-seal or bloodwort, because it stops bleeding. The leaves have a peppery taste." She peeled one from a plant and popped it in her mouth.

"No, not you!" Dovey exclaimed as Mathry went to do the same. "It's given to bring on menses, among other things. We're working too hard to keep the little *pwt* in there."

Mathry's eyes widened. "*Coc y garth!*" she swore. "There's so much I can do wrong! How'll I ever learn?"

"Practice, and listening," Gwen said. "We harvest the whole stem, like this, and will dry it upside down in the stillroom. You can soak the leaves and wrap them on wounds for healing, or make a tea that will settle the stomach. It helps stop spasms and aids sleep. I use it often when Tomos gets upset or when Mother Morris is tamping."

"Put it in remedies for a putrid throat or rheumatism," Dovey added.

"And I'll distill some flowers into an oil," Gwen said. "I like it for soap, and a drop or two for sore muscles or bruising. We went through quite a lot of it with Pen."

"Mr. Pen," Mathry said with a coy smile, "is sweet on you. What are you going to do about it, Gwen?"

Gwen hid her heated face among the yarrow blooms. What, indeed? *Sweet* was too light a word for what blazed between them, scorching her senses pure of everything but him. No doubt he'd feel something equally blazing when she finally told him the truth. She knew no way to sweeten the revelation that she'd lied to him, had been lying for weeks. Even while she allowed herself the pleasure of his company, the mind-blotting bliss of his bed.

"We have to tell him," she said to Dovey.

Dovey froze, fingers clasped about a clutch of yarrow stems. "But nothing has changed. They say the violence is only getting worse, more rough men every day."

"We can't keep him here any longer," Gwen said. "It's not right."

Mathry frowned. "What do you mean, keep him here? Does Mr. Pen have somewhere else to go?"

Gwen drew a deep breath. "Pen is—"

"Indebted to us," Dovey said quickly. "Does he know that, though?"

Gwen sat back on her heels. She wouldn't forgive herself if Dovey or any of them came to harm because of her. But she couldn't continue with the charade.

"I'll—"

"Gwen *bach!*" Widow Jones's voice floated across the garden. "*Saeson* at the door. The solicitor again, and he's come with reinforcements."

"St. Aled's eyeballs," Gwen muttered, locking eyes with Dovey.

"We don't have the money," Dovey whispered, voicing her fear.

"Where's Mr. Pen to?" Mathry looked about.

"Over at St. Woolos with Evans and the boys. They're seeing what slates Mr. Stanley needs for the roof."

She rounded the corner of St. Sefin's church to find Mother Morris glaring down the front drive, hands on her thick hips. She and Widow Jones had run out of bushes in the back, so were draping linens over the strawberry tree that grew near the old stone wall that outlined the property. Gwen spotted two of Pen's shirts and an image streaked through her mind of helping him dress that morning, scattering kisses and caresses over all that splendid bare skin and muscle before she had to hide it from the world.

She wasn't ready to lose him. She never would be.

"*Twll din pob Saes*," Mother Morris muttered.

Barlow stood beside the low front porch, as if it were beneath him to set foot on it. Next to him was a younger man in a brown riding coat and breeches with thick cinnamon-brown curls crammed beneath his hat. Panic slammed through Gwen as she recognized him. Penrydd's secretary.

He was saying something in English to Barlow but stuttered to a stop as the three women approached. Gwen twisted her hands in her shawl to hide her tremors.

"Miss ap Ewyas." The secretary's eyes widened.

"*Prynhawn da*, Mr. Barlow, Mr.—"

"Ross," he supplied. He watched her with fascination, as if she were some exotic plant he'd discovered. He'd been there at the interview, this man, laughing up his sleeve as Gwen tried to barter for St. Sefin's and Pen tried to make her his mistress. Had he come with Barlow to turn them out at last?

"Mr. Ross." She gulped and addressed him in English. "We are grateful for your offer to buy St. Sefin's. We are collecting the fifteen hundred pounds. I hope you can allow us more time. It is a—substantial sum for us, as you might guess."

"Er—yes. I was rather hoping you had the funds already. His lordship is eager to see the transaction concluded." Ross glanced at Mathry as she strolled up behind Gwen, then sheared his eyes away as if the sight burned him.

"His lordship?" Gwen asked, confused.

"Will gladly be rid of it," Barlow said with irritation. "Particularly if the Vaughns bring a suit."

Gwen's throat went dry. "What do you mean?"

"Mr. Calvin Vaughn has gone before the justice of the

peace saying he has evidence you are running a disorderly house out of St. Sefin's." Barlow glared as if he had no doubt this were true.

"Who is the other accuser?" Dovey spoke up. "For there must be at least two."

"Mr. Daron Sutton, gentleman," Ross said.

"He's not even a resident of this parish!" Mathry squawked. Ross's eyes shifted back to her and stuck.

"This is not a disorderly house," Gwen said, clenching her fists in her shawl. "There is no drinking, no gaming here, and certainly no—nothing of what he implies. We have separate dormitories for men and women." The only person engaged in bawdiness was her.

Ross knew of the proposition Pen had made her. And here she was, enjoying Pen's bed. What must that look like to Ross? Or to Pen?

"The judge will make that decision, should Mr. Vaughn decide to bring a suit. He gave me the impression he could be persuaded from pressing the case, with good enough reasons." The solicitor frowned. "We will find it difficult to sell the property if you have made it notorious."

"I will confer with his lordship to see if he will make a concession on the price," Ross said loftily. "Though you must give him time to reply."

Gwen reached to take Dovey's hand, squeezing it tightly.

"We can ask him now," she said, feeling the earth shift beneath her. "Here he comes."

Pen stalked like the master of the land across the overgrown lawn that led from St. Woolos, matching his strides to those of Ifor, who rambled beside him. Gafr bobbed between them, munching on a cluster of grasses. Pen and Evans were deep in conversation with the vicar, while Tomos trudged behind them clutching a handful of daisies.

They paused in the shadow of the looming stone porch. Evans fell silent. Pen stood calmly, weight on his heels, shoulders square. Lordly.

He looked at the men as if he knew exactly who they were.

"M-m-milord!" Ross stammered. His expression was priceless, a Trojan scout counting the Greek armies massing on the shore.

"Lord?" Barlow's bushy white eyebrows flew toward the brim of his hat.

"Penrydd," Pen said.

Gwen's stomach splashed into her shoes.

"The *Viscount* Penrydd?" Barlow yelped.

Pen nodded. "Fourth of that title. Hullo, Ross. Took you long enough to find me."

He knew.

"Er." Ross gulped, his eyes bulging behind his spectacles. "Well. I suppose it hadn't occurred to me that you would be here, milord. Surveying your, ah, property."

"My property?" Pen's brows lifted in a more regal version of Barlow's surprise. "Ah. *My* property. That explains a great deal."

His gaze pinned Gwen, and she clung to Dovey's hand so she didn't collapse. The scenery whirled around her. Dovey's fingernails digging into her palm kept her anchored.

She wanted to say so many things to him, but foremost was a hopeless plea. *Forgive me.*

"Well," Pen said, his voice neutral. "I've had time to survey my property at length."

Tomos shifted on his feet, growing agitated. Evans put a calming hand on the boy's shoulder.

"We want to buy it," Gwen said to Pen, her throat tight with anguish. "But you—know our situation."

"Fifteen hundred pounds." Pen regarded Ross, who

coughed into his hand. "I recall your telling me it couldn't be worth more than a thousand."

He remembered everything. *Everything.* Gwen's heart started working its way down her chest, aiming to join her stomach. Dovey held her up.

"Yes, well, I thought you should ask an extra five hundred to cover loss of prospective rent," Ross said.

"I see," Pen said. "And what other properties have you sold while I was—away?"

Pen hadn't dressed in the laborer's clothes she'd given him, the rough woolen coat and trousers. He wore his own clothes, the tailored coat with its clawhammer tail, the buckskin breeches, the cravat more complicated than anything he'd attempted before. With his attire and his mien, there was no questioning he was a man of stature.

Barlow at last remembered to sweep off his hat. "My lord," he stammered.

"We've not gone behind your back, sir," Ross squeaked. "Nothing can be finalized without your approval. But I've been —importuned for money. From—you know."

"Yes, I know," Pen said.

The others in his group stepped away from Pen, acknowledging they were no longer equals. He was lord of this land and they were his subjects, entirely at his mercy.

Gafr, uninterested in the ways of men, nosed at Pen's boots, but Ifor, attuned to the tension in the air, pulled him back.

Pen plucked a tall flowering stalk that grew in the shade of the porch. He studied the white bell of the flower, the scarlet specks at its heart, then put the bloom on his finger like a thimble. Gwen wondered if he knew it was foxglove, flowering early this year. She should tell Mathry, she thought with the fluttering, leaping part of her brain that was not frozen in shock. Foxglove was very useful for nervous disorders or to stem bleeding, but too much could stop the heart. She ought to remove the clump to the poison garden.

Pen examined the plant as if he wasn't sure whether he wanted to heal or to kill.

"Let me guess," he said. "The moneylender lost track of me after his men attacked me as I sailed for Newport. As far as I can ascertain, after beating me senseless in pursuit of my purse, his men tipped me over the side of the boat so they mightn't be hanged for murder. By sheer good luck, or their stupidity, I fell into a boat alongside the ship instead of drowning."

He glanced at Gwen, but his expression was guarded, revealing nothing. "Finding my purse insufficient, I gather this same moneylender then approached you, Ross, insisting you pay the debt my brother owed him. A debt I suspect I am not, after all, responsible for."

Pen turned to Evans, as if continuing a conversation from before. "This moneylender and his men are the cause of the violence we've been seeing in town. The man lives in Cardiff, but for some reason has lately become keen on collecting his debts, and not loathe how he goes about it. He had some grudge against the Jew from Merthyr Tydfil, a successful financier whom he regarded as a rival. And we know how that ended, may his poor soul find peace."

Mr. Stanley crossed himself, watching Pen with wide eyes.

Penrydd turned back to Gwen. "Our friends we met on the bridge, Minikin and Gap-tooth—his real name is Pedr—they worked for this lender. They were part of the gang sent to shake me down, in fact. But they were spooked by his methods so struck out on their own. I found them in the pubs and we've been discussing how to end their boss's reign of terror. They call him Y Gwyllgi."

"The Black Hound," Gwen whispered. Y Gwyllgi was a mythical beast that roamed mountain passes and isolated roads.

His red eye froze his prey and his breath was poison. Any mortal who had earned that name had done so by being a monster.

So Pen, during his days in town, had been making friends along the wharves and mingling with the shopkeepers and merchants of Newport. He'd not only remembered his past but was laying plans to deal with the man who attacked him, the man who was threatening others as well. She understood now why he had sought out Gossett after that first thrashing and convinced the man, a former bare-knuckle boxer, to teach him to fight.

A cold cloud froze her heart, as if she'd taken the foxglove. Those men had meant to kill Pen if he wouldn't pay them money. She would have lost any chance to know him. To love him.

How long had he known who he was?

"Pen," she managed to say. "Let the authorities deal with him. You must have nothing to do with such a man." He could be killed in truth next time.

His eyes tightened. She'd used her name for him, not his title. She didn't get to call him Pen, or even Penrydd—that was a luxury reserved for his peers. He was Lord Penrydd now, his lordship or my lord to someone like her. The Right Honourable The Viscount Penrydd did she wish to write him a letter. She didn't even know his given name.

And she had no right to learn anything more about him. Not after what she'd done.

Pen, forgive me.

Barlow's eyebrows had taken up permanent residence near his hairline. "Can we call the constable on this Gooey—" He gave up trying to pronounce the Welsh syllables. "In no way are you bound to discharge this debt, milord. If I know the money-lender to whom you refer, he charges usurious, ruinous rates.

The law cannot compel you to uphold an illegal agreement your brother made."

"The law cannot compel me," Pen agreed. "Which is why he's trying other means." He winced and rolled his injured shoulder.

"When he lost you, he contacted the viscountess," Ross said unhappily. "She came here to pay him, thinking to free you all, but of course, with you absent—"

"She doesn't have the funds." Pen's studied calm slipped. "Do you mean Lydia is here? Or Prunella?"

Ross lifted his hands in a shrug. "Er, both? The money-lender told them both he could seize their jointures if he wasn't paid, which you and I both know he can't do, but they believed it." He cleared his throat. "They are currently staying in Chippenham with the family of Miss Carruthers."

"Who the deuce is Miss Carruthers?" Pen scowled.

"The—er—girl your mother wishes you to wed. The one with the rather large dowry."

"*Coc oen*," Pen swore, and Mother Morris's lips twitched. The older women, laundry forgotten, hung close by, listening as intently to the conversation as everyone else. Gwen had stopped breathing. Pen knew who he was. Pen had a mother and sister and possibly a betrothed waiting for him in his real life. What came next?

As if she'd spoken aloud, he turned to her. "Gather your things, Gwen. You're familiar with my rooms at the Green Man —we still have them, don't we, Ross? I can only imagine how delighted the dowager viscountess, my stepmother Lydia, and my brother's wife, Prunella, will be to meet you."

He snapped the stalk of foxglove in two and threw it at his feet. Gafr sniffed and turned away.

Gwen held to Dovey's hand as if it kept her from drowning. "What of St. Sefin's?" she whispered.

Pen scowled. "We will discuss that. Among other things."

The arrogant lord was back, the one who could wave his hand and men, and women, would spring to his bidding. He was a *viscount,* of all things. What she had done to him was punishable. He could have her whipped and put in chains. He could have her transported.

Gwen lifted her chin. She couldn't go with him, not even to save St. Sefin's. She had no bargaining power with the arrogant lord.

"My place is here," she said quietly.

She missed him already, Pen, the man who had shared this place with her. He'd disappeared, and she hadn't had a chance to say goodbye.

His face froze with that flat expression she couldn't read. Dovey, dropping a brief curtsey, tugged at her hand. "We'll gather your things, milord. Only give us a moment."

Lifting her leaden feet with conscious effort, Gwen followed Dovey to the men's dormitory and Pen's room. The room where she'd spent all those blissful, wondrous hours in his arms.

While he was betrothed to someone else. Or about to be.

Pen was already wearing his own clothes, so all that remained were the few trinkets he had gathered during his sojourn with them. A scarf that Mother Morris had knitted for him. A set of stockings from the donation box that Widow Jones had embroidered with beautiful rows of the letter P, like elegant clocks. A cockle shell from the handful he'd brought back for Tomos the day she sent him to gather seaweed, and a shell from the oysters he'd brought Ifor.

Gwen picked up a smooth stone he'd found along the Severn. Below it, pressed between old newsprint, was a bluebell.

Her heart clenched, a little hiccup of despair escaping.

"How long do you suppose he's known?" Dovey reached to

strip the linens from the bed. Gwen, recalling what had transpired on those linens a few short hours ago, stopped her, swapping the cloth bag of Pen's small relics for the housekeeping task.

"I don't know. Perhaps when I showed him the Penrydd estate." Though that had been a fortnight ago. Surely he wouldn't have stayed all that time if he'd known. "Perhaps when Vaughn and the Suttons visited. He seemed very agitated after they left."

But that had been yesterday. Wouldn't he have said something the moment he realized they'd tricked him? Railed, shouted, accused, threatened—

Or laid in wait for her to be truthful with him, at long last. A cold certainty splashed through her, like she'd fallen into the river.

"And you don't wish to go with him?" Dovey asked.

Oh, she wished. Her heart scraped in her chest with the longing to go with him. Toss everything aside and follow with nothing but her shawl and her shoes. To live with him however he wished, without shame or recrimination, basking in his attention for as long as he chose to bestow it.

She'd put herself at a man's mercy before, and look what that gained her. And if she left, what would Dovey and Cerys and the others live on? How would they make do without her? While she was off enjoying the bliss of Pen's arms, her friends at St. Sefin's would be subject to the scorn and whispers of the town. Merchants might deny them business, shops deny them custom, if they thought St. Sefin's was a disorderly house. They could starve.

She couldn't protect them if she left. She had to stay here and bargain for their lives.

"I won't go with him," Gwen whispered. "I can't."

"But his family." Dovey's eyes widened. "What if he wants to marry you?"

Then her worries for the fate of St. Sefin's would be over. Gwen's laugh was feral. "How could he? He's a *viscount*. I'm—" She held out her arms.

"There might be a child," Dovey said, frowning.

Gwen's heart lifted and slammed against her ribs. How she would adore sharing a child with Pen. "But I can't conceive again, not after—" She swallowed hard. "I'm sure of it."

Gwen left the heap of linens on the bed to retrieve later. They lay crumpled and empty, like her heart. She'd stolen time with Pen, and now she had to account for it.

Dovey handed her the cloth bag. "At the least say goodbye." *And see what he means to do with us*, she didn't need to add.

Ross stood in the kitchen, looking baffled and ill at ease. Was he inspecting the place? Wondering if he ought to raise the asking price?

"We still want to buy it," Gwen said, forcing out the words. "If he'll allow it."

Ross's brows drew together. He was a young man, but there were already habitual creases on his face. What worry he must have been through while she'd hidden Pen away from the world for her own selfish purposes. Even his mother and sister—well, stepmother and sister-in-law—had come looking for him. What she had done to him, to those who cared for him, was unforgiveable.

"Penrydd doesn't keep mistresses," Ross said.

Gwen gave a strangled snort. "He's not celibate." The man had experience and great skill as well as ingenuity. She had reason to know.

"No, but—he's never—er, kept anyone," Ross said. "What he offered you—" He trailed off as Mathry came out of the still-room with a small jar.

"Camphor for his lordship's wounds," Mathry said. She held the jar out to Ross with a shy smile. "Miss Gwen gave it him, and it seemed to help."

Ross stared at Mathry as if he'd never seen a female in his life. "Er—thank you."

Gwen went outside. Clouds rolled up from the bay, streaking the sky with lead. Pen stood beside Barlow, on the side of his people, while apart from them stood hers, Evans and Mr. Stanley with the boys. Widow Jones and Mother Morris sheltered under the strawberry tree with Cerys. Ross and Mathry followed behind her. Everyone she cared about on earth was there to witness her betrayal. And her judgment.

She shuffled, her feet heavy with dread, across the dirt and grass toward Pen. She held out the bag.

"I deceived you," she said. She, who insisted she prized truth. "I doubt you can forgive me."

He'd tricked her in return, but it wasn't the same. She didn't know how to tell him that coming to his bed hadn't been an attempt at bargaining. It had been nothing but the wish to be with him, as free as Adam and Eve in their first days.

His face was hard and flat. She'd never seen him so unapproachable. She swallowed against the hot agony in her throat.

"I wanted you to see us." She forced out the words. "I wanted you to..."

Stay here. Be with me. St. Myllin's arms, she couldn't say *that* in front of all these people.

He raised a brow in that contemptuous way she hated. This wasn't her Pen. He'd reverted to the haughty viscount. His eyes narrowed for a moment, making her think he tensed against some unwanted thought of mercy. But he pushed it down.

"Wanted me to fetch and carry for you, I presume," he drawled. "I hope I earned my keep."

Tears of shame stung her eyes. She'd hurt him. She never meant to.

"Punish me," Gwen said, bowing her head. "But not them." She waved a hand toward the others, a helpless gesture.

Pen's eyes flicked to Barlow, then away. "I must confer with Ross about the state of my finances," he said. "I'll be in touch."

He meant to keep her in suspense over what he intended to do with St. Sefin's? With her? The world spun around her. Barlow waddled off, muttering something about reporting to the constable, but Gwen paid him no heed. It took everything in her not to crumple to the ground as Pen gave her one last, cold look, and then turned away.

She watched him stride out of her life, his back straight and strong, his stride again the confident swagger of a lord of the realm. He held the bag of assorted trinkets he'd gathered during his stay, but she didn't doubt the Viscount Penrydd would dispose of them at the first opportunity, just as he'd shed every other association of his time with them.

He was gone. She'd never see him again.

Her knees folded to the hard-packed earth and she stared down the hill where Pen had disappeared. She had left all her tears in the cold ground where she'd buried her daughter. She had none left for a man she'd duped and betrayed.

Gafr reached her first, snuffling her cheek, his fur tickling her ear. Then Ifor's hand came to her shoulder, stroking softly. The others came too, offering her comfort. Her family. At least she had them. And her home, until Pen decided what to do with her.

But he had taken her heart with him, and she would have to live the rest of her days without it. Without him.

CHAPTER SIXTEEN

E ngland wasn't as lovely as Wales, Pen thought as his ship sailed up Bristol Channel, bearing him first to the offices of Mr. Barlow, solicitor, and then beyond to the rooms Ross had kept for them at the Green Man.

True, the plunging sides of Avon Gorge were a more dramatic frame for the river than the flatter hills that sloped down to the Severn. But atop Stow Hill, the view spread for miles, following the Usk as it meandered into the great oak forest of Wentwood. From Brynglas one could see the hills that rose with their ores of coal and gold into the rich Welsh midlands, or look south to the gleaming mouth of the Severn where it stretched to the sea. At St. Sefin's, a man could fill his lungs with deep breaths. Sailing up the Avon Gorge, Pen felt boxed in, his future a mummy's casket closing around him.

The minute they entered the inn, he ordered that a glass of grog be sent to his rooms. He could practically taste the sweet, mind-erasing alcohol already. Gwen would be disappointed in him, but he didn't care. If she were concerned about his welfare, then she ought to have come with him, rather than spurning him in front of everyone at St. Sefin's and Vicar Stanley, too. There were only so many blows to his pride that a man could be asked to sustain.

"How desperate am I for money?" Pen asked, throwing himself into the upholstered chair of the private sitting room. The chair he'd occupied when Gwen had first approached him, seeking to buy St. Sefin's.

He'd fallen for her snares when he knew who she was, and he'd fallen for her snares when he didn't. While she had been true to one thing throughout all her dealings with him: Everything with her was about how to keep St. Sefin's. Damn her eyes.

Ross sighed unhappily, regarding the pile of correspondence on his desk that had quadrupled in Pen's absence.

"If we can be rid of your brother's debt with the money-lender, you won't be destitute. I've been looking into improvements we can make on the estates that will allow us to raise the rents. You can lease the hunting box and perhaps Penrydd, if you're not going to use it, and—"

"I plan to open the house at Penrydd," Pen said. "In fact I think I'll make it my primary residence."

Ross opened his mouth and then shut it. Pen knew what he had been about to ask—*because of the girl?*

No. His decisions from now on would have nothing to do with Gwen. How dare she let him walk away as if he meant nothing to her. *My place is here*, she'd said. Not with him. He had nothing she wanted. She'd lied to him, dallied with him, wrapped him in her heady spells, and then handed him his things and sent him on his way as if she'd forget about him the moment he walked down the hill. How *dare* she?

"It's an interesting house," Pen said. "I fancy living there a while."

"Of course, sir," Ross said, his tone bland and polite.

A lad delivered the grog, and Pen reached for it eagerly.

This was going to taste so good. A salve for all that he had been deprived of the weeks without his memory, and then the weeks after. But as he brought the glass to his nose, the sour scent made his stomach turn over. He set the glass aside for the moment.

"Speaking of which," Pen said. "I want you to make inquiries about a Carew family from Llan—Llan Festiniog." His Welsh was improving, though Gwen probably wouldn't care. She ought to. "He was a farmer, and his wife's family ran the inn. Penguin Arms or something. Find out everything you can."

"Very well. Carew." Ross smoothed away an expression of surprise. "Anything else, sir?"

So many things, Pen thought. He wanted to make inquiries about the death of Dovey's husband and see if the Dutch Navy had made any provision for her as a widow. He wanted to find the miner who had worked Mother Morris's sons to death and lock him in a cavern. He wanted to buy a funeral monument for Evans's wife and children and set up an annuity for Widow Jones. He wanted to ensure that Tomos and Ifor would be taken care of, and he wanted to make a fat donation to St. Woolos church so the vicar could make all the improvements he wanted.

Besides that, Newport was a city on the cusp of expansion, so many opportunities. He could buy shares in the new stone bridge they were planning to build to replace the wooden one over the Usk where he and Gwen had been accosted by Gap-tooth and Minikin. He could invest in the tramways being built to ferry coal and ore from the inland mines to the Monmouthshire Canal. He could build a proper school in the town so the Gossett and Trett children had somewhere to learn their letters. And refurbish St. Sefin's. It needed so many repairs, and if she saw he meant to take care of her, perhaps Gwen—

That way lay madness. Pen reined in his thoughts. He

brought the glass of grog to his nose, and again his stomach rebelled. He couldn't stand the smell of it.

We're drying you out, Pen.

The infernal woman had turned him off rum. She'd *ruined* him.

"Why did you never find me?" he asked Ross, uncurling from the chair and stalking toward the table to sift through the yards of parchment. "Did you make no inquiries? I wasn't that far away."

"I made inquiries, sir," Ross said, stung. "The Vaughns could tell me nothing, as they hadn't seen you. Remember, though, you hadn't told me you were setting out for Newport that morning. I thought you were going to Weston-super-Mare with Mr. Turbeville. He also asked around about you," Ross added, "and ended up getting rather badly beaten for his efforts. I gather he fell afoul of the moneylender's men."

Pen paced across the room. He neared the grog, then veered away. He had no appetite for it any longer. Even the smell was vile.

"I have a notion of how to deal with the Black Hound," Pen said. "But I left everything I was working on at sodding St. Sefin's."

"You're not limping any longer," Ross observed with surprise.

Pen had grown so accustomed to feeling at ease in his body that he'd nearly forgotten the constant pain that had been his companion since Tenerife. In tending him after his various thrashings, Gwen had healed those old wounds, too.

His time with her had transformed him in so many ways. After all she had shared with him, how could she simply let him walk away?

He'd make her regret that. He would find an appropriate response to her treachery. It would involve having her in his bed, stripping off every piece of her clothing, moving his mouth over every delicious inch of her body until she was mindless and quivering and begging him to fulfill her.

She'd known he was a viscount and that hadn't moved her. She'd known he held St. Sefin's, and she'd still not chosen to come away. What would make her want *him*?

Pen handed the glass of grog to Ross and gestured for him to send it away. He ran a hand through his hair and glared toward the mountain of correspondence.

"The first order of business is to put down the Black Hound. Send for Lydia and Prunella, and tell them to leave Miss Who's-it where they found her. I'll deal with them next."

If Gwen were his viscountess, she would deliver him from matrimonial schemes. She would save him from dealing with women in general. *See the viscountess*, he would say to his step-mother and sister-in-law and every other woman who impor-tuned him. And in return he would give her splendid houses, carriages and gowns, jewels and horses—as soon as he could afford them, anyway. He would ensure she wanted nothing, that she need never work again.

Would it be enough to win her?

Perhaps she had merely thought he meant for her to be his mistress. She didn't know what he could offer her. Somehow, he had to make her trust him. Choose him. Put her faith in him, instead of thinking she could do everything herself, all of the time.

Pen stared out the window, across the Bristol Channel to Wales and its dark hills. "The hound, and the women," he decided. "And then I will call Miss Gwenllian ap Ewyas to account for her crimes."

. . .

"NEXT CASE," the clerk called. "Gwenllian ap Ewyas of St. Woolos parish, Newport. Accused of keeping an ill-governed and disorderly house and entertaining diverse men and women of suspicious and ill repute, to the common nuisance of her neighbors."

The bailiff motioned her forward, and Gwen obeyed, sweating beneath the blonde lace. The bodice of her redingote felt tighter than usual. This justice, Sir Robert, controlled her fate.

Mr. Stanley had explained the workings of English law, after the constable came to St. Sefin's with his writ summoning her to appear. Her case fell under summary justice, in which case the justice of the peace could act alone, examining the evidence and pronouncing what sentence he wished. At a whim he could convict her and demand a fine, imprisonment in the workhouse, or a whipping, and it was unlikely he would be challenged.

If he found her guilty and there was an indictment, her case would go to the petty sessions. There she would come before two or more magistrates, and the punishment could be harsher, a steeper fine or imprisonment of six months or more. And if the offense were considered a serious threat to public peace, her case would move to the quarter sessions and the assizes, held every three months. There her sentence could be much worse, perhaps transportation. The thought turned her blood to ice.

She could be cast into the bridewell for years and her friends turned out of St. Sefin's. Once again Daron Sutton could destroy her life and cast her into the outer darkness. And Calvin Vaughn, whom she had thought an idle menace, might manage what she had once feared Pen would do: end St. Sefin's entirely.

Sir Robert Salusbury was a man she'd had no business with. Mr. Stanley could tell her that he'd studied at Trinity College and Cambridge and Lincoln's Inn. Gwen had passed Llanwern, the manor house he'd inherited through his wife, on her way to harp at Pencoed Castle. Sir Robert had recently been elected mayor of Newport, but he was also MP for Brecon and had Parliamentary duties, so she couldn't vouch that he knew of St. Sefin's and the people she'd helped.

The travelers they lodged when the inns were full, earning much-needed extra coin. The girls like Mathry they took during their lying-ins for children they would be forced to give away. The foreigners they housed while they looked for work in the mines and coalfields and shipyards. The widows and orphans turned out of their homes, the men deprived of work, the ailing who had found refuge under their roof until better circumstances arrived, or they were transferred quietly to the pauper's section of the graveyard in the cemetery at St. Woolos.

The room fell silent as she shed her hat and moved toward the wooden table where Sir Robert sat. He looked like a decent man. He wore a white bag wig, the sign of his office, and was dressed in a somber black wool suit. But he had children, daughters. Surely his heart could be moved in her favor.

Gwen looked about hesitantly. Sir Robert had chosen to hold court in one of the upper rooms of the Fleur-de-Lys, a pub just off High Street. In Tudor times the house had belonged to powerful Herberts, high sheriffs and lords of St. Julian's Manor outside of town. St. Julian's was an ivy-covered ruin now and Herbert lands had been absorbed by other lords as Dame Fortune turned her wheel.

Gwen cast her eye over the plasterwork ceiling and shivered. She recognized the Aragon pineapple in the bas relief. Wales had celebrated when their Tudor prince, Arthur, was betrothed to the beautiful Katherine, princess of the powerful realm of Aragon. But Arthur died before his prime and Katherine passed to the cruel hands of his brother, Henry VIII. The once-admired princess had ended her life impoverished and divorced, denied by her husband, stripped of her pride and her child when another woman caught Henry's eye. He had riven England from the Roman church in order to have Anne Boleyn, and then chopped off Anne's head when she displeased him. A chill ran down Gwen's back. The fortunes of the powerful were changeable, and the fates of women more fragile yet.

She lifted her chin and wondered why the silence stretched out. A small crowd of people was gathered in the room, other plaintiffs and defendants awaiting their turn, witnesses waiting to be examined, spectators there for a diversion. The May afternoon promised sun after the morning mist rolled away, and dust motes glittered in the air. The clerk of the peace stared at her. Sir Robert stared at her. Even the bailiff, craning his neck for the source of the quiet, couldn't take his eyes off her face.

"Don't be taken in by her beauty, judge," Calvin Vaughn said. "There's a tart's heart beneath that lace."

"Hold your tongue, Vaughn." Daron Sutton stepped forward. The two men had been standing in a corner, shielded by the ostrich plumes on the hat of a woman wearing a heavy veil.

"I meant for her to be my wife." Daron reached for Gwen's hand. "I would still have you, Gwen. Say the word, and the charges against you will be dropped."

Gwen stared into his face. His petulant, self-satisfied face. Even now he thought she was his for the asking.

Deliberately she moved her gloved hands away from his outstretched one. "I decline the honor of your hand, Mr. Sutton," she said, and then ruined the dignity of her reply with a muttered Welsh curse. A gasp told her someone in the back knew she'd compared him to sheep's poo, though Sutton didn't.

He scowled, but his retort was drowned out by the man behind the table.

"You will address the court as Sir Robert or Your Worship, Mr. Vaughn," Sir Robert said. "And you, Mr. Sutton, will stand back. This examination will proceed, considering the charges are already written out and on the rolls." He pointed to a tiny lectern where perched the clerk of the peace, scribbling across a scroll of paper.

"The evidence is false, Your Worship," Gwen said. She stroked her fingers, the way she calmed herself when playing before a new audience. "It can only be false. St. Sefin's is not what they say."

"I am here to judge that." Sir Robert glowered, and Gwen bent her head.

The clerk cleared his throat. "The charges include drinking."

"Rhubarb cordial and dandelion wine," Gwen said. "We cannot afford spirits."

"Tippling," the clerk continued.

"How is that different from drinking?" Gwen asked.

Sir Robert scowled. "Proceed, Mr. Lewis."

"Carousing at all hours of the day and night," the clerk read.

"We go to bed at dark." Gwen's cheeks tightened with a blush. "All of us."

"Suspicious conversation—"

"Suspicious to whom?"

"Miss Ewyas! Let the man do his work," Sir Robert barked.

"Huh—ahem—whoring," the clerk stuttered. Calvin Vaughn smirked. A hot wave of anger splashed through Gwen.

"Not once."

Sir Robert gave her a stern glower. "You deny the charges?"

"All of them. Particularly the last. We are not—that kind of house." Gwen managed to keep her temper, though she wanted to rain Welsh curses down upon their heads.

The clerk hid behind his roll. "There are accusations of men coming and going at all hours. A Mr. Stanley—"

"The vicar," Gwen said, scandalized.

"A young, stocky man, fair-haired—"

"That's Tomos. He is grown like a man, but in his mind he's as a boy. Five, six years old at most."

"There are reports of keeping company with boys as well, leading them into a path of vice and sin."

"Does he mean Ifor?" Gwen stared. "Our goat boy?"

"And there has been of late, under your roof, a particular person, origins unknown—a large man, very rough-looking, who has roamed at large about Newport, engaged in fighting, drinking, and general disruption of the peace—"

"That's Penry—Pen." She chopped off his title, not sure if Pen would want it known that he'd spent weeks cloistered with the unfortunate souls of St. Sefin's in a rough, tiny town in Wales. The hind-end of Britain, he'd called it. A hard thread twisted around her heart and pulled tight. She hadn't heard from him since he'd walked away, nearly two weeks ago. She hadn't dared send to him, not even when the writ appeared, for she recalled the cold look on his face when he left.

What if he regretted his time with her? Thought it shameful. What if all they had shared had meant nothing to him—

"What have you to say to these last charges, Miss Ewyas?" Sir Robert demanded.

This whole spectacle was a farce. They didn't even know her real name. At least it couldn't shame her father, and her poor mother too, to have the Carews on the rolls with such ridiculous charges. When Gwen had done so much worse in her life.

"Who was keeping company with me?" she asked.

"This stranger. Pen," Calvin Vaughn said roughly.

Gwen stared at him. Even now he had no idea. "That wasn't

whoring," she said to Vaughn. "Men and women keep company all the time outside of marital relations, and not in criminal conversation. Unless he's forced a girl against her will—"

Vaughn flushed at the accusation. "It's whoring even if there's no money involved! And you've done it before."

Daron, beside him, grew rigid. He must have said something to Vaughn about their past relationship. He'd dug a hole for himself now; he couldn't take her hand or her supposed inheritance if Vaughn dragged her name through the mud in a court of law.

The thread around her heart tightened. What she'd shared with Pen was beautiful. It came near to being holy, the highest design of their Maker, two human hearts ennobled and bound together in adoration, in service, and in love. For her, it was love.

She'd wager no woman had ever known that sense of wholeness and completion in Calvin Vaughn's arms. And not Daron Sutton's, either.

"All this to the effect," the clerk went on in a strained voice, "that the neighbors were vexed and disquieted and grieved."

"What neighbors?" Gwen laughed, a short, bitter sound. "Our land abuts the St. Woolos churchyard, a ditch, and marshland owned by the Morgans. There's nothing but empty land between us and Maes-n-Gaer, the old hillfort."

Sir Roger glowered at the plaintiffs. "Mr. Vaughn, you led us to believe that this St. Sefin's was a rowdy pub filled with all manner of debauchery."

Vaughn swung on Gwen. "It is!"

"Your Worship," Gwen said. "Let me acquaint you with the present inhabitants of St. Sefin's. A young boy left blind as a babe who earns his keep as our goatherd. A young man who is a natural, an innocent, whose parents could not afford to keep him. A widow turned out of her house by her children and a grandmother turned off her land when her sons died. A veteran of the British Army maimed in the siege on Gibraltar. A young widow who lost her husband in the service of the Dutch Navy. And a young maid recently in service at Greenfield—"

Here Calvin Vaughn cleared his throat loudly, drowning out what she might say next. Gwen knotted her fingers in the lace apron she had worn instead of her shawl, because Dovey insisted it looked more English.

"All of these souls would have nowhere to go if we did not give them a home at St. Sefin's, Your Worship," Gwen said.

"I should say not," said Sir Robert. "Good Lord, they'd be in the workhouse, or demanding outdoor relief from the parish."

Gwen nodded. This was a tactic that might yield fruit. "I believe you were supplied a letter from Mr. Stanley, the vicar of St. Woolos? He attests that St. Sefin's has been a great relief on the poor rates around Newport. We rely on donations and our own earnings, you see. Not taxes."

The clerk handed over a letter. Sir Robert's eyebrows rose as he read it.

"Housing for indigent—foreigners—that is concerning— young mothers giving birth out of wedlock? Hmm. Taking all manner of ill and diseased—asking no fee or surety for their care —but you are not a religious institution." He peered at Gwen over the paper.

"No, Your Worship. St. Sefin's was a priory of the Carmelite nuns, and then passed into private hands at the Dissolution. We are a secular community. Our only rule—"

She hesitated. This was not the place to discuss her superstition about death. A hollow ache pierced her womb, an old memory. She'd borne and buried a daughter, and not two yards away stood the man who had fathered the babe, planted his seed and never thought again of the infant or its mother. He had walked free and unburdened in his life of luxury, spending coin as it came, while Gwen wore her fingers to bone to feed herself and Dovey and Cerys. She trembled with wrath, alight with it.

"None of this matters," Vaughn butted in. "Miss Ewyas owns the place and is therefore responsible for the goings on there. Charge her, threaten her with imprisonment, and let her throw herself on the mercy of her—friends." His pale eyes, red-rimmed, glimmered with malice. This was the next step in his blackmail, to make her cave to his demands to marry one of them.

She could protest no longer that she was worth nothing. Just that morning she'd received the letter from her father's solicitor in North Wales. She was worth more than Greenfield and Vine Court put together, and she was daughter to a man knighted for service to the Crown.

She lifted her chin. "I do not own St. Sefin's."

"She can still be charged," Daron said. "The law says she does not have to be owner to be held accountable."

"What an odd law for you to be so intimately acquainted with, Mr. Sutton," Gwen said.

Sir Robert frowned. "I know what the law says. But in my court the owner is answerable for what takes place on his property." He peered at Gwen. "Who owns St. Sefin's?"

"I do."

Pen stepped through the door. Every gaze in the room swiveled to him as if they were iron shavings and he the magnet that drew them all in a line.

He was overpoweringly elegant in a double-breasted tailcoat of blue wool over a waistcoat embroidered with red. Instead of breeches he wore buff pantaloons and a pair of gleaming tall boots. The well-tailored, expensive clothes showed every powerful line of his frame, and he swept off his black wool hat as he entered, transferring it to the hand holding a bronze-tipped cane. Gwen wondered if he needed the stick to walk, but his confident stride into the room suggested it was merely an accessory. This man had no weaknesses.

"Rhydian Price, The Right Honourable Viscount Penrydd," Ross announced from behind him. Ross too was well-dressed but wore a harried expression, while Penrydd was every inch the haughty lord. He nodded in acknowledgement to Sir Robert, who half-rose in respect at the title before recalling that, as presiding judge, he owned the room.

"How did my family come by a Carmelite priory? An interesting story," Pen said, though no one had asked. "My ancestor, Gereint ap Rhys, was a Welsh knight and great friend to Jasper Tudor. He supported Henry Tudor's troops at Bosworth and earned a barony for it. At the Dissolution, Henry VIII gave St. Sefin's to the family, by then calling themselves Price, and it's been bound up with the Penrydd estate ever since, though I regret to say that not much care was taken of it. Miss Ewyas, happily, has rectified that oversight."

At last his eyes moved to her, and a rush of air filled Gwen's body like the fuel of a hot-air balloon. The shifting world settled. Pen was here. He was here to witness her disgrace, the last thing she wanted, and yet his being here made everything hurt less.

"You own it!" Vaughn yelped. "But you—you're the man—"

Penrydd watched him with the cool curiosity he might show a new kind of insect. "The rough, worthless man described as causing fights and—how did you put it—keeping company with Miss Ewyas?"

Oh, yes, company was kept. She carried those memories on her skin. Gwen enjoyed watching Vaughn's Adam's apple bob up and down his throat as he attempted to find the words to redeem himself. "But you—you—"

"I was lodging on my own property to discover its state of

repair before attempting to sell it," Pen drawled. "I doubt that is a chargeable offense, Your Worship."

The spectators tittered. Pen had won them all in a moment. It seemed by Sir Robert's chuckle that he'd won him, too, by his name alone. Indignation and gratitude sparred in Gwen's breast. She wanted to win this case on her own merit, but Pen swept her accusers before him in a way she never could, as if they were so much rickrack on the Severn's tide.

"Penrydd," Sir Robert said with respect in his tone. "Heard you fought under Nelson at Tenerife. Rather a bad time, wasn't that?"

"Rather," Pen said. Every line in his body went taut, and Gwen ached to soothe him. All those nights he woke screaming, transported back to that living nightmare—who came to him now, in his rooms at the inn, to whisper him out of his dreams?

"That Penrydd." Daron finally made the connection. "You made Gwen your mistress?" His nostrils flared.

"On the contrary, I mean to make her my wife," Pen said. "I'll wed her as soon as she consents for the banns to be posted."

The crowd rustled like shorebirds when a morning fisherman set them to flight. Gwen's eyes tightened against a sudden threat of tears. Marriage was taking things too far. No one would believe this magnificent man would want her, in her dowdy gown and mended lace.

Daron snapped his jaw shut. "You can't marry her. She's—"

"She's what?" Pen crossed the room in a few bold strides. Gwen caught the trace of a limp and wondered what he'd been doing to strain himself this early in the day. Concern melted as he lifted her gloved hand and kissed the back of it. Sighs rose from the females in the audience. Gwen curled her fingers around his out of sheer instinct.

"Ruined!" Sutton exclaimed. "She's been—I, a long time ago —and this place—the business there—"

Pen lifted one brow, waiting, and Gwen adored his supercilious mien at the same time she cringed at it. The viscount was out in full display. This wasn't Pen, the man who made her laugh, the man who surprised and delighted her, the man who brought her to heights of pleasure and then picked fennel for her besides.

But it *was* him. These were all aspects of him, and if she loved the man, she had to accept all of him. She couldn't pick and choose the parts to leave and the parts to keep.

"Vaughn told me what goes on there!" Sutton sputtered. "Day and night. She's available to any man who pays for her and trots all about the countryside at their bidding. And the company she keeps, the dregs of society—it's hardly respectable! My lord," he added, belatedly realizing he was swinging at an opponent far above him in weight.

"Choose your words wisely, Sutton," Penrydd said. "You are making claims against my future viscountess and doings on my property, and the clerk of the peace over there is writing all of this down. Sir Robert, remind me—is there still a penalty on the books for insulting a peer of the realm?"

Ross coughed into his fist. "*Scandalum magnatum*," he said.

Sir Robert's eyebrows shot up. "Slander of the great? Not prosecuted much these days, but still a chargeable offense, yes. Need a jury for that trial, though. Have to go up to quarter sessions at the least." He turned toward the plaintiffs. "And a much higher penalty, if the slander is proved."

Vaughn, impossibly, turned even paler and took a step backward. Sutton's lip curled as if he'd swallowed something sour.

"A case for another time, then," Pen said, his voice as silky as the morning mist that rose from the basin of the Usk. "To the one at hand—have you had time to consider the evidence, Your Worship? Keeping a disorderly house, nuisance to her neighbors, and all that."

Sir Robert fidgeted with the piece of parchment before him on the table. "According to Mr. Stanley, a man from whom I have never known an untruth to be uttered, the establishment of St. Sefin's is a public good and has kept any number of people out of the workhouse and off the poor rolls. As a private home that does not charge fees, I see no licensing requirement that must be met. And I find it unlikely a collection of widows would be running a bawdy house, with children about. As to the matter of Miss Ewyas and her personal conduct—" He gave Gwen a sidewise glance. "I feel certain, Lord Penrydd, that you would only offer for a woman of the highest moral character."

He pounded on the table with his gavel. "Defendant is not guilty. The charges against Miss Ewyas are dismissed." As an immediate babble resulted, Sir Robert raised his voice and fixed a protuberant stare on Vaughn and Sutton. "The surety of the plaintiffs given as recognizance is forfeit to this court," he shouted. "And—there is a fee for my services, gentlemen."

It was over. Not guilty. Case dismissed. Gwen's knees went as watery as goat's milk, and she clung to Pen for support as he drew her away.

"Surety?" she murmured.

Pen nodded. "Sutton and Vaughn had to pay the constable twenty pounds each in bond as testament they had a valid complaint. Keeps the justice from wasting time with frivolous suits. Since the evidence didn't stand, they lose the forfeit. And as justices of the peace don't have a stipend, they are at liberty to request fees for their services. Robert has daughters to support."

Gwen stifled a laugh. "Thank goodness I wasn't levied a fine. We've no money." She tugged at Pen's hand, so strong, so firm around hers. "You must let me buy St. Sefin's nevertheless. We will find the funds somehow." It seemed miraculous that she'd been spared. Now, finally, she could settle the thing she'd wanted from the beginning: his promise that St. Sefin's would be hers.

He lifted one eyebrow in that manner she hated. "And deny me the pleasure of defending you in court? I quite enjoyed this little fracas. So rare that I get to win. Besides, any property of yours will become mine when we marry."

He slipped an arm around her and nodded as people clustered before them, delivering congratulations along with curious stares. He'd made a wonder of her with his claim that she would be his viscountess. Baronets were the biggest titles they saw in Newport, and he was Penrydd, one of their own.

"As to the matter of marriage," Gwen stammered.

"Milord Penrydd." The prim, silent woman in the corner rose and pulled back the black netting of her veil. Though lined with strain, her pale face was more bewitching in its beauty than Gwen had ever seen her.

She flowed across the room and lightly touched Pen's arm. "Anne Sutton. Milord, I had no part in my brother's schemes. Please believe me."

Pen's jaw tightened. Gwen recognized the flare of anger. Anne Sutton had seen Pen in his workman's jacket and cap and had looked past him like a fencepost, as had her brother. Put him in fancy garb and address him as milord, and she was clinging to his hand.

As was Gwen. She squeezed his fingers, treasuring that silent marker of their connection. Their belonging to one another.

"What do you want of me, Miss Sutton?" Pen said in a measured tone.

"Please, milord. Take me with you. Away from him. Away from here. I long to go to England, and I'll do anything you ask of me. Your mistress. Your—I'll be your viscountess. I'd be a sight better at it than Gwen could."

The girl she'd known could never be so heartless toward an old friend, Gwen thought. Anne's swift, despairing glance, laden with apology and defiance, softened Gwen's heart even as the insult pricked her ire.

"But you see, I have offered my hand to Gwen," Penrydd said.

"A farmer's daughter? Don't you desire a good match for you, milord?" Anne, in desperation, followed them out the door to the top of the stairs.

Gwen strove to hold her tongue. If she were to spend any time around Pen, she would have to steel herself to women flinging themselves at him before her very nose. He was a lord of the realm, and eventually he would need to think about heirs. He was handsome, assured, titled, and wealthy. Many women would bear a surly temper or overfondness for rum from such a marital prize.

Could she bear it, though, her entire life? Always feeling that she was stealing him from his real life, his true place as a lord and peer? The very notion that she, so unequal in rank, could be his viscountess—his offer could only be a performance for the court, meant to shield her from Sutton's schemes. As a mistress she could be with him openly and no one would think the less of him for her inferior wealth and birth. But as wife— her mind veered away.

"Miss Sutton," Pen said. "Are you familiar with the ancient Greek legend about how the original humans were split in two, so each spends their mortal life looking for their other half?"

Anne watched him warily. "Milord? There is no such Christian belief."

"I quite liked the tale," Pen said. "Though I cannot recall now where I read it."

"Plato's Symposium," Gwen murmured. "Surely you remember, Anne, when your tutor tried to teach us ancient

Greek?" She turned to Pen. "It was Zeus who divided humans into their current form, fearing their power. And I am quite sure the moral had something to do with philosophical completion. With Plato, the moral is always philosophical."

"Love is a form of completion." Pen laced her arm around his, his eyes glowing as if he were lit from behind. "I think it a sound philosophy, too."

Anne's lower lip trembled. "I cannot stay in Llanfyllin."

"Then perhaps you ought to have thrown yourself on me, and not Penrydd," Gwen said. "Come to St. Sefin's, Anne, and we will make up a room for you. It's not grand like Vine Court, but you will be free of your brother's shadow."

"I am taking you to Bristol," Pen said. "There are two viscountesses who are very eager to make your acquaintance."

Anne fell back in dismay as her brother shouted her name. Pen drew Gwen out of the room, down the stairs of the pub and to the street outside, where Ross stood holding the reins of a pair of expensive-looking horses.

"Pen," she said. "I need to return to St. Sefin's. They need to know—"

"Yes, and you may tell them our happy news. I expect they will be thrilled that I have finally succeeded in my suit."

Pen swung atop the larger animal as if he did such things every day, which, Gwen realized, in his real, lordly life, he did. She stared with apprehension at the enormous gelding, who eyeballed her back with disdain. She flinched as Ross, with apologies in advance, put his hands at her waist to lift her into Pen's arms.

"Pen, I didn't agree—"

"I will persuade you," Pen said. "Come, my Welsh warrior princess, courage! This horse and my stepmother are not the worst things you will face as a viscountess."

"What could be worse?" Gwen said, but she allowed Pen to

settle her before him in the saddle and place his arms around her, and she realized that this could be her life, if she chose it: Pen's arms around her, and untold dangers ahead.

She couldn't live like that. She couldn't ask him to. But she didn't know how to stop him as he clucked to the horse to take them first to St. Sefin's, and then to God knows where after that.

CHAPTER SEVENTEEN

S t. Sefin's had visitors. Pen felt Gwen tense in his arms as they trotted up the path and around the stately front of the church. A small cart sat in the back yard, near the outbuildings, and a pony he recognized from the King's Head stables browsed among the goats. Birds swirled and settled back to retrieving seeds from the newly sown garden when the horses clopped to a stop.

"Haia, Miss Gwen!" Ifor called from his perch atop a low wall, the foundations of a former building long scavenged for its stone. "Two fancy ladies here to see you. They're the viscount's people, they are."

Pen groaned. "Of course they wouldn't stay in Bristol, though I told them I would bring you to them. Ifor, I'm putting my horse and Ross's in the pen. Will Gafr have it?"

Ifor's face broke into a broad smile. "*Croeso*, Mr. Pen!"

"That means welcome," Pen said to Ross as he swung Gwen down from the horse. She gripped his forearms in terror, and he smiled, pleased at this tiny sign that she needed him. His stubborn Gwen pretended to need no one, but she'd needed him today in the courtroom. He had to prove she required him in other ways, too.

"Still holding to your courage, I hope?" he murmured in her ear, catching her arm again as he dismounted and Ifor helped Ross pen the horses. He sensed Ross's discomfort; his secretary didn't know what to make of the unusual community of St. Sefin's, or Pen's interest in it. But Pen's concern was for Gwenllian, whose face was white with terror.

"You'll see how they will receive me," she warned him. "It will be the same everywhere. No one will ever allow you to make a Welsh farm girl your viscountess."

"I don't need anyone's approval," Pen said. "I need you."

He detected a softening at the corners of her mouth in response to his words, and debated whether to kiss her. Instinct won out over propriety and at the door to the chapter house, where the others had gathered, he bent and pressed his lips to the enchanting curve of her cheek. She pulled away but couldn't repress the small smile that told him she was delighted by his declaration.

An instant clamor arose as Gwen stepped into the room, shouts, cries of welcome, exclamations of relief. His stepmother and sister-in-law rose from two upholstered chairs, holding themselves apart from the rest. Prunella looked intrigued, and Lydia furious.

Evans stepped forward and held out his hand to shake Pen's. Lydia's lip curled at this gesture of familiarity and Pen added a thump on Evans's back for good measure.

"Miss Gwenllian didn't end in the bridewell, I take it," Evans said. "What did Sir Robert decide, then?"

"Not guilty," Gwen said. "By reason that the Viscount Penrydd appeared and made Mr. Sutton and Mr. Vaughn think very carefully about the accusations they wanted to level against a peer."

She hugged Dovey, who wiped a tear of relief from her cheek. Dovey, Pen guessed, had been in Gwen's confidence this whole time, while she had told him nothing, even though it was his property under discussion.

The thought should have made him furious. But it made him simply more determined to prove that he, too, was worthy of her trust.

"We're free of them?" Dovey asked. "Truly?"

"Doubt they'll be back," Mother Morris cackled, rising and hobbling to Gwen to claim a hug of her own. "No use lifting your petticoat after you've peed."

"Will we see the girl, though?" Widow Jones asked, giving Gwen a squeeze of welcome. "Anne?"

"I told her to come to us, though she's used to better," Gwen said. "She threw out her scarf for the viscount, and I can't say I blame her. I imagine Calvin Vaughn won't take her without a dowry, and she is better off free of him."

Mathry moved in for an embrace, but Cerys dived in first, clinging to Gwen's waist. Mathry threw her arms around them both. Tomos, holding to Gwen's apron with one fist, beamed at them all.

"Well, she can't have me. Lydia, Prunella," Pen greeted the two women. Prunella was a lush woman with large, sweeping curves, just the shape Edwin preferred, and she had a habitual sleepy, languid air from which it was difficult to rouse her. Pen was frankly surprised she had bestirred herself to travel from the comfortable London townhouse, and in the company of Lydia, whom she did not particularly like.

"What brings you here, Lydia? At least you have finally relieved yourself of Miss Carruthers," Pen said. "I found her very tedious."

"Mr. Turbeville took her with his sisters on an excursion to his family's cottage in Weston-super-Mare," Lydia said in a tight voice. "Penrydd, we must speak with you at once. Ross advised me of your ridiculous intentions, and I have come to make you see sense."

"Very well." Pen seated himself in the bishop's chair, of which he'd grown fond. He urged Gwen to perch on the carved lion's paw arm, hooking his elbow around her hips. She blushed at the blatant signal of possession, but didn't argue, for once.

Lydia narrowed her eyes. In opposition to Prunella's generous lines, she was a thin, shrewish woman as tense as a coiled spring. She'd brought an admirable dowry and an impeccable bloodline to her marriage, and she had suffered her stepson's rowdiness during his breaks from school or visits home. Now, with no children of her own and that family of impeccable bloodline having no inclination to take her in, she depended on the income she drew from the estate that Pen controlled, and her every interaction with him bristled with her resentment for living at the mercy of the boy she had always despised.

"You might as well have it out here, Lydia," Pen said. "I daresay Gwen has already gone over all your objections." He enjoyed the way everyone was listening avidly to the exchange, including Ifor, who had come in from outside.

"Very well." Lydia gathered her dignity. She wore an open robe of striped grey silk with white flowers embroidered at the hem and a lace fichu tucked into the bodice. The ensemble was plain for Lydia, but he saw Gwen eying the finery. Dovey in turn was studying Prunella's robe of white muslin spotted with tiny red flowers, cinched with a pink sash at her waist and ruffles of lace about her neck.

"You must think of your family, Rhydian. You cannot sink us this low. To marry a Welsh woman—"

"You forget your husband's family was Welsh, and had been for centuries," Pen said.

Lydia was the daughter of a lesser son born to one of the

oldest English earldoms, so she could and did boast of her high connections. Prunella too was a gentleman's daughter and could be sure of her reception anywhere. They were not of the fast, dashing set that would laugh at conventions and thumb their nose at the strictures of the moral middle class.

No, they were of the sort that guarded carefully the borders of class and rank, and they would do their best to ensure that someone like Gwen was kept out. They would be the first to criticize her conduct and her birth, to ridicule her Welsh ways and forthright manner of speaking. They would somehow make it shameful that she had run a refuge for the destitute and cast-away, and if they ever found out she had borne a child out of wedlock—he had a sense, as most men did, of the cruel, strict way women held other women in line. Bringing Gwen into this world would be like throwing a virgin martyr into the Coliseum to be devoured by lions.

Lydia's eyelid twitched, a sure sign of annoyance. "You must realize we couldn't hold our heads up to the gossip," she said. "You'd never be taken seriously in Lords or anywhere else. She'd be cut everywhere, and you would too. You might have to leave the country. Is that what you want?"

Of course not. What he wanted was to live in bliss with the woman he loved, and the rest of the world could go hang.

He tightened his arm, feeling Gwen stir in protest. A mistress would be the easier choice. She would be accepted among the other women of the demimonde, the woman like her who earned their keep with their favors, and he would be applauded for capturing a rare beauty. Men of his station were expected to keep a ladybird. They were also expected to marry among their station and breed children to take up the reins of power once they had passed.

Children. With Gwen. He'd never before wanted to bring a child into this cruel world, had in fact taken pains in all his liaisons to avoid that outcome. But a child of his and Gwen's, or several—his lungs clenched at the thought, empty of air.

"Your wife must be bred to the position, Rhydian," Lydia said. "You can't make a Welsh farm girl a viscountess. You'll shame us all."

"Is that your main objection, Lydia?" Pen said. "Then allow me to present to you Miss Gwenllian Carew, also calling herself Gwenllian ap Ewyas." He sensed the gasp of surprise that went around the room as he said Gwen's name. She rose and delivered a stiff but proper curtsey.

"Gwen, my stepmother Lydia, the Dowager Viscountess Penrydd, and Prunella, the current Viscountess Penrydd, my brother's bride. There will be two dowagers once you wed me, which I judge will cause no end of confusion about town, but I could not care less."

"Penrydd," Lydia said, a set to her mouth that promised she would give no quarter. "It's shocking enough what these people have done to your property, your family's property. But to unite yourself in marriage to—"

"A knight's daughter," Pen said, forcing his voice to remain level. "Badge presented for service to the Crown in supplying copper from his mines to line the hulls of ships for the Royal Navy. Who's to say but that our ammunition at Tenerife might have stayed dry if Bowen's ship had been so outfitted. Now, it's not a title of a hundred years' standing, I grant you, but if Sir David Carew has saved one life with his copper, that's more than I can lay claim to doing in all my years of service."

An utter silence fell over the room. Shards of colored light drifted through the stained glass set high in the wall. Gwen's face caught the colors as she stared at him.

"That's not enough," Lydia said. "The money—"

"Yes, my brother's debts. Poor Prunella. Our respectable Edwin turned up rather more unsteady than we thought him, didn't he? I'll have you know, Lydia, that I've been wise enough to let myself be leg-shackled by an heiress. How much did they tell us the mines yield a year, Ross?"

Ross tore his eyes away from Mathry, who was lounging in her usual spot in the window, her curved form limned with light. "Ahem. Ah. The copper and lead-silver together, on the combined properties, produce about thirty thousand in any given year, depending on the price for ore. Gross income before salaries and supplies, that is. Sir."

Lydia paled beneath the lead paint of her makeup.

"Thousands, you say?" Prunella looked as if she'd just been handed a pretty new hat.

Gwen scowled. "How do you know this? My father's solicitor only replied to me this morning."

"Ross made inquiries," Pen said. "Now don't go in a taking. I'll ask you to repair the Penrydd fortunes, yes, but beyond that I'll let you have a say in how the income is used."

A joyful light broke over Gwen's face. "I can buy St. Sefin's."

"Which will do you no good, since it will be mine again at our marriage. I told you this," Pen said. "Besides, I have other plans for the place. I intend to sell St. Sefin's to Mrs. Van der Welle for the price of—what do you think fair, Ross? One pound?"

Ross, overcome by a choking fit, could not respond. His reply would have been drowned out anyway by the uproar in the room. Pen was aware only of Gwen beside him. She trembled like a dancing flame and her expression of admiration as she looked down at him made him wish he could do something to win that look from her every day.

Dovey lifted her chin with eloquent pride. "I can pay you a hundred pounds, milord. We have savings."

"Ten pounds it is," Pen said to her. "I'm not convinced it's the best move, mind, since what's yours will go to Evans, do you ever accept him. But we could draw up papers that upon your marriage put the property in trust for Cerys, or some such. I'm sure Ross can find a legal recourse, and if he can't, Barlow will."

"Dovey?" Gwen blinked. "Marry Evans?"

"There are ways to keep it in her name, sir," Evans said in a mild voice belied by the furious red blush of his ears. "And make it her jointure, of course, if something happens to me, with provision that the property go to Cerys in the event that—"

"I have not consented to marriage," Dovey said, her nose pointed toward the ceiling. "Mr. Evans has not made me an offer, proper or otherwise."

"Dovey?" Gwen cried, staring at her friend. "And Evans?"

"My word, Gwen, how did you miss that? And here I thought you so clever." Pen tightened his arm about her. She was so strong, so fierce, but she betrayed herself in how she unconsciously leaned toward him. Her body knew she belonged with him, even if her solid good sense still protested.

"Dovey and Evans," Gwen repeated. "But they're always chopsing. He's forever scolding her, and she says he can't do anything right, and—"

"Gwenllian ap Ewyas, my ridiculous daft garden warbler. That man would give his every remaining limb for her. And if I'm not mistaken, she's a particular tendre for him, haven't you, Mrs. Van der Welle? She needs only be convinced another marriage won't break her heart again, or leave her destitute, like last time. And if she has property with some income, that's one problem solved."

"We haven't any income," Gwen said.

"We'll deal with that in a minute." Pen withdrew his pocket watch and regarded it. "It's been two weeks, aye? Time enough to age that special batch of St. Sefin's brew I made. And long enough to season our mixtures, wouldn't you say, Evans?" At the other man's nod, Pen snapped his watch shut and tucked it back in his pocket.

"Very well. Let's have a fine dinner and I'll tell you what I plan to do with the Black Hound. And then, Gwenllian ap Ewyas," and he pulled her close against him, where he no longer felt the constant hollow ache, and with her beside him might never feel such again. "We will discuss posting the banns."

CHAPTER EIGHTEEN

"Laverbread," Pen said to Ross, breaking off a piece and handing it to him. "Gwen's specialty."

"Seaweed?" Ross poked at it doubtfully.

Pen caught Gwen's eyes as they sat around the large refectory table. "*Saes*," he said, shaking his head. His smile sent warmth channeling through her.

"I'm a Scotsman born and bred, and you ken that, sir," Ross said with reproach in his tone. Down the table, with Mother Morris on one side of her and Widow Jones on the other, Mathry giggled.

Pen had persuaded Sir Robert to dismiss the charges against them. Pen meant to sell St. Sefin's to Dovey. Not her. Dovey. Gwen's heart pinched with a kind of hopeful agony she didn't know how to decipher.

He didn't want to marry that other girl. Despite the strenuous objections of his stepmother, he said he wanted to marry Gwen. Lydia and Prunella sat a bit apart at one of the long tables, and Lydia's face said what she thought of the simple fare. She'd wanted to find a decent inn in town, or go back to Bristol that evening, but Pen said he was otherwise occupied and could not take her, so she and sweet, languid Prunella were obliged to lodge at St. Sefin's for the night.

She'd never get on with them. She'd never survive in Pen's world. Better to stay here, the world she knew, and ask him to visit now and again, to breathe life into her.

"I do wish you'd let the authorities deal with the Black Hound." Gwen heaped another helping of steamed cockles on Pen's plate.

"That's the thing. I spoke to all the authorities, including Sir Robert Salusbury." Pen cracked open a shell with relish. "No one dares try to bring him to trial. They're all too glad to let me address his crimes in any manner I see fit."

"You know Sir Robert?" She handed the platter down the table to Dovey, who sat with Cerys and the boys, having their own giggled conversation. Evans sat across from Dovey, blushing every time he looked at her. Gwen tore her gaze away.

"Robert studied under my Uncle Broderick at Lincoln's Inn," Pen said, splashing vinegar onto his cockles. "Uncle gave a good report of him, far as I could decipher. Second Price sons are supposed to study law, you know, not buy an officer's commission."

"I—I suppose I didn't realize there are more of you." But Lydia had spoken of the family. When she'd kept Pen at St. Sefin's, she'd thought she was doing no worse than keep an idle rouseabout from fondling maids and drinking too much grog. She hadn't thought a moment about women who depended on him for their livelihood, about aunts and uncles and cousins.

How could he ever trust her after such a deceit? How could his family ever let her in?

He'd only come up with that daft claim of a betrothal to rout Vaughn and his suit, and perhaps get out of marrying the other young lady his stepmother had selected for his bride. She couldn't hold him to it. Although as she watched him sitting at the table, as easy as a lord as when he'd been simply Pen, she wished with a high, wild longing that she *could* make this man hers in the eyes of the world. He was imprinted on her heart, so why couldn't she claim and keep him?

"There are any number of uncles and cousins and nephews and second cousins waiting to see what might finish me off." Pen carefully cut a truffle and gave her half. She rolled the morsel over her tongue, delighting in the rich, complicated taste. Much like Pen. "I'd love to tweak their noses by producing a brace of heirs. Maybe a round dozen of them."

She swallowed the truffle past a suddenly thick throat. He had to know she was barren. Barren women had no right marrying men who were expected to pass along titles and estates.

"Sir Robert knew all along you were the owner of St. Sefin's? I would have wagered his surprise was real when you appeared."

He poured himself a small dose of small beer, the beer she'd made earlier. A lord of the realm, sitting at a table with paupers, drinking small beer.

"I approached Sir Robert about a week ago for his advice, and he warned me I was unlikely to find a second plaintiff to lodge a complaint against the Black Hound. People seem notoriously unwilling to accuse the man of anything, possibly because they usually hire him to cover up some peccadillo they don't want known. With just the testimony of two former convicts, Robert didn't think I had evidence enough to make up a formal complaint of my own. Though he said he wished I did, since the only interesting case he had coming up was a woman supposedly running a disorderly house in an old convent."

Gwen's stomach shifted, and she looked down at her plate. "You're wondering why I didn't notify you myself. Since it was your property I had brought into ill repute."

"And since I am a landowner of some stature in this area, even if the Morgans own more acres than I do," Pen said gently. She couldn't meet his eyes. "I *am* one of the authorities around here, as it turns out. But I was hoping you would come to me."

Her eyes stung. How could she ask anything of him, after the way she'd betrayed him? How could he forgive her so easily?

His voice dropped to a low murmur, and he moved his hand to cover hers, which trembled. "I won't hurt you like he did, Gwen."

She couldn't tell him this wasn't about Daron Sutton. That man had no hold on her. No, what lay between them was her lies, what she'd become. He couldn't lift her up with a silk gown and a diamond necklace; she'd always be what she was. She couldn't hope for such wild happiness as a future with Pen.

Besides, she was needed here. She'd built St. Sefin's with her bare hands. Even if it were safe under Dovey's ownership, Dovey still needed her help.

There was a Cymric word for the ache that pierced her: *hiraeth,* that longing for something beautiful and lost. It built in her as she listened to Pen's laugh, the deep timber of his voice, that sweetest of music. It built as he rubbed a hand over her back and the calluses on his fingers, gained from honest labor, snagged in her hair. It built as his heat wrapped around her, feeding an inner fire, one that was going to burn her to ash. He had pierced his way into her heart, this scarred, shattered man who was putting himself back together, and the loss of him was going to break her forever.

"I have to—pick some wormwood. And make up the beds." She bolted as the meal drew to an end. She would let Dovey and Widow Jones clean up while she busied herself making up the best rooms she could find for their guests.

Later, as dusk fell, she made her way to the tiny chapel in the church. Before the stained glass window she took up a spill and lit a candle, the flame fluttering wildly in her trembling fingers. *Gwladys, mother and saint, give me the strength to bear this*. Gwladys had helped her once before, infusing her with the courage to stay and sit with the pieces of her life. But this time, there was so much more she would lose. So much more she would miss.

"I'm glad to find Gwladys right where I left her." She heard him first in her chest, her heart humming like a plucked harp string, before his words registered.

Gwen, too, would stay right where he left her. A walking husk of a woman animated only by his nearness, his touch.

"Have you been to the tower yet?" he asked.

"I told everyone to stay away. I'm sure it's not safe."

"Good. Then they won't find us."

He held out his hand. What a shapely hand he had for a man, the wrist fine-boned, the fingers long and agile. She recalled every time that hand had brushed her skin, and her insides swirled with heat.

She took his hand. These might be her last moments with him. She would dwell in this bliss for as long as she could, brand him into her memory so deeply that he would remain part of her beyond death.

There was a folded woolen blanket and a bag of rags that passed for a pillow at the top platform of the old belltower. Without the bell, the slits of the tower opened to the sky, a drape of black velvet shimmering with thousands of pinpricks of light and a lazy river of stars.

"You slept up here?" Gwen asked. In the enclosed space his body brushed against her, and her nerves flared like a sulfur match.

"Sometimes. When the nightmares bit hard. But when you were with me—" His mouth brushed her temple, as if he were sampling the taste of her. "I didn't dream."

He turned his body toward her and Gwen fell into his embrace without a qualm. His arms held her and her soul lifted into his kiss. She helped him haul her skirts around her waist and he sat her on the railing, one arm like a steel band holding her fast. She wrapped her legs around his flanks and caught his groan in her mouth when his erect member pressed against her, rubbing, teasing.

She didn't need flirtatious words or slow kindling caresses, not this time. She urged him with a hand on the taut muscle of his buttock and he reached under her skirts again. This time the flap on his breeches fell away and she wiggled toward him, tilting up her hips, and smiled at his murmur of satisfaction when he probed at the entrance to her body and found her wet and waiting. He entered in one slow, smooth, sure glide and she wondered if that was her hiss of pleasure, or his.

"Ah, God, Gwen." He held still a moment and she reveled with him in their connection. The seal on their need, and their joy.

"Yes." The pleasure built from nothing but the feel of him inside her, of knowing he wanted her as urgently as she desired him. She slid a hand to the back of his neck and kissed him with everything she had, drawing his tongue into her mouth and sucking. His hips bucked against hers, then he shifted his weight and clasped one hand to her breast and began thrusting in earnest, and in moments she was hurtling off the edge into the sky, flung into a bliss so shattering that stars burned upon her eyelids, a river of sparks erupting inside her. He shivered in her arms and she knew her climax had spurred his, that he spun with her inside this perfect ecstasy, that the same force that bound the planets held them together.

With Pen, held and fused, she was complete.

After a while they unwrapped their bodies and burrowed under the blanket together. There they lay quietly, hands moving beneath their clothes. She touched him as if still not certain he was real, despite the solid warmth that crept from his body into hers. He stroked a hand from her hips to her shoulder, his touch possessive and reverent, and paused at her throat with the thumb resting on the dent between her collarbones, his fingers sliding into her hair behind her ear.

"You must marry me," Pen said.

She stilled in the act of tracing his ribs, finding the small lump where the bones had knit after his fall into the dory. The night that had changed his life, and hers.

"I can't be a viscountess." She tried to laugh, but the sound was a wince of pain. Here in this tower in the wilds of Wales, beneath a rough blanket and an ancient sky, she belonged to him completely. Outside St. Sefin's, his world was as different as could be.

"Tell me why." He wrapped a lock of her hair around his fist and tugged lightly.

"Where to begin? I'm Welsh. Your countrymen hate mine." She let her fingers follow the scars over his shoulder and arm. "I'm a farmer's daughter." The fact that her father might have died a knight didn't change the fact of her humble birth, a class far below his, and Pen lived in a world where birth meant everything.

"I'm not pure, which you already know. I don't have the breeding of those English ladies. I'll do nothing but disappoint you."

"All you have to do is love me."

She spread her hand over his heart, letting her palm absorb the firm, steady beat. He moved a hand to cover hers.

"That I do," she said quietly. "It is the only requirement I could meet, Pen."

"Then nothing else matters."

"Perhaps not to you. But it will matter to your world. Your

people won't have someone like me. I'll be an embarrassment. The woman you lowered yourself for."

"But we'll have each other. We'll have *this*." He rose swiftly and rolled atop her, his groin settling atop hers. She shifted her hips to cradle him, her body an invitation. She couldn't deny that in this way they fit, this most primal and elemental connection. She'd never try to deny it. He could come to her at any time and no matter where he had traveled, who else he had loved, she knew she would open and yield to him, draw him hungrily, gladly back into her arms. She hadn't the power to end this craving and wouldn't try.

"But what about children?" she whispered. "You have a title and estates you need to pass on. I can't—I doubt I'll have another child of my own. Something happened at the birth of my daughter, and it left me barren."

Hot tears seeped from her eyes, sliding down her temples. She put her hands on either side of his face, trying to read his eyes. They were shadowed, only his cheeks and lips catching the starlight, and the faint pink line of a scar high on his brow.

"You would give up everything to be with me, Pen. I can't ask that of you."

"I gave it all up before." His voice was rough and low, scraping against her chest. "I lived here with you as a nobody."

"That was a lie." Despair clutched at her throat. "Because I didn't tell you who you were. It was selfish and dishonest, and I —I kept you from where you belonged."

She thought of Penrydd, that lovely little castle in its field of lush green. She'd barter her soul to belong there with him, raising their children in spacious rooms, entertaining their friends with hunts and musical evenings. But that place had been barred to her from birth, even before choice and circumstance made it impossible for her to be worthy of him.

"Then come with me as my not-viscountess." He muttered

the words against her throat, kissing a line from her ear down her neck. "I made you an offer months ago, didn't I? It stands. It will always stand." His clever hand worked at her breast, knowing how to bring her desire to thrumming life with a stroke or two.

"I'm needed here." She couldn't just hare off in pursuit of her own pleasures and leave everyone here to shoulder on without her. Her income sustained them, paltry as it was.

Her fingers stilled on Pen's back. She'd forgotten about the mines. She could arrange for a stipend for St. Sefin's. She could repair and expand the place, take in even more people. The project might sustain her when Pen left. It would give her a reason to keep breathing.

"*I* need you." He rolled his hips against her and with a little moan she bent a knee so his growing erection slid between her legs.

She let her head fall back, helpless to resist him, but knowing that even when the night ended and they must part again, her answer must be the same. She had been exonerated from her trial. She might indeed be an heiress. But she had seen the disdain in Lydia's eyes, knew what barriers would confront her, them, if she were so foolish as to give in to love and passion. Her answer must always be the same.

"Look at the sky," she whispered. "What do you English call that? The silver wheel." She pointed to the river snaking its way across the spangled expanse.

"The Milky Way? We learned this in school. The *via lactea*, so called because one Greek god or another tore a child from Hera's breast, and the droplets spattered into the sky." He dropped his mouth over her naked breast, tonguing the nipple.

Gwen shook her head, even as little fires arrowed through her veins. "We call it Caer Wydion, the castle of Gwydion, an ancient hero known for his strength and cleverness."

Pen moved from the moistened tip of one breast to the other, licking and nuzzling. "I thought Gwydion was a pig stealer and the father of his sister's child."

She sighed and tugged the blanket over his back, enclosing them both. "He was a powerful warrior and knew magic. He made a woman once out of nothing but flowers."

"You taste like a flower." He tugged a nipple between his teeth. "I don't see your point, besides these two."

She cradled his head in her hand, sifting her fingers through his hair.

"Two different stories," she said. "Two different worlds. Two different pasts. They can never come together."

"We've come together. Several times." He reached between them and led his cock to the slit of her body, the slick, firm cap nosing against her entrance. She was ready for him, hungry again. She would always be hungry for him. It was her curse.

She cupped her hand around his and guided him inside and he obeyed, sinking his length into her. He dropped her forehead to hers, breathing heavily, holding himself taut as she accepted his swelling fullness, the ache and its relief together. She could never have enough of him. She could never have him inside her long enough, deep enough, to quell the demand. She would always want more. If she could pull him inside her and keep him there, she would.

Leaving him what? Her?

"I will always want you, Pen," she whispered, rocking against him, grief in her voice.

He moved against her in leisurely strokes, watching her eyes, and she knew he would try every angle, every variety of pressure, until he brought them both to bliss and beyond.

"Then at least we have this," he muttered.

"Yes." She had him for now, this man who made her feel as if she were knit of flowers and stars. This astonishing man with his clever mind and gentle hands, his determined spirit, his fierce and battered heart. She braced her feet to take him inside her more deeply, loving how his breath hitched in pleasure, wishing she could hold and please him always. Desire reached from her belly, clenching around her heart, a candle now burning bright that would be wasted and empty when he left.

"At least we have this."

CHAPTER NINETEEN

"It's just tea, Gwen," Anne Sutton said. "My brother and Mr. Vaughn won't be there. Lady Vaughn wants to entertain the Dowager Viscountess and Lady Penrydd while they are in the area, and to make her apologies to you." Anne pouted. "Please come."

She was wearing the frilly muslin dress she'd wore on her first visit to St. Sefin's, but the dark circles beneath made her eyes look haunted and she smoothed her fingers over the ribbon at her waist in a nervous gesture. Gwen sighed.

"It's late for tea." She'd have to travel to Greenfield in the company of the ladies Penrydd, who had not warmed to her after Pen's startling announcement in the chapter house the day before. She'd be back far too late to help with the evening meal, leaving Dovey and Widow Jones to see to everything, and then what was she to feed two picky, overbred English viscountesses? "Does she want me to harp, then?"

"Just you. Come, Gwen. The others are already in the carriage." Anne paused, fingers fluttering at her throat. "Lady Vaughn feels terrible for what her son put you through. As do I."

The best thing Lady Vaughn could do was let her forget the

entire courtroom scene, Gwen thought. She'd much rather stay here and acquaint herself with whatever schemes Pen was working up. He and Ross and Evans had been in the back pasture all day, engaged in a project they wouldn't disclose, but the occasional muffled explosions and whoops of joy that emanated from that quarter told her they were up to mischief.

He'd asked her to let him deal with the Black Hound in his own fashion. So far his fashion, as far as she could gather, included making darnel beer and dung bombs. Gwen harbored great reservations.

Anne tugged on her sleeve. "Gwen. Please."

Gwen sighed and went to the kitchen to leave her shawl and a word to Mother Morris about where she was going. She was dressed in a plain cotton day gown, the second best she had, but Anne urged her to the carriage without giving her time to fetch a bonnet. At least Anne wasn't lingering to throw out her scarf for Pen, Gwen grumbled to herself.

The coach wasn't one she recognized, a barouche in glossy black lacquer with red trim around the wheels and door, and red leather seats inside. It appeared new.

"—at least some semblance of civilization," Lydia was saying as Gwen climbed in.

Prunella offered Gwen a pleasant smile, and Gwen manu-factured one in return. She sensed Prunella might be more approachable on her own, but Lydia stood guard over her like a wolfhound, protecting the family honor. From people like Gwen.

The pair of blacks weren't Greenfield horses, and instead of setting out to the west towards Bassaleg and the patches of red oak and sycamore that encased Greenfield, the coach jolted down the rough track leading south over the salty marshes that lined the low-lying Usk. Gwen grabbed for a leather handle near the ceiling as the carriage jostled.

"Greenfield isn't this way." Lady Vaughn must have hired a coach and driver who didn't know his direction. Perhaps her own coach wasn't large enough for all four of them.

"Oh—she wished us to join her on a boat. On the river." Anne's smile seemed forced, and her eyes wouldn't settle in any one place. "A sort of pleasure cruise."

"A late afternoon pleasure cruise?"

"We go for punts on the Thames all the time, Miss Carew," Lydia said. Her smile stretched even more thinly than Anne's. "In fact Miss Carruthers was hoping she and Penrydd would marry on a small boat on the river."

Reference to Pen's conjectured betrothal silenced Gwen, as Lydia intended. Prunella grimaced as the carriage wheel fell into a rut, then jounced free. "I wouldn't like it," she said. "I'd daresay I'd be seasick the entire time."

"It would merely be for an hour, Prunella, and the boat would not be moving," Lydia snapped. "Miss Sutton, you said Lady Vaughn was from Wrexham? I know Sir Foster and Lady Cunliffe. In fact, they have invited me to Acton Park on more than one occasion."

Gwen held her tongue and looked out the window, wrinkling her nose against the many odors that crowded the carriage. Rising above the pungent scent of new leather and fresh paint were warring scents of flowers. It appeared the other ladies had known about the invitation before she did and had taken care to dress their hats with fresh blooms she recognized as being taken from St. Sefin's gardens.

Her heart clenched tight. St. Sefin's was going to feel so different when Pen left. It would be Dovey's, not hers. Could she leave it to become his mistress? How long could she remain immune to the scorn of his world? At St. Sefin's, she had friends, the children to look after, a community. In Pen's world, she would have no one but him. It was bound to become lonely, especially when his duties as a viscount pulled him further and further away.

"I've seen this ship. It's been anchored here for weeks. Is it one of Sir Lambert Vaughn's?" Gwen said with surprise as the river came into full view.

She wouldn't set foot on a slaver. But the sleek two-masted brig anchored in the curve of the Usk was small and light, made for maneuvering in coastal channels. Four squat, round cannons pointed their noses at them as the carriage stopped on the sandy shore.

"I don't know. Just come inside. Hurry."

"Will the tea get cold?" Gwen snapped. Anne's nervousness was starting to infect her. Her boots sank into the sand as she struggled out of the carriage. The breeze from the channel, though the sun shone warm, held a playful bite. There was no proper dock or wharf at this curve in the Usk, the shore having such a gentle slope that crew could merely carry their goods to the edge of the water and hoist them into the ship using the small rowboat they called a yawl. She saw several men at such work, rolling casks and carrying crates. In fact two of them, one quite large and one markedly shorter, seemed familiar.

"I'll ruin my half boots," Prunella complained. "And I just got these this Season. It was so pleasant to leave off mourning at last."

Gwen scanned the brig with rising alarm. It was fully rigged, the square sails lightly belling in the breeze, the triangular jibs pointed toward the Channel as if eager to be set free. She saw no sign of Lady Vaughn on the main deck, and no servants either, only the busy work of sailors in their rough canvas garb.

"I don't think we—"

She faltered as a sudden ring of men formed behind them. The carriage driver tipped his hat and urged the horses to walk on, taking away their avenue of escape. An enormous man with a black gap in his teeth stood directly behind her.

"You!" Gwen hissed.

Minikin, the little man beside him, flashed her a cocky grin in greeting. "*Shwmae*, Moll?"

"They are not taking us to Lady Vaughn," Gwen said loudly.

"Aye, but we'll be taking you to the boat nonetheless, and you won't give us trouble, you won't," said Gap-tooth—Pedr, Pen had said his name was. These men had been working for the Black Hound all this time. They'd walked into a trap.

"Anne, I don't know what they told you, but—"

"They'll kill Daron." Anne's pupils were tiny blue dots in the huge whites of her eyes. "They told me they will kill him if I didn't bring all of you, and if we fight or struggle—" She pressed a fist to her mouth to stop a whimper. "They'll kill all of us."

Prunella shrieked and her eyes rolled back in her head. Gwen was ready to applaud the girl's cleverness until she realized her swooning was not a ruse to give them a chance to rush their guards and escape. As Prunella's body folded, Pedr lunged forward to catch her before she toppled to the ground, and Gwen could have laughed at the comical look on his face as he found his arms full of round, soft woman. Lydia screeched and stepped away as if Pedr, or Prunella, had something catching, but she couldn't go far with another of the Black Hound's henchman crowding in from the side. Pedr scooped Prunella into his arms, grunting a bit as he adjusted his grip, and his cohorts herded the rest of them toward the shallow wooden boat that had been lowered to the ground.

"Hey, now, into the jolly-boat with you all!" Minikin barked. He caught Gwen's eye. "The Moll doesn't have the—this time?" He made a motion toward his waist.

"The what?" Gwen shot a glare at one of the men shouldering her toward the tiny boat. He had pox scars on his face and only a few stumps of teeth. He looked hungry and angry.

"The—achoo!" Minikin pretended to open a pouch at his waist, then sneezed.

The sneezewort she'd used on him before. *Twpsyn!* She always traveled with it, except when she was invited to tea with society ladies.

"I don't have it," she bit out.

Minikin, strangely enough, looked disconcerted. "Ah. Well, then." He shared a glance with Pedr and, with a wince of apology, shooed all four women into the yawl and indicated that they sit. The hard wooden plank pressed against Gwen's rear and the tiny boat jolted as men above cranked the winch to haul up the ropes. Like water being fetched from a well the boat carried the four women and their captors up the side of the brig, and men on the main deck unceremoniously hauled them over the rail like so many sacks of flour.

Gwen was too busy cursing herself to take proper note of her surroundings. It was a regular ship, strung with a spider's web of ropes and riggings, instruments with unaccountable functions scattered here and there. Pedr's compatriots reached into the yawl and heaved out two small firkins, the half-sized casks used for ale. Gwen's stomach jumped as she recognized a mark on the side. The casks came from St. Sefin's, and they held the brew Pen had made with the infected darnel seeds. She'd carefully marked the firkins so no one opened one by accident and drank the poisoned brew. What was it doing here, with Minikin so cheerfully rolling a cask before him, as if he hadn't a care in the world?

"Master wants to see you." He whistled as if calling a dog. "Come along, fair ladies, come along."

Gwen, herded by the much larger and clearly armed men, had no choice but to follow. Anne trailed behind her, whimpering and fretting. Lydia marched with her head up, going to the gallows with pride, and Pedr caught up the rear with a groggy Prunella in his arms. Minikin pointed to a short stair at the back of the deck leading downward. "There. Try not to anger him, chick. He's in a foul temper to begin with."

Where was Pen? What would he do when he learned what had happened? For that matter, what did the Hound want with them? Gwen's courage quailed as she stepped down the short, dark stairwell into the unknown.

The captain's cabin spread over the entire rear of the ship, and a more sumptuous boudoir Gwen had never seen. Half a dozen narrow arched windows let in a buttery spring light, and on a small raised platform tucked against them stood a large feather bed clothed in silk damask. Shelves and cupboards with polished brass handles lined the walls. In the center of the room stood a large walnut dining table draped in a crisp white linen cloth, and around it sat several Gillow armchairs in gleaming walnut. Comfortable chairs, with shepherd's crook arms and tapestry seats. Nestled in one was an older man dressed head to toe in black, save for a flash of startling white at his shirt collar and a red silk cravat.

"Y Gwyllgi." Gwen said it like a curse.

He rose and bowed. He was a large man, stocky, and he wore his own hair, white and cupped around his ears. His cheekbones stood out like knobs, his mouth was a thin straight slash across his face, and his eyes were so deep-set beneath heavy coal-black brows that Gwen at first couldn't discern the gleam of malice in them. Altogether, he was terrifying.

"The Black Hound, is that it? I didn't choose the name for myself. My real name, if you want to know, is Bryan." He moved around the table to regard them. He was very tall. "But I believe the Black Hound suits me, for all that. I am single-minded in my pursuits. I enjoy a fight. And I never give up until I have what I want."

"Hardly a fair fight when you hire thugs to beat a man senseless, or kidnap ladies," Gwen said. Pedr and Minikin left, but other men stood guard in the tiny stairwell. These were the rough men they'd heard reports of roaming Newport, causing fights and hassling merchants. Who was this man to command a small army of henchmen, all to do his will?

"Gwenllian ap Ewyas," the Hound said softly, regarding her intently. He spoke English but with an accent she couldn't place, lilting and rhythmic, but not Welsh. "I've heard of you. Princess of an ancient kingdom that no longer exists. Warrior in a world where females are meant to be gracious and silent." His thin lips flattened in a sneer. "I cannot think of a worse torment for a woman of pride. It must be purgatory on earth."

"Where is my brother?" Anne choked out, stepping forward. Behind them Lydia and Prunella clung together, wide-eyed and silent, their skirts rustling like a pair of dainty stonechat.

"Why, he's right here waiting for you." The Hound gestured toward a shadowed corner where a chair sat before a built-in desk. Daron Sutton sat bound to it by long thin ropes. His blue coat was torn, his cravat rust-stained, and his head hung heavily on his chest, his golden hair matted with blood at one temple. Anne rushed to him with a low cry.

"Is he dead?" She looked at Gwen with anguish.

Gwen's heart twisted despite herself. She hadn't wished Daron *dead*. Mauled by corgis, perhaps, but not blotted from the earth. "Check his pulse," she said roughly.

"I don't know how to do that." Anne gazed on her brother forlornly, touching his shoulder as if fearing to find him cold.

Heaving a sigh, Gwen stepped forward and pressed two fingers beneath Sutton's fleshy chin. "Alive." She dropped her fingers, loathe to touch him, and instead snatched a linen serviette from the table, snapped it open, and bound the length around Sutton's head. "Does he owe you money, too?"

The Hound grinned. The expression resembled the gape of a skull removed of flesh. "He approached me with a bargain. I'm ensuring he maintains his end of it."

"What bargain?" Gwen swallowed a sour taste in her mouth.

The Hound nodded towards the two viscountesses, watching white-faced and silent. Gwen had to commend Lydia's ruthless self-control. She appeared outraged at the indignity being done her. Poor Prunella looked prepared to faint again.

"These two," the Hound said, "bring the viscount to me. He owes me a debt. He," he nodded toward Sutton, "keeps you."

"And me?" Anne gave a soft yelp.

The Hound watched her with his tiny, piercing eyes. "I fancy a wife," he said. "I've always been partial to those English blue eyes and that skin, like a—what's that white flower you see in the spring?"

"Wood anemone," Gwen said shortly. "Penrydd owes you nothing. He is not responsible for his brother's debt."

"He is if I say he is," said the Hound, his gaze still on Anne. She gave another small cry and ran to hide behind Gwen.

"What happens next?" Gwen asked through a throat gone dry with fear.

The Hound gave his rictus smile. "My message has been sent, so now we pass the time until his lordship calls. Do you enjoy ombre? Vingt-et-un? I am fond of faro."

He seated himself at the table and gestured the ladies forward. "Come, I've sent for refreshments. We're not savages, even if we do live in Wales."

"You beat that Jewish man from Merthyr Tydfil until he died," Gwen said. "An act of savagery if I ever heard of one."

The Hound shook his head. "Ach, Daniel. Such a stubborn man, so hard to persuade. I regret that some of my men like their work too much. I pay better than the mines, you see, and less risk of life and limb."

A knock sounded at the door. "Spot of tea for the ladies!" It was Minikin, bearing a polished salver with a pitcher and tall pewter goblet. "Ha, only jesting. It's small beer for you, *drewgi*."

Gwen watched in amazement as Minikin advanced to the table and slid the platter onto the linen cloth. The Hound didn't look up from the deck of cards he was shuffling, apparently not realizing that his minion had just called him a smelly dog.

"Does he not speak Cymraeg?" Gwen asked in Welsh.

"Na, he's *Gwyddelig*," Pedr spat.

Irish. Just as the English considered the Welsh uncivilized, many Welsh thought of the Irish as barbarians. Iolo Morganwg, the self-appointed modern Welsh bard, said the Irish loved only violence, deception, and poetry.

"But you serve him," Gwen said, still in Welsh. The Hound looked sharply at her but said nothing. No one else understood their conversations. Anne knew only a few words that Gwen had taught her, mostly the names of flowers and birds.

"We serve the man with no name," Pedr answered in a slow rumble.

"A gift from the publican at the King's Head, your Hound-ship." Minikin switched to English and poured from the pitcher into the goblet. Gwen swore she detected the sharp, sour scent of darnel. "The men are enjoying a dram or two, and there's more at the Head if they nip in there tonight whilst going about their business."

Gwen's heart raced with sudden hope. Pen was the man with no name. He said he'd been working with their attackers from the bridge. He had brewed the darnel and if Pedr and Minikin served it here, they would disarm the Hound's men. Mr. Trett at the King's Head had the only thing in Newport that served as a lockup, a rickety lean-to in his stable yard. Though she seemed to recall Pen and Evans, in their work at the stables, had reported reinforcing the lean-to with new timber and a great new iron padlock.

Pen meant to lure the Hound's henchmen to the pub, lock them up, and have the constable deal with them. The rough-hewn army, dispensed with in one blow. But what, then, of the bombs he had Evans and Ross making?

"What are we to do?" Gwen whispered in Welsh. What was the rest of Pen's plan?

Minikin gave her a reproachful look, speaking out of the side of his mouth. "You was supposed to have the sneeze weed."

Gwen almost laughed. They had counted on her not walking into the trap, yet here she was, in the Hound's lair, with three helpless women and a wounded Sutton still unconscious in his chair. Could she overcome the Hound if he drank the poisoned beer? Could Pedr and Minikin alone help them escape if their cohorts grew drunk and rowdy? Sounds of revelry spilled from the main deck where, she assumed, the first firkin had been tapped. But the side effects of darnel were unpredictable. Who knew what a man prone to violence was capable of under the influence of intoxication, much less hallucination?

The Hound didn't glance at the goblet. "I dislike beer, Morys. Open a bottle of wine."

"Aye, but 'tis a gift, your Houndship, and you know they say that—"

"Wine, Morys," the Hound said.

"For me as well." Lydia glared at the little man. She sat without touching the back of her chair, shoulders stiff, chin high. "We might play vingt-et-un to begin, Mr. Bryan. I am not one of those fast faro ladies to lose thousands of pounds a night at the table."

"You have a harp," Gwen noted with surprise, at last spotting the instrument housed beside the rack of wine bottles where Minikin browsed the selection, then picked out a set of faceted glass goblets. "Shall I play for us?"

The sound would disguise any noises from above, of the men's carousing or Pen's arrival, if indeed he were coming to rescue them. And harping would help her think. The Hound wasn't drinking the beer. She didn't have her sneezewort. A rack of guns gleamed above the desk, long-barreled, lethal-looking weapons, but she didn't know the complicated sequence required to load and fire a gun, much less what went into it. She needed another weapon.

As coolly as if she were at tea, Lydia unpinned her hat and set it aside. Prunella cautiously followed suit, hanging her bonnet on the back of her chair. Anne sat near her brother, keeping a nervous eye on him. Gwen studied the three women and the adornments they'd unknowingly retrieved from St. Sefin's poison garden.

Lydia's hat brim was decorated with blooms of hellebore. A quite toxic plant, the ingestion of which could cause burning in the mouth, purging of the stomach and bowels, and potentially halt the heart.

Prunella had embellished her bonnet with blooms of cheerful purple-blue lobelia. In small doses effective for breathing difficulties or bouts of sadness; in high doses, responsible for nausea, vomiting, and cardiac arrest.

And Anne, bless her delicate heart, had decorated the corsage of her pretty muslin gown with a stem of foxglove.

The Hound looked up from dealing cards as Gwen casually swept up the ladies' hats and asked to see Anne's posy. "You mean to play for us while you await your doom?" He grinned.

"By all means."

"They say Nero fiddled while Rome burned." Gwen seated herself in the shadowy corner, nearer Sutton than she liked, but the desk held what she needed. She pulled the harp to her, an Irish harp with only two sets of strings, not her beloved Welsh *telyn,* but a fine instrument with a smooth body fashioned of willow wood and brass strings that produced bright, resonant tones. Under pretext of settling with the harp she withdrew a small candleholder from the table and placed it in her lap.

"I'll start with 'The Lament of the Rejected Maiden,'" Gwen said. "A sad little ballad about a girl who finds herself pregnant out of wedlock and is cast out by her family, left friendless and destitute."

Anne cut her eyes away, looking embarrassed, which was just what Gwen hoped to achieve. She didn't want anyone watching. As she sang and plucked with one hand, with the other she managed to strip the leaves and petals from her plants, collecting them in the bowl. Then she set the dish near her feet and, as if she were pedaling a harp, used the hollow brass tube of the candle holder to crush the pieces, breaking free the oils and the compounds that would create the ill effects.

The sharp scents assailed her nose, crying a warning, but no one at the table seemed to notice. They'd switched to a game of ombre and the Hound attempted to teach Anne and Prunella the rules, with no great success. Prunella was apparently unable to grasp the logic, and Anne was too frightened to think straight.

The noise from above kept increasing, shouts of merriment, taunts, and snatches of song drifting from the main deck as the men consumed the free beer. For all that the volume was louder, Gwen thought she detected fewer voices. There were occasional thumps and creaks as if the yawl had been raised and lowered a few times. If men were departing, their chances of escape improved. But how was she to pour the poison into the Hound's drink so they might get away?

"I'd like a glass of wine," Gwen said. "I'm rather parched from singing for so long."

"Pour it yourself," Lydia said acidly. "You're not a viscountess yet, to have our servants to wait on you."

The Hound's eyes flickered over her, and Gwen tried to hide the dish of pounded leaves beneath the hem of her skirt. "I thought she was for that one," he said, nodding at Sutton, who had slipped into sleep, lightly snoring.

"He only wants her for her mines," Anne squeaked.

Now the Hound looked fully at her. *Coc oen!* "What mines?" he said.

Gwen made a show of selecting a glass goblet from the hanging rack. It seemed strange that a sailing ship, prone to vagaries of weather, would carry an assortment of fragile glass items, but the Black Hound apparently liked his luxuries.

"Ask Anne," she said. "She knows more about my supposed wealth than I do."

The Hound focused on his reluctant guest, and Gwen bent to swiftly pick up her dish of poisons. A small puddle of liquid had formed in the bottom, the oils pressed from the leaves and flowers. How much did she need, with all three plants together? This was her first attempt at poisoning someone. She wanted to make him ill, but she didn't want the stain of murder on her soul. She couldn't be with Pen if she were hanged for manslaughter.

Her hands trembled as she tipped the dish into the goblet. She wanted to be with Pen. Desperately, with every nerve and fiber of her being, she wanted a future with him. No matter what it looked like. Slowly the liquid trickled into the glass. She carried it to the table.

"Copper," Anne was saying. "And lead-silver. Brand new veins, I was given to understand."

"I foresee a difficulty with your plans," Gwen said, and gestured broadly toward the bank of mullioned windows set into the back of the ship. Outside, clouds massed to the north, and a warning wind had kicked up, shaping the placid Usk into herringbone waves. "It bodes rain."

She had only a second while his attention was diverted. "More wine, your Houndship?" She filled the poison goblet to the brim before he could answer.

"It's always raining in this bloody country," the Hound said, turning back to the table. "Lady Penrydd, I believe it is your turn?"

"Mine?" Prunella said uncertainly.

The Hound's eyes flicked down the table in annoyance, and Gwen, her heart beating wildly, withdrew his first glass, leaving the poisoned cup in its place. All he had to do was notice the slightly different position. Or her clear signs of guilt. She was no Claudius, coolly plotting to kill his nephew Hamlet. But in the play, Gertrude the queen drank the poisoned goblet. Gwen, hands shaking, nudged Lydia's unadulterated goblet a bit closer to her, so there could be no mistaking. She didn't want a tragic scene of bodies sprawled everywhere, like a Shakespearean play. She wanted all of them to escape with their skins and for the Black Hound to come to justice.

"The other Lady Penrydd," the Hound said in irritation. "By God, your bloody English titles are confusing." He picked up the poisoned cup and took a long drink. Gwen stopped breathing.

He set down the goblet and stared at her. "Aren't you going to harp some more? Rome's not burning yet."

She was certain everyone in the chamber could hear her heart beating as she returned to her chair. Pedr, who had relieved the guard at the door, must hear it. She sent him a pleading look as she returned to her chair. He lifted his hands in a helpless shrug.

He didn't know when Pen was coming, either.

She was on "The Song of the White Piper" when a low, bellowing *boom* sounded from below. The ship rocked slightly, the glasses gently clanking in their rack.

The Hound loosened the cravat at his throat. "Go see what that was!" he bellowed at Pedr, who, with a wide-eyed look at Gwen, disappeared from the door.

"Thunder," Gwen said. "It's starting, the *glaw gochel,* the heavy rain."

"I'm going to be sick if the rocking doesn't stop." The Hound's pupils had dilated and sweat shone on his craggy brow. "By God, that's a bitter wine."

It was working. Gwen stood and carefully put away the harp. "It's time to unbind Mr. Sutton, don't you think?" They needed to wake him to make their escape. None of the women could carry him.

Two short explosions sounded in a row, rattling the window-panes. An enormous stench floated into the room, the smell of singed wood and sulfur. The trick with a dung bomb, Pen had explained, was not so much the mixture but the firing mechanism. St. Teilo's toes, he was blowing up the boat, and they were still on it.

"Time to go," Gwen said, urging Lydia and Prunella to their feet. Anne, looking scared and bewildered, helped her fumble with the knots of Daron's ropes. "I think we'll be taking our leave of his Houndship."

"You're not going anywhere." The Hound gasped and reached for the table as he rose, then doubled over, clutching his gut. "I've—I've a score to settle."

"Settle it with me," Penrydd said from the door. "Stop preying on helpless women."

Gwen wanted to melt at the sight of him. He wore a rough woolen waistcoat, no jacket, and his working trousers and boots. A clump of something very smelly had lodged in his hair. His expression was thunderous and she wanted to kiss every inch of his beautiful face.

"Helpless!" was all she could think of to say.

"Get them to the main deck." He glanced around the room, a brow lifting in surprise when he recognized Sutton. His gaze settled on Gwen, warm and steady. "Get off the boat now."

"What about you?" Though she'd rather fling herself into his arms, she instead grabbed Daron Sutton's arm and shook him awake.

Pen rolled up one sleeve of his linen shirt. "There's the matter of my brother's debt. I won't leave until I've paid."

"You can't—" Gwen started to argue, but Anne Sutton grasped her arm.

"Gwen, can we please leave? Like he said?"

A series of explosions ripped through the hull. Pen's eyes widened. The Hound clutched the table, dry heaving. "I—I didn't harm them," he gasped. "Leave the money and go."

"Oh, I don't have money." Pen rolled up his other sleeve. His hands were filthy and he reeked as he stepped into the room.

Gwen slipped under Prunella's arm as the woman sagged, close to another fainting spell. "Don't get hurt," she said to Pen. "I need you."

His eyes met hers, and the flicker of heat, of promise, licked through her to her knees. "I'll be there. Now go away, my love."

Pedr and Minikin stood on the main deck, cranking up the yawl. Minikin gestured wildly as the women ran toward him. Another explosion rocked the boat, shouts of alarm following. From shore came the whinny of a horse. Gwen glanced over the side and saw the pony cart from the King's Head waiting on the beach, the tired old gelding she recognized in its traces. It wasn't an elegant carriage, but it would get them to safety before the entire boat blew up.

"Over the side with you now!" Minikin cried. Pedr picked up Prunella and slung her over the rail of the brig into the waiting yawl as if she were a sack of grain. Lydia slapped his hand away and tried to clamber over herself. Anne gave her dazed brother to Gwen as she flung herself into Pedr's arms, nearly sobbing in relief as they reached the boat.

"Gwen?" Daron Sutton sagged against her, blinking in confusion. "Where am I? What are we—God, my head."

"You," Gwen said furiously. "You put us all in a fine pickle, and you'll pay for it, Daron Sutton. Get them to shore," she ordered Minikin.

"His lordship—"

"I'll be back with him in a minute!" Lifting her skirts, she sped back toward the stairway.

"Gwen!" Evans shouted. He hauled himself up from the hatch that led belowdecks, throwing his crutch onto the deck before pulling his body up. "Worked a little too well. We blew more than we meant to. We all need to clear this ship, now."

"Pen is with the Black Hound." Gwen watched without surprise as Ross, equally filthy, hauled himself up behind Evans.

"Then get him and get out! We'll hold the last boat for you." She turned as Pedr and Minikin hopped into the boat with the women and Sutton, while Evans and Ross ran to the winch to lower them to safety.

Another explosion ripped through the hull, and part of the desk exploded behind her as Gwen ran for the captain's quarters. With a huge groan the brig rolled, rigging creaking as the masts tilted and the sails shifted weight. Gwen regained her footing and flung herself down the stairs.

"Pen, my darling! Time to abandon ship!"

The two men were locked in combat amid the wreckage of the walnut dining table and upholstered chairs. The mullioned windows had blown out, and a jagged hole had appeared in the floor. Gwen smelled the flames before they danced through the opening. The rug caught fire at once.

"Pen!" she screamed through the boom of another explosion. The men weren't setting bombs now; these were out of their control. The overhead chandelier with its burning candles swung precariously.

"That," Pen roared, landing a punch, "is for Edwin. You killed my brother, you bastard. He never would have taken that bet if he hadn't owed you!"

The Hound was larger and heavier by a stone, but the poison had clearly reached his guts, and Pen had trained for this. "For Prunella!" he shouted, landing a right jab to the man's ribs. "For Lydia." A left.

For a moment, from some deep and primitive part of herself, Gwen thrilled to his physical strength, his domination. The Hound gasped and staggered to his feet.

"Christ," he croaked, "have mercy."

"Mercy? The same mercy you showed me?" Some transfiguring rage had overtaken Pen. He began a flurry of punishing blows, shouting incoherently. "This is for the Jew. This is for Arwen. This is for Bowen—for Nelson's arm—for every man at Tenerife who—should—be—here—"

The Hound's face had nearly disappeared under blood. Pen's fist shot out again, fingers clenched around the man's throat. "Do you know what you *did* to me?"

The Hound's fingers weakly scrabbled at his arm. He couldn't answer with his airway choked off. Gwen fought down her fear that she was about the lose the man she loved and ran forward over the pitching floor.

She laid a hand on Pen's iron forearm. "Pen. Don't kill him. We have to get out of here."

"He doesn't deserve to live." This wasn't a Pen she knew. This was a feral animal.

"Then let the courts hang him. Pen! Please!"

Her cry was lost in another explosion as the rest of the room disappeared. Pen lurched against her, dropping the Hound and shielding her with his body as the ship came apart around them. A beam crashed across the stairwell, narrowing their only avenue of escape. The rest of the room was a wall of fire.

With one hand, Pen grabbed the collar of his enemy, and with the other he shielded Gwen as they fought their way up the stairs. On the main deck one of the masts broke and fell, its huge cross beams swinging through the air. They half-stumbled, half-crawled over the disintegrating deck toward the yawl where Evans and Ross gestured wildly. Pen launched the Hound's inert body over the side, then spread himself against Gwen as another explosion erupted.

His body lurched against hers as he took the hit. Grasping her arms about him, Gwen threw herself against the rail as the deck tipped, tumbling both of them into the boat. Evans and Ross heaved wildly at the ropes, letting them down as fast as possible, while the crossbeam of the mast followed them, plowing through splintering wood. One last explosion filled the air with smoke and ash, and Gwen's entire body jolted as the boat hit the ground. She waved her hands before her face, choking, then reached for Pen. Evans and Ross helped her haul him onto the sand. Rockets of light from the exploding ship fell about them like streamers at a market fair.

"Argh!" Pen groaned as Gwen examined his shredded back.

"Not as bad as canister shot. And the right side this time. Balances things out."

"You." Gwen swallowed a sob. "Didn't I tell you the third time I found you like this, I'd roll you under a hedge and leave you there?" She searched his body for other wounds, wiping away blood and what appeared to be scorched manure.

Pen staggered to his feet and let Evans help him toward the cart, laden with the rescued. "You can't. I have your selkie skin. I found it and kept it, and now you are bound to me." He turned his head, his face changing expression. The feral animal was gone, and he was her Pen again, only chagrined. "But then I gave St. sodding Sefin's to Dovey, and now you've no reason to stay with me."

"My love, I'll never leave you. I'll go anywhere you wish."

"Is that Penrydd?" Sutton leaned forward from among the women seated in the back of the pony cart.

"You!" Pen limped to the side of the cart. Before Sutton could recoil, Pen grabbed his cravat in a bloodied hand. "You worthless son of a bitch. If you ever raise a hand against my wife —if you ever *think* about my wife—"

"I won't! I won't," Daron bleated, batting at Pen's fist, his eyes huge.

Pen breathed through his teeth. "If you say one word about my wife, to anyone—"

"She's dead to me. Dead!"

"She never existed for you at all," Pen snarled. He let go, and Sutton sat back, gasping for air.

"But the Hound?" Anne asked uncertainly.

A low roaring sound rose from the river, and as one they turned to see the dark, high wave, like the fin of some great water monster, rolling up the Usk. It broke apart the last hulk of the brig, which fell into separate pieces that quietly burned themselves out in the water. The wave lifted the yawl bearing the Hound's unconscious body and carried it northward, toward Newport, toward Caerleon, toward places beyond, faster than a man could run.

"Well," Evans said into a silence edged with the sound of burning wood and the smell of sulfur and ash. "A new moon tonight, isn't it? So that'd be the Severn bore, with the high tide behind it."

"Where's he going?" Ross asked in a hushed tone.

"I don't care." Pen turned to haul himself into the plank seat of the cart. "Let's to the King's Head and see what Trett's done with the men we sent him. I'm for Gwen's nursing and a good stiff drink, so long as it isn't rum."

Gossett met them at the King's Head with roughed-up knuckles and the report that, intoxicated on the darnel beer, the Hound's men had been easily rounded up by the constable— with some coaxing by Gossett.

"The villains are mewed in the lock-up, which is the noise you hear yonder," Trett added, looking pleased with the part he had played in bringing peace back to Newport. "Sir Robert's clerk will have a busy morning, writing out all the charges."

Pen grunted with satisfaction. "I am therefore allowed to say I told you so," he said to Ross.

They left the Suttons to shift for themselves at the King's Head, and Gwen took her people back to St. Sefin's. Lydia consented as, she said, her luggage was there, and Prunella for her part did not want to be parted from Gwen. The dowager viscountess caught Gwen as she came to the kitchen for another basin of hot water and herbs for Pen.

"We owe you our thanks, Miss Carew. You saved our lives."

"It was Penrydd—Rhydian, my lady."

"And how uncharacteristic of him, too." Lydia looked as if she were struggling to smile but was unsure how to move her mouth that way. "The old Rhydian didn't care a sot for others. You've—changed him."

"I can't take credit, mum. 'Tis more that he's become himself, I think."

"The man he was meant to be," Lydia murmured. "I believe I can live with that man. And—with you."

It was very nearly a blessing. Gwen's eyes smarted with tears as she hurried back to Pen's room.

She found him struggling out of his shirt. The candle in its holder on the high shelf showed the jagged cut in his back. Another scar for his fine, splendid form. Her heart burrowed into her throat, sealing off words. He had survived so much. He had come to her, her fair unknown, her gift from the sea, and he had seen beneath her own scars to the woman hidden there, had called forth a love she hadn't known she could feel. Hadn't known she was healed enough to ever be capable of feeling.

She was his, body and soul. Like that silly myth of Plato's he mentioned. She would be his mistress. She would be anything he wanted, just to be near him, in his life. She'd been putting too much stake in all the things that wanted to separate them—their stations and birth, their countries, their pasts. When the truth was simply this: his heart calling to hers, and hers responding.

"What happens next?" Gwen whispered.

"To the Hound? Let him wash up where he may, and let the mercy shown to him be the kind of mercy he's shown to the other poor souls he's left in torment." Pen stretched out on his bed, turning his injured back her way.

"To us, my heart." Gwen wrung out her cloth in the basin. The water turned filthy in an instant.

Pen caught her hand. "I thought we settled that."

She moved to swabbing his neck and felt his fast pulse. He had over-exerted himself, or he was desperate for her answer.

"I thought you might want to reconsider," she whispered. "If you've been blown to your senses, or some such."

He bent his head and laid his forearm against her arm. The gesture of surrender flattened her as nothing else could.

"I came to my senses the minute you walked into my rooms at the Green Man," he said. "Everything's pig's poo without you, Gwen. You make everything hurt less."

She loosed a trembling laugh at his Welsh curse. Could that be enough, that they could simply try to shield each other from the hurts of the world?

She stroked his back. Everything she wanted was bound up in the shape of this man. Just him. As he was. And he needed her.

"Let me be clear, Pen. Rhydian." She tried his name in her mouth, finding she liked the full, properly Cymric shape of it. "I don't want to marry the viscount."

He tensed, as if awaiting the killing blow. She dabbed her cloth against his wounded cheek. She didn't know what their future held, any more than he did. But she trusted him completely.

"However," she said, her breathing shaky, "I very much want to marry *you*."

His eyes kindled with wonder, and his face transformed into the most beautiful smile she'd ever seen. He lifted his hand to cradle hers against his cheek. "Thank God."

CHAPTER TWENTY

"We'll travel north for our honeymoon to inspect her mines and ensure all is in order." Pen's voice floated down from the bell tower of St. Sefin's where he was repairing the wooden platform where he had made love to Gwen under the stars. "My viscountess and I won't let our workers be abused the way Mother Morris's sons were in the coal mines."

"Viscountess," Dovey murmured. She buffed the stained glass window that held the portrait of St. Sefin, one of the many daughters of the legendary Brychan, Welsh king and saint. "Will I have to call you milady?"

Gwen gave a last loving pat to St. Gwladys, whose window gleamed beneath her cloth. "I'll only ever be Gwen to you. Will you want me to call you Dovinia Emerald Van der Welle Evans?"

Dovey smiled. "You might call me Mrs. Evans once in a while. Until I get used to the name."

Dovey's wedding to Evans would take place in a week, after the last banns were posted. She wanted the ceremony done before Gwen left. There would be less gossip and suspicion,

Dovey thought, if St. Sefin's were run by a proper married couple.

Gwen would marry Lord Penrydd the week after, and so they were polishing St. Sefin's church to its highest gleam, sprucing up every guest room. Penrydd had invited all his family and friends, everyone he'd pushed away in his mourning and self-isolation after Tenerife. He was ready to return to the world.

The children were supposed to be helping clean, but they had got up a game with their brooms and mops that involved batting a ball around the floor. Tomos was currently the man in the middle, chuckling each time the ball sailed past him. Ifor proved the most proficient player, as he tracked the ball by listening, while Cerys was more interested in shouting taunts and challenges.

At the back of the church, Mathry and Widow Jones discussed where to place flower arrangements, while Mother Morris sat knitting in a shaft of sun falling through the open front door. Prunella and Anne Sutton were huddled in the chapter house over a bottle of canary wine. Lydia was visiting Greenfield, but Prunella preferred to entertain Anne at St. Sefin's, where Miss Sutton was welcome though her brother was not. Prunella had made it clear that, after what she considered her heroic rescue, Gwen could do no wrong in her eyes. The rest of Penrydd's family might not accept her, but Prunella's cheerful companionship would make up for a great deal, Gwen hoped.

"I want to ensure the mines have safe working conditions," Pen went on, answering the question Evans had asked. Evans and Ross, with Mr. Stanley's help, were repairing the hole in the roof over the north transept. "Fair wages," he explained. "Medical care and decent living quarters for the workers. And I won't allow the overseer to employ small children."

"Such progressive notions you have, milord," Gwen called to him.

He paused his hammer, his head appearing in the opening. His hair was tousled and his neckcloth wrapped in a simple twist. He'd recovered from the explosion with only residual aches, the old battle scars which he would always carry. But he was hale and hardy, restored to health, and had so far drunk nothing stronger than rhubarb wine. Gwen's entire chest glowed at the sight of him.

"I thought you'd agree." His gaze met and held hers.

She smiled. "I do. I'm pleased you feel the same way."

"Most mine owners feel it an unnecessary expense to take care of their workers," Mr. Stanley said. "Since they are so easy to replace."

"It's good business to have a strong workforce," Pen said. "Sick workers don't perform as well, and if you wear them out and kill them, it takes time to replace them and train up someone new. Better to preserve the workers you have and capitalize on their skills. Plus that keeps widows and orphans off the poor rolls."

"Glad to hear you feel that way, sir," Ross called.

Mathry bumped Gwen's hip as she circled past, counting the niches where she planned to put bowls of blooms. "You won't have time to run mines. You'll be too busy nursing a *baban.*" She patted her belly, quite noticeably round.

Gwen shook her head. "There won't be a babe for me."

Mathry sent a pointed look at Gwen's breasts, swelling against the bodice of the old flannel gown that had always fit her. "They're just growing on their own, then?"

"She's left off wearing her stays," Dovey murmured. "Don't fit."

Mathry grinned. "Time to start a red raspberry leaf and nettle tea."

Gwen clasped her middle. "I can't—it's not possible—"

Dovey lifted a curving black brow.

"All right then, it's possible I caught, but to see it through to delivery—" Fear and wonder gripped her in twin claws. "I'm sure my womb was damaged from what happened before. What if I can conceive but not carry?" Her eyes filled with tears. What if she were forced to relive her nightmare again and again, bearing a babe but not being able to hold it?

Dovey touched her arm. "Dearling. Mathry will have been through her own travail by then, and I know a bit. You'll have help this time."

"But it will be seven months or more," Gwen said, calculating. "You'll have Evans and St. Sefin's to see to, and Mathry's to be our housekeeper at Penrydd." Pen had set men to work repairing the estate and engaged staff to open and prepare the house. They'd return to it after their honeymoon.

Mathry cradled her own belly with a grin. "Have a little lord, and the dowager will go all sweet on you, I be thinking."

Gwen stared up at the bell tower where Pen uttered a muffled curse. An English viscount, wielding a hammer, whistling through the nails clenched in his teeth. If she could bear children, the last reason she oughtn't marry him fell away. Her birth wasn't equal to his, and God knew her past wasn't that of a pure, sheltered maid. But he hadn't been born to his title, either. They would learn together. And build a life they chose for themselves, not one dictated to them by others.

"I want a girl," Gwen whispered. "Is that wrong?"

Mathry tossed her head. "All that's wrong is that *tymffat* up there who trips over his feet when'er he sees me, but won't make a declaration." She pointed to the platform where Ross and Evans moved about. "Be nice if he made an honest woman of me afore the *baban* comes."

"You can't have my man," Dovey said placidly, scouring the dust from her window.

"*Wfft*, the Northman," Mathry said. "Thought a Scotsman might have more in his head, but too much English blood up there at the border, that's what it is."

"Speaking of Evans, Dovey *bach*," Gwen said. "If you cared for him, why didn't you marry him long ago?"

Dovey dabbed her cloth at St. Sefin's purple gown. "Fear, I suppose. That I'd lose someone again. Besides, I couldn't be sure he was sweet on me. 'Twas safer not to let anything change. But then you showed me the way, casting your heart on his lordship, and I thought—how can I be less brave?" She smiled, her face soft with enchantment.

A sliver of guilt nibbled at Gwen's conscience. She and Pen had agreed they would support St. Sefin's, so Dovey never need worry for income. But Gwen was leaving her friend with all the burdens, the worries, the knocks on the door in darkest night, and Dovey was both proud and strong—what if she didn't ask if she needed more help? "Dovey *bach—ow!*"

Gwen yelped as the ball bounced off her ankle with a sharp thwack, then caromed away. "Now you've done it, my potato flowers. It's gone for good if you've lost your ball under the altar." St. Sefin's altar was a solid hunk of ancient English oak set on four stone slabs. They couldn't move it and had never tried.

"I'll find it." Ifor threw himself to the floor and began poking about with his shepherd's crook.

"By the by, I heard an odd tale from the vicar of St. Mary's in Abergavenny," Mr. Stanley remarked. "Seems a stranger in a small dory floated up the Usk many days back. His fine clothes were covered in filth, smelling of sulfur and dung, and he'd been so knocked about he couldn't recall his own name. They sent him to the workhouse, and like he'll be put to work in the mines of the Black Mountains as soon as he recovers. Can't expect he'll last long there, poor creature. It's a great mystery where he came from."

"All sorts of traffic on the Usk, newcomers and such," Evans said.

"Wasn't St. Mary's once a Benedictine priory?" Gwen asked.

Pen set a fresh wooden board in place and hammered it down with several loud blows. "Unlucky bastard. Hope it all turns out well for him, though I doubt he'll have the good fortune I did." He gave Gwen a saucy wink.

A few hollow thumps echoed behind her, then a loud click. Gwen turned to find Ifor struggling with a wooden panel on the side of the altar.

"Cerys," Ifor called. "There's a compartment in here, there is."

"I knew that." Cerys hurried over. "I found it years ago. Nothing in it but some lumps of old pottery."

Ifor reached in and ran a hand over the shapes inside. A grin stretched over his face. "Old pottery, is it?"

Gwen knelt and peered inside the compartment. "The nuns might have hidden things here they didn't want soldiers or thieves to find. Ifor! Perhaps we'll find records, or an old scrap of altar cloth, mayhap even—"

"St. Sefin's treasure," Cerys said with a gasp.

"Ooh." Tomos leaned over her shoulder, his eyes round.

"Cerys, *calon bach*, I know you love the tale, but it's not... possible that..."

Gwen fell silent as Ifor pulled an item from the dark hollow. He handed her a large shallow platter, covered with hastily made clay, not even properly fired in a kiln. "Now why would they hide lumps of old mud?"

Dovey reached around her and broke off a piece of the red-brown clay. "Because there's something beneath," she said.

Through the break shone another color, a dull buttery gleam.

"The paten," Cerys said. "The poem said there was one."

Gwen couldn't speak as Ifor handed her the next item, shaped like a goblet. Following Dovey's lead, she nicked a piece of the masking clay with her fingernail. It broke apart, and in her hand gleamed a silver cup inlaid with delicate carvings and precious gems.

"The chalice." Cerys clapped her hands. "What else?"

There were half a dozen pieces, including an intricate ciborium, the vessel that held the bread used for communion, and a gorgeous monstrance shaped like a golden sunburst on a long stem, bristling with gold and gems, a worthy backdrop for the host it was meant to display. The men came down from their heights and joined the women and children as they clustered around the altar and stared at the holy relics as they emerged from their cloaks of clay. They were old, expertly fashioned, and extremely valuable.

"I *knew* it was here," Cerys said with satisfaction.

"Gold," Pen said in surprise as Gwen handed him a censor and he ran his hands over the delicate carvings. "Finely made."

"You can sell these, Dovey, and be set for life," Gwen said.

"Sell them? I'll have copies made and put on display for pilgrims," Dovey said. "I'll have St. Sefin's treasure put in all the guidebooks. Travelers who come to climb the ruins of Newport Castle or see the Romanesque arch at St. Woolos will come here to see the priceless relics that St. Gwladys brought with her when she founded her hermitage."

"St. Gwladys's hermitage was at Pencarn," Gwen felt obliged to point out. "She lived on vegetables and bathed in the Ebbw. Her grave is there."

Dovey shrugged. "Those old stories of saint's lives never agree, do they? You were worried about abandoning us, Gwenllian ap Ewyas. I know you were. And now you needn't fear we can't make do. You can sally off with your light o' love and never look back."

Gwen hugged her friend, her ally for so long. "We'll live at Penrydd most of the time. You'll never be rid of me."

As she released Dovey and straightened, a new thought struck her. "But the papers haven't been signed yet. The treasure—" Pen could claim it, and he had the right. The items on this table would obliterate his brother's debts and restore the Price family's fortunes in full.

Pen raised his voice so that it reached Anne and Prunella, hovering in the doorway of the chapter house with glassy eyes and cheeks pink with the flush of wine. His voice was firm and authoritative.

"The papers Barlow is finishing as we speak entrust Mrs. Van der Welle Evans with the property of St. Sefin's and all its lands, furnishing, and movables. I'll not change a word of it. Whatever lies within these walls will be hers."

Dovey dipped her chin in a gracious acknowledgement. "Thank you, milord."

"You'll want a safe place to store them," said Ross. "And several copies made, as they're quite likely to be stolen."

"As many as need be." Dovey picked up the paten and scraped the last of the clay from the inlaid gems. "I won't quarrel with the blessings St. Gwladys chooses to give me."

Gwen cradled Pen's arms around her and wondered how soon she should tell him what she suspected, that she might have conceived a child. He'd insisted he didn't need heirs; how would he feel about having them anyway? She leaned against his shoulder, listening to the firm steady beat of his heart, and watched the colored light fall through the window of the saint who had watched over her for so many years.

St. Gwladys had whispered to her to stay here, stay alive. She had given her shelter and then she had given her help, and then she had given her, one at a time, people to heal her heart and teach her again how to love. And when she was ready, the river had carried her this man, her future, her joy, and the whole of her heart.

"All right?" Pen whispered in her ear. He must have felt the shiver pass through her.

She hugged his arms around her. "Better than all right," she whispered back. "Very, very happy."

From her window, St. Gwladys smiled.

ABOUT THE AUTHOR

Misty Urban fell in love with stories at an early age and has spent her life among books as a teacher, scholar, editor, writer, and bookseller. Her favorite stories take you new places, teach you new things, and end with a win. She especially likes romances about unconventional heroines who defy the odds and the unexpected heroes who woo them, so that's mostly what she writes. When she puts down the book she likes to take long walks, drag her family to new places, or hang out around water, dreaming up new stories.

Visit the author's website
Join the author's newsletter